Clary and the Chained

King

By: D.A. Martin

Clary and The Chained King

Text Copyright © 2018 by Duncan A. Martin

This is a work of fiction. Names, characters, places, and incidents either are the product of the author's imagination or are used fictitiously. Any resemblance to actual persons, living or dead, events, or locales is entirely coincidental.

Illustration © Tom Edwards

TomEdwardsDesign.com

Editing by: Tim Major and Cynthia Martin

ISBN-13: 978-1-7329810-1-0

D.A.M. PRODUCTIONS, LLC

Table of Contents

For Patricia, my loving grandmother.

For Cynthia, my mother, without whom I never would have written my stories.

And for Cornel, my father, who believed in my writing above all others.

Chapter 1

Clary ran down the dirt road towards the village square, panting with excitement in her attempt to keep pace with her two friends, Sisti and Terra. The news that Vinvale, the westernmost village of the kingdom of Belderan and, in her opinion, the most boring place in existence, was to be visited that day by a member of the royal family had given Clary something new to look forward to for the first time in months. While she was not usually the type to get excited by gossip, the town was consumed with rumors regarding the identity of the visitor as of late, making the topic near unavoidable. It was not uncommon for the identity of nobles to be kept secret while traveling in order to thwart would-be assassins, so all but the mayor of Vinvale were left to guess. The most prominent theory circulating was that prince Valen, the youngest of the Drakewil line, was using Vinvale as a rest stop on his pilgrimage to Saroza.

This prospect excited Clary and her friends, though for very different reasons. If Valen was taking his first pilgrimage, it would mean that he was seventeen or eighteen – that is, he would have been considered a *man* for over four years now. This meant that he would be looking for a wife, and while noblewomen were required to marry other nobles, no such rule fell on noblemen, save for the eldest prince. It was not unheard of for noblemen to meet their wives on occasions such as these, a fact which many of the girls in town had repeated to one another over the past few days in delighted conversation. Clary, on the other hand, could not have rolled her eyes harder when Sisti and Terra first informed her of their desires towards the prince or any other young knights or nobles who might be accompanying him. She was, however still just as excited at the idea of the visit, if not more.

For Clary, the excitement lay in the idea of the pilgrimage itself. It was well known that anyone of age could join the nobles on their journey beyond the Arid Sea in the followers' camp. Unlike the disgusting camps of those civilians following the royal legion on conquest, these camps were well taken care of and peaceful. The Church and the various magical orders closest to the nobility sponsored the wagons and security in order to gain followers throughout the kingdom. Though this was the true reason for their sponsorship, it was performed under the guise of charity given by the nobles. Clary wished to join them. She had always dreamed of traveling. She yearned for adventure, excitement, and danger. If this truly were the pilgrimage, she would not let the opportunity slip by. She would meet with the entourage and make efforts towards receiving the favor of one of the magic guilds.

Life with her father and mother on the outskirts of town had always been peaceful. Clary's father was the only true mage in Vinvale and used his medical magic, skills learned during his time as a medic in the Royal Militia, to act as a doctor for the village. He owned a small store in the center of town, which sold various simple goods from shoe polish to snacks to kitchenware. He was a large, round man – the largest person Clary had ever known, in fact. He stood at least a head taller than the next tallest man, and had a great mustache and beard, which were both beginning to grey slightly. He was loved by everyone in the town and was known for his booming laugh and his generosity towards the villagers. He was strong as well. It was a popular story among the villagers how he had once, before Clary was born, rescued a fully armored knight and his injured horse, whom he had come across whilst fishing far to the west of the village. According to the story, he carried both knight and horse, as well as all of the knight's belongings, back to the village – a full day and a half of travel without rest. Clary was not so sure how much truth there was to this tale, though if such a feat were possible she was sure her father would be the man to do it. Despite this strength, however, he was a gentle man. Never once had he yelled at his daughter, though he did often lecture her about her antics.

Clary's favorite memories were of the stories her father told to her as a child. Every night he would recount a different tale of the two grand leaders of his militia, Balthazar and Cartus. They were unrivaled warrior-mages who had been best friends since birth. According to Clary's father, they were unparalleled in physical combat and led the king's most prized militia. As her father told it, his militia was so favored by the king that it was held in equal status with several of the knight's legions. Clary loved hearing about the militia braving mysterious lands, facing all kinds of enemy hordes and dangerous creatures. She often fantasized that her own adventures would be like theirs.

Her mother, like her father, was extremely kind and caring. She worked as an assistant to her physician husband, and was known for her expertise in magical botany. She'd even written a few books on medical uses of certain herbs and plants found in the region. She had a warm smile, which

Clary had frequently been told she had inherited. She had also inherited her mother's flowing light brown hair, which fell midway down her back.

Clary was sixteen and on the tall side, though not too far off from most of the girls in town. She was slender with soft pale skin, not the type one would expect to see out in the fields collecting grapes and berries to make the wine for which the town was named, as did most of the other young women. No, Clary was more interested in studying her parent's medical texts, something her mother and father were all too happy to help her with. Despite her appearance and her love of reading, however, Clary was by no means a timid bookworm. Ever since she was little Clary had always attempted to find new ways to make village life more exciting. This often involved exploring nearby caves and forests, attempting to buy magic spells and charms from travelers, and pulling pranks on the boys in the town.

Fortunately for Clary, her two best friends were always there for her. Though they did not share her grand dreams, they did care for her and always accompanied her, if only to make sure that she didn't accidentally kill herself running around the forest alone. Sisti was a real beauty, sought after by all the boys in town. Terra, on the other hand, was plainer and had curly red hair and chubby cheeks, and though she was just as boy crazy as Sisti, she was still an excellent judge of character, which Clary always liked about her. The two of them were happy with life in the village, though their wish to be swept off their feet by a handsome prince had been obvious to Clary even before the news had reached the village. That very wish, though, was the reason Clary liked them. It meant that they weren't afraid to leave Vinvale as everyone else was.

Finally, the trio reached the town square. The royal envoy would not be there for an hour or so, if they were lucky. The girls knew that the watchman in the bell tower would be the first to see any approaching horses or carriages. The girls found a spot on the steps of the statue of the king in the center of the square.

"Do you think he'll be handsome?" asked Sisti.

"Of course he will. He's a prince! Don't be stupid," said Terra "I'm more interested in those strong, manly soldiers that'll be following him. I don't think I could deal with a pampered little prince."

"Well, that does sound more your level," Sisti responded.

"What's that supposed to—"

"Do you two ever stop talking about boys?" Clary interrupted, laughing. "You don't even know who it is yet." She was used to this routine. They bickered every day about which guys were worth their time. By now she could probably have recited every jab and comeback that would follow without missing a line.

"Well sooorry. We can't all be satisfied with fake magic books and climbing trees like *someone*," scoffed Sisti. "But don't forget, these boys won't know about any of your little games, will they? You should take this chance and find yourself a husband!" She grinned. "Who knows? You might actually have fun."

"Never!" Clary exclaimed, turning away to hide her reddening cheeks. As much as she loved her friends, she couldn't stand how frequently they talked about boys, nor the fact that they were so good at pushing her buttons whenever they did. She didn't see the point. If the greatest adventure they could imagine was running off with some man, then they would just end up raising kids in some other town and otherwise their lives would be exactly the same as in Vinvale. Not Clary. No. She would make it out and find a real adventure. She would see it all. Magic! Sword fights! Amazing creatures! It'd be everything she'd ever dreamed of!

At just that moment, there came a call from the tower. "There's a large group approaching from the eastern bridge!" The watchman paused for a moment. "They are bearing the royal symbol... There are also two others... I see it! It's a mage's banner, and the shield of the High Church!"

"That's it! It's a pilgrimage!" Clary shouted, her face lighting up.

"There's more!" the guardsman called down. "A royal banner!"

"Well, what banner is it?" Sisti called up. "Is it the gold and purple? The elk?" she asked excitedly. This was the symbol of the youngest of the royal line.

"Maybe his brothers are with him!" Terra suggested.

"I hadn't even considered that!" Sisti shouted. "Maybe his brother Lorious is here. I hear he's unimaginably handsome."

"I think I'd prefer Prince Bjorn, the second eldest. Everyone says that he's the strongest, a huge muscly soldier."

"Could be the oldest, Prince Kadrien. He might want to escort his youngest brother. Word is he's pretty close to him."

"I doubt it." Sisti replied. "Kadrien just got married a few months ago. He's probably still honeymooning."

Clary laughed. "It always amazes me how much you study the nobles. If only you studied just as hard for class, then you'd outscore even me."

Sisti stuck her tongue out at her friend and turned to call up to the guardsman again. "Is there more than one? Do you see Prince Lorious' silver and blue ram? Or maybe the bronze and green bear of Prince Bjorn? Or Kadrien's iron bull?"

"Give me a minute. They're still rounding the bend. Too many trees in the way right now." the watchman replied, straining to peer through the spy glass. "Looks like just one. It's gold… and purple! It's the golden bull-elk! It's the youngest prince!"

Sisti and Terra giggled with anticipation as they waited for the first of the visitors to arrive at the village gates. After a short while, the procession began to pass into the village square with all the pomp and circumstance of a grand parade. In the middle of the procession was the boy whom Clary assumed could only be the youngest prince, Valen Drakewil. He was adorned in silver armor that shone like a mirror – she imagined it must have been polished frequently during the journey. Atop his wavy blonde hair sat a small golden crown. Valen was everything one would imagine a prince to be, as though he were an image torn from the pages of one of Clary's books. He was, she thought, quite handsome. She had never thought that about a boy before. Her heart thumped as he looked her way. He caught her eye and winked, and she went red.

"Did you see that?" asked Sisti. "He winked at me. I told you I'd catch a prince."

"I don't know. He seems kind of snobbish to me." Terra replied. "Clary… you're still all red. Are you okay?"

Clary suddenly snapped out of her daze. "I'm fine… just tired from running all the way here. I think I'm going to head home."

"What?" Sisti groaned, grabbing Clary by the hand and pulling her back. "At least stay for his address to the village. You have to hear my future husband's voice with me!"

Before Clary could protest, the horns blared again, and everyone fell silent. Unfortunately, the crowd around them was now too thick and, given the stillness, any attempt to push through would cause quite an obvious commotion. Clary knew she would simply have to wait and endure, though she was not quite sure why she felt so uncomfortable.

"People of Vinvale!" Valen began. "As I'm sure you all know, I am Prince Valen Drakewil!"

The crowd applauded, and it was clear that the villagers weren't used to such excitement.

He continued, "I'm sure most of you have already realized that my reason for stopping in your little village is to rest before crossing the Arid Sea on pilgrimage!"

The crowd applauded again, for even longer.

"My arrangements have already been made. I will be staying at the mayor's estate while my men will camp in the field on the north side of the village. My men and I will be here for three days. We will try to be as little hindrance as possible, so I ask that you be patient and bear with us for the time being. Now, I am weary from my travels, and will be joining the mayor for some much-needed refreshment. Grand Bishop Samson will now address those wishing to join us on this blessed journey." He gestured to an old man wearing scarlet robes who stood behind him and to his right. "Once again I thank you. Glory to the King!"

As the crowd cheered, Valen stepped down from the podium, accepting varous bows, handshakes and other expected courtesies before following the mayor and the village council into the town hall.

Once he was out of sight, Clary focused on the speech given by the Grand Bishop. After a few minutes of warnings about the danger and perils of the trip, followed by a long-winded explanation of the importance of the event and the process of joining the Church on the pilgrimage, Clary finally got what she was waiting for.

"If, however," the bishop said, "you wish to delve into the mystic arts, the elder mages have asked that you bring to them, at their station in camp, something which you find personally valuable. This is not to say that you need to pay them or give it to them. They will, however, judge the capability of your spirit based on your choice."

Clary's mind began to race. Something valuable? What could she bring? Obviously she treasured her family and friends, but no object in this boring town had any particular value to her.

After the speech the girls agreed to meet later at the inn so that Sisti and Terra could hunt for the new bachelors in town. Then they went their separate ways.

As Clary walked home, she tried to think of anything of value in the village. "In the village…" she said out loud. "That's it!"

She ran towards the forest on the western edge of town, remembering her first adventure with Sisti and Terra when they were little, in which they had discovered their secret hideout. At the time, the girls had been looking for buried treasure, hoping to run into bandits from the Arid Sea. Though the Arid Sea lay many days west, at the time the girls had not understood the concept of distance. Instead of bandits, they found a beautiful meadow filled with violet flowers.

It was only slightly past midday when Clary arrived and she was exhausted. This summer had been extremely hot, and she feared that the purple flowers would be dried up or not yet in bloom. Much to her relief the meadow was full, as it had always been, of violet flowers. The field was surrounded by large trees, yet a beam of sunlight fell directly onto the crystal-clear pool in the center of the meadow, which was formed by a stream passing through it.

She calmed herself, remembering that she had three days until the mages left. Before picking her gift for the mages she decided that she would rest and cool down in the stream. Even though she did not like to dress herself up for others, she knew she had to do whatever it took to ensure her place in the followers' camp. Knowing that no one in town knew of this meadow and that it was completely secluded, she began to strip down. She bathed in the pool, scrubbing her body with the purple petals that smelled almost as beautiful as they appeared. She made a mental note to walk back home rather than run, so as not to sweat, and then change into her nicest dress. Maybe she would bring extra flowers with her just in case. Then she laid out on the flowerbed in the shade and relaxed, allowing the sunlight to dry her skin.

The sky was dark. Clary realized she had fallen asleep. She shot up when she heard for a second time the noise that had disturbed her. As her eyes adjusted to the moonlight she now had a full view of the meadow. She looked in the direction the noise had come from, and her stomach dropped. She froze. There, at the point where the stream entered the meadow, were two large yellow eyes. The area was in the shadow of the trees so she could not make out what the creature was. All she could see were the eyes hovering at the height of a man. Then, much to her dismay, the eyes rose to double the height, and though she still could not see it, she now knew what was staring at her, and it caused tears to roll down her face. A monolith bear.

Chapter 2

Why? Clary thought. *Why is it here?*

While monolith bears could be found far from their home in the southern sands of the Arid Sea, it was extremely uncommon to encounter such a creature as far into the green lands as Vinvale, where the most dangerous animal was the occasional crop snake. Monolith bears were titanic creatures, over twice as tall as any man. Known for their extreme aggression and power, they were feared throughout the land. No one would dare take one on without a few well-armed warriors, or at least a great mage to help bring it down. The hide was too thick to be pierced without great strength. A simple spear thrown or a shot from a bow would not be enough.

Clary slowly shuffled backward, hoping the creature was just trying to scare her off. She had no weapons or even clothes to protect her, and the best offensive spell she had ever learned could only change the color of someone's hair for a few minutes as a prank. She was completely defenseless.

The beast stepped out into the moonlight, matching her pace.

This is it, she thought as more tears rolled down her face. *This is how I die. No adventure, no magic, nothing.* She imagined Terra and Sisti finding her. If there was anything left to find.

A twig snapped under her foot.

"Rrrrraaaarrrrghhhh!"

"NOOOO!"

The bear charged forward with lightning speed. Clary tried to jump out of the way but was struck in the chest by an enormous claw. She flew across the meadow, crashing into a tree and falling to the ground with a thud. She felt hot wetness on her chest, then stomach, then legs. The ground, previously dry due to the heat, was now damp beneath her. She looked down and saw where the long claws had pierced her chest, or at least what she thought was her chest. It was too mangled to tell at this point. Suddenly the pain struck. It was a searing burn like nothing she had ever felt before.

The burning was a result of the monolith's defense mechanism. Though they were the most dangerous creatures in the green lands, they were not the top predators in the Arid Sea. The venom in their claws fended off larger predators by causing intense pain with a single scratch. And Clary was rent open with them.

The pain kept her from passing out, though she was sure she would succumb shortly. As the animal charged she only wished it would end the pain sooner.

A man leaped straight into its path.

Papa? she thought. No, this could not be him; this man was the largest she'd ever seen, even taller than her father, though the monster he confronted still towered over him. Had he not been clad in armor, she would have thought the man to be an ogre or perhaps a young giant.

The man and the bear collided with a thud, which to Clary sounded like thunder. The bear caught the man across the chest with a swipe, yet he did not stagger. He grabbed the bear by the arm. The bear bit his bicep, tearing the armor from it. The man wrapped his arms around the creature's waist and, to Clary's disbelief, lifted and slammed it to the ground. At this point, Clary found the man to be almost as intimidating at the beast. He got on top of the bear, striking with blow after blow, like great hammers falling from the heavens. The man reached for a large rock, which seemed almost too heavy for any human to lift and—

Everything went black.

*　　*　　*

Once again she awoke looking at the sky from the meadow floor. *Was it all a dream?* she thought. She felt no pain. In fact she felt fine. She was glad. Surely if everything she remembered had truly happened, that brave hero would have died for nothing. She was, she thought, beyond saving at that point. She sat up and looked down at herself.

Pure horror. She choked as she saw the amount of blood covering her body. She looked around and saw the meadow, her beloved safe haven, covered in gore. She screamed, grasping at her wounds. Her wounds.

What? Where...

She searched her now smooth chest and stomach. There was nothing there. Though covered in blood, she was otherwise unscathed.

Suddenly a deep voice sounded. "Are you alright?"

A man was bathing in the pool. Though he was still armored and clothed, he had removed his hood and cloak, allowing her to see his face. What she had taken to be a titan of a man was, in fact, but a boy. Though he was larger than any man she'd ever seen, he must have been almost the exact same age as her. His face was soft and endearing. He had two scars over his left eye and one over his right cheek yet they didn't seem out of place, as if they belonged there. He had short messy brown hair though not in the same elegant sense as Prince Valen. She couldn't help but think of the word *handsome*.

"I… I'm n-not sure," she stuttered.

"You're in shock," he replied.

"W-w-what's g-going on?" She was now shivering intensely.

"I'm sorry, I should have washed the blood off of you first, but I used the last of my phoenix tears on you and needed to rinse the venom from my chest and arms, you see. It's quite painful, though I'm sure you know that by know." He laughed awkwardly.

Phoenix tears? she thought. *Impossible!* Even she knew that phoenix tears were almost impossible to come by unless you were a top-class mage or extremely wealthy. Even then it was still incredibly difficult to make phoenix tears, from what she'd read and heard. This elixir was said to cure any injury. Even if one could obtain it, to use it on a total stranger was unheard of, especially if you yourself were suffering from monolith bear venom.

Her rescuer clearly understood that she was trying to decipher the situation. "We need to get you washed before you get sick."

"No!" Clary blurted out. She suddenly realized that she was completely naked in front of a man she didn't know. "I can do it myself!"

She stood up slowly, took a step and became dizzy and collapsed. "Oof!"

"See?" he said, chuckling a little. "They work wonders, but as close to death as you were, even phoenix tears won't let you just walk it off after only a few minutes."

He stepped forward and reached under her knees and arm, lifting her as if she weighed nothing. She looked away, frowning. She was glad of the darkness which meant that he couldn't see her red face. He lowered her into the pool and, still holding her, began to gently cup the water in his hand and pour it over her. Though the water ran red, it quickly cleared as the stream carried it from the meadow. He then reached his arm over and grabbed a handful of clean purple flowers, squeezed them tight in his hand and began to rub the perfumed remains along the areas where the blood had been. Once she was completely clean he lifted her out of the pool and placed her on the opposite bank to where the carnage had taken place. Next he fetched her clothes, which were still hanging where she had left them earlier that day, and placed them at her side.

She started as he turned and began walking towards the forest. "Wait! Where are you—"

"Don't worry, I'm only grabbing my bag. I have some things in there that should help."

"What if that thing comes back?" she asked nervously.

"I don't think that'll happen."

"How can you be sure?"

He continued walking, and before she could protest he reached behind a nearby tree, and with one hand lifted up the corpse of the monolith bear. She gasped.

"Sorry," he said with a sigh. "I didn't want you to wake up and think it was still attacking you so I threw it away." He put it back behind the tree and continued toward the place from which he had leapt. After a few minutes he returned with a large bag with what appeared to be a gigantic sword attached to it. When he rejoined her he pulled from the bag a pink fruit, the likes of which she had never seen.

"Here," he said, handing it to her. "Eat this. It will restore your energy after a few hours." He smiled.

Clary had nothing to lose. This boy had killed an unkillable monster with his bare hands. If he wanted to kill her, he needn't use a poison fruit. She ate the fruit, which was extremely sweet yet surprisingly delicious.

"It'll take a while to work, so I'll wait here with you." The boy walked back towards the stream with his bag in hand. Once there, he removed his chest plate, pauldrons, tunic and his remaining gauntlet. Strangely enough, removing his armor somehow made him seem even more massive.

Then she saw it. A mark of black ink on the back of his neck. Though no one in Vinvale bore this mark, and she had only seen it once before, there was no mistaking it. This was the magic seal of a slave. *No,* she thought, *a former slave.* The seal was broken, showing that the contract, which had subdued him, had been broken.

Clary's vision returned to her. In the moonlight that shone off of his back, she could now see a myriad of scars covering it. They were the only imperfections on the man's enormous, glimmering muscles, yet they were many. She wondered what kind of horrors he must have been through. Her stomach churned with guilt as her gaze fell upon the bloody claw marks on his lower back. He had been tending to her this whole time without regard for the searing pain of the monolith venom, which had no doubt been shooting through his system since the battle. To endure such agony without even flinching should not have been possible. On top of this he seemed to be losing a lot of blood. Given that he had used the last of his phoenix tears on Clary, he would have no choice but to stop the bleeding himself and wait it out. Though Clary had learned a good deal of medical magic from her father, she was in no condition to perform any kind of treatment.

When the stranger reached into the bag at his side she saw more tattoos on his forearms. These, however, were not the marks of a slave. They were in a form of writing that she could not decipher. She could tell that they were some other form of magical seal. Though she was certain she did not recognize the writing, the tattoos looked oddly familiar. Before she could dwell on it any longer he removed a needle and thread. Realizing what it was he was about to do, she shut her eyes and looked away. She had seen enough pain for one night. After a few minutes two large, rough hands pulled her up and she opened her eyes to find that her head was resting on his right thigh. He then reached into his bag again, this time retrieving a blanket, which he used to cover her. Then, smiling at her he said, "Wake me when you're ready to walk home," as he, himself lay down to sleep.

Wait, what's your name? she thought to ask, but she found herself unable to speak as she drifted off.

<u>Chapter 3</u>

Clary awoke with the sun beating down on her face. She was alone, fully clothed in the western field between the village and the forest. She felt something on her wrist and looked down to find a large pouch tied to it. Upon examining its contents she discovered four things: a bundle of purple flowers; a foreign pink fruit; a vial covered in runes, which could only have been a container for phoenix tears; and – she jumped at the sight – the claw of a monolith bear.

Standing, she found that she was completely rejuvenated, though admittedly still shaken. She rushed toward the village. As she drew closer she reviewed the night's events in her head. Had she not had the remnants in the pouch now tied securely to her waist band, she would not have believed it to be anything more than a vivid dream. She had so many questions. Who was the stranger? Where did he come from? How could anyone kill a monolith bear with his bare hands? Why was the bear even there? Her stomach turned over as she remembered looking down at the mangled hunk of flesh that was her chest, before her mysterious savior had sprung into action.

She came across Sisti and Terra, who marched towards her, clearly furious.

"How could you ditch us like that?!?" Sisti started. "Look I get that you're all obsessed with finding your adventure, but some of us just want— Ow! Hey!" Terra had slapped Sisti in the chest hard enough to stop her.

"What happened to you?" Terra asked. "You look like you just watched someone die."

Clary imagined that her face must be even paler than usual. She had watched someone almost die, but that someone was her. However, she was certain that attempting an explanation would only make her sound crazy.

"What? No... I'm fine, really. Just... uh, started feeling a little sick last night, that's all."

Terra glared at her intently. "Okay, if you say so." She clearly wasn't buying it.

Sisti, clueless as usual, finally jumped in. "Well, even if you were sick, you should have said something. We waited outside the inn for two hours when I could have been warming up to Prince Valen at the party at the manor!"

As usual, Sisti's mind was on only one thing. As she droned on about the importance of the previous night, Clary zoned out, thinking, *The prince ... the prince. The pilgrimage. The mages. My valuable item!*

"I've got to go!" she blurted out before running off toward the tent camp where she knew the mages' station would be. "I'll be there tonight! I promise!" she shouted back. She could vaguely hear the others shouting behind her, but she ignored them. She was heading towards her destiny. She knew it. Regardless of whatever was happening, she would still achieve her dream. She would leave this town and experience the world.

She was in such a rush to reach the mages' station that she'd completely forgotten her plan to wear her most beautiful dress. She was, in fact, still wearing the work clothes she had been wearing the previous day, and which still smelled of sweat. At this point, however, she didn't care. She was determined.

She stopped at the edge of the eastern side of the village. She gazed down at the field of tents in the followers' camp, mesmerized. She had never seen anything like it. Just behind the camp, towering even over the tree line, were three titanic garrison buildings on giant sets of wheels. They almost resembled ships. These enormous wooden structures, she imagined, were the mobile shelters which would carry the pilgrimage across the vast sands of the Arid Sea. One would be for the followers of the church, one would be dedicated to the mages' guilds and their new recruits, and one would house the nobility and their protection.

When she arrived at the set of tents bearing the mages' seal – the three crossed talons of a raven, an owl, and an eagle respectively – she found two villagers already waiting there. "Am I late?" she said, panting and trying to catch her breath. "Have I missed it?"

"They're going to be here for two more days!" snapped a squeaky, rat-like voice which she knew all too well. "Of course you haven't missed it. You should use your head for once."

Great, she thought, as the bespectacled boy turned to face her. It was none other than Gerald, son of the mayor and the biggest snob in the village. He was an insufferable know-it-all who always antagonized Clary in school because they were the top students, though in a town as small as Vinvale this was not much of an accomplishment. She scowled at him.

The other person was a woman who appeared to be in her sixties, and was not familiar to her. It was odd for Clary not to recognize someone from the village. Though the village was not so small that one would know everyone personally, Clary at least knew the faces of almost all the residents.

The three were silent for what must have been an hour. The unknown woman broke the silence. "I assume you are here to join the mages' guilds as well?" she asked, smiling.

"Yes," replied Clary excitedly. "I've been waiting for this my whole life."

"Oh, I know just what you mean. I've always dreamed of it as well."

"Aren't you a little old to be doing this now?" Gerald cut in rudely. Clary was embarrassed at Gerald's question, though she wasn't surprised to hear it. This kind of behavior was expected whenever he was around.

The woman looked a little taken aback but smiled again. "Well you see, because of my children I couldn't leave the village, and now that they have children of their own and my husband, rest his soul, has passed on, I feel that it's time to start a new adventure."

"I'm sorry for your loss", said Clary. "But I'm glad to know there are others in this town like me."

"What about me?" Gerald interjected.

"Yeah, right." She laughed sarcastically.

They fell silent for a moment.

"Excuse me," the woman said, "I'm actually a little worried as to whether or not I followed the rules correctly. What kind of items did you bring to present to the mages?"

Before Clary could respond, Gerald whipped out a silver ring with a large white crystal set in its center. It seemed he had been waiting for a chance to show off his item. "I bought this when I visited the capital last year!

It's expensive, and the crystal lets the user turn invisible for a few minutes. I bet no one in town could afford something as valuable as this!"

"Oh my!" responded the woman. "I only brought a letter my husband wrote to me when we first met. It's nowhere near that valuable." Clary had the impression that the woman was just being polite, though the triumphant grin spread across Gerald's face indicated that he hadn't noticed.

"And what about you?" the woman said to Clary.

"Well," Clary said, reaching to her hip. "I brought these fl—" She stopped herself as she peered into the pouch. What was the most valuable item? Was it the one-of-a-kind violet flower? Yesterday she would have said that these were the most precious items in the village, but now… she just wasn't sure. She possessed a rejuvenating fruit, a claw from a deadly monolith bear and even a rune-inscribed bottle, which was, no doubt, essential in the storage, if not the creation, of the legendary phoenix tear potion. The latter item was so unique that it could make her family rich beyond measure even if sold at the lowest price. The value of the item was only dawning on her now. No doubt the enchanted container was the only item in her possession that would put Gerald's ring to shame and impress any mage, maybe even earning her a place within a mages' guild, yet for some reason she felt that only one item seemed right in this situation.

"I have this monolith bear claw." When she thought about it, she hated the claw. It was a reminder of the pain she had undergone the previous night, of the fear and desperation she had felt. Now that the venom from the claws had been used up on herself and the stranger, it was of relatively little value. She wasn't sure why she had chosen to show them this item.

Before she could change her selection, the woman said, "Oh wow, that is an interesting find." She was staring at the claw, one eyebrow raised. A few seconds passed. Then the woman looked up. "I'm sorry to change the subject, but I'm actually feeling a bit tired. This boy and I have been waiting here since very early this morning. Do you think you can help me find a place to sit down nearby? Then if the mages' guild comes out you will know where I am and fetch me."

"Oh, right. Of course," Clary responded. She was happy to help. After all, this woman seemed kind and, as Gerald said, the mages would be there for a while.

The two walked off in search of a place for the woman to rest. As soon as they turned the corner the woman turned to face her. "I'm dreadfully sorry about this."

"Oh it's no prob—" Clary began, but before she could even finish her sentence she was jolted in the chest. The woman had shocked Clary with some form of spell. Clary felt her muscles tense up. Losing her balance, she fell back into the entrance of the tent behind her. She closed her eyes in anticipation of her head bouncing off the ground, but the impact never came. Instead she felt herself slowing mid-fall, until her back gently touched the wooden floor of the tent. *Wood floor?* she thought in her confusion.

Now wasn't the time to be pondering this puzzle. She opened her eyes and jumped up, her fists raised, prepared to fight her attacker if she had to. But the woman wasn't there. In fact, the entrance to the tent wasn't there either. Instead she found herself facing what seemed to be a cabin wall in a dimly-lit room. She heard laughter behind her and swung around, ready to defend herself, but was surprised to discover that she was surrounded by a large group of hooded figures.

"What's going on?" she shouted. "Where am I? Who are you?"

Ignoring her questions, one of the figures – though she couldn't tell which – began to speak in a dry, stoic voice. "Is it not your wish to travel to Saroza? Did you not come here seeking grand adventure and magic?"

Clary suddenly understood what was going on. She had been transported to one of the land ships she had seen when she'd first arrived at the camp. Furthermore, these were, undoubtedly, the mages who were to examine her valued item and judge whether or not she was worthy enough to join them and start her journey.

"Well, are you ready to begin or not?" the voice asked, more sternly than before.

"Y-yes sir! I am!"

This was the only chance she would get. Strengthening her resolve, she reached into her bag. "I have brought this for you to review. I hope that I understood what was asked properly." Looking down at the claw in her open hand, the group erupted with laughter.

Clary was beginning to panic. "Please, accept this. I am prepared to do whatever it takes to earn a place here. This is where I belong!" She felt tears welling up in her eyes.

The laughter started to die down and the voice spoke again. "You misunderstand, child. The strength of your heart has already been measured."

"And I'm so glad!" replied another, familiar, voice. "I don't know what I would've done if that spoiled little boy had made it instead."

It was the woman who had been waiting outside the tents. As she stepped out from a shadowed corner of the room where she had been hiding, she began to change. Her skin became smooth, her greying and stringy hair became silky and blonde. She was becoming younger before Clary's eyes. She now appeared to be in her early thirties, or maybe even her late twenties, and she was beautiful. Once her miraculous transformation was complete, she walked straight up to Clary and gave her a warm hug, kissing her cheek. "Congratulations!"

"Wait... so... I'm in?" Clary asked, still confused at this rapid succession of events.

"Yes!" shouted the woman, an enormous smile spread across her face.

"But, how—"

"Hilda here is an extremely gifted empath." replied another one of the mages, lowering his hood and gesturing towards the woman. "She can read the true emotions of those around her and in some cases, manipulate them. When someone exerts particularly strong emotions she can even read thoughts to a certain extent."

Hilda curtsied to Clary. "I'm dreadfully sorry for lying, but it was necessary to see your true feelings."

"I don't understand. Why did I need to retrieve an item if you can read minds?" Clary was beginning to feel slightly annoyed. Couldn't she have been spared the excruciating events of the previous night?

"Well, it's not that I can read minds exactly," Hilda replied. "Magic like that is nearly impossible. In order to read someone's thoughts, I need them to be emotionally attached to a focal point which allows me to reach in and see what their heart is capable of."

· "And what does that have to do with being a mage?" Clary wasn't getting it at all.

"Well... everything." replied Hilda.

At this point the first mage removed his hood. He was everything one would imagine a mage to be. He had a long grey and white beard, a curled mustache and glasses.

"Being a mage is all about emotion." he said. "One cannot simply study books and become a true mage. It takes strong emotion to truly access magic. Mages frequently exhibit strong senses of justice or adventure. These things give us our greatest power, yet they can also offer us our greatest weaknesses. For every handful of mages who are fueled by righteousness, there is one who receives strength from rage, hatred or, worse still, from sadness or self-loathing. Consequently, it is often the case that mages are damaged individuals. They feel constrained in communities such as yours. The have experienced loss, pain, suffering. Any number of traumas can awaken power within a mage. It is for this reason that it is so important for mages to be guided properly. They must be educated in techniques for controlling such emotion. These are some of the first things all mages must learn."

Until this point the old mage had been somber and serious. Now, perhaps having noticed the nervous expression on Clary's face, he suddenly chuckled and smiled. "I suppose that may have been a little too much to process all at once. There will be plenty of time to discuss all of this after we begin our trip. You should be celebrating. After all, you've just been accepted into the mages' guilds. You've achieved the first step towards your dream, and we have all gathered here to welcome you to what will be your new home for the next several weeks…"

He raised his hands in the air, and as he did so, hundreds of crystals ignited, illuminating what turned out to be not a small cabin, but a grand hall filled with mages, all applauding Clary.

The mage concluded, "…as well as to what we hope will be your new family for a lifetime."

<u>Chapter 4</u>

After being greeted by the entirety of the mages' community within the followers' camp, Clary was taken aside by the elder mage and instructed on how to proceed over the next few days. She was told to pack everything she would need and to settle all her accounts before departing, and she was given the information for what time to meet, where she would be staying, as well as all of the other basic preparatory information one would expect to receive before embarking on such a long journey.

Hilda accompanied Clary on her way home. As they left the camp Clary couldn't contain her excitement. She had a million questions, and Hilda, who seemed fond of her, was all too happy to indulge her. She told Clary about the basic lessons she would receive as well as some of the more advanced focuses that would become available to her later on. She described some of the differences between each of the three major guilds, each of which was represented by a different talon on the mages' seal. Hilda even recounted a few stories about her encounters with other, smaller guilds throughout the kingdom.

The sun was setting as the pair drew near to Clary's house. Hilda sidestepped Clary's continued questioning, saying that she needed to return to the mages' camp. Just as Clary began to protest, Hilda cut her off. "I'll be back tonight. We can meet at the village square. There're all sorts of festivities going on, just like last night. From the looks of it, you're going to need some time to get ready." She laughed.

Clary blushed, noticing her own attire for the first time. Though she had not been wearing her clothes at the time of the monolith bear attack, some of the blood must have gotten on her outfit. The smell of it, combined with dried sweat from all the running and hiking, was not helping.

"Yeah, I guess you're right," she said. "We can talk more tonight."

The two parted ways.

Clary was glad that Hilda wanted to meet up that night. She felt guilty for having forgotten about her promise to Sisti and Terra. This would be a way to kill two birds with one stone. She could join in the partying, without actually having to follow the pair around and help in their "manhunt".

When she arrived home her mother was waiting in the kitchen. To Clary's dismay, she was giving her a disapproving scowl. Though this was not a common sight in her house, and Clary was irritated at the idea of an impending argument, she had to admit that her mother's mood was justifiable. Clary had, after all, been gone for over a day and a half without having said anything to either of her parents. Her mother's worry at Clary's disappearance was even more justified considering what had happened to her the night before, though Clary did not see any reason that her mother needed to know about that. Before her mother could begin her argument, however, Clary ran upstairs to her room to get ready, pretending she hadn't noticed.

After she had finished getting ready she tried to rush down and out of the house as fast as she could, calling out, "Love you Mom, going to the square." But before she could reach the front door she ran into what she thought for a moment was a brick wall. The wall turned out to be her father.

"And where are you off to in such a rush, princess?" he said, laughing his usual booming laugh. "We've only just got you back!"

"I'm headed to the inn with Sisti and Terra."

"Are those two off chasing boys again tonight? If they're not careful, one of them might actually succeed!" He laughed again.

"Does this mean you're going out looking for one too?" her mother interjected. Her mood had lightened with the arrival of her husband. "It's about time! I can't wait to have grandchildren!"

"Ew! Mom!"

"I have to side with Clary on this, dear." agreed her father. "It's far too early for me to hand over my baby to some brute!"

"Dad!" Clary was so embarrassed. "I'm just going because I promised Sisti I'd be there for her while she tries to catch her prince."

"You shouldn't be hanging around that man," her father said. The serious tone was unusual for him. "That family is dangerous."

"It's not like it matters," she responded. "I'll be talking with Hilda for the most part anyway. Plus it's not like I can avoid him much once I'm on the pilgrimage."

"But you have to be accepted into a pilgrimage first," her mom said, obviously trying to ease the tension, "and that is not so common for someone your age, so it shouldn't be an issue."

This was an extremely unusual situation. Clary was not used to seeing her father upset, especially towards her. "Well I... I already was accepted. Hilda is a mage, and she's helping me prepare for the trip."

Her father's face turned red. She had definitely never seen that before.

"You what? Is that what you were doing? I was worried, but apparently not enough!"

"Honey, please," his wife pleaded. "It's not that big a deal. We knew this was a possibility."

"Yes, but we were supposed to have a few more years. She can't go now! Not this time."

"Excuse me?" Clary interjected. "What do you mean I can't go? I'm old enough! And this is my dream. We've been talking about it forever!"

"Yes we have, but you were supposed to go with a smaller group of nobles, if you went at all." It was clear he was trying not to lose his temper. "Not with one of them."

"I can't believe you, Dad! I thought you wanted to help me be happy, but you're just like everyone else here. You've been laughing at me this whole time!" Now Clary was crying.

"No sweetheart, that's not—"

But it was too late. She had rushed past him and run out the door.

How could he? she thought. Her father was the only one who had truly supported her. He was the one who had told her all about the wonders of his adventures. How could he build her up like that and then suddenly tell her she couldn't go? What had she done to be treated so cruelly? She deserved this opportunity! Not only had she dreamed about it her whole life, but she'd come within an inch of losing her life to attain it.

She stopped for a moment to wipe her eyes. She didn't want the others to see her like this. It took a while to regain control over herself. After all, she had never fought with her father before, and she was devastated. She tried to put the thought away and focus on the night ahead. She knew it was going to be a long one.

In the village square she was greeted promptly by Sisti and Terra. They had never been good at hiding their eagerness and had clearly been there for quite a while. The thought of the two of them sitting there waiting for the first boy to show up was enough to cheer Clary up a little.

The square was surrounded by buildings, which made it perfect for festivals. Each venue had its own special house wine, as did most public establishments in Vinvale. Even those not meant for food and beverage maintained a house wine, to be poured out for guests. It was considered common courtesy in Vinvale to provide at least this much. As the buildings in town were more frequented the closer one got to the center, it was only natural that those buildings in the square would have enough wine to support not only the populace but also any royal procession – or in this case, pilgrimage – that passed through the town. On the north side of the square were the village inn and the old tavern. To the east was the town hall with its bell tower overseeing the entire village. In the early days of the village the town hall had been designed as a mead hall. Though its title had become more refined in recent decades, its use had not changed much. On the southern side was the new tavern, Farthing's Froth-House, frequented more often by Clary's generation than its northern counterpart, the Grumbling Grape. Farthing's was large enough to take up one entire side of the square. Finally, to the west was the village lawn, a large field and garden, which was at the moment, covered in canopies housing food stands and competitive wine vendors, as well as many laughing soldiers, nobles, mages and villagers all having a merry time.

The girls decided that first they would stop at the new tavern and see who was there. Clary figured that Hilda would recognize this as the place where most people her age congregated and would know to search for her there. The smells of fresh bread, hot meat and ale filled the air as they entered. A crowd of young villagers and soldiers were gathered around the small stage, which housed a lively group of musicians all stomping and singing. Terra spotted a large empty booth by the front window, which must have only just been vacated considering how packed the place was. She quickly dragged the other two over to it.

They ordered their drinks, and Sisti immediately began scanning the room and divulging every bit of information she'd gathered on any boys whom she considered to be worthy of her attention. Clary and Terra, who after all these years were quite used to her one-track mind, both rolled their eyes and laughed. By the time their drinks had arrived the girls had moved on to discussing Clary's ordeal in the followers' camp. She told them about Hilda and how she would be joining them later. Sisti and Terra were excited to meet the mage, especially after hearing about her distaste for Gerald. Sisti in particular took this to be a good display of character.

The girls giggled and gossiped for a short while until Sisti, ever observant, shushed them, drawing their attention to the tavern entrance. A new group of soldiers was pouring in, their uniforms making them easily identifiable. They were members of the Royal Guard, though they lacked formalities and armor. They must have been off duty, Clary surmised. Had the prince been with them, one of the guardsmen would have announced his presence before the others had entered. This was a perfect chance for Sisti. She knew that the prince's personal guards would all be noble knights and not simply soldiers like most of the men in the bar. She fluffed her hair and adjusted her dress, pulling it up in an attempt to accentuate what she viewed as her most valuable assets. Once again Terra and Clary rolled their eyes and laughed, and once again Sisti shot them a dirty look.

While most of the guardsmen went straight for the bar, five of them stayed back, looking around for a table until one knight, the shortest of the group, spotted the booth where the girls were seated. They started making their way over toward the girls, weaving their way through the crowd. Sisti turned to the other two girls and smirked, clearly proud of her accomplishment – though whether the approach of the guardsmen was due to Sisti's efforts or simply because there were no other seats available, Clary wasn't sure.

"Good evening. I would like to introduce myself," said the short knight as he and his men arrived at the booth. "My name is Sir Harvel, and these are my men Sirs Cloin, Edgrum, Ingrum and Garrett. May we join you ladies this evening, or have these seats been taken by some other lucky men?"

Though charming, this was only a formality. Being nobles, no one in the tavern had the right to deny these men a seat, even if the seat was occupied – not that Sisti would have allowed anyone else to join them.

"Well, they are empty, sire, and it is your right." Sisti replied. She was confident as ever, though Clary knew that she had probably practiced these lines over a million times in her mirror at home.

The four knights shuffled into the seats beside the girls. A flustered waitress, who had been following these men since they had first entered, stood at the head of the table to await their order.

"Bring us your best ale!" Harvel commanded.

Clary took note of their order. Drinking ale with peasant girls – an interesting choice. Most nobles, in order to impress a woman, would have ordered the best wine available, especially in this town. This man, Harvel, instead had ordered ale, a peasant's drink. He was humbling himself in their presence.

As the night progressed Clary found herself glancing out the window more and more frequently. She was enjoying herself watching Sisti and Terra doing their best to impress these young knights, who were responding in kind with impressive stories of their fighting prowess and valiance, stopping thieves and aiding the capital police during their training. Usually stories such as these would have Clary completely enthralled, but she was starting to wonder when Hilda would arrive or if she would be able to find her within the immense crowd. Eventually she heard something that dragged her attention away from the window and back to the conversation.

"Well it's nothing grand, but once I faced the Exiled Regiment in battle!" It was Sir Ingrum who spoke.

Clary gasped. "What? Really? What was it like?"

"They were terrifying, of course!" he boasted, clearly pleased with this reaction. "Obviously the heroes of the former great Royal Militia would be."

"Traitors of the great Royal Militia, you mean," Harvel corrected him, before Clary had the chance to.

"Y-yeah, that's what I meant."

Clary's father had told her that the Exiled Regiment was made up of members of the King's Militia in which he had served. They were the reason the militia had disbanded. After turning on and then murdering their two commanders in mutiny, these treacherous men raided the second largest city in the kingdom, the port city of Thandessa on the eastern crest of the southern ocean. Since then they had rarely been heard from. Thandessa had become a wretched place, a kingdom of its own, housing the worst sorts of pirates and marauders. The Exiled Militia itself, who now owned the city, had become something of a legend. They occasionally attacked eastern settlements and royal supply lines in order to disrupt and generally harm the kingdom. No one knew what spurred their hatred of the Drakewils, but it was common knowledge that they would do anything to destroy their kingdom.

"Did you see the Treacherous King?" Clary inquired, more excited than ever.

"Who?" Terra asked. She was clearly more confused than anyone, save Sisti.

"The Treacherous King." Terra and Sisti still looked bewildered. "He was the greatest warrior to serve under Balthazar and Cartus, the legendary commanders of the militia. They say he was the one who led the mutiny and took charge after he killed his two mentors." Clary turned to Ingrum, still wide-eyed.

"You mean you haven't heard?" he said.

Now Clary was confused. "Heard what?"

"The Treacherous King was killed ages ago. The man I saw leading them was far more terrifying." He paused to relish Clary's shocked expression. "Their new leader is hailed as the Chained King. They say he killed the Treacherous King in one-on-one combat, and that he is a man who cannot be killed."

"Impossible!" Clary protested. "There's no way one man could have beaten the Treacherous King. He killed both Balthazar and Cartus."

"I wouldn't have believed it either if I hadn't seen the culprit in battle myself." Ingrum replied. "He was a giant of a man. Clad from head to toe in black armor. It looked like something out of a nightmare."

"So why do they call him the Chained King then?" Sisti asked.

"Well, probably because of the iron links that hang from his armor," he replied. "Rumor has it he was shackled into his armor by the Treacherous

King because underneath he was more beast than human. If you saw this man fight, as I did, you wouldn't doubt it either. When they attacked the eastern trading post outside of Grandwell, I watched him throw a siege cart over a wall of soldiers into an enemy phalanx. He took down four men at once with a single swing of his sword. I would have fought him myself had his forces not pulled back when the Third Cavalry arrived. I did still fight valiantly, of course," he added with a smirk.

"Is that so?" came a familiar voice. "Because the way I remember it, the raid at the Grandwell trading post took place when we were only eight years old, and correct me if I'm wrong, but I seem to remember watching it from the wall where one could barely see the action, let alone make out a single man. Ah yes! That's right. If I recall correctly there was another boy with me crying about how scared he was." The newcomer grinned. "Now what was that boy's name? Do you remember, Ingrum?"

Ingrum's face was bright red as he turned to look at the owner of the hand resting on his shoulder. "No, milord. I… uh… I don't quite recall." It was Prince Valen.

"Hmmm, is that so? Well, I believe he was crying because he missed his older brother Edgrum—"

"I think it's time for a dance! Care for a dance?" Ingrum shouted. He jumped up, cutting off the prince. He grabbed a flustered Sisti's hand, pulling her up and into the crowd. The prince and his other guardsmen erupted into laughter. Terra and Clary couldn't help but giggle too.

The prince took Ingrum's vacated seat and looked at Clary. "My name is Valen. Valen Drakewil."

Clary was blushing. She hadn't expected this and, judging by the exclamations of amazement of people at the tables surrounding theirs, neither

37

had anyone else. The three girls had been so absorbed in Ingrum's story that none of them had noticed the silence which had fallen on this side of the tavern upon Valen's arrival.

"And might I ask your name, milady?" Valen continued.

"Oh. I'm er… Clary, sire," she stuttered.

"Please, don't mind the formalities. Just Valen will suffice. We are all here to enjoy ourselves." He paused and then, in an exaggerated voice, said, "Though it would be easier to have fun without an audience!" Suddenly everyone turned back to their food and drink, and the noise resumed. Once again the guardsmen erupted into laughter.

"Don't mind Ingrum," Harvel continued. "He's always exaggerating. But he does have a good heart."

"My brother's been like that since we were kids," added Edgrum. "Always pretending to be something he's not. You shouldn't believe a word of his stories."

"So it's not true, then?" asked Clary. "The Chained King doesn't exist? He made it all up?"

"Well I wouldn't say that," Valen admitted. "You'd have to ask one of the soldiers who was on the battlefield."

"He may be a bit of a liar, but unfortunately he isn't smart enough to come up with something like that…" Edgrum agreed. "No, that story was told by one of our father's men."

"But still, you know how old soldiers can be," said Valen. "I'm sure he was just telling tales. There's no way a beast like that could exist."

Clary was relieved. The idea of running into such a monster was terrifying. "So how do you know you're well protected if your guards have never seen battle?"

"I don't remember saying that they hadn't," responded Valen. "Each of them has at least a little combat experience. We may have grown up together in the city, but our fathers insisted that we receive the greatest training possible. Honestly, I don't think that there are any men alive to whom I would better entrust my safety. Harvel is an amazing strategist, and I've never met a more chivalrous man in all my days."

Harvel seemed embarrassed at such praise. "Please, my liege, you flatter me. I am only as good as the men who serve under me."

"Nonsense!" shot back the prince. "You are far too humble sometimes. Is it perhaps that you are trying to impress someone?"

Harvel instinctively glanced at Terra – only for an instant, but it was enough for the prince to understand what was going on. "Well, my lady, it appears our noble captain would like to ask you something."

Harvel's cheeks turned red. "N-no… I mean yes… I mean… sire!"

"Now Harvel, it's rude to keep a lady waiting. Go on, or do I need to pull rank!"

Clary could tell the prince was someone who liked to meddle, though it seemed more out of fun than spite. She'd never seen anyone control a room as he did.

Harvel was clearly embarrassed, but he quickly stifled his reaction and announced, "Miss Terra, would you please honor me with a dance?"

Terra, who wasn't one to be so easily embarrassed, responded immediately. "I thought you'd never ask." She stood up and grabbed a dumbfounded Harvel's arm, pulling him into the crowd.

Valen smiled. "There's no helping that one. As I said, when it comes to the battlefield there is no greater mind, but when it comes to women he is clueless. A bit too honorable for his own good. As for me, I'm not one to waste time with idle chit-chat." He stood from his chair and extended his hand. "Why don't we follow their lead?"

Clary was shocked. No boy in town had ever asked her to dance before. To think a prince would be the first to do so... "Yes your majes— I mean... yes, Valen," she stammered.

Cloin and Edgrum whistled and clapped as Valen led Clary towards the stage. Clary was embarrassed that her lack of experience was obvious next to Valen who, as a prince, would have been educated in many forms of dance. She felt burning stares from all over the room. Being the center of attention at such a time was so awkward for her.

"Don't worry, you get used to it," said Valen. "Relax, just have fun."

It was reassuring. Valen must have to deal with this feeling all the time. They continued dancing for a few songs. Eventually Clary managed to block out the rest of the dancers and began to have fun.

The lively atmosphere changed after a while, as the music turned somber. She was relieved for the opportunity to have a break. Valen pulled her closer and slowed to a sway. "Your friend Miss Terra seems to be enjoying herself," he said. Clary glanced over and saw Terra and Harvel seated close together at a table in the corner of the tavern, laughing.

"Yes, well, she always wanted to find herself a handsome knight," Clary responded.

Valen laughed. "And you?"

"Well, I— I've never really had time for things like that." She was sure she was blushing.

"That's a shame. I'm sure the boys in the village would stand in line for a chance to dance with you."

She didn't want to admit to him that she scared off most of the boys in town. In an attempt to change the subject, she said, "Where's Sisti?"

"Oh, she probably ran off with Ingrum somewhere. Don't worry, she's safe with him. All of my men are respectful. He knows the kind of trouble he'll get into if he besmirches the name of the Royal Guard."

Clary wasn't really worried about them. She knew Sisti was exactly where she wanted to be, swooning over a manly noble knight who seemed just as self-absorbed as she was. Still, she saw an opportunity to get off the dance floor. She had never felt this desire before, but she wanted to be alone with this man. She wanted to talk to him, to know more about him, so she took a chance. "I don't know... maybe we should go look for her."

"Well, if it would make you feel better, then sure. Do you know where they might have gone?"

They stopped dancing and headed towards the exit.

"I'm not sure, but I know a place where we can go to look for them."

Valen looked a little confused.

"Just come with me."

They left the tavern and crossed the square. She was leading him towards the town hall. She knew it would be empty at this time, and from there they would be able to see the whole village, though she had to admit she didn't have much interest in looking for Sisti. As they entered the town hall and made their way up the stairs Clary thought about what she would ask him. Now that they were alone she felt herself becoming more and more nervous. When they reached the top of the tower the prince looked out upon the town below. It was clear that he knew why Clary wanted to come here to search.

After a few minutes of pretending to search the city in silence, Clary finally spoke up. "Your men seem to be very fond of you." It was the first thing that came to mind.

"Aye, and I of them." He turned to face her.

"Are they really as skilled as you say? Or were you simply being kind to your friends?"

"I would never lie about the skill of my men." he replied. "Each one of them has a unique skill that makes him invaluable."

"Like what?" Clary asked. "I know Harvel is a brilliant strategist, but what about the others?" The way the prince talked about his men made them seem like the heroes out of her father's stories. It made her excited to hear about them. He held them in such high regard.

"Well, take Cloin, for instance. He is unrivaled with two swords. He has won every tournament in which he has competed. He's the youngest champion in the history of the capital."

This was hard for Clary to imagine. From what she had seen at Farthing's, Sir Cloin seemed a huge clown. Throughout the evening he had done nothing but joke and make everyone laugh. She simply could not imagine him being so violent.

"What about the two brothers, Ingrum and Edgrum?"

"Those two are definitely interesting. Their family specialized in long-range weaponry. Edgrum can hit a target with anything you put in his hands; a bow, an ax, a dagger, you name it."

"And Ingrum?" she asked, noting the omission of his name.

"Ingrum was always more of an outcast. He's a good marksman but he's never excelled the way his brother has. Instead, he spent a lot of time developing his ability to deceive. It may not seem that way, but he makes an excellent spy and he's managed to get us out of quite a few tight spots with his quick tongue."

"And Sir Garrett?"

Valen's face fell. "He's a bit more difficult. I would suggest asking him about his history. It's not my place to share his story."

Clary was curious as to what he meant by this. Sir Garrett was the only one of the knights who seemed out of place. He had been silent the whole night, showing minimal reaction to anything that happened, only occasionally sipping from his drink. There was something frightening about him, though she wasn't sure what.

Valen moved closer and sat on the ledge by her side. "I'd really much prefer to hear about you, if you would indulge me. We leave the day after tomorrow, and I wouldn't want our time together to be spent talking about my men."

Clary was glad for the darkness so that he couldn't see her face go red again. She had blushed more tonight than she had during the entirety of her life.

"Well, it doesn't have to be that short," she said. "I've been accepted into the mages' guilds so I'll be coming with you on the pilgrimage."

The prince paused for a second, then took her hand. "Well, you are just full of surprises. I knew there was something different about you."

Clary's heart was racing. They were incredibly close. She couldn't believe what was happening as she felt herself being drawn in towards him. She closed her eyes and leaned in, her heartbeat increasing with every inch. Their lips were so close and then, *BOOOM!*

<u>Chapter 5</u>

Vinvale was silent for the first time that night. The laughter ceased. The musicians halted. The crowd, which only moments ago had been steeped in smiling faces and revelry, was now frozen in silent confusion. Everyone – man, woman and child – was now staring towards the eastern side of the village with expressions of fear.

Finally murmurs began to spring up.

"Was there an accident with the fireworks?"

"Are the mages mucking around in the camp?"

The sheer terror was clearly visible in Clary's face as her hands shot to her mouth. *This cannot not be happening here!* she thought. *It's not possible!* Had she not been gazing upon this horrifying image from the bell tower, she too would have been trying to come up with some benign explanation, just as the villagers below were. Not a single person in the entire kingdom would ever have imagined that this could be witnessed in Vinvale of all places.

Clary and Valen had sprung apart at the sound of the blast. The Followers' Camp was illuminated by the enormous ball of fire shooting up from where one of the mobile-garrisons had been. It was the land vessel which was to house the prince and his nobles. A swarm of men flooded into the campsite from the forest, setting ablaze every tent and cutting down anyone who tried to flee.

Shouting from below broke the silence. "Sire! Sire!" It was Ingrum. He was bleeding from his side. "It's them! It's the Exiled Regiment! They're here for you!"

The crowd exploded in panic. Screams filled the air as everyone rushed to escape, grabbing loved ones and stampeding toward the western wall. It was all in vain, however. Clary could see torches emerging from the western forest as well. The torch bearers appeared to be waiting, watching for anyone who might try to escape. No doubt they were waiting for confirmation that the Camp had fallen before advancing on the walls. Clary tried calling to the villagers below to warn them, but the panic was such that nobody paid her any attention. Unsure of what to do, she turned to Valen. He appeared to be still in a state of bewilderment. "Valen!" she shouted grabbing his arm. "They've surrounded the village! We need your men!"

At her touch, Valen snapped out of his trance. "Yes, right. Er… you stay here and hide. I'll gather my men and make a stand. It's our only hope."

"You should head to the Mayor's estate," Clary suggested. "In emergencies, all of the town guards are supposed to meet there for instructions. I'm sure most of your men will know to go there."

"Thanks," he replied. He leaned in and kissed her on the cheek. "Until next time." He turned and darted off down the stairs.

Clary felt slightly relieved. She trusted Valen. If his men were as good as he had said, perhaps they stood a chance and could hold out until reinforcements could arrive. The fire and smoke billowing from the Followers' Camp must have been visible for miles. Surely someone would take notice.

After a few minutes gathering her composure, Clary made her way down the stairs. Though Valen had told her to stay put, she couldn't simply hide while everyone else was in danger. She had to find her friends and make sure they were safe and, more importantly, she needed to get home and warn her parents about what was going on. Their home was close to the town's southern wall. She would not have much trouble getting there while the majority of the crowd was rushing to the western side. Also, her best chance of finding Terra and Sisti was to head in this direction as their houses fell between the village square and her home.

Exiting the town hall through a small side door Clary was relieved to find her route mostly unobscured. As she had hoped, most people were avoiding the side from which the explosion had occurred. She decided to take the back alleys in order to avoid the mob. This would be the fastest way home, and as long as the village gates remained closed, she would be safe as well.

Clary took off at a sprint. She was weaving her way through the side streets as fast as she could until—

Smack! Thud!

She had run headlong into a fully armored man. Her immediate fear that the wall had been breached was short lived. She looked up to see a familiar face.

"Sir Cloin? Is that you?"

"Clary? Oh thank the heavens!" the knight responded, helping her back to her feet. He was searching the dark street behind her. "Where's the prince?"

"He went to gather with all of you at the mayor's estate, I think."

"What? All the men have been waiting there this whole time. We rushed there immediately to grab armor and weapons."

"Then why are you out here?"

"Our commander sent some of us out to find him and any other men we could for reinforcements. Have you seen Sir Harvel? No one can find him either." Sir Cloin spoke fast and he kept glancing around, hands at his swords, ready to strike at anyone who might be waiting in the shadows.

"He was with Terra last I saw him," she guessed. "She's probably headed for her house."

"Knowing Harvel, he wouldn't let a woman who was out with him return home by herself in such a dangerous situation," Cloin explained. "Where does she live? I need to search wherever I can."

"I'm headed there now. Come with me."

Clary led him towards Terra's house. As they progressed she recalled how Valen had described Sir Cloin, which made her feel much safer. A master swordsman such as Sir Cloin was the perfect escort to keep her family and friends safe, and the possible addition of Sir Harvel to their company only added further reassurance. This confidence might have been sustained if not for the crashes and bangs which reverberated throughout the city, and which had been steadily increasing in frequency since she left the tower. It sounded as though the invaders were attacking the walls from every gate.

"Here!" she shouted, pointing to a house ahead of them.

"This is your friend Terra's house?" Cloin asked as Clary reached for the door.

"No. It's Sisti's. Her father's a Vinvale guard. We need to take her with—" Clary gasped as she looked upon the horrific scene before her.

On the floor, clutching a bloodied kitchen knife and lying in a pool of her own blood was one of her two dearest friends. It seemed that whoever had done this had murdered Sisti's mother and father while they sat in their chairs by the hearth. Neither seemed to have known what was coming. It appeared only Sisti had the chance to defend herself. The lack of a fourth body suggested that, though Sisti had injured her assailant, she had not done enough damage to kill.

Clary felt her cheeks grow cold. She wanted to throw up, but she couldn't muster the strength even for that. She would have screamed if it weren't for Sir Cloin who, sensing the impending screech, forcefully covered her mouth.

"Shhhh! Do you hear that?" he whispered.

Clary heard the sound of footsteps of a couple of men approaching from outside.

Her eyes opened wide in realization. *They're inside the wall!* she thought.

"Get down, and whatever you do, don't make a sound," Cloin whispered frantically. He grabbed the bloodsoaked blade from Sisti's lifeless hand and pressed it into Clary's. "If anyone comes through that door other than me, do not hesitate. Ram this blade into his heart!"

Clary was so shaken, she couldn't respond.

"Don't worry, my lady. I will protect you."

Cloin turned and cracked open the door. He must have known that they were heading towards and not simply passing by the house, because he stepped out to face them before they could come any closer. Clary crawled over to one of the windows and peeked through the curtain. She was still terrified, but she couldn't bear to look at the tragedy behind her. She had already seen enough, and she didn't want the last memory of her best friend's face to be a cold and lifeless one. She felt hot tears streaking down her face, but she did her best not to make any noise.

"State your purpose!" Sir Cloin demanded. He was standing at the ready. His arms were crossed in front of him, his hands placed on the hilts of his two trusted weapons. At this moment, Clary knew that everything Valen had said about this knight was true. She had never in her life seen a man look more at home with a pair of blades. He had seemed on edge earlier, but as he stood now with his opponents, in the open before him, he appeared to be totally calm.

One of the three men standing before Cloin turned and shouted, "We've found one over here!"

Clary heard more footsteps approaching from the next street over. *These men must be hunting down the guardsmen,* she thought. She felt her heart twinge. These were probably the men responsible for Sisti's death. More tears poured down her cheeks.

There was no doubt about it now. These men were going attack as soon as their backup arrived. Sir Cloin leaped towards the man closest to him. The man fell before he had even noticed the knight's movements. Clary had never witnessed such speed. She hadn't even seen him draw his blades. As far as she could tell, they were simply sheathed at his sides one moment and then the next they were spread out in the open, dripping with the blood of their victim.

The other two assailants had finally realized that the battle had begun, but it was too late. The closest of the remaining pair raised his sword but was slashed three times – at the thigh, the chest and then the neck – before he could even bring it down. The man who had alerted their comrades upon arrival was fortunate enough to get two swings in, but to his dismay these were deflected with precise parries, and he was quickly run through. Watching Sir Cloin fight was like watching an expert surgeon, Clary thought. He moved with such grace and precision that he seemed to be dancing rather than fighting to the death.

All three of these deaths took place within a few seconds. The last man fell just as their reinforcements turned the corner. Clary could see eight men, but she was certain there was another, staying back in the alleyway from which the others had just emerged. She could not see him but she heard his armor shifting as he approached. It was an odd sound. He must have been wearing full heavy plate armor, unlike the hodge-podge of men who bore mail, leather and light plate armor.

If these men were really the Exiled Regiment, as Ingrum had said, then they would be well trained. Even so, Clary was confused at the expression that crossed Sir Cloin's face. It was only for a moment, but he seemed unnerved and maybe even scared. *But why would he be?* she thought. There may have been eight men before him, but this was Sir Cloin. She had just witnessed him fell three well-trained attackers in mere seconds. Surely a few more men would not intimidate him. Maybe she was just imagining things.

The men squared off for a few moments. Sir Cloin would not be lucky enough to catch this group off guard, especially with three bodies lying at his feet. Eventually, one of the men made the first move, charging at Cloin. His eagerness, however, was his downfall. It seemed that the master swordsman had been hoping that a stray would separate himself, and he started his lethal dance once again. The rest of the men followed suit, charging in, hoping to catch Cloin while he attacked their fellow Exile, but wherever one of his swords wasn't striking, the other was parrying. To Clary it seemed as though Cloin must have had eyes in every direction, for not once did he let an opponent's weapon breach his defense, even when they struck from behind. The man was, in short, a prodigy.

I must have been imagining things, Clary decided as Cloin ran his sword through the last man. But as soon as she had come to this conclusion, Cloin's nervous expression flashed once more.

"Well, I'd say it's about time you came out," he said. The strange armor sounded once more. "Have I proven myself worthy of your sword, then?"

Clary began to shake. Now she knew what had caused Sir Cloin to second-guess himself. The final Exile was massive. His feet fell with a thud every time he stepped closer. The beast before Clary reminded her of the monolith bear in its imposing stature. He wore black, iron armor the likes of which no man should be able to carry. She understood, finally what was making the strange rattling noise on his armor. He truly did appear to be something out of a nightmare. The Chained King had come to Vinvale.

He reached his massive, chained arm towards his back and retrieved a large sword. While most men would have struggled to wield this sword with both hands, the Chained King needed only one to handle it.

Sir Cloin's only chance at victory would be his speed. He began to flow as he had done before. This was not an opponent whom he could allow to make the first strike. He swept in on the giant's left leg, hoping to catch him off guard with a low slash at the joint with his left blade, impairing his movement. But the King was faster than he let on. He brought his sword to guard just in time. Cloin did not seem fazed but spun back over the defense and brought his right blade down on his opponent's midsection. He connected, but unfortunately it was the back of the Chained King's gauntlet that caught the blow. He backed off and tried another flowing combination, this time from below. He repeated this a few times, attempting to beat the monster with finesse and speed, but each time the knight was thwarted.

He had to think of a new strategy. Cloin could always feel what would and wouldn't work when fighting an opponent. It was this gift of analyzing others' fighting styles that he felt gave him the edge. He shot in again. He decided that if he could not go around the guard he would have to go through it. He waited for the King's center strike, which he knew would come, and attempted to parry. Surely a massive man like this would not imagine a foe would try to parry him. This would leave him surprised, giving Cloin an advantage. The downward slash came, just as Cloin had expected, but as his sword met the paddle of a blade it simply bounced off. The attack crashed to the ground, slashing through Cloin's shoulder. He let out a scream. Had he not been wearing pauldrons, he was sure his arm would have come off.

Sir Cloin was hurt but not badly enough to give up. At this point both he and Clary knew what was going to happen, but Sir Cloin didn't give up. He charged in again and again. He received a new wound every few assaults. His left arm, his side, his back. Each injury only seemed to increase his fighting will. Unfortunately, this kind of drive could only take one so far when confronting such power.

Cloin was worn down. He knew his next attack would be his last and that he had to make it count. His back was to the house where Clary now hid. He glanced back for a moment. "I'm sorry."

He dove in one last time. Just as before, the massive blade came crashing down. At the last minute Cloin slipped to the right, chucking his left blade into the chained helmet above him. It glanced off the side of the giants mask, providing Sir Cloin with a much needed moment of distraction. He leaped up and with both hands on his remaining sword he brought it down, piercing the joint in his foe's armor at the shoulder. He had finally landed a blow.

Though the strike had forced him down, the Chained King did not make a sound. The strike had not been deep enough to be fatal. Cloin understood this. He wrapped his legs around the massive, armored torso and attempted to force the blade deeper.

One enormous black gauntlet closed around the struggling knight's hands and began to crush them. Cloin grunted in agonizing pain as the crackling and popping of his own breaking bones rang out. The King pulled the blade out of his shoulder even as Cloin's hand still grasped it. Pushing Cloin's throat back with his other iron glove, the Chained King stared into his defeated enemy's eyes.

"You have earned this," he said as he pressed the Knight's own blade into his heart with such force that he broke through the door behind him.

Clary knew it was now or never. She jumped forward and jammed the blade under the Chained King's arm. He had been so focused on the death of this worthy opponent that he had not taken the time to check the room he had just burst into.

"Raaaaarghh!"

Clary had sunk the knife into an area not covered by armor. She knew her aim was true, but at the same time it was like stabbing a tree. She knew it had not been enough to kill him. The King turned towards her, enraged, lurching forward, grabbing her by the throat and pinning her against a wall. She was choking now, but she thought she could hear people talking and armor clanking. A crowd was approaching. She hoped it was the knights, but she knew none of them would be in this area. By now they were probably out fighting by the wall, led by their valiant prince. No, there would be no rescue party. She would die here – if not by this terror's hand, then by the hand of his men.

Everything was beginning to fade away when the Chained King suddenly let her go. He leaned forward, examining Clary, who was now gasping and unable to stand.

"Quickly, you need to calm your breathing!" he said.

"Get away from me!" Clary shot back. Maybe it was the knights after all, she thought. That would explain the King's sudden fear and urgency. Even he couldn't take on a large group of elite knights by himself. "You think I'm just going to let you kill me and get away?"

"I said be quiet! If they hear you, they'll kill you."

Clary tried to shout for help, but he covered her mouth before she could do so.

"What a mess this is!" came an unfamiliar voice from outside. "King! Hey, King! You in there?"

The Chained King looked out towards the door and then back at Clary, who was still struggling to catch her breath. "Please do as I say, and do not make a sound."

Clary knew now that these weren't guardsmen or knights. They had to be Exiles to be addressing the Chained King this way. She wasn't sure why he was suddenly trying to keep her alive but she believed him when he said that his men would kill her.

He lifted her up and quickly placed her in the blood on the floor next to Sisti. This made her breathe even harder.

"Please, they will hear you. I know it's awful, but you must calm yourself."

She may not have understood his reasoning but she did understand his plan. He meant for her to play dead, another murder victim. She tried her best to control her breathing but nothing was working. She had barely survived his assault.

"King?" came the voice once more.

"Yes, I'm in here."

Clary could see the newcomer's feet between the Chained King's.

"You made a right good show of it, didn't you, King? What happened?"

"I came across this stubborn knight killing our men. He refused to come quietly."

"Oh hell, he actually got your shoulder!" the man exclaimed. Clary couldn't see the man's face but she could tell he was shocked.

"He was a strong opponent," the King said.

"What's all this then?" the man asked, stepping around his master. Clary shut her eyes, hoping he hadn't noticed the bodies.

"Our men were attacking this house. I suspect the knight knew the residents."

"They all dead then?"

"I believe so. There was no sound when I ended the knight."

"We must be getting close then. That knight there's got a royal guard seal on his armor. Must be a noble, then."

"Yes, he was," replied the king in a somber tone.

"Right shame that is, probably would've fetched a good price, that one would. Let's try to be a little more careful with the next one then, eh?"

Clary was becoming more nervous. Her breathing was still slightly elevated. If the man examined her in the slightest, she would be discovered. She could only hope that he would lose interest.

"Alright then, let's get out of here."

Clary breathed a sigh of relief as the two men left the building. She sat up and started making her way towards the back window as quietly as possible. Now that the house was clear, she figured that this would be the safest exit. She dropped out of the window into the back alleyway.

There was a startled scream followed by a loud, shocked, "Clary, is that you?"

Clary had been trying to make her way toward Terra and Harvel all night, but at this moment she could not have been less happy to hear her friend's voice.

"I heard someone over here!" said a voice at the other side of the house.

"Be quiet!" Clary whispered. "Run!"

But it was too late. There were men on either side of the alley. They were trapped. Sir Harvel drew his sword, ready to make a stand.

"Wait!" Clary shouted. "We are nobles! This is our guard!" Though Sir Harvel was not wearing his armor, his linen dress clothes still bore the royal guard's emblem, just as Cloin's armor had. Not only was Harvel dressed the part but the girls had worn their finest clothes in order to mingle with the knights at the festival. They may not have been worthy of royals, but their garments could pass for the attire of nobles. Clary knew that the Chained King was nearby, and if he were summoned, he would defeat Harvel with ease and probably kill the girls. Harvel seemed to understand the

56

disadvantage he was in, having to protect both unarmed girls in such a cramped setting, but he still refused to lower his sword.

"Harvel, they killed Cloin," she said. "You can't take them."

From the crowd of soldiers came an unpleasant, weasel-like voice, which Clary had hoped never to hear again. "Well. What's all this then?" It was the man who was had been inside the house. Though he was a soldier, he reminded her more of a rodent than a man. "Alright, alright. Got ourselves a couple of nobles here, boys." The men laughed. "Looks like this young girl understands how things are working out on this fine evening. So, listen here then, pretty boy, I understand you want to act all chivalrous, what with you being a knight and all, but if you do, we are going to have to kill you and them two pretty little things you got there. However, if you do put your weapon down, we will simply take you and hold you for ransom which, as you know, the kingdom will be forced to pay. Fair enough, then?"

It appeared that Harvel was silently debating what to do.

"Please, Harvel!" Clary pleaded. "He's telling the truth. I heard them talking about it earlier. They don't want to kill any nobles."

Harvel closed his eyes, furrowing his brow. It was clearly painful for him to do, but lacking any other option, he lowered his sword.

<u>Chapter 6</u>

It had been over an hour since the wall had been breached. Though no one was sure how it had happened, the Exiles had, at some point, found a way to get the gates opened from the inside. The village guardsmen and the few knights and soldiers assigned to protect the pilgrimage may have been able to hold out in a war of attrition if they had had the luxury of awaiting aid from the capital. But once this horde of men had flooded into the streets, there was no chance of victory. A great number of mages and soldiers, who had decided not to take to the night's revelries or had simply gone back to camp early, had already been lost in the initial surprise attack. Those men who were lucky enough to be in the village were not only ill-equipped for battle, many were still drunk from the festivities. Any resistance was quickly stifled, and the village was overrun within minutes.

Though it was the dead of night, the sky over Clary's hometown was orange. She had to squint to look back at the blazing village. By this time tomorrow it would be nothing more than a pile of ash. Tears rolled down her cheeks as she thought about the night's turmoil. She was scared. She had still not seen her parents. She wondered if they had made it out, or if they had managed to survive until the guards surrendered. Surely they must have. She could not imagine her father allowing her mother to come to any harm. He would have fought tooth and nail to protect her.

A sudden realization made her chest tighten. The last conversation she had with her mother and father had been a fight. She wanted to collapse in anguish, but at that moment she received a sharp boot to the center of her back.

"Oi! Keep it moving then!" It was a man whom they had learned was named Turk. He was the one who had taken her, Terra and Harvel hostage. From what Clary had gathered, he was of higher rank than the other men in the group. Considering how informal he was with their leader, Clary could only assume that he was close with the Chained King.

Clary shot him the most enraged look she was capable of, but kept moving. She felt she was glowing hot from anger. She'd never wanted so badly to attack someone in her life.

As the trio approached the burnt remains of what was once the followers' camp, they could see other groups of Exiles leading prisoners in the same direction. Clary had overheard Turk instructing his underlings not to kill any more villagers after the surrender. "They'll fetch a fine price as slaves. If we can't sell 'em in the Arid Sea, we'll bring 'em back to Thandessa and sell 'em for cheap. Don't want to be wasting free merchandise. Even a cheap slave is worth something."

Clary looked up at the mages' garrison as they approached it. It was the only one of the three massive mobile structures left standing. She spotted the area where she had first met Hilda earlier that day. It was hard to believe that only a few hours ago she had been experiencing the best day of her life. Now the former mages' section was unrecognizable. Piles of smoldering ash, burnt wood and charred bodies lay everywhere.

Before the mages' garrison was a large chair upon which sat a huge figure clad in black, chained armor. His men surrounded his throne on either side. Kneeling before them were dozens of villagers, guards, mages, and knights. Clary did not see any clergy members. She assumed that they must have all been caught in their mobile garrison as it burned.

All of the prisoners were either shackled in chains or had their hands tied behind their backs, as Clary, Harvel and Terra did. The three of them were forced to their knees when they joined the crowd. Clary looked around, hoping to identify which of her friends and family had survived. From what she could see, most of the survivors were nobles and knights. She knew that the Exiles were trying to spare the nobles at first, but she had hoped the surrender would have saved more of the villagers. She could see a few familiar faces, though. She saw Sir Garrett and Sir Edgrum. Garrett looked quite bloodied. He must have taken a serious beating. Edgrum did not appear to have fared much better.

She could also see a few members of her class from school, including Gerald. He was crying openly. She scanned the crowd and then realized why. His father, the mayor, was at the front of the crowd of prisoners, kneeling before an Exile who stood between him and the Chained King.

"Where is he?" the Exile shouted.

"I don't know! I swear!" the mayor squealed.

Smack! The Exile had brought the pommel of his sword down across the cowering man's temple. "Tell me now or I'll strike you with the other end!" *Crunch!* He struck him again. There was blood dripping down the mayor's face. He seemed delirious from the blows to his head and couldn't answer. The Exile raised his sword once more.

"Stop! Can't you see he doesn't know anything?"

Clary knew the defiant voice all too well. Her father had been hidden in the depths of the crowd but now stood towering over everyone. It was clear he'd had a rough time tonight, judging by the blade wounds across his cheek and chest.

"Well, since you seem so sure of that then I guess this one isn't of much use after all," replied the exile. He looked back down at the mayor and swung his sword. "Bring that one here," he said, pointing at Clary's father.

"Careful with that one!" said another of the Exiles. "He's pretty strong. Took a few of us to bring him in. He's a mage, he says."

"If he's a mage then why didn't you kill him, then?" This time it was Turk who spoke out. "You know our orders!"

"He says he's the town physician. He's not a battle mage. Figured he could be useful. He'll be worth more than the rest."

A few Exiles stepped forward to lead her father toward the front, where the mayor's body now lay.

"Turn around and kneel down." the interrogator shouted.

Her father complied. Clary realized what was going on as two of the Exiles ripped open the back of her father's shirt. She wanted to help, but she knew she couldn't do anything.

"Let this be a warning to all of you!" he shouted. "If you defy us, if you question us, if you so much as utter a word against us, this'll be you!" He pulled out a long studded whip and brought it down across Clary's father's back. Blood oozed from the laceration, but he did not scream. The interrogator, clearly displeased with this reaction, struck him again. *Crack!* Again there was no reaction from Clary's father. *Crack! Crack! Crack!* The interrogator seemed determined to make an example out of him. Finally, after the eighth or ninth strike, Clary's father's fortitude waivered. It was only a slight acknowledgement of the pain, but the slight wince and scowl did not go unnoticed. The interrogator smiled.

Clary could not stand to see her father in such pain and was relieved when the lashing finally stopped. Or so she thought… but the interrogator was not done yet. This sadistic Exile wanted to savor the pain he was causing. Once again he raised his whip. Clary lost all reason. She was going to charge this interrogator and stop him. She did not care what happened to her. She needed to save her father.

Before she had the chance, someone else did exactly what she was planning. It was her mother. She had apparently also reached her limit and sprung forth to attack the man who was hurting her husband. She was immediately intercepted by Turk.

Screams rang throughout the crowd. Everything happened so fast that Clary still hadn't realized what was going on when her mother fell to the ground in front of her. She simply stared down in dazed disbelief. The thing that finally snapped her out of it was a cry of pure rage that seemed inhuman. It was louder and more terrifying than even the monolith bear. For a moment Clary was sure that a dragon out of a fairy tale must have been descending upon the village. At this point she felt that nothing could shock her, but when she looked towards the source of the noise, what she saw was more surprising.

Clary's father bent over and spewed white-hot fire from his mouth, down upon the chains that bound his wrists together. Somehow, though, his hands were unscathed. He reached up to the wound on his chest, covering his fingers in blood, which he used to quickly inscribe some runes on his left arm. Suddenly tattoos appeared on his forearms and his hands began glowing bright as a sword in the blacksmith's forge.

The surrounding Exiles had jumped back at the sight of the fire but now charged back in to subdue the old man. However, there was no stopping him. He discharged his flames once again upon the Exiles to his left and then turned towards the two on his right. He grabbed the first by his helmet, which melted under the heat of his burning hand. The other attacker swung his sword at Clary's father only to have his blade caught in the old mage's free hand. The blade, too, melted at the point where he had grabbed it. He grasped the frightened Exile by the arm, and the man screamed. Then he rained fire down on him. More of the Exiles charged in. Clary's father threw them around like rag dolls, burning any man he could get his hands on. The heat that burst forth from his mouth was enough to drown six men in flames at once.

He was nothing but rage and fire at this point and seemed invincible. It seemed no one understood where this was coming from. Clary's father had always been the kind, loving physician. He never raised a hand against anyone. Clary knew her father was strong. She knew he was a mage, but magic like this was beyond high level. Not only was it extremely powerful, there was only one mage in the world who should be able to wield it.

"Cartus!" came a booming shout from the front of the crowd. The Chained King had finally risen from his makeshift throne and was making his way towards the mage who had been laying waste to his men.

Clary could not believe it. Cartus, one of the two legendary generals who had led the King's Militia was not only alive, he was her father. The stories he had told her as a child had not been about the men whom he had admired and served under, they were about him and his best friend. Every battle, every act of heroism, every tragic event, had been his.

Her father – Cartus – still held the smoldering body of the interrogator. He turned to face the charging King, then threw the armored corpse at him. It burst into a cloud of ash upon impact, causing the King to lose sight of his target for a moment. Cartus smashed into him with a sound like thunder. He threw the Chained King to the ground, but the King jumped back up and caught him across the right side of his face with a blow that sounded like a hammer striking an anvil. The immense power emanating from each strike these titans threw was so intimidating that no one even attempted to interfere. The two were evenly matched. Neither man even attempted to guard himself. They simply threw blow after blow, each one smashing the other in turn. Every time Cartus' fists struck the black armor before him, sparks exploded from the point of impact.

Though everyone else's attention was still focused on the terrifying clash in front of them, Clary turned to her mother. The spot where Turk's blade had met her stomach was growing damper and redder by the second. Panicking, Clary tried to remember every medical spell her father had ever taught her. She placed her hands on the wound and started muttering incantations. Tears dripped from the tip of her nose. "I'm so sorry, Mom! I'm so sorry for everything I said! I love you so much. Please! Please stay with me." The bleeding slowed, but Clary wasn't sure if it would be enough.

"It's okay, baby," her mother responded. "I know. We both do. Your father and I are both so proud of you." She coughed. "It'll be okay Clary. I love you." She coughed again.

Clary could tell she didn't have much time. In her panic she turned back towards the fight and shouted, "Papa, help!"

Her father broke from his rage for a second and turned to face her. Unfortunately Turk, who was still standing nearby, had taken notice. He grabbed Clary and put his blade to her throat.

"Come on then, Cartus. It's over," he shouted. "Make one more move and I'll slit her throat. Don't you push me! You know I'll do it! You remember what I'm capable of, don't you?"

Her father seemed more enraged than before, if it were even possible. There was fire coming from his nostrils with every breath. But he must have realized the truth in Turk's words. He gave up. His face fell, and he went down to his knees. "Please, don't hurt her," he said. There were now tears in his eyes – another sight Clary had never seen before, and she wished she never had. "Don't hurt my daughter. I'll do whatever you want." He was defeated.

The Chained King came up behind Cartus and struck him in the back of his head with his gauntlet. Cartus dropped to the ground unconscious.

"Well how 'bout that then, King?" said Turk in his squeaky voice. "Never thought we'd run into old Cartus out here then, did we? Guess this venture was more profitable than we thought then, eh? Hardly recognized him with that grey beard. Seems to have gotten a little pudgy in his retirement too."

"You bastard!" Clary shouted.

"Shut it, you!" Turk shot back, raising his fist.

"Stop!" shouted the Chained King. "That's enough! We'll need her in order to keep Cartus under control until we can get him back. I'll not have you harm her." It seemed even the Chained King himself feared what would happen if Cartus awoke to discover his daughter was dead. "Get any medics we can spare and try to save that woman on the ground. If possible we should keep her alive as well."

Clary felt a surge of relief.

"But King!" Turk said.

"This supersedes any prior orders. We will do everything we can to keep the Firedrake of the North contained until he is brought in. Do I make myself clear!"

Turk was clearly frustrated but he backed off. "Alright then." He hoisted Clary up to her feet and started forcing her over toward his master.

At that moment there came another call from the rear of the group. "We've found him sir!"

Eight men now entered the camp; six Exiles and two prisoners. They were Valen and Ingrum.

"Spotted them in the fields to the south just after we breached the wall," one of the captors said. "Seems they were trying to escape."

"Then why are you only now bringing them to me?" the Chained King demanded.

"We had to chase them down through the forest. This injured one here fell behind so we caught him quick enough, but the prince didn't seem to want to wait around so he took us a little longer."

Clary couldn't believe it. Valen was a noble and kind man. There was no way he would have abandoned his men to save himself. The Exile must have been mistaken or lying. The prince had told her he was going to gather the troops and defend the wall.

Valen stepped forward. "Please sir, you know who I am. If you treat me well I'm sure my father will pay you whatever you want. I'll even pay you more myself if you want. Just please don't hurt me."

"And what will he pay us for the rest of his people?" the Chained King asked.

"What? Who cares? Just make sure you help me, and I'll do whatever it takes to help you!"

Clary was disgusted. The prince was a fraud. To think that, for a moment, she had felt something for this coward. He really had abandoned the city. When he left the tower, he expected her to stay there and die. He was nothing more than a spoiled brat who cared only for himself. He wasn't even trying to help the others even though the whole reason the Exiles attacked the village was to find him! She looked over to Harvel who was hanging his head in shame.

"Unfortunately for you, we don't give special priority to our prisoners unless they are dangerous enough to warrant it. And clearly a coward like you could not be a threat to even our lowest warrior." At this, the rest of the Exiles began to laugh.

The prince looked terrified. "No, please! I'll make you rich! I swear!" But he was ignored.

"Turk!" the Chained King called, taking his leave.

"Alright then boys, you heard the king! We've got what we came for! Now let's pack 'em up then!" came the squeaky voice.

The men started hoisting up the prisoners and walking them through the fields to the north.

"Where are we going?" Clary asked.

"We are taking you to the camp. To get you all stowed and ready for travel." Turk laughed, urging Clary forward by jamming a knuckle between her shoulder blades.

"You're talking about us like we're objects. You can't treat people like this!"

"Don't you worry your pretty little head then. You're not going to be staying in a cheap cart or cage like the rest of these peasants."

"What do you mean?" Clary asked.

"You're the daughter of the Firedrake then, ain't ya? We've got a special new place picked out for our priority customers like yourself."

"What are you talking about?"

Then Clary heard loud creaking and groaning. She turned back to see the last mobile structure, where she had been officially accepted as a mage, begin to trudge forward in their wake.

"A very special place indeed then."

Chapter 7

None of the prisoners aboard the mages' garrison were able to sleep on the night of the attack, save for those who were seriously injured or who had lost consciousness during the struggle. For most, the fear of the days to come was far too great. Those who were deemed by the Exiles to be of higher value were kept on different floors in this mobile castle. It no longer resembled a wondrous hall with luxurious rooms, as it had when Clary had first visited the vessel. Though it had survived the assault, the structure was unable to avoid damage completely. The rooms had been torn out and reconstructed with iron bars to form makeshift cells. It now resembled a prison more than anything else. The magic, which controlled the climate and protected the inhabitants from the elements, had also been neglected, lacking the service of the many mages for whom it was originally intended. The wind now flowed freely through the corridors. Rainwater dripped through the cracks in the ceiling and the holes sustained during the battle.

Clary sat on the hay-lined floor, mulling over the events of the past several hours. She was devastated at all she had lost. The only thing she had left was the small pouch containing her valued items. She was glad that she'd thought to keep the small bag tucked away under her dress where it would not be found. She had been caged alone on the top level, in the second to last cell of sixteen, farthest from the staircase leading to the floors below. The two cells on either side of hers were empty. It was clear that the Exiles intended to keep her separate from everyone else, though she was not sure why. The other thirteen cells were occupied, but it was too dark to make out faces, and it seemed that everyone was apprehensive about speaking out in such uncertain circumstances. In fact, it was this uncertainty of their fate that was the most frightening aspect of the whole ordeal.

It was dawn before the prisoners had any contact with their captors. Clary heard their voices as they ascended the stairs, and took them to be Exiles. As they entered the room, however, she could see that they were leading a group of prisoners to the other cells. Clary's door opened and two figures stood in the entrance. She scrambled to her feet, ready to defend herself if necessary, but no attack came. Instead, the smaller of the two was shoved into the cell, colliding with Clary.

"What the— Ouch! Hey!"

"Clary? Is that you?" asked the figure. It was a voice which Clary recognized, but one that she had never expected to hear again.

"Hilda!" Clary responded, happy to finally be in friendly company. "How did you—"

"Oi! Shut it you!" said one of the Exiles.

Clary turned on him, furious. "Don't you tell me to shut it, you dolt! Where are my parents? What've you done with them?" Clary didn't know where this sense of bravery was coming from. She was burning with anger. All she could think about were her parents. She felt hot all over.

"Why you insolent little—" The guard raised his hand to strike her, but just before he could do so, the other Exile who had entered the cell grabbed his wrist.

"Are you bleedin' mad Thymey? We're not supposed to touch this one!"

"And why is that?" responded the man called Thymey.

"Cause she's old Cartus' daughter!"

Thymey paused for a moment. He must have realized his mistake, but he was still not willing to let the insult go. "So what? I've heard we just needed her to control him. It's not like she's the only leverage we have. If anything, we should kill her like the rest of those dirty mages."

"You know good and well that old bag probably ain't gonna last the night – and even if she does, she's nowhere near as valuable as the girl. She's the daughter of one of the original two, the daughter of the legendary Firedrake of the North. She's one of the Fjorendel. Another chance, don't you understand? Boss says if we do things right, then we might be able to—"

"Then you might be able to learn when to shut your mouth then, Ammle!"

Clary shivered at the words of a third Exile who had just arrived. As if she didn't have reason enough to be angry, now the weasel was here again.

"Uh, right, sir! Sorry 'bout that, Captain Turk!" replied Ammle quickly.

"Oh, it's not me you should be apologizing to, then." Turk responded, a clear sense of superiority in his voice. "Imagine if King had been around to hear you talking so openly about that then?"

"Well er… I uh… I h-hadn't thought about that, sir."

"Well that's obvious then, now isn't it, you idiot." Clary got the distinct impression that Turk enjoyed talking down to those beneath him. "I don't think even I'd be able to stop him, then. You know how unreasonable he can be when you talk about those things that you shouldn't, then."

"It's not a problem, sir," Thymey interjected. "He won't be doing it again."

"Yeah, you better not, then. And you better listen to your partner as well, then. If I see you placing hands on this girl, I'll have you flogged and then thrown in with the lot of them. Understand?"

"As you command, sir." Thymey responded begrudgingly.

"As you were, then." Turk walked off, clearly satisfied with the opportunity to impose his will upon this man.

"Alright, the last of you, get into those three cells at the front! Now!"

The other prisoners quickly shuffled into the open cells that remained – but the two on either side of Clary were still kept vacant.

"Wait!" she called out. "What about my mom! I heard —"

"I told you to shut it!" Thymey slammed the gate in her face. "You may be under the protection of the higher ups, but make no mistake, your time will come, and I'll be there when it does. Then we'll see how far that sharp tongue of yours gets you." He stormed off down the stairway.

Clary was still hot with anger at the exchange, but at least she had gathered a bit of information. Much to her fortune, the man called Ammle didn't seem too bright and had let slip a little more than he meant to. For one thing, she now knew her mother was alive and, even if it were only slight, there was a chance she might pull through. Her father was also alive, and as long as her captors kept *her* alive, she could assume that he was too. She was sure that if he expired, they would either kill her or throw her in the carts with the rest of the villagers who were being sold as slaves, unless something else made her valuable apart from her use as a bargaining chip. They talked about her like they needed her for something else. He had even said that she was a Fjorendel, whatever that was. But perhaps Ammle was just overstating things. Maybe he didn't know what he was talking about.

"Clary, are you alright?" Hilda, whose face was now more visible as the sunlight increased ever so slightly, looked worried.

Clary realized that she had been standing in silence for several minutes since Thymey and Ammle had left. "Y-yeah, I'm fine," she lied.

"Clary, you and I both know that's not true."

"Right, empath, sorry. But anyway it doesn't matter right now. How did you escape? I thought they were killing any mages that stuck around." It made sense that they would have done this. No one would pay ransom on mages, and as useful as having a mage for a slave would seem, controlling them would be so difficult that no traders would want to risk purchasing one. On top of the direct danger they would pose to the Exiles, this all made keeping them extremely impractical.

"Well you just said it didn't you? I'm an empath." Hilda responded frankly, as if this explained everything. Clary frowned in confusion. "Well, I was almost at the village square when the attack happened, so when I was found by a group of Exiles I just lied and said I was a noble."

"And they didn't press any further?"

"No. Don't you remember what the head mage said? Skilled empaths can control people."

"You mean you completely hypnotized one of them? That's great! Maybe we can—"

"It's not exactly like that. Like I said, you have to be exceptionally skilled to control others like that. I may not be that good, but put a sword to my throat and even I can at least calm the emotions of an attacker or two and make him a bit more trusting. It's not something I could do if the lies were

73

more elaborate or unbelievable, but I think their urgency to gather up as many nobles as they could helped me get a pass."

Even though Hilda was trying to pass it off as something simple, Clary was impressed. "And what about the others? The rest of the mages."

"As I said, I was in the city when it started. I haven't seen most of them, but the few that I have seen were already dead. Hopefully some of them got out in time."

This saddened Clary even more. The mages she had met yesterday had all been so kind and welcoming. They seemed truly happy to have added another member to their family. The thought that so many of those smiling faces had been snuffed out was heartbreaking.

"But you, Clary, you never mentioned you were the daughter of Cartus. He's one of the most powerful battle mages who ever lived. His use of fire magic is legendary."

"The thing is, I had no idea. My father has always just been the town physician. He owns a general store. He said he was in the royal militia but that he was just a medic. Besides, even if he was Cartus, what's the big deal? Why would they want him dead? I mean, the only one who hated him was the Treacherous King, and he's gone. And why does being his daughter make me valuable? He hasn't taught me anything but a little medical magic here and there."

"Clary, I don't think you quite understand. Your father, Cartus... he's Fjorendel."

"Yeah, I heard that Ammle guy say so. What is that?"

Just as Hilda was about to answer more voices came from the stairs. Clary and Hilda shuffled to the corner of the cell, trying to get a look at what was coming. A light was coming up through the stair port. Whoever it was, they had torches. This was a good thing, Clary thought. From the sound of clanking chains and tired panting, she surmised that they must be bringing in more prisoners. The fire would finally bring a little illumination and warmth into this dark, dank room and would allow her finally to be able to survey the situation a little better. Not to mention the addition of a few new prisoners might help to provide a bit more information. But as the Exiles emerged from the stairwell, all of Clary's attention turned to the prisoner they were carrying.

There was a handful of Exiles this time, but they weren't directing a group of prisoners as before. Instead, there was only one prisoner, and they were carrying him. Though his head hung low with the sway of a dead weight, she could tell from the size of the massive man that it could only be one person.

"Daddy!" she shouted. "Daddy, are you okay?"

"Quiet, prisoner!" one of the Exiles shouted, rapping the bars with his club while the others continued to load her father into the cell next to Clary's. It smashed her fingers and she fell back to the floor. Though the pain was great, she didn't care. She needed to talk to her father. Not only did she want to make sure that he was okay, but she also had many questions that needed answers.

"Daddy! Dad, wake up!" But he did not move.

The Exile stomped over towards her cell. "Hey! What did I just say?"

"Wait!" shouted another Exile. It was Ammle. "Don't touch her. This is the one we're supposed to grab."

Clary was confused. She wanted to shout again, but Hilda grabbed her shoulder, whispering, "You need to calm down. You know they need you and your father. They won't let him die. Don't go causing unnecessary trouble, or they might hurt one of you."

The guards were now in the process of nailing down the many chains that bound their former leader, throwing the links over the large wooden rafter and hoisting him up. Clary hated the way they laughed as they secured her father. He was the most kind-hearted man she had ever known. He did not deserve to be treated like this.

Next, the men moved to the cell holding Clary and Hilda. Clary knew they would be taking her next. She wanted to fight, but there were so many of them that she wouldn't stand a chance, and they might hurt her father if she did break free. She wasn't scared, though. As Hilda had pointed out, the Exiles needed Clary. They would not risk the rage that her father might unleash if she were to die. She stood up and followed them quietly.

From the stairs Clary could view each floor as they descended. She tried to make the most of this, gathering whatever information she could, but unfortunately the lower corridors were even less well-lit than the one in which she had been held. She would have to remember to take a look around on the way back up, when more light would penetrate the tiny windows.

As they exited the building she could see that the Exiles had set up camp. What had appeared last night to be just a small marauding band of one or two hundred men was now visible as an entire army numbering closer to a thousand men. Clary figured that during the attack many of them must have been either holding a perimeter in the forest or protecting their base camp. She surveyed the camp as best she could, but the men kept pushing her forward every time she stopped to look around. Though she was not able to see much, one thing did catch her eye. Just on the edge of the camp, near the part of the forest to which the men were leading her, was a large cage. Clary's heart sped up as they approached it. For a moment, she thought that they might have meant to throw her in the cage along with the gargantuan beasts within it. She had an all too familiar sense of terror at the sight of the eight sleeping monolith bears. Her momentary panic did not go unnoticed.

"Oh, don't you worry your pretty little head, dearie. Like the captain said, you're too important. We ain't going to let you be bear food." It was the Exile, Thymey, walking up and joining them. He had an eager, sinister look about him, as if what he was planning for her was going to be just as bad. Clary closed her eyes and groaned. *Why does it have to be him?* she thought.

They reached a small clearing next to a stream, and Clary stood in silence for a few minutes while the soldiers settled themselves around the edges of the clearing. They were waiting for someone. Clary simply stood in the middle, trying not to provoke them, fearing the worst. She was trying not to look at Thymey, who was still staring at her with that evil grin. After a few more minutes of rising apprehension, the person they had all been waiting for arrived. She never thought the day would come when she would be happy to see him, but she felt oddly relieved. It was Turk. Though she hated him, she knew that he had a good deal of power as well as an interest in keeping her alive and unharmed.

"Alright, get on with it you coward. Why am I here?" She felt her confidence returning. As long as Turk was there she knew she would be kept safe from whatever Thymey was planning.

A flash of anger crossed Thymey's face as he looked up to his captain. Turk only smiled and nodded. Thymey's grin returned as he turned to pick up two swords from the ground; one wooden and one steel. He walked towards her, holding out the handle of the steel blade, ready for her to grasp.

Clary was apprehensive, but Thymey was egging her on. "Go on, girly. Take it, and give it your best go."

Clary decided it would be best to give it a shot. She didn't want to give him the opportunity to use the blade against her. She reached for it when *SMACK!!!*

"Oops, sorry 'bout that, girly. Me hand must've slipped. I thought you had it," Thymey said. The men around him laughed. He had hit her across the face with the back of the hand which was clutching the blade, using such force that she had fallen to the ground.

Clary glared up at him, filling with rage. She was starting to get hot again.

"Well, since you don't want to take it from me, I guess you can just pick it up off the ground." He grinned, spitting on the handle and throwing the blade into the dirt. He turned back to face his men, laughing.

Clary saw her opportunity. Without hesitation, she reached forward, grabbing a handful of sand. She threw it in her opponent's eyes as he turned back to face her, then utilized Thymey's temporary state of blindness to attempt to rend his head from his shoulders. But as her sword burst through the cloud of sand, it met only air.

"There's the fighting spirit we was lookin' for!" Thymey cackled. He was now at her side. *When did he—* she thought, but before she could turn around there was a loud *CRACK!* as he brought his wooden sword down across the other side of her face. She hit the ground again with a thump. She could feel herself getting angrier by the second.

"Come on now, lovely. You didn't think I was just some prison guard now did you?"

Clary thought hard, trying to devise a strategy to defeat him. She remembered the fight between the Chained King and Sir Cloin. Leaping forward, she struck at Thymey's leg, expecting it to be blocked, and when it was, she spun around to strike at his neck. She was nowhere near as fluid as Cloin had been. In fact, the movement seemed quite awkward and slow when performed by her, but she was sure that this sort of strike would be unexpected and might still connect. Unfortunately, however, her blade once again met nothing but air.

"So you've seen a bit of sword play, have you? That was pretty clever, but you're a hundred years too early to try that on me." *Bam!* This time he struck her in the back, and once again she crashed to the floor. Her skin stung as though she'd been whipped, and her spine started to throb where it had been battered. This man was fast. He was clearly skilled, and had no problem showing off this talent against her.

"It would've worked if I had a second sword!" Clary shot back, panting as she got up.

"Is that so?" Thymey chuckled. "Very well then, seems we've got an expert swordsman in our midst boys!"

All the men laughed. Clary was burning red with anger and embarrassment. Thymey looked towards one of his men and gestured for his weapon. He threw the new blade on the floor at her feet, as he had the first. Then he did something that Clary thought very strange. He dropped his wooden sword to the ground and turned to face his men. Did he really think so little of her that he would show his back towards an enemy with a weapon?

She seethed. Regardless of the reason, she was not going to let this opportunity pass her by. She would take advantage of his overconfidence.

She charged forward, grabbing the second sword as she went. She tried once again to picture Sir Cloin's flowing movements. She drew nearer and nearer, yet the Exile did not turn. *This is it! You shouldn't underestimate me!*

The first blade flew from Clary's hand with a *clink!* as it was met by the tip of Thymey's boot. But Clary was not done yet. She swung her other sword with all her might as quickly as she could, but it was stopped mid-swing. She was confused. Thymey hadn't been holding a sword only moments before. How could he have blocked her strike? Then it clicked. After kicking her blade upwards into the air, he had caught it and defended at the last moment. This man's swordsmanship was at an extremely high level. Clary wondered if even Sir Cloin would have been able to defeat him.

Clary was stunned as all of these thoughts raced through her head. She expected another strike to her face, but instead Thymey moved to the side again, allowing her to fall forward, and slashed her across the back. She let out a scream. The wound burned badly, sending throbbing pain shooting throughout her entire body. The laceration was deep, though she could tell it was not deep enough to be fatal, nor crippling. No, this wound was meant solely to cause pain.

Thymey grabbed Clary's hair and pulled her head up to look into his eyes. "Now you listen here, girly. You are worthless. Worthless and stupid just like that bitch mother of yours. And just like her, you're going to die here, all because you are weak. But me captain over there, he's a kinder man than I. He's got a special deal for you, once in a lifetime opportunity in fact. If you can ever beat me, that is to say, if you can ever kill me, we'll let you go. How's that sound?" He grinned that same evil smile.

Clary was searing with rage, at his making fun of her. She hated this man more than she had ever realized it was possible to hate someone.

"Well girly, didn't that fat father of yours ever teach you to say thank you when someone offers you a kindness?"

Clary reached boiling point. She felt as if she were nothing more than rage. She was weak from the beating and the wound on her back, but she grabbed this evil man's wrist, wishing she could crush it solely with her anger.

"Gaaah!" There was a sizzling noise and Thymey let out a howl of pain, pulling his arm free and clutching at his wrist.

He raised his sword high, and Clary was sure he was going to end her life right then and there, but before he swung, a weaselly voice interrupted them. "That's enough, then, lieutenant!"

Captain Turk was still sitting in the same place, as calm as ever. He knew that Thymey wouldn't dare disobey his orders.

Thymey looked almost as mad as Clary had been but, reluctantly, he obeyed. He leaned in close to her and whispered in her ear. "I probably should've mentioned, I'm the best swordsman there is round here. Don't think you'll be able to catch me using cheap tricks or copied moves that you haven't mastered. You will never beat me. It's as I said before. You will die here. You and your whole, wretched family. And I will enjoy causing you pain every day until that moment comes."

He stood up, and just as Clary thought it was over, he raised his boot and then everything went dark.

<u>Chapter 8</u>

The following weeks passed in a similar fashion to that of the first day. For the most part, the prisoners were kept in a confused state. The guards would not offer any information as to their whereabouts or where they were heading. In fact, it seemed that Clary alone was permitted any movement beyond her cell, though she was not all too thrilled due to the torment which came with it. Each day she would be taken from her floor within the mages' garrison, and would be forced to fight with Thymey. Over and over again she would be humiliated by the Exile while his men watched and laughed. Whenever she became so enraged that she couldn't bear the weight of her anger, Captain Turk would call a halt to the spar and have her returned to her cage. Unbeknownst to the captain and his men, however, Clary was utilizing each of these outdoor excursions to gather what little information she could. She wasn't sure why the Exiles were putting her through these trials, but she wasn't simply going to let them have their way.

From the thinning of the forest and the great increase in temperature with each passing day, Clary could tell that the caravan had been traveling southwest towards the most dangerous part of the Arid Sea. It was nearly impossible for normal humans to inhabit such an area for long, not only due to the extreme heat and sandstorms which plagued the lands, but also due to the great amount of deadly creatures that lived there.

Clary had heard some of the Exiles mention a trade city called Beyond. From what she could tell it was a slave city where the Exiles meant to sell off whatever they could to lighten the load of their haul. This news frightened her. The only beings that could hold a city in such a place would be the Varhalla. Though she had never seen one, she knew that they were not to be trifled with. All children in the westernmost settlements of the kingdom were told stories of the Varhalla. Parents would warn that if a child disobeyed and wandered off, they would be sucked into the desert by these humanoid creatures. While the threat of the Varhalla might have been used as a ghost story to discipline children, they were as real as day. From the accounts Clary had heard, they stood as tall as regular men but with grey skin, like hard folded leather. They were quiet and secretive creatures, but when provoked they became ferocious, using their long, clawed arms, which reached down to their ankles, to rend their enemies' flesh from the bone. Clary hoped that she would never have the misfortune of encountering these traders.

She had also heard talk of a large group of cargo ships waiting on the western coast of the Crescent Ocean to the south. Clary surmised that this was how the Exiles managed to evade discovery as they made their way to Vinvale. No members of the royal fleet would have had any reason to patrol so far southwest. The idea of any attacks occurring in the peaceful western part of the kingdom would have been considered ridiculous. Even if a foreign nation had planned an invasion on the kingdom, the western villages would offer neither strategic advantage nor valuable resources. It would be suicide for an army to corner itself between the Arid Sea and the main capital.

Back in the mobile garrison, Cartus was still unresponsive. When he had finally begun to stir in his chains, the guards descended upon him and forced him to drink elixirs and mushrooms which kept him in a drowsy stupor. As such, Clary had been unable attain any information from him. Her attempts to converse with Hilda were also in vain, as there was a guard posted in front of their cell every second of the day. They were permitted to talk; however, when their chatter turned to anything of importance, the guard would shout them down and threaten them. Though Clary often wanted to snap back at the guards, Hilda, being the level-headed person she was, would urge her otherwise.

Clary had seen more and more of the caravan with each passing day. In fact, she believed that she had seen most of the Exiles, as each time she fought with Lieutenant Thymey there were more and more men in the audience. It seemed that everyone who was off duty would gather to watch her being tormented, as if it was some sort of demented entertainment. The one person she hadn't seen in all this time was the Exiles' notorious leader. In fact, he seemed to be entirely absent from the area where she was held captive. This was made all the more perplexing by the sheer number of times in which Clary and Thymey had fought. They crossed blades on at least three separate occasions per day. Clary was sure the Chained King must have at least heard of what was happening, even if he had not approved the actions himself.

What was more, Clary found it odd that the Chained King had not once visited her father. She would expect that such a prized captive would have invited some examination or interrogation by the leader of these men. Admittedly, she was grateful for this absence. She feared that he would come and hurt her father, or perhaps he would hurt her in order to gain some kind of leverage.

About halfway through the fourth week of their travels, just as Clary had begun to get used to her routine, something strange happened. After her morning session with Thymey, Clary returned to her cell to find that the guard, who was always stationed there in the mornings, was gone. Not only was he gone, but there was no other guard in his place. As her escorts forced her inside, she glanced at Hilda inquisitively, but Hilda simply shrugged. It was obvious that she was just as clueless as Clary regarding this new development. Clary assumed that one of the other Exiles who had brought her back to the cell would take his place, but once they locked the door behind her, the men returned down the stairs from which they had come.

Clary and Hilda were both stunned at this turn of events. Though the Exiles were cruel and brutish, they did still retain their militaristic order in the manner in which they conducted their daily lives. It was very unusual for them to vary from the schedule.

"What happened, Hilda? When did the guard leave?" Clary asked.

"I'm not too sure. After you left I went back to sleep, and when I woke up he was gone. That was only just a few minutes before you got back. Is anything happening outside? Did you notice anything strange?"

Clary thought for a moment. Nothing had seemed too out of the ordinary. "We've completely left the forest. That's the only difference I can think of." She had noticed that the thinning forest had now become nothing but dry shrubs. The dirt and grass had given way to sand and rock. Now that Clary thought about it, she hadn't seen a stream or pond in several days.

"We must have passed the kingdom's boundaries then," said Hilda.

"But what would that change about the guards?"

"I'm not sure. Maybe they believe that we have travelled too far now for any of us to run for help, or that we will be too scared of becoming lost in the desert to escape." Hilda looked slightly concerned about this new development, but then seemed to push it from her mind. "Have you found out anything about what's going on? Where are we headed? How many are still alive?"

It was the first chance they'd had to really talk in a long while, and she couldn't afford to let it pass them by. Clary told Hilda of all that she had seen. She told her about where they were headed and how the Exiles planned to take them across the Crescent Ocean to Thandessa.

"Oh, and I've found some of my friends who might be helpful if we ever find a way to slip out of here. They're members of the prince's royal guard – a man named Harvel and a few other knights. They're two levels below us and right by the stairs." Clary had also seen Terra on the same floor, but she didn't think that would be important to Hilda at the moment. If she got the chance she would free Terra immediately – or, at least, immediately after releasing her father.

A loud thumping noise came from the stairwell. Clary thought it might be the guards, but it sounded more like someone was slamming the floorboards with a sack of bricks. *Thunk… Thunk… Thunk!* When Clary saw who emerged from the porthole she felt her stomach turn over in fear. The Chained King, accompanied by Turk and Ammle, was walking towards her cell, lumbering slowly as if he were exhausted. With each step closer, Clary prayed that he would stop at another cage. She hoped with every fiber of her being that he wasn't here for her. But as he passed by each set of bars, one after another, she knew he would not stop. Finally he stood before her and turned to gaze upon her. Clary was frozen in fear as he peered at her through the soulless black holes of his helmet. He began to raise his hand to gesture toward her before he was interrupted.

"Hey! Move it, then, King! You're holding us up! I haven't got all day to be tending to your lazy ass!" Turk said as he kicked the giant in the small of his back. The jolt made the Chained King take a step forward. He continued into the cell next to Clary and Hilda's. The two girls stared at the giant in in awe as he collapsed against the wall.

"Now you listen here then, King," Turk ordered as he closed and locked the door. "Keep an eye on these two then, and make sure they don't get up to anything funny. We'll come and get you if we run into any problems. But you're in here until we reach Beyond. Got it?"

The Chained King only nodded silently.

"Good! We're off then."

After Turk and Ammle departed all of the prisoners sat in silence. It seemed to Clary that the Chained King was asleep. She didn't understand why he would let his underlings talk to him like that. If he truly were there to keep an eye on the other prisoners, then what was the reason for being in a cell himself? Clary's mind whirled with questions but she could not think how to get the answers. As things stood, it didn't seem safe to question the man, so the girls fell silent and remained that way. They did not want to risk disturbing the sleeping terror that was so close.

Clary examined the Chained King through the bars that separated the two cells, and listened to the shallow breathing emanating from within the black iron armor. He almost seemed peaceful – but then she thought of the last time he had been so close to her, and her head was filled with images of Sisti's body and the light fading from Sir Cloin's eyes. Fear turned to anger. Though the memories stirred up hatred and sadness, they also brought with them slight confusion. Maybe the excitement of the night's attack was causing Clary to exaggerate things in her mind, but if she didn't know any better, she would swear that this monster had gotten smaller. She pushed it from her mind. She needed to rest if she were to be ready to face Thymey once again.

*   *   *

It had been several days since the guards had deposited the King in his cell. By this point Clary and Hilda had stopped paying him much attention. It seemed that all he did was sleep and eat when his rations were brought to him. Other than the addition of this new inmate, things did not change much. Every day, Ammle would come to retrieve Clary for her fight sessions, and then he would return at a later time to bring food. The other guards never showed their faces in the garrison.

Now that they had reached the thick of the Arid Sea, Clary was able to see the entire camp without obstruction. At night two areas were filled with tents; one at the very front of the caravan and one at the rear. She imagined that these tents must have been very nice inside, perhaps even enchanted. This would explain why the men preferred them to the mobile garrison. She was grateful that she was placed inside with the high-value prisoners. The alternative was to be chained in the overcrowded cages pulled behind large bull-drages, which were like some form of cross between a mammoth and a crocodile. The massive, scaled herbivores were slow, but they had the advantage of being able to tow great weight behind them. They were quite common on the edges of the Arid Sea. Predators avoided them for the most part, their instincts telling them that the armored scales were too thick to pierce. The ones Clary had seen were not only carrying the slave cages but large cargo sleds as well. The Exiles even used them to help pull the large structure in which Clary and the others were kept, to help supplement the shortage of mages within the Exile ranks.

Clary was resting that afternoon after having finished her bit of stale bread and water for the day. Hilda had been trying to work out a spell to open up the locks.

"I heard about it in a lecture once," Hilda said. "It was a seminar on simple spells for everyday life. To be honest, the archemage who headed our guild made me go after I got into a spot of trouble drinking with some friends downtown. He said it would do me some good to focus on my studies, but… I kind of slept through most of it."

Clary laughed at this. She could picture it clearly, Hilda being scolded by the old bearded wizard whom Clary had met on the day of her trial, her head ringing from the revelry of the night before.

Clary and Hilda had grown close during their time in captivity. Perhaps it was due to her skills as an empath, but she was quite adept at lightening the mood. She always knew exactly what to say.

"Don't suppose you'd be able to help with that?" Hilda said, addressing the Chained King. He didn't make a sound. "Yeah, didn't think so," she sighed. It was almost funny how little the Chained King reacted to anything they did. He simply didn't seem to care. Even when he was awake all he did was stare straight ahead. Occasionally Clary thought she caught him looking at her, but it could have been just her mind playing tricks. She didn't like to think that he might be watching her when she wasn't looking.

A rattle behind Clary almost made her shriek in shock. She turned around immediately. Her father was starting to stir.

Cough, Cough— "C-Clary? Is that you?"

"Dad! Yes! Yes, it's me!" She rushed over to the bars. She wanted to reach out to him, to help him, but he was too far away.

"How long has it been? Are you okay? Your mother... is she...?"

"I know she's hanging in, but just barely. They're trying to keep her alive as leverage over you." Clary could see the guilt in her father's eyes. He was definitely blaming himself. "Don't think like that. If it weren't for you, they would've either killed her or sold her to the Varhalla. Oh, and that's where we're headed, I think. The Exiles want to sell off as many slaves and goods as they can in a place called Beyond before taking us to Thandessa by ship. We've already been in the southern part of the Arid Sea for almost a week."

"Has it really been that long? I know it's been a while since I've used real magic but I shouldn't have been out for more than a couple of days."

Clary wasn't exactly sure of his meaning, but she assumed that by *'real magic'* he was referring to his battle with the Chained King. Either way, this was what she'd been most anxious to discuss with her father since they'd been captured, and she wasn't going to allow the moment go so easily. "Well, that was the Exiles. They were keeping you sedated, feeding you potions and mushrooms. But about your magic – what was that? That was the same as Cartus from your stories. Everyone keeps saying you're him. I know he was supposed to be the only human who could breathe fire. No one else could heat up their body and melt steel like that. But you always said you were just a medic. What's going on? Who are you?"

Though she had intended to remain calm as she spoke, Clary could feel tears welling up in her eyes. With each word her feelings intensified. She had waited so long to ask him these questions. She had so much wanted to speak to her father, and now that she had the opportunity, the emotion she hadn't yet been able to convey was spilling out.

The expression of guilt returned to the old physicians face. "I… I'm sorry, sweetheart. I know I shouldn't have lied, but I had no choice. Your mother and I, we wanted to wait until you were a little older to tell you. This isn't how we wanted you to find out. The truth is—"

Hilda cut him off. "Wait! I'm sorry Mr. Cartus, sir… but we have someone here watching us. You might want to hold off on saying anything too important." She gestured towards the Chained King, who was sitting upright, facing the three of them.

"Who? That sorry pile of metal? Ha!" Though it was sarcastic, Clary was happy to be able to hear her father's booming laugh again. "I've got nothing to fear from him! He's nothing more than a babe! He's a slave, and not a very good one at that. I can sense his hatred for these Exiles a mile away. He doesn't even know how to control his powers fully."

The Chained King had lowered his head in shame. Clary knew her father was right.

"You hear that? If old Balthazar knew what you were doing he'd be ashamed!" Clary could see steam rising from her father's hands.

"Father! Calm down!" she urged him.

"I'm sorry, it's not every day you're forced to fight another Fjorendel. It's not something I ever wanted to have to do."

At this statement Clary became even more confused. There was that word again. She wondered what it meant.

As if Cartus could read his daughter's mind, he caught himself. "I'm sorry, Clary. I forgot. There were a few important details I left out of the stories I used to tell you. You see, Balthazar and Cartus – that is to say

Balthazar and I – were not just ordinary mages. We came from the Northlands, from a people called the Fjorendel. They're powerful mages who for centuries have passed down special magic unique to specific bloodlines. In a sense we bred body augmentation into our families with magic over hundreds of years. That's why, in Belderan, I alone was capable of using those temperature-altering abilities. Well, at least I was the only one left capable, until you were born."

Clary couldn't believe it. Suddenly many things were starting to make sense. "But why didn't you tell me?"

"After the Exiles turned on us, Balthazar and I were forced to flee. We were separated during our escape but I knew he would be headed back home to the north. On my way back I decided to return to the capital to gather information and warn the king, but I was set upon by members of the royal guard. They had heard of the sacking of Thandessa and tried to have me killed. I'm still not sure if it was confusion that led to their behavior or if they had been infiltrated by the Treacherous King's spies. Either way, I knew it was not safe there. Just as I was leaving the city, I received a raven from Balthazar telling me he'd been followed. He told me not to return to the north for a while. I decided to hold up in Vinvale until things blew over. The town was even smaller back then, and I knew no one would look for me there. A short time after that rumors were circulating, saying that the Treacherous King had killed Balthazar. When people began to assume I was dead as well, I decided it would be best to leave it that way. By then I had met your mother and fallen in love. She was pregnant with you. We decided it would be best for all of us to leave the past be and raise you within a normal family. Truthfully, I know it was partly for my own selfish joy that I did things this way, but I would do anything to keep you safe. I'm sorry I wasn't able to protect you, Clary."

Clary looked away from her father for a moment. Though it had become apparent that he was, indeed the Firedrake of the N orth, she couldn't truly accept it until she'd heard it from the man himself. Nothing could have prepared her for this. She'd been told stories of Cartus throughout her entire life, and they had always brought her such joy. Now, for the first time, it brought her pain and confusion instead. For a moment she was angry at having been lied to for such a long time, by the man who she was supposed to trust above all others. But as she collected herself, refocusing on him, she could see that Cartus was suffering even more than she was. His poor defeated expression filled her with guilt.

"It's okay. It's not your fault. They came for the prince. They would've been there anyway." Clary wasn't sure how to console her father. She had never seen him like this. He was always such a happy man. Though now she felt foolish. Surely, he'd been through times of sadness remembering his past, his home. He must have put on a strong performance so many times, just for her. She felt horrible. It seemed obvious now that her father had regaled her with his stories as much for himself as he had for his daughter. It must've been the only way he could truly share who he was. How could she not have known her own father was suffering so?

"They haven't hurt you have they?" her father asked after a short silence.

"Oh, uh… no, not really, not outside of the sparring sessions." It occurred to her that it was a little sad that her regular torment now seemed almost normal.

"What sparring sessions?" he asked, concerned and confused.

Clary explained to her father everything she had been through. She even told him about Thymey and Captain Turk and how they treated her during the sessions. When she finished describing the events silence fell. She could see that her father had become alarmed and even angry. It looked as if he was still working it out in his mind. She thought he was going to explain why the Exiles had been doing all of this – but it was Hilda who broke the silence with a terrified gasp.

"Clary, guys!"

Hilda was facing the other cell, backing up toward them. When Clary looked in the same direction she saw what had Hilda so scared.

"So much rage," Hilda squeaked.

The Chained King was standing now, grasping the bars between the two cells. He was taking deep, fast breaths. He appeared to be shaking with pure anger. His face may have been covered, but it didn't do anything to hide the raw emotion.

"TUUUUUURK!!! THYMEY!!!" he shouted, as loud as he could.

Crap! Clary thought. They must have given away some information he was looking for. Maybe he had been placed in the cell in order to ease them into a false sense of security. Was he waiting for her father to wake up? What had they said to upset him like this? Whatever it was, Clary feared that it spelled disaster.

He kept shouting the names over and over again. The sound was bloodcurdling. "TURK!!! THYMEY!!! TUUUURK!!!"

After a couple minutes the two men arrived, bringing with them a group of Exiles. Thymey was carrying his club. He always had it when it was his turn to guard the prisoners. "What's all this, then?" Turk shouted back.

"Oh, hello Commander Cartus. Glad to see you're awake, then." His smirk made him look even more like a rat than usual.

"Shut up!" the Chained King shouted. "You're doing it again! I know what you're doing. I won't let you! You can't make another!"

At this, Turk's expression changed drastically. The usually calm and confident look he sported had completely vanished. He now appeared as angry as the Chained King. He raised a finger and gestured towards the giant who was now bending the cell bars open. Thymey stepped forward and swung upwards with his club, striking the King as hard as he could under the chin. The blow was so strong that it knocked the man's helmet off. Clary tried to catch a glimpse of his face, but from her angle she couldn't see past his ear.

Turk pulled out a small whip from inside his vest. He muttered a few words, drawing invisible symbols on it with his finger. Something like red electricity seemed to be flowing inside the leather whip, only visible in certain creases of the tool. Turk lashed out, catching the Chained King in his face. The King finally let go of the bars, falling back and covering his face with his hands.

"Now you listen, and you listen well you mongrel," said Turk. "I don't care what we pretend you are for everyone else, but in here you're just a slave. You may think you're a valuable weapon, but I guarantee you this, we don't need you. You are simply a convenience. If you ever talk to me like that again, I swear I will exercise my full authority. Or did you forget that our true leader gave me permission to end your life whenever I see fit? That contract is still valid, and I do have the ability to terminate it in an instant if I so choose." He turned to the others. "And let that be a lesson to all of you. He is barely able to feel pain, yet I can leave him in agony." He focused his attention on Clary. "Imagine what my whip would do to you, my Chained Queen." The smile that now stretched across his lips made Clary want to throw up. He left with the rest of his men, all laughing as they exited.

Clary leaped over to the other side of the cell and grabbed the bars. She wanted answers, and she wanted them now. She started to shout at the downed man who was still clutching at his face. "What was that? What did he mean? Why did he call me the—"

The Chained King lowered his hands to look up at her. Clary was petrified in her disbelief and shock. Immediately many things made sense to her yet, at the same time, so many more things became less clear. One thing was certain, though – Clary never could have imagined, not in a hundred million years, that the person staring up at her right now, the most feared man throughout the entire kingdom, would be the same boy who had saved her from a monolith bear little more than a month earlier.

Chapter 9

"Oi! What you doing?"

Feryl had been daydreaming again. Perhaps it was the proximity to his homeland, but for some reason he'd remained aloof throughout this whole mission.

"Get back to work now, or I'll call the captain and have you flogged!" Thymey shouted. "You great lump of metal!"

"R-Right! Sorry sir!" Feryl stuttered.

Thymey was particularly hard on Feryl. He wasn't completely sure of the reason, but he had once heard Turk, his overseer, say that Thymey couldn't stand Feryl's strength. He didn't like that a boy his age could contend with such an accomplished swordsman. When he asked Turk directly about it, Turk threatened him with his torture magic for eavesdropping, and that was the end of it.

It had always been this way for Feryl, even back when he was first conscripted into the Exiled Regiment as a boy, twelve years ago. For some reason, the Exiles wanted to ensure that he always had as little information as possible. They didn't trust him. It made no sense to him why they would be so wary of him. As long as he was bound by contract, he had no choice but to do what they said.

Strange as it was, though, he was constantly reminded of his place. Sometimes, when he had been good for a while and had avoided punishment for a long period of time, he would be disciplined anyway. Either the captain or Thymey would suggest that he must be up to something and would have him flogged. By this point, he had become used to the lash. Between the constant assaults and his Fjorendel blood, most injuries would not bother him anymore. He was sure that there was something sick about that, but he thought it best not to dwell on it.

The one thing Feryl did fear was the lash of the captain's flail. Turk had been given the position of captain by the Treacherous King himself. He utilized an uncommon brand of magic designed for one thing: inflicting pain. It did not matter how strong you were or how tough you thought you were, the little weasel's torture spells would have you crying for your mother in minutes. It tapped directly into the nerves, shocking them to life and sending the strongest possible pain signal racing to the brain.

Feryl had even once seen Turk's magic used on a man who had been born without feeling in his legs. He imbued a small letter opener with those dreaded red streaks of his and stuck it behind the poor cripple's kneecap. It was sad, really, Feryl thought. The man experienced sensation in his legs for the first time in his life, as the magic forced the nerves to activate, but instead of joy, all he felt was immeasurable agony. Feryl couldn't even remember what the man had been withholding from Turk. It was something of little importance, but he had made the mistake of refusing the captain something he wanted. Turk would never stand for anyone not bowing to his will.

On this day the Exiles had set up camp outside of a small village called Vinvale on the western front of the kingdom of Belderan. One of their informants within the kingdom had let loose that the youngest son of the Drakewil line, Prince Valen, would be passing through on his first pilgrimage. They knew that he would be arriving sometime this morning, if he hadn't reached town already. They were to raid the village on the second night of

Valen's stay, taking with them every noble they could to be sold at ransom upon their return. Any other survivors were to be sold as slaves to the Varhalla before returning to their ships to the south. Feryl didn't much like the idea of meeting with the Varhalla. Even with his immense strength, he knew that if he had to face a group of them alone he definitely wouldn't come out unscathed. He gathered that there was something else going on with the raid, but ulterior motives were part and parcel of everyday life amongst the Exiles and once again he was kept in the dark.

This day was particularly hot, so much so that it almost felt like they were back in the Arid Sea, that horrible, sweltering ocean of sand which had already taken the lives of several of their men. Days like this were particularly hard on Feryl. His armor, which he was almost never permitted to remove, was not suited for warm climates as the black iron absorbed a great deal of heat. For him, it was like living in an oven. He again had to thank his sturdy Fjoren constitution, for he was sure that a normal man would not be able to survive such conditions.

Feryl, Thymey, Ammle and a few other men had been assigned to move the nine monolith bears, which they intended to bring back to Thandessa, into a new, larger cage while the older one was being repaired and prepped for the slaves they would take in the raid. Monolith bears were a rare find in the eastern markets, and these would definitely fetch a good price. There were four breeding pairs and an extra male. They'd had an extra female as well but it had died along the way due to injuries sustained during its capture.

The plan was to drag the beasts from one cage to the other by feeding the chain through the front door, into the other cage and out of the back. This was easier said than done. In fact, if they hadn't had Feryl among them it might not even have been possible. The cage in which the bears were currently residing was not an option anymore. The bars on one side had loosened at the bottom when one of the bears had a tantrum. The Exiles could not risk one of them breaking free on the ride back to the ships. After the raid, they would need Feryl to remain on guard until they were able to cross the border of Belderan again. Using up that much power, especially for that amount of time, would drain even Feryl entirely, for a while. They needed to ensure that there was no risk of one of the bears breaking out of the enclosure while they didn't have their muscle on hand. "Heave!" Thymey commanded. He was overlooking the effort.

Feryl, Ammle and some of the other Exiles pulled the chains tight as two of the work slaves released the locks on the cage doors. The animals burst through the gate, fighting violently in their attempts to move in any direction other than the one in which they were being pulled. Even the Chained King himself was struggling to keep his grip on the chain links.

"Heave!" Thymey called again.

Feryl pulled with all his might to secure the line once more. It was working. The bears were clawing at the gravel, trying to hold their positions, but it was futile. More men joined the ranks, each one grabbing a handful of links and pulling as if their lives depended on it.

It seemed as if the bears had finally given up, realizing that their efforts would not allow them to escape. The extra male, who was the last on the chain, was slowly inching his way through the gate.

One of the work slaves began carefully making his way toward the animals to close and lock the latch. What he didn't realize was that the lone male had its eyes on him. It bared its claws, ready for the attack. Thymey caught sight of it and shouted, "Hold on to the latch, you idiot! Not yet!

Don't close it yet!" – but it was too late. The slave was supposed to wait until the men could stake down the chain on the other side and allow the fully armored Feryl to handle it. Instead, he was now standing before the open door, staring at Thymey, trying to hear his orders over the thunderous roars of the predators.

The lone male bear jumped forth from the cage, taking a swing at the slave. One swipe of its claw stripped the man's arm from his shoulder. He lay in the dirt screaming in pain as the bear advanced on him. The slave was surely about to meet his end.

It all happened so fast that there was no time for orders to be given. Feryl went into a fit of pure instinct. He unsheathed one of the two large blades holstered on his back and stabbed it down through the chain in his hand, pinning it firmly to the ground. Removing the other oar-sized blade as he moved, Feryl raced forward in an attempt to cut the animal down, before it could cause any further damage. However, as he swung, his blade slicing down onto where the mighty bear's head should have been, the creature's course suddenly shifted. Instead of meeting fur, bone and flesh, the blade clashed with chain and gravel.

This creature was clever, for as soon as the sparks shot out from the point of impact, the beast took off running towards the trees. It knew full well that it would not be able to survive an assault from the army of men that surrounded it. Within seconds the bear had disappeared.

Feryl weighed his decision only momentarily. The bear was of some value but, given that it did not have an accompanying female, it was not an imperative in terms of value. Instead of scrambling to chase the animal down, Feryl turned to the slave flailing in pain beside him. Just as he began putting pressure on the bleeding nub and pulled out his bottle of phoenix tears there came an angry shout behind him and a strong blow to the back of his head.

"You stupid boy!" Thymey steamed. "You let that beast go over a work slave! How can one person contain so much idiocy?" His eyes widened as he saw the small bottle in Feryl's hand. He struck Feryl once more with his club. "How dare you! That was given to you for emergency use only! The Treacherous King told you specifically only to use if necessary! That means only if you or an officer is dying! Are you stupid *and* deaf?"

Feryl couldn't stand the lieutenant's lectures. "Look, sir, he's going to die if we don't do something. We may still be able to save his—"

"Did I ask you for excuses? That thing is nothing more than a slave. He doesn't even have a contract seal! Nothing but chains and cowardice bind work slaves. It may not seem possible but they're worth even less than you are! They don't cover anywhere near the cost of a full-grown monolith bear!"

"But Lieutenant, we can always capture another monolith on the way home, or we could send out a hunting party, or—"

CRACK!!! Once again, Thymey struck Feryl with his club. "You think I'm mad over a few lost coins? Where are we, boy?"

"We… we're outside the target zone, sir," Feryl looked down. He hated being patronized, but he knew he had to sit there and take it.

"Yes, that's right, we're outside the goddamned target zone! And what is that target zone?"

Feryl was silent. He realized what the lieutenant was getting at.

"Come on, boy! Speak up! I want specifics. How exactly was it described in your briefing?" As mad as he said he was, Thymey seemed to be enjoying the opportunity to lay into Feryl.

"It's Vinvale, a Belderanian village located on the western front. The area is heavily forested with no major threats, militarily or environmentally."

"That's right, slave. Now what do you think is going to happen if a large dangerous predator, that is supposed to live over two weeks travel away from here, is found wandering around in some nana's garden?"

Feryl sighed. "It will raise alarm, and they'll step up security."

"There! Was that so hard? Now that you've decided to use your brain for once, I want you to take a group of men and get your bleedin' candy ass out there and fetch my bear now!" His voice seemed to rise in volume with every word he spoke. Feryl could see all the veins on his neck, temples and forehead pulsating with rage.

Swallowing his pride, Feryl begrudgingly let out a, "Yes, sir."

Just as Feryl turned away to start gathering a group he heard a small rodent-like voice. It was the last voice he wanted to hear right now.

"Stop right there, King." Captain Turk always liked to call him 'King'. He said he liked being able to assert authority over the most feared man in the entire kingdom. "I think someone's getting a bit ahead of themselves."

This is it, Feryl thought. *Here comes the lash order.* But instead, the captain turned his gaze on the lieutenant standing behind his ward.

"Lieutenant, what exactly were you planning on doing just now, then?"

"Oh, er, Captain Turk, sir, I didn't see you there." Thymey stammered, caught off guard by the captain's sudden appearance. "Well, I was just reprimanding the slave—"

"The Chained King, then, Lieutenant. Do not refer to him as anything other than that when we are this far in country. Or do you want to let the entire royal force know our little secret, then?"

Thymey sighed in obvious frustration. "Right, sir. Well I was just about to send him with a group of men to retrieve the property he just let escape before it alerts the locals." It was clear that he hated this power game that the captain was playing with him. Feryl could see the frustration in Thymey's visage as the lieutenant endured the same belittling patronization he had just inflicted on Feryl only moments ago.

"And tell me, Lieutenant, what would happen then if a lone fisherman or hunter saw a group of heavily outfitted men led by somebody wearing the most iconic and feared set of armor in the world trekking through the forest?"

Thymey winced at the realization of his mistake, as if the admission physically hurt him. "It will raise alarm, and they'll step up security."

"Right, then. So, what are we going to do about it, then?"

"I don't know, sir. Why don't you enlighten us all?" Thymey's anger was so apparent in his red face that Feryl almost laughed. Knowing that this would be a straight shot to a lashing, he thought it wise to stifle it.

"Gladly, then." Turk was loving every second of it. He lived for these moments of subjugation. "We will send one man, without any identifying standards or armor, then. One slave, to be more precise."

Thymey's jaw dropped. "But sir! He's not supposed to be out of his armor! Ever! The Treacherous King ruled that—"

"I know what he ruled, Lieutenant." The rat said, now strangely serious. "He also said that, on this mission, my word is his!" It was clear that there would be no further discussion. If Thymey pushed back any more than he already had, even he would not be safe from the captain's lash.

"Now then, King, you are to remove your helmet and grab a spare set of armor from the supply wagon. If anyone asks who you are or what it is you are doing here, you are to say that you are a hunter for hire, then, heading to the Arid Sea to claim bounties. If they see the bear, you are to inform them that you have come from the Arid Sea and are tracking the monster to kill it. Tell them you are alone, then. If you get even an inkling that they don't believe you or are suspicious, you kill them and make it look like an accident as best you can. You got all that, then?"

"Yes, sir." Feryl memorized each word as if it were scripture. He would not risk messing up direct orders from the captain himself.

"Well, what are you waiting for, then? Get on with it, then!"

Feryl immediately began his preparations. This hunt would be difficult. For any other man, completing the task alone would be near impossible. Though Feryl was sturdier than the average man, there was still a large possibility that this would not go in his favor. He departed on his mission as swiftly as he could, just wanting to get it over with.

Feryl was irritated at being sent on this errand so close to the attack on Vinvale. Sure, it was his fault that the bear escaped, but what did it matter? Even if they did step up security, it would probably just be in the form of a few local hunters trying to track it down. Monolith bears weren't native to the region, but it could have been rabid or sickly or something. The locals would never suspect that it was lost by a group of raiders. He hated how he always got caught between the captain and lieutenant's pissing contests.

He had to admit that there was one upside to this venture. For the first time in months — no, probably years when he really thought about it —

Feryl was allowed to spend an extended period of time without his helmet or heavy iron armor. From the time he was first brought into the Exiled Regiment as a boy, Feryl had been forced to keep himself covered at all times. He wasn't sure why, but they had always made him wear some form of armor whenever he was in groups. He'd understood that now he had to be perceived only as the Chained King, but he wasn't sure why it was necessary as a child. He thought perhaps it was another way to train him, or to subjugate him by removing his identity. Either way, he'd had it on for so long that he wasn't entirely sure what his face looked like today. He had never been allowed any sort of mirror in his holding cells.

The monolith would be dehydrated after the journey, so Feryl sought out a water supply. He was sure the animal would sniff out a stream or pond first, then rest to regain energy. After that it would probably search for food. Most likely it would end up in a meadow or field to the southeast. Unlike most bears, monoliths did not like forested areas. They were accustomed to vast, open desert plains.

By the time Feryl came across the creature, it had already fallen asleep. Just as he was about to make his move, he realized that once the bear was caught, he would have to return to the base camp. He did not know when would be the next time he would be afforded such freedom. Though he could have killed the bear right then and there, he thought it would be better to enjoy his freedom for a few hours without monolith venom coursing through his veins.

Finding a nearby spot to rest, Feryl removed the swords from his back and strapped them to his bag. He wanted to enjoy this opportunity as best he could. Even if he killed the beast and returned in record time, it most likely would not save him from a flogging. Faced with the prospect of returning to the hell that was the Exiled Regiment, he savored every last second of freedom. He wondered to himself if this was what regular people felt like every day.

After he had lain against a particularly comfortable tree for a few hours watching the sky, the sun descended behind the horizon. The sky was totally clear, making visible the full moon and nearly every star in the sky. Feryl set up traps around his area to alert him to any intruders, bear or otherwise. Upon waking, the bear would smell the meat which he had brought from the base camp and laid out as bait. It would definitely come for Feryl tonight, and he was ready for it... or so he thought.

He shot up as he heard it. The creature's roar had alerted him, but the sound that shocked him and caused him to rush in the direction of the sound without caution or plan was a single word: "No!" It sounded like a girl and was almost ear-piercing in its volume. It was obvious that the bear was charging her, and when Feryl arrived at a small opening in the treeline, he saw exactly what he expected. The girl was sitting against a tree before him, body mangled, blood strewn across the meadow. *Shit, I'm too late!* he thought. *No, wait! She's moving.* The girl appeared to be trying to call for help or to scream, but she was too weak from the blood loss. All that came out was a gurgle and a cough.

The choice he was faced with now was a difficult one. He wanted to save the girl, but he knew that during a kill, monolith bears were at their most violent, overcome by bloodlust. This would be the most dangerous time to attack, and the girl would most likely not survive anyway. Not to mention that, in his excited state, he'd forgotten that he'd removed his blades and left them behind. It would be best if he just left to retrieve his weapons and attacked while the bear's attention was focused on devouring its kill. But he did have his phoenix tears. If it were discovered that he'd used them on an enemy, he would be in serious trouble.

The bear turned on the girl and began to charge. It was now or never. Feryl sighed. Gathering his courage, he stepped out from the trees.

<u>Chapter 10</u>

Clary still didn't know how to react. If the truth were not staring her in the face right this moment, she wouldn't have believed it. She couldn't make sense of it all. She wanted to know why this boy had helped her, both in the meadow and then again in the village. She thought that perhaps he'd had some idea of who she and her father were, only that would not have made sense. Surely he would have brought her to the other Exiles if he'd realized.

Believing that she would never see the boy again, she'd often wished she could thank him. She even considered at one point that he might have been a guardian spirit of some sort. He seemed such a kind and gentle person. So how could he turn out to be one of the most violent and ruthless killers ever to plague the western continent? The only way to find out was to ask him, but she was not sure how to approach the conversation.

Since Turk had struck him and left with his men, the boy hadn't moved even once from the spot on the floor where he had landed. Clary couldn't tell if his paralysis was due to humiliation, pain, or exhaustion. Perhaps it was a combination of all three. Either way, he lay still with a look of defeat covering his face.

Hours had passed in much the same fashion, and Clary knew it was time to do something. She couldn't ignore him any longer. There were a slew of questions flying around in her head, but she decided to start simple. "Who are you?" she asked in a shaking voice.

The boy sighed. He sat up, faced her and said simply, "My name... is Feryl."

Clary wasn't expecting much, but she was determined to learn more than just his name. "Why are they keeping you in a cell? You're the Chained King, aren't you? Did your men turn on you?" She knew that there hadn't been a mutiny, but she wasn't quite sure where all the pieces fit.

"No, they didn't. I serve them... I've always served the Exiled Regiment."

"That doesn't make any sense." No matter what the Chained King did, every encounter with him muddled Clary's life even more, and left her less informed than she was to begin with. "You killed the Treacherous King. You took control of the Exiles single-handedly."

"No, I didn't. That's just what we wanted everyone to believe."

"Then who killed him?"

"No one did."

"Then did he just die on his own? Who's leading the Exiles?"

"The same person as always – the Treacherous King. He never left."

"What?" Hilda interjected. "Then why are you leading his armies?"

"It's for protection. They created the myth of the Chained King to deter vengeance seekers, to create fear over a monster who doesn't exist. But mostly, to make sure he never came for revenge over the man who killed my father." He gestured towards Cartus as he spoke.

"Your father?" Clary asked.

"Balthazar," Cartus said from behind Clary, his voice still weak yet filled with anger. "The Stone Giant. And he'd be turning over in his grave if he knew what you'd become. His own son, a killer and banner-man for the very people who took his life. For once, I'm glad he's dead. It spares him such disappointment."

"My father would understand!" Feryl shot back. "You have no idea what you're talking about, old man!"

"Ha! You think he'd understand you turning on your own people? He'd rather you take your own life than see you become a monster."

"I was following his orders!"

"He never ordered you to kill innocent people for his enemies."

"He ordered me to protect our family!"

At this, Cartus stopped his verbal assault. Clary noticed that both he and Hilda looked down, an odd mannerism as if someone died.

It was awkwardly quiet for a few moments. Then Clary finally spoke up. "What do you mean by that? How does all this help your family?"

Feryl just looked away, a deep anguishing pain becoming more evident on his face with each passing second.

"You've gone and done it, boy, haven't you?" Cartus said in a hushed whisper.

"What? What has he done?" Clary pressed.

"He's sold his soul to those demons."

"I… I didn't have a choice," Feryl whimpered. "They held blades to my little sister's throat, and my mother's. If I didn't agree to the contract ritual, they would have killed them."

"And what were the terms?" Cartus asked solemnly.

"If I ever disobey them, or make any attempt on them… if I even fail to carry out orders in a way that they like, they can activate the seal, and my family will be killed by it." Feryl hesitated for a moment. "I have to live with what they make me do every day. I see the terrified faces of the people I've killed every time I close my eyes. I hear their screams when I sleep. The countless men and women I've killed... the children..." There were tears welling up in his eyes now. "You don't have to tell me what kind of monster I am. I know better than anyone else. But what would you have done if it were your wife... or your daughter?"

Cartus didn't say anything. He just stared at the floor, ashamed.

Feryl continued, "I'm a disgusting waste of life! I know that. I don't even know if I qualify as human. But I'm doing the best I can."

Clary couldn't believe it, but she actually felt sorry for him. She had imagined the creature beneath the black iron armor of the Chained King to be a disfigured monster who only loved death and carnage. Instead, all she saw before her was a sad, frightened boy, just as trapped and tortured as the rest of the Exiles' victims.

"Then why would you risk fighting with Turk and Thymey if they still can activate the contract?" Clary asked. "Why would you shout at them like that?"

Feryl sat for a moment, collecting himself. "Because they are going to turn you into the same thing as me. They are going to use your father and mother to force you to make a contract and become a weapon for them. They wanted you to become the Chained Queen... I couldn't let them do that to someone else."

Clary's eyes went wide with shock. Panic ensued as she thought of her mother being used as a threat, forcing her to make a similar contract to Feryl's. Would her mother be kept prisoner for the rest of her life? If so, then it would be Clary's fault. The thought made her feel ill. She hadn't been expecting to hear something like this. She looked at the lash mark on his face and felt as guilty as she had on the night of their first encounter. She now knew it was her fault he had gone through that. He had done it for her. *No! Don't feel sorry for him. Remember everything he's done!*

"But why didn't you freak out like earlier?" Hilda asked, shakily. She'd turned a sickly shade of green at the revelation of Feryls strife. No doubt, she was being affected by the various dark emotions swirling around the room. "Didn't you know what they were doing already?"

"No. I didn't. They don't like to tell me what's going on. They probably knew how I would react. I didn't know until you told the old man about how the Exiles have been making you fight."

"That sick bastard. He probably put you in here just to let you find out," Cartus said. "He loves causing pain like that. I always hated him, even when he was just starting out, back when we were still the Royal Militia."

Feryl nodded in agreement. It was still strange for Clary to hear her dad talk this way. He was usually so kind; he'd never talked badly about anyone like this before. As much as she despised the little weasel, she'd been thinking of Turk as a sort of safe signal when he was around. He always prevented Thymey from taking things too far. She hadn't taken time to think about his reasoning. She'd thought it was all the Chained King's doing up until now.

"So why did you save me?" Clary asked.

"Which time?" Feryl asked, frankly.

"Wait, you've met him before?" Hilda cut in.

"Oh, right," Clary only just now remembered that she hadn't told anyone about their encounters yet. After all that happened and then the silence forced by the Exiles, she had never gotten the chance to mention it. "During the attack, he protected me from the other Exiles."

"So you met during the assault?" her father asked.

"Not exactly… On the night before, when I didn't come home, I was attacked by a rogue monolith bear while out in the forest. He saved me and then…" Images from that night surfaced in her head. She remembered how he nursed her back to health. When her thoughts turned to how he had bathed her, she blushed in embarrassment. "I was hurt and he healed my wounds. He got hurt pretty bad, too. He had to…" She perked up as she recalled him preparing to sew himself up. "Wait, King— I mean Feryl. Have you had any other contracts put on you? I mean besides this one."

Feryl seemed blindsided by the question. "Uh no… Why?"

"And where is your contract bound?"

He looked even more puzzled. "It's on the back of my neck. Why do you want to know?"

Clary was standing at the bars again, right above him. She had caught him.

"The contract mark on the back of your neck, it's already been broken. You lied to us!" He hadn't been forced to do any of this.

"What? What do you mean? No that's… that's not possible." He reached a hand back towards the tattoo. It was covered by the collar of his armor. "How would you even…"

"On that night, the night when you first met me. I saw it when you took off your armor. You really are the Chained King. Was that all an act? I bet your Exile buddies have been listening this whole time! You probably did kill the—"

"Clary!" Hilda cut her off. Clary looked at her, confused. Hilda only nodded towards the boy. He was leaning forward on his knees. His expression looked as if his entire world had been shattered, as if he had lost all sense of emotion. He looked numb, his gaze empty.

She had been wrong. She now knew, without a doubt, that he had been telling the truth. If the contract mark had been broken, it left only three possibilities: first, that Feryl had been freed by the Exiles, something that obviously hadn't happened. Second, that he had broken his end of the contract, resulting in his family's death and his execution. Given that he was alive and breathing before them, they knew this to be false as well. The only remaining reason for the mark being broken was that the Exiles had failed to hold up their end of the bargain. They had killed his family. He was free, but that news came with tragic implications. All of the atrocities he'd committed over the years – the pain, the torture, the genocide – it had all been perpetrated under the pretense that he had no choice. Now he knew that it had all been for nothing. He could have stopped at any time, even if they killed him for it, but instead he had followed their every order, thinking that he was protecting the ones he loved. But the worst of it was the knowledge that his family, his sole reason for continuing on, was dead.

"Feryl, I... I'm so sorry, but how did you not know? I mean in all this time did you not once check the mark?" Hilda asked, in a calm, caring voice. "Has no one ever seen it? Or maybe someone told you?"

Feryl finally understood the purpose for his isolation. "No, no one was ever permitted to see me without my armor outside of the officers and trusted Exiles. They kept me covered at all times. I have been forced to wear armor every day from the time they contracted me. Even when I shaved, I wasn't permitted a mirror. And now I know why."

He reached his hand toward his cheek and wiped away the still streaming tears. Feryl stared at his hand as though he were shocked that his eyes were still capable of producing them. Clary suspected that it had been years since Feryl had cried. Through all the pain and struggle he'd undergone, he'd never been forced to tears. It was almost ironic that the great Chained King, feared throughout the western continent, could be brought to tears by the simple word of a girl.

But the moment of sorrow and pain quickly left him. It was replaced with a visible unyielding rage, along with something he'd never had the luxury of feeling before: a thirst for revenge. Clary did not have to be an empath to figure out what was going through the boy's head at this moment. As a slave, Feryl would never have considered the possibility of being able to live his life for himself. He must have always thought only of his family, suffering for their sake. He had always assumed that he would die under the thumb of the Treacherous King, but this could no longer be the case. Now he had a new drive, a new purpose, and it became clear that he would not stop until he killed his former ruler for what he had done.

Feryl stood to face the girls and Cartus. He asked only one question. "Where are we going when we get out?"

*　　　*　　　*

Another week went by without incident. Feryl knew that they would have to leave within the next day or so, whenever an opportunity presented itself. By now the caravan was no more than a week's travel to Beyond, as far as Feryl could tell. The longer they waited, the deeper into Varhalla territory they would be. Unfortunately, Feryl needed to wait at least that long to recover his strength. After using up so much power bending the bars in his rage, he was exhausted. He had already used up more than he was supposed to on the journey. Fortunately, however, Clary had saved the strange energy-replenishing fruit that Feryl had left with her on the night he saved her. He wanted to wait so he could take it just before their escape.

Feryl told the girls that they could only take a few people with them. If the group were too large, they would be easily noticed and would be caught immediately. They planned to take with them only the knights that Clary knew, since Feryl and Hilda had no friendly contacts on board the garrison. They feared that if they attempted to free other captives with whom they were unfamiliar, there would be a chance that they might reject the escape attempt and sound the alarm for fear of punishment.

Cartus had decided to stay behind, much to Clary's dismay. "I am far too injured to make the journey. I'd only slow you down. On top of that, much as I hate the bastards, the Exiles are the only thing keeping your poor mother from bleeding out right now," He Said. "Even if we did free her and I tried to treat her myself, there is no way I would have the energy to brave the Arid Sea at the same time. And if I leave without her then they'll just kill her. The only reason they're keeping her alive and free from the Varhalla is because of her value as leverage over me. You need to get help. It's the only way I'm afraid."

"Should we head to the capital?" Clary asked.

"No, not directly – they would catch you along the way. It's too dangerous."

"But surely the kingdom must've sent someone to Vinvale to investigate. Plus, I'm sure there should be some sort of royal force chasing us down in any case," Hilda argued.

"No, by now they would have abandoned the investigation," Feryl said. "The Exiles don't usually take prisoners. We burned the bodies and left a message. We wanted them to think we killed everyone so they wouldn't follow. We even made the camp outside of the town seem bigger than was necessary to fool them into thinking our force was larger. We didn't want them to have a reason to risk coming after us until we were safe in Thandessa. On top of all that, we also left traps, as well as about thirty or forty hired mercenaries along our path to stop anyone."

The girls looked at him, clearly in awe at the way he talked about it all in such matter-of-fact terms. Though Clary still could not accept him as a friend, even she could not deny that having the Chained King on their side was an invaluable advantage. If they had tried to escape without him they would never make it.

Cartus chuckled, clearly relieved to know that Feryl was at least privy to the battle tactics of the mission, if nothing else.

"So, what do we do?" Hilda asked.

"Well, the way I see it, we only have one choice." Clary answered. "We have to go to Saroza."

"Guess we'll be going on the pilgrimage after all," Hilda laughed.

"Unfortunately, it's not quite that simple," Feryl said, reluctantly. "You have to remember, we must carry with us everything we need. We won't have much food or water. A distance like that most likely won't be possible. That's not to mention the dangerous creatures we'd have to face traveling through the heart of the desert like that. It's much safer if we stay close to the border on this one."

The girls looked down. Clearly, they hadn't thought about the issue of surviving once they were free of the Exiles' caravan. They were visibly upset but they knew he was right.

"In that case, what option do we have left?" Clary asked.

"Well, there is one. It won't be easy. In fact, I'm sure it is the longest possible route, but it should provide the least risk," Feryl responded. He paused for a moment, wrestling with whether his idea was actually an option or not.

"So, where is it?" Clary urged.

"He wants you to go to the Fjorendel capital at Harsgard," said Cartus, answering for Feryl.

"You want to go that far north? That's even farther than Saroza!" Hilda exclaimed.

"Yes, but along the way there is water and game. We can actually survive. As hard as it will be, it's the only option we have."

The girls both seemed apprehensive.

"You're going," Cartus said. "It's either that or stay here. When you arrive, tell the other Fjorendel who you are. They'll help you and escort you to the capital so that you won't have to worry about the Exiles. When you get to the capital, you can give word to the nobility of what happened, so that the royal fleet can intercept the Exiles before they return to Thandessa and save the rest of us."

Clary accepted her father's word without further argument. Though it was no secret that she didn't completely trust Feryl, her father's approval of the idea seemed to assure her that it would be their best hope.

"And there's something else," Feryl said. "If this is going to work, we are going to need the prince with us." Feryl had overheard the girls talking about him a few times. Clary had not been secretive about her distaste for the cowardice he had displayed on the night of the attack.

"What!?" Clary shouted. "No way – not him!"

"I know you don't like him, but we are going to need him. He's our only chance of getting into the city. Security will be on high alert everywhere we go. If we run into any royal police, they are just as likely to kill us as traitors as they are to welcome us."

"What are you talking about? We don't need anything like that. We're citizens of the kingdom. Once we get to the capital, we can just go up and tell the king what's happening."

"Clary... not to be rude," Hilda said, obviously trying to tread lightly, "but you've never been to the capital city, have you?"

"Well, no, but why does it matter?"

"The thing is, the center of the kingdom is a much different place from the outer rim. You can't just walk up and receive an audience with the king. It's a very structured and organized place. There are guidelines and precautions at every turn. Everything is highly regulated. Getting close to the king would be near impossible without the prince. I know you don't like him, but we don't have much of a choice."

Clary was clearly irritated, but from the serious looks Feryl and Hilda displayed, it was evident that she'd been outvoted. Still, Feryl understood where she was coming from. It wasn't as though Prince Valen's life was in danger. Unlike everyone else, he wasn't expendable to the Exiles. His capture was their whole reason for this venture. In his time in the cell, Feryl had overheard a bit about Clary's distaste for the prince and was sure she would much rather have freed a few more of the regular people who were about to be sold to the Varhalla. But, understanding her lack of choice in the matter, Clary let out a begrudging, "Fine."

Chapter 11

The time had finally arrived as the sun set, and the caravan had stopped for the evening. The Exiles were due to hold a large meeting in the forward camp to brief and prepare for their dealings with the Varhalla. When Clary asked why they hadn't been prepared for it beforehand, Feryl informed her that they had, but encounters with the Varhalla were so dangerous that they needed to make sure to be as careful as possible.

Feryl had bored a small hole through the wooden wall at the back of his cell, just big enough to see what was going on outside and below. It was too dark to see the actual soldiers, but as he told Clary, he could at least see their torches. When it came time for the meeting, he would be able to see the lights moving towards the front of the caravan.

He and the others were all terribly nervous. They really didn't have much of a way to gauge their chances of actually succeeding. The only thing that was certain was that their chances would be much higher now than they woud be later, when a large number of prisoners would have been sold off.

Clary was especially nervous. She had been afraid ever since escape had become an actual possibility. For almost two months now, she had done nothing but fight with Thymey over and over again. Not once had she managed to best him. In fact, she hadn't even come close. After being beaten so many times without success, she wondered if she really would be able to help out should they find themselves in a tight spot. It was no secret that Feryl was capable of handling himself, and Hilda was in possession of a decent amount of battle magic herself. Clary, on the other hand, had never even been in a real fight before all this, at least not one where her life was truly on the line.

"I think it's about to happen," said Feryl. "I see movement."

Clary started to panic a little. "Are we doing it now?"

"No, not yet, it'll be a while before the Exiles from the rear make it all the way up front. They're taking their time."

Clary sighed in relief. They only had a little time left, maybe a few minutes before they had to act. They needed to make every moment count. With all her worries, she was beginning to wonder if maybe she should stay behind with her father. She didn't want to become dead weight and hold Hilda and Feryl back.

"Clary, sweetheart, come here for a minute." It was her father. He'd been out of it for a while, resting. He was still exhausted. The small amount of food they were each given was never enough for him, especially considering the injuries from which he was still recovering. He'd been insisting that Clary and the others take some of his rations to build up their strength before the journey. Clary must have shown more of her fear than she meant to because he seemed to understand what she was feeling.

She moved over next to the bars. "What is it?"

Though he was in pain and completely drained, for the first time since they'd left the village he managed a warm endearing smile. "Look, I know you're scared. That's okay. If you're frightened, then it just means you understand how serious this is — but you need to know that once you leave this cell, there's no turning back. You all have made a decision, and you need to stick with it. Since you've come here I've seen you confused, scared and unsure of yourself, but now that has to stop. That is not the daughter I raised. That is not the Clary I know. The Clary I know is strong, and confident, and adventurous. She wouldn't let a couple of ruffians like these stop her. You can do this. I know you can."

"But father, I—"

"Alright, it's time," said Feryl. "There are still a few torches at the base of the structure, but I think that is the best we are going to get."

No! Clary thought. It wasn't enough time. She wanted to stay a little longer with her father. Feryl and Cartus both seemed to sense her distress, however. Cartus looked up at the boy and nodded. In response, Feryl ate the pink fruit which Clary had returned to him. He stood up and stepped over to the front of his cell. Magically expanding the size of both arms, he gripped the two bars either side of the lock, then pulled them apart. The lock broke with a snap and a ring, and the door swung free. Feryl moved over to the girls' cell and did the same thing.

Then, just as he began to make his way over towards the stairwell, Cartus called after him. "Wait, boy!"

Feryl stopped in his tracks and turned to face the old man.

"Before you go, come and break my restraints. I need to give Clary something."

Feryl looked alarmed. Clary knew he was worried about their time, but Cartus' order, combined with the desperate look she now gave the Chained King did not leave much room for debate. Cartus groaned in pain as his arms thudded to the floor. Clary rushed over to help him up. He caught his breath and said, "Give me your hands."

Clary wasn't sure what this was all about, but she did as he asked. She hoped that he was going to change his mind about staying behind. She'd wanted him to come with them so badly, but she knew that as things stood, it would be impossible. Suddenly her chest sank and she began to tear up as It occurred to her that this might be the last time she ever saw her father.

"Shhh, shhh, shhhhh. It's okay, my angel. I had hoped I wouldn't have to do this until you were a bit older, but things don't always turn out the way we plan them."

"W-What are you..." But before she could get the question out, her father bit down onto his hand and, with the blood from his wound, began to inscribe upon her forearms various symbols which she could not read. When he was done, he began whispering under his breath. It was a chant but it meant nothing to her. After a few seconds, he took a deep breath and opened his mouth wide, letting flames fall from his lips and onto the inscription. Clary winced and closed her eyes, expecting to feel the white-hot burn of the fire. Strangely, however, she felt only a cool tickle, as if she'd put her arms into a gentle stream. She felt a euphoric sensation as a surge of pleasant energy coursed throughout her entire body. Her fear and shock dissipated and she was left feeling calm and relieved. When she opened her eyes she saw that the flames did not come raging out of her father's throat as they had the first time. This time, they trickled out, flowing like water down upon her wrists. The fire itself seemed to change color as it fell, at first a pale blue, then orange and red, then gold.

When he finally stopped, the flames coated her arms and hands from the elbow down. It settled to become a bright white, then began to move as if it were being sucked into the letters. When it was gone, the runes burned red like embers for a few moments, though they still did not harm her. Finally, they turned to black ash. The ash seemed to sink below the skin and then resurface around her forearms and wrists as a black tattoo.

"Papa, what did you…"

Her father raised his own wrists up. His tattoos were identical. She finally understood. He had given her the same power that he had.

"Besides me, You are the only living person outside of the Fjorenlands who can wield our clan's flames. I hope you never have to use them, but when the time comes you will be ready."

"But how? How am I supposed to know how to control it?" she asked as panic began to take hold of her once again. This was a lot to take in all at once. Clary had never considered the weight of such power, and she doubted whether she would be able to wield it as the mighty Cartus had. Now that she would need her father more than ever, she had to leave him behind.

"Trust me, you'll know when the time is right. Until then, that boy will help you. Do you understand?"

Clary nodded. She thought if she tried to talk, she might cry even more. She could hear his energy fading as her father spoke. Clary realized that he must have been saving up as much magical energy as possible, right up to the last minute, in order to bestow this gift upon her.

"And one last thing, sweetheart. No matter what happens, no matter how bad it gets, even if you aren't able to get to us in time, just always remember that your mother and I… we love you more than anything on this earth or any other. We are both so proud of you."

Clary couldn't contain herself anymore. Crying, she grabbed her father, pulling him into a tight embrace. "I know, Papa. I love you too, you and Mom. I promise we'll come back for you. I promise!"

Cartus hugged his daughter back and then pulled away. "Alright, it's time you get going."

The trio took off down the stairwell as fast and quietly as they could. The first task was to collect their friends without being discovered. Fortunately, it appeared that most of the guards were either at the meeting or outside, so they wouldn't have any interference. The last thing they wanted was for the alarm to be raised while they were caught inside the mobile garrison. If the Exiles were able to block the exits, escape would be impossible.

Just as they reached the floor below theirs, Clary began to pull Feryl toward the cell where she knew Harvel and the others were being held. Once again, Feryl bulked up his arms with the same ritual as before and pried the door from its lock.

"What's going on? Stay away! I'll kill you with my bare hands before I let you near my men!" It was Harvel. The lower floors lacked any ceiling cracks which might allow for some illumination; as such, it was much darker at night the further one descended into the structure.

"Shhh! Harvel, it's me, Clary. We're leaving, but we need your help."

"Clary? Oh, thank the gods. Come on men, let's go." Clary knew that Edgrum was in the cell with him, as well as two other knights with whom she wasn't familiar.

"Clary, is that you?"

"Yes, yes, Terra, I'm here," she whispered. "We're getting you out. Just wait a moment, and keep quiet." The cell adjacent to the knights' contained Terra, as well as four other noble girls. Fortunately the Exiles didn't seem to have taken much interest in who was placed in each cell when they stowed the other prisoners. Instead they simply separated the males and females throwing them in the cells as they arrived in the garrison. This made things much easier for Clary and the others, since Terra and Harvel were together when they were captured and thus, imprisoned within close proximity to each other. Once Feryl broke open the door, Terra rushed out and jumped onto Clary, hugging her tightly. One of the other girls came out as well, but the other three weren't moving.

"What are you waiting for? We have to go now!" Feryl said.

"No, we're staying here," responded one of the three.

"What are you talking about? This is crazy. We're setting you free!"

The three girls still did not move.

"We're going to Harsgard to get help." Clary whispered. "Come on, let's go!"

"You fools are going to get everyone killed!" the girl said. "You can't escape from them. It's best if we just stay here. My father's a rich nobleman. He'll pay the ransom and get us home."

Clary opened her mouth to argue but then felt both Hilda and Feryl's hands on her shoulders. She understood. This was the kind of reaction they had been worried about – the risk they would run if they chanced breaking out too many people. Clary became even more nervous as she realized that they not only had to fear the alarm being raised by the guards, but by the scared prisoners as well.

Two floors down they found another cell close to the stair entrance housing three knights and a civilian. Garrett and Ingrum were the two Clary had come to retrieve; the extra soldier was an added bonus. As much as it irritated her, Gerald was the civilian in the cell. He was no noble, but the mayor's family was known to be very wealthy, and the Exiles knew that Gerald was his son, so he would also raise a high ransom.

127

This time, they had no trouble gathering the group. Harvel's presence was reassuring to any who knew him. His skills as a tactician were well known, and he had a reputation among the royal guard for being trustworthy.

From what Feryl had ascertained, Valen was being held in a separate cart a short distance ahead of the garrison. A small guard was kept on him at all times. When they finally got to the front door, Feryl hushed everyone and slowly cracked it open.

There were three guards waiting outside. They had expected one or maybe two, but no one expected the Exiles to be led by Thymey himself. Yet there he was, sitting on the steps right in front of the door, drawing with the tip of his blade in the sand.

Fortunately enough, however, there were two bottles of rum with him. One lay empty on the ground, while the other was half empty in the lieutenant's hand.

"Can you believe that pompous bastard?" Thymey spat, taking a swig and passing the bottle to the man to his left. "Where does he get off making me stay here to guard the prisoners while he gives an important briefing to the rest of the men? It's not like they're going anywhere. What, does he think they're just going to rip the bars out and run for it? Of course not! He just wants to rub it in my face that he got the promotion instead of me, especially while we're away from the real King. He just wants to throw his rank in my face now that he's a captain. I'm a lieutenant, damn it! If I have to listen to one more order from that little rodent-voiced runt, I swear I'll kill the bastard!"

"You got that right, sir. He's full of nonsense, he is!" one of the other guards agreed. "And that stupid way he talks! *'Then* this, *then* that'. What's he on about with that crap?"

The third man laughed. "Yeah, he acts all pompous like he's something special, but I know for a fact that's a Durvin accent. Nothing but ice and sheep up there."

As the three men complained and laughed, Feryl signaled to Harvel. Harvel in turn signaled to Garrett and the other knight who had been in the cell with him. The pair moved closer to the door. Feryl tapped Garrett, pointing left, and then to the other knight he pointed right. He then held up his fingers and mouthed, "Three, two, one."

Feryl kicked open the door, smashing the heel of his boot firmly into the back of Thymey's head. At the same time, Garrett and the other knight leapt onto the backs of the two guards. The knight choked his victim unconscious. From Sir Garrett's victim came an unpleasant snap. Clary looked at him in shock as he stood up with an emotionless expression, grabbing the dead guard's sword for his own. He had always seemed so quiet, and his smile was so friendly. It was strange to see him kill a man in such a brutal fashion and treat it as if it were some mundane chore.

Before Clary had time to think about it, they were on the move. They had been lucky that they were able to catch Thymey and his two guards unawares, though, admittedly, she wished that the evil lieutenant would have turned and put up a fight, forcing them to kill him rather than just leaving him unconscious, but there was no time. She would have to swallow the visceral hatred she harbored for the sake of expediency.

They moved as a group. Feryl remained beside Clary. For some reason, he seemed determined to keep her at his side. As much as she didn't like him, it was reassuring to have the Chained King protecting her.

They needed to get an armory cart before going after the prince. Feryl had been forced to store his swords inside the nearest one just before he'd been put into his cell, so he led the way, dragging Clary close behind.

Luckily, they didn't come across any guards along the way as they ducked from wagon to wagon. When they reached it, they found no guards. The Exiles were clearly confident in their plan. They didn't expect any intruders this far in.

They began to unload the wagon, grabbing swords, knives, spears, axes, even bows and arrows. Many of the weapons inside were ones taken from the knights after the assault. Clary remembered Feryl saying how they had wanted the superior steel of the royal forces and how they were sure to grab every weapon they could from the village. Once everyone was fitted up, they began moving in the other direction, towards the prince's cart. Clary, however, gave one last glance at the weapons, and something caught her eye – a glint of gold that she recognized. She leaned in closer to see a pair of ornate swords which had once belonged to a champion of swordplay. The thought of Sir Cloin's precious tools being tossed in with the rest of the weapons enraged her. Despite their hurry, she couldn't just leave them there. The brave knight had saved her life, and she felt like she owed him.

She began to climb over the scattered weapons inside the cart until she was finally able to reach them. She had to be careful about it, as the swords were underneath a pile of weapons and armor. She didn't want to risk the noise that would come if a couple dozen large pieces of metal came crashing down on top of each other. Gently moving the weapons one by one, she finally freed her prize.

As she began to crawl backwards out of the cart, she suddenly felt a tug. Her skirt had caught on a stray nail. She pulled hard, but couldn't get loose. She was starting to panic. She had already been in there too long. It was only a matter of time before someone came and discovered her.

The fear left her as a hand appeared, grabbing the fabric and tearing it loose from the nail. She sighed with relief as she stepped back outside. She was so grateful to whoever it was from the group that had saved her.

"Thank you, I was scared someone might find—"

But it wasn't one of the other escapees. Clary was standing face to face with a very angry-looking Exile. He raised his sword ready to strike. Clary panicked again.

There was swish and a clang. She had blocked his strike.

She didn't even realize what she'd done at first. It was like a reflex. The Exile looked as confused as she felt. The Exile swung again; this time, Clary stepped out of the way at the last minute. The man was a clumsy swordfighter. She swung back with one of Cloin's swords. The Exile just barely blocked it. He seemed worried, almost scared. Now he took a serious stance and lunged for her. The two clashed swords a few times. The Exile was definitely stronger than her. Every time their swords connected, hers reverberated intensely, bouncing backward, yet still she was able to keep up.

Finally she realized what was going on. She had gotten so used to facing off with Thymey every day that even an average swordsman such as this low-ranking Exile seemed poor. After realizing this, she was less scared. They were evenly matched, neither one able to land a blow. After a few moments of fighting he seemed to become irritated that he couldn't put the little girl before him away. He took a big arching swing out of anger. It was clumsy and slow. This was too easy for her. She parried the strike with her left blade and stepping in to close the distance, caught the man with her right.

The Exile grunted in pain as he jumped back just in time to avoid a fatal gut wound. He clutched at his side, which was bleeding heavily. He dropped to a knee.

I did it! I beat him! Just as Clary let her guard down the Exile jumped up, raising his arm. She didn't have time to react. He had retrieved a dagger from his boot and was in the midst of throwing it when he froze. Another knife had come from the darkness and pierced the man's throat. There was a squelching noise as he clutched at his neck. He tried to scream, but only blood came from his mouth, as he fell to the floor, dead.

It was Edgrum who had saved her. He ran over to her and took her hand. "Oh thank the gods!," he cried. "We thought you were dead."

Clary laughed. "A second later, and I might have been."

The two hustled towards the wagon where the prince was being held. When they arrived, they found that the fight had already been won. Six guards lay strewn on the ground, all either dead or unconscious. Feryl was already starting to pry open the door of the cart.

Sir Edgrum turned to Clary. "That big guy you brought, who is he? I don't remember him being with us when we were forced into the camp on the first night." He peered at Feryl with suspicion.

"Oh, er... he's a slave they took prisoner before they got to Vinvale. He was in the cell next to us," Clary answered. Hilda and Clary had advised Feryl to remove his armor before they began their escape. They all agreed that it would probably cause problems and argument, were they to suddenly show up to rescue their friends with the very man whom they thought had ordered their imprisonment. The explanations could wait until after they made it out of the Exiles' clutches.

"Well as long as he's with us, I'm glad to have someone that strong on our side. He looks like he could even be as strong as the Chained King!" Edgrum chuckled.

"Yeah, ha ha, I'm sure," Clary agreed awkwardly. She felt bad, but she technically hadn't lied.

Two figures emerged from the cart. One was unmistakable as Prince Valen, and the other was a middle-aged man who was clearly some sort of warrior. The prince took no time to start complaining. "What are you idiots doing? They are going to sell us back to the kingdom. My father will ensure that I'm taken care of." He was being obnoxiously loud. It was like the girls in Terra's cell all over again.

Clary could hear Feryl and Harvel shushing him and whispering to him, though she couldn't make out precisely what they were saying.

"What!" the prince shouted. "No, I'm not going anywhere!"

His shouting triggered something that made every single one of them jump in fright. A guard who had heard the commotion had come to investigate. When he heard Valen talk about leaving, he yelled, "Prisoners have escaped! Prisoners have escaped!"

"Someone stop him!" Feryl shouted back, but it was too late. The guard had fled behind the nearest group of wagons.

"There! See what you've done!" Valen shouted. "You've gone and—"

BAM!!! Feryl planted his fist firmly in the prince's face, knocking him out cold and throwing him over his shoulder. "Anyone got a problem with that?" No one said anything. "Good. Now let's go."

Just as they turned to depart, a bell started to ring nearby.

"Damn," said the knight who had been imprisoned with the prince. "That bell will wake half the camp. There's no way we'll outrun them now."

"Wait," said Clary, thinking quickly. "I have an idea. Follow me."

With no other options, they all followed Clary back to the mobile garrison. In front of the structure were four sleeping bull-drages. The massive animals were unbothered by the noise in the now bustling camp. So long as they were not being ushered and whipped by Exiles, the stubborn creatures would not move. Clary started to explain her plan, but Harvel had already grasped her intentions.

The knights lined up behind each of the bull-drages and cut loose the reins and restrains. Together they readied their swords and then, all at once, stuck the sleeping beasts between the plated scales in their rears. The drages sprung to life, charging forward and tearing through wagons, carts, and tents. One of them even crashed into the cart carrying the monolith bears, busting open the cage door and releasing them into the camp. Screams rang through the caravan as the bears descended upon unsuspecting Exiles. Fires started to erupt as torches were knocked into the various temporary structures that the Exiles had erected, igniting canvas and wood.

It had gone better than Clary had hoped. With the rampaging beasts loose in the camp, and smoke rapidly filling the air, the Exiles were in complete disarray, and would be unable to figure out that they had escaped. It would give Clary and the others enough time to put some distance between them and the camp.

Now was the time to make their escape. The group took off into the desert. Clary hoped the chaos of the bull-drages' assault combined with the darkness of the night would be enough to keep them completely hidden. Just as they passed the last wagon there was a scream. "Aaaah! Help me! Please, wait!" It was the one girl from Terra's cell who had elected to come with them. She had been struck in the leg by an arrow. A small group of Exiles, led by the one who had rung the warning bell, was in pursuit. Apparently he had managed to recruit a few nearby reinforcements to hunt them down before their distraction became too great. Harvel turned round and began to make his way back to the girl, but one of the knights from his cell stopped him. "I'm sorry, sir, but you can't. These people are going to need you. Let me handle this."

Harvel looked at his brother-in-arms, clearly wanting to reject his suggestion, but the knight pushed off of him, yelling, "Go now!" and charged to face their pursuers.

Staying would only make the knight's efforts pointless, and so without once glance back he turned, grabbed Terra's hand, and ran after the rest of the group. They may have gotten free of the camp, but their escape was far from over.

Chapter 12

"Guh! Phht! What the bloody hell is that about? You shit!"

Thymey awoke to a bucket of water being splashed in his face. Blinded by the sun beating down on his face, head banging, he was completely disoriented. He knew he was drunk, but he definitely hadn't drunk enough to be in this much pain. He looked to his right where he saw his guardsman also sitting up, bewildered and drenched in filthy water. When he looked left, his eyes went wide. The other guardsman was lying face down on the ground, his neck bent at an odd angle. His face retained his expression of shock from the moment he had met his end.

"Have yourself a nice nap, then, Lieutenant?" came that rodent-like voice, which he had come to loathe with a passion.

"What's going on... sir?" He was already feeling irritable, but the appearance of the captain only made it all the worse. He knew by the smug grin on the captain's face that whatever had happened was about to be blamed on him.

"Well, I was hoping you'd be able to fill us all in on some of that, then." Turk gestured to the group of men surrounding them.

He's going to drag this out as much as he can. "Would you just tell me already? Enough of your games, Turk!"

At this, the captain's usual calm, collected facade dropped. "Watch your tone, Lieutenant. Look around then. This is all your fault."

"How is this my fault? Who attacked us?" By now Thymey could see the smoke and burnt tents.

"The prisoners who you were supposed to be guarding, that's who!"

For the first time, Thymey found himself frightened of Turk. Sure, Turk had authority over him for a while now, but even within the Exiled Regiment, an officer needed to have a reason to kill a man below him. Now Turk had all the reason he needed. If he didn't do it, then the Treacherous King would. Any mistake that resulted in the death of a fellow Exile would place the life of the man responsible into the hands of the highest-ranking officer present at the time.

Thymey hoped that he might be able to chalk it up to a hazard of the job. If it was just one guard who had died, he might be able to skate by.

"How many did they get?" he said.

Turk turned and signaled to one of the men who stepped forward and answered, "Sir! One man on rounds by an armory cart they raided, four men assigned to protect the prince and his royal security commander before they freed them. Three were killed in pursuit by an escapee who stayed back. Twelve were killed in the stampede and resulting fire started by the rampaging bull-drages, seven by the escaped monolith bears and, finally, one guard in front of the prisoner's garrison while his commanding lieutenant and fellow guardsman were passed out drunk on duty."

Shit! That's twenty-eight. There's no way I can swing that. Thymey wanted to argue, but the empty bottles at his feet thwarted the possibility of blaming it on a simple ambush.

Turk leaned in close. "Now then, you're going to tell me which prisoners did this, and then we'll see what fate has in store for you."

That was it, the nail in the coffin. Thymey closed his eyes ready for what was about to come and said, "I… I don't know, sir."

"That's what I thought, then. Prepare them!" Turk ordered. "And the rest of you, I want that prison searched top to bottom! Find out who else has escaped!"

All at once the men lunged on Thymey, kicking and punching as they struggled to restrain the thrashing lieutenant. Though he knew he wasn't going to make it out of there, he resolved to go out fighting. This didn't last long: within seconds, he was being dragged off outside of the camp. Three sets of posts had been set up side by side, and one pair already had a man strapped to it. He was covered in blood, whip marks covered the front and back of his torso, and his head hung limp. Thymey guessed that he was one of the escapees.

"Oh don't worry, he's still alive," Turk said with a smile. "We couldn't afford to lose any more product after all the gold you just cost us. It's more than I can say for you, then," He may have been upset, but he was taking every bit of joy he could from Thymey's impending death.

They strapped the lieutenant's wrists to the top of two posts, hoisting him up so that his arms were stretched out, putting all the weight on his shoulders. The pain was a mere irritation compared to what he would soon be facing at the end of the captain's whip. He had seen Turk perform this sort of execution before. He enjoyed playing with his victims beforehand, ensuring that they experienced the maximum amount of pain before he killed them with a dull rusty dagger that he kept on his person.

Turk had already positioned himself about fifteen paces in front of him. He liked to lash people from the front when he was going to kill them. He enjoyed savoring their last moments of pain. He would analyze each expression, so that he knew exactly when to strike in order to keep the pain levels at their peak throughout the entire process.

As soon as they finished stringing up the other guard to Thymey's right, the captain raised his whip and swung. *Crack!* The first lash hit the other guard. Turk would play with him first, letting his screams draw out the lieutenant's fear, to build as much anxiety and apprehension as possible. *Crack! Crack! Crack!*

"Aaaagh!" The man's screams were ear-piercing. Turk's plan was working. Thymey was beginning to panic, though he did his best to hide it from him.

After about a minute of lashing, the screaming stopped. The guardsman had passed out. Thymey knew that this was only the first round. The man would be woken up and then whipped into unconsciousness two or three times more, until either his heart gave out or Turk decided to go to work with his blades.

The lieutenant braced himself, trying to prepare for the pain that was to come. He closed his eyes and then he felt it. The pain was so intense that he couldn't even hear the crack of the whip. All he could hear was ringing. Every place the whip touched felt as though it were being stuck with a white-hot poker. No, that still wouldn't come close to the searing pain he was feeling now. Again and again the leather cut across his flesh. He began to pray for death. It couldn't come soon enough.

Just as he was beginning to fade out, another soldier appeared, shouting, "Captain! Captain, you need to hear this!" Turk turned on the man and looked as though he might strike out at him for interrupting his ritual, but the man came in close to him and started to tell him something. Thymey couldn't make out what he was saying over the ringing in his ears, but suddenly Turk pulled back, enraged. He turned toward Thymey and started to storm over towards him. He removed the dreaded rusty knife from its holster, and Thymey was sure this was his end. He relaxed, closing his eyes, ready for death. *Anything would be better than this*, he thought. Then he heard a terrible ripping noise followed by squelching and more screams. He opened his eyes and looked left were he saw the captain ripping out the other guard's innards from his stomach. He stabbed violently again and again, and roared in anger.

Then he stopped abruptly. Taking a deep breath and slicking his hair back with the blood that covered his hands, he looked at Thymey. "Looks like you're in luck today, then, Lieutenant. I'm going to give you another chance."

Thymey's mouth was agape. He couldn't believe what he was hearing.

"I've got a mission which – unfortunately – requires your expertise at tracking as well as your abilities with a sword. If you succeed, I will forget about everything that has happened, and we will let this man beside you take all of the blame. However, if you fail, we will hunt you down and be sure that you spend the rest of your days under my whip. I will experiment on you with new kinds of torture the likes of which even I have not tried yet. I assure you, it will mean pain. Do you understand?"

In his amazement at how quickly things had changed, Thymey let out a weak, "Yes, sir. What do you need me to do?"

"I need you to take a large group men, hunt down the Chained King, and bring him back to me dead or alive. Now clean yourself up and get out of my sight."

*   *   *

Clary and the rest of the escapees hadn't stopped running throughout the entire night and into the following morning. Fear and desperation had kept them going far beyond their usual capabilities. By the time the sun had almost reached its highest point they were reaching their limit. It had been several hours since then, and the draining effects of the heat had forced them into a slow walk. They tried to push as hard as they could to put some distance between themselves and the caravan, but they weren't sure how much they could create. The commotion caused by Clary's quick thinking surely would have caused some confusion within the camp, postponing the initial discovery. This was only a temporary buffer, however, and they couldn't truly gauge how much time this would buy them.

"Feryl, we have to take a break. We can't keep this pace up much longer," Clary urged.

"No! Every second we rest is another step closer to the Exiles." He was at the head of the group and was still keeping up a fast pace.

"Feryl, please. We can't keep up."

"And we're still in Varhalla territory. It's not safe here."

"Feryl!" This time she shouted his name and finally caught his full attention.

"What?" He stopped, looking back to see that the rest of their group was a ways behind. Terra was sitting on the ground. Harvel was tending to her. Gerald and Ingrum as well as one of the other knights were also on the ground. Everyone was soaked in sweat and taking deep, labored breaths.

"Feryl, we're not like you, we can't keep going for that long," said Clary. "We need to rest for a bit or we're going to start losing people."

"And you need to rest too," said Hilda, catching up with them. "If you keep pushing your powers like that when you haven't been able to recover, you'll die. I know you're scared but even if you survive, none of us have the strength to carry you."

Feryl was visibly embarrassed. He'd been so terrified of being brought back to the Exiles, he hadn't been considering the others. "Y-yeah, you're right... Sorry." It dawned on him that he'd never been in a position like this before. The people with whom he was traveling were friendly, which meant that he had to concern himself with their wellbeing. Usually, he would trudge on until he was ordered to stop.

"What's got you so jittery?" Clary asked, having noticed Feryl's nervous fidgeting. "There's no way the Exiles could catch up with us this quickly." She looked back clearly trying to make sure none of the others were near enough to overhear and then continued in a hushed voice, "Even if they did, you're still the Chained King. It's not like they could take you down without a contract controlling you. Right?"

Feryl looked at her in confusion. Though he knew she was saying this only to reassure herself that they were safe, it was the closest thing to a compliment that she, or anyone else for that matter, had ever paid him.

"You're seriously overestimating me," he said. He wanted to help with her reassurance but he had learned from his years with the Exiles that false confidence could be a grave mistake. "If I had enough time to recuperate, I could probably hold off a good number of them, but weakened as I am, and without armor, I couldn't fight a larger group, especially if they have archers. Even I couldn't survive a volley of arrows without protection."

At this, the girls' faces became sullen. Feryl felt bad for having frightened them. "But as you said, we do have a sizable lead on them, and without my armor, they won't figure out it was me who led the escape, so they won't expect us to be headed to Harsgard." He gave a halfhearted smile.

"Why are you still so worried?" Hilda asked. "I can tell the Exiles scare you, but something else is riling you up."

Feryl sighed. She had seen straight through him. "The Exiles will be difficult to deal with if they catch up to us, but they don't have enough supplies left to send the whole force. More than likely, a large group of higher-ranking elites will split off to track us down. Even so, without horses or some sort of desert transportation, they shouldn't be able to catch up to us too quickly."

Clary cut in. "So what's the problem?"

"The problem is that the Exiles are the least of our worries. We are very deep into Varhalla territory. Even fully powered and equipped, I don't know how I'd fare against a group of them. They are vicious and extremely deadly. On top of that, they're much stronger than men, and some of their magics are as deadly as they are ancient. If we run into one of their hunting parties, let alone a decent-sized group, we'll be in serious trouble."

Clary was looking more panicked by the second. Desperate to find some sort of solid footing, she suggested, "Well, maybe that can be a good thing. If we get lucky, the Exiles might run into a group of them and be taken out since they're split up and weakened, right?"

Feryl almost laughed at her optimism. "No, not likely. They have a deal set up with the Varhalla. They were expecting us to bring them some goods from our raid, as well as first pick from whatever we brought for sale, in exchange for safe passage. That brings my second fear. Once the captain reaches Beyond, he may inform them of our escape and hire Varhallan trackers and mercenaries to come after us. They'll have gandovors."

Gandovors were large desert-dwelling birds that grew to be roughly the size of horses. They were fierce predators with razor-sharp beaks. While they could not fly, they did have wings, which helped them to leap to great heights and distances. Also, they had an extra set of arms which hung forward beneath their wings, allowing them to grab hold of prey. Not only were they incredibly fast, they could also travel great distances without water, making them ideal as desert mounts. Horses could not survive long within the Arid Sea – it was for this reason that the Exiles had neglected to bring any with them.

"If we don't put enough distance between us and them, the Varhalla will overtake us, and that'll be the end of it."

"The Varhalla are nothing but exaggerations by old soldiers and travelers. In reality they're just a bunch of drunk savages. Don't listen to this overgrown buffoon. They haven't been a real threat since the war." It was Prince Valen. He had just arrived from farther back, only overhearing the tail end of the conversation.

It was fortunate that he had not arrived sooner, Feryl thought. Though they knew that eventually Feryl's true identity would become known, the three of them thought it better to delay that revelation until they were further from the Exiles. Dissent within the group so early on could cause some serious problems.

"They're just a bunch of normal, filthy pirates, living in holes out here in the sand somewhere," Valen concluded.

"I wouldn't let them hear you say that, Prince," Feryl suggested. "They take pride in their origins – they even consider it a sacred story. To utter something like that would be considered blasphemy. They'd cut out your tongue before even questioning you, and that wouldn't be the worst of it."

The prince's face went red. "The day I take suggestions from a common slave like you—"

"On second thought," Feryl interrupted, "it might be an improvement."

"You impudent—"

"Shut it, boy!" cried the older knight they had rescued along with the prince. Valen tried to protest, but the old knight was having none of it. "There're a few things you need to wrap your thick skull around if you plan on making it through. First is that out here, no one cares who your dear old daddy is. So until we get back home, you better watch that attitude of yours. If you can't do that, this big one here won't have to teach you a lesson, because I'll be putting my own boot up yer arse the whole walk back. Understand?"

Valen was steaming, but he obviously knew the man's threats were real. He stormed off to the rest of the group.

"Sorry about the brat," the knight said, taking a seat across from Feryl. "The King was always way too soft with that one," he chuckled.

"Excuse me," Hilda said, "but I don't believe we ever got your name."

"Ah, right. I am Sir Rorian, high commander of the royal guard. Pleased to make your acquaintance."

This explained why the prince didn't fight back when Rorian put him in his place, Feryl thought. He, Clary and Hilda made their introductions in return.

"So, I heard you talking about the Varhalla," Rorian said. "I was hoping you could give up a bit more information about them."

"Well, I'm sure I don't know as much as the royal guard does, sir." Feryl responded modestly.

"Oh, I doubt that, boy. It's a large kingdom. Most royal forces never deploy so far west, and we in the inner provinces don't suffer many dealings with desert dwellers. Besides, from what I gather, the Exiles had an exchange deal with them, so who better to ask than the Chained King himself?"

Feryl and the girls stared at the commander wide-eyed. Their secret had been figured out so easily.

"I-I don't know what your—" Feryl began.

"Come now lad, I may be old but I'm not daft," Rorian said, grinning. "I do fancy myself a bit sharper than these young bucks, anyway. You're far too massive and well-trained to be just a slave. Not to mention I saw you rip the door off our cage like it were made of parchment. And don't think I didn't notice that bit of Fjoren body alteration magic you did with your arms. It was the same as the Chained King used on the night of the attack."

Feryl looked at the other two, as though he were asking for help, but they both looked just as unsure as he was. "Look, we can explain."

"Bah! No need. If you really were the one leading that lot, you wouldn't have set us free. Reckon you had some kind of control magic on you, right?"

"A slave's contract, sir."

"Aye, that'll do it."

"Please don't tell the others."

"Don't worry, I wasn't planning on it. Not yet anyway. Those children will probably misunderstand, and we don't need that kind of trouble at the moment."

Clary sighed in relief. The commander seemed to be a good man. He also appeared knowledgeable and experienced. Having him on their side would certainly aide in their endeavor.

"Now, about these sand-men… anything you've got. What exactly are they? Where do they come from?"

"First off," said Feryl, "they aren't men at all. At least, not anymore."

"What's that supposed to mean?" Clary asked.

Feryl looked back at the rest of the group. Terra and Gerald were still panting, and the rest of them seemed to need at least a few more minutes of recovery. It would be a while before they could move again. "I'm not sure it's anything useful, but the way their legend goes, they were once a seafaring people. They had a powerful empire stretching across many islands."

"Wait, so they aren't from the Arid Sea?" Clary asked. She didn't understand why anyone would leave a prosperous land just to come to this forsaken desert.

"In a sense they are, but not as it is now," Feryl replied. "Just listen, I'll explain everything. According to them, the Arid Sea was at one point an actual part of the Crescent Ocean, called the Great Western Sea, and the Varhalla were men who had conquered it. They had created a vast empire under the rule of a genius war chief by the name of Hallumsha. He started by uniting all of the peoples of the Southern Crescent and then pushed back west and north to expand their borders. By the time they had reached the northernmost point of the Western Sea, the Varhalla had amassed an enormous army. Unfortunately, it was here that they encountered another ancient people, who wielded powerful magic, fueled by nature. Most people believe these magic-users to be the original ancestors of the Fjorendel. The Varhalla themselves had not discovered much in the way of magic, and so they struggled in the face of their new enemy. After many attempts to storm the frozen tundras that these northmen called home, they were unable to push the Fjorendel back. Eventually, the Varhalla decided to continue west, recruiting small island nations and villages to their empire as they went, but Hallumsha never forgot the humiliation he suffered at the hands of the northmen, vowing to return once he had acquired the power to defeat them.

"At one point they came across a very peculiar island; one made entirely of crystal and gems, like a grand castle of jewels jutting up from the ocean itself. There were people there, but oddly enough they had no villages and no chief – only men who called themselves priests. Hallumsha asked the priests to speak to their leader so that he might negotiate their terms of surrender and bring them in as part of his great nation. The priests explained that their leaders were not of this earth, and suggested that if Hallumsha wished to converse with them, he should vow to serve them, as he was a visitor in the gods' great nation. At this, Hallumsha and his advisors laughed and mocked the priests for worshiping shiny rocks and false gods. In order to convince the Varhalla of the validity of their gods so that the invaders might join them in peaceful devotion, the priests decided to display powerful magic, the likes of which the Varhalla had never seen. Hallumsha and his men were astounded at the sight.

"Unfortunately, however, they did not view the magic as coming from the gods. Instead, Hallumsha's advisors told him that it was the crystal palace that gave these priests their abilities. They told Hallumsha that it would be wise to take the crystal palace from its inhabitants and use it to defeat the northmen. Though the priests wielded great magic, they knew that they were too few to defeat Hallumsha's vast forces. Instead they warned the war chief that if he continued down his path, he would receive the magic he desired but that it would come at great cost, turning his empire to dust and subjecting him and his people to an eternal and horrible fate. Taking this as a threat, Hallumsha decided to have the priests executed and ordered that the island be stripped completely of the magic stone.

"After months of work, the island was bare, and the remaining crystal was too far under the water's surface to be mined. Just as the war chief and his fleet began to pull away from what remained of the island, there was a great rocking within the sea. The fleet was tossed and shaken with the waves, though there were no storm clouds in sight and no wind to speak of. Then the rear half of the armada was suddenly sucked back towards the place where the crystal palace once stood – only it was not just the ships that were being drawn back. It was the very ocean itself. All the water in the western sea was being pulled into a great whirlpool, at the center of which was the island. The sight was something unimaginable, and finally the war chief had realized his mistake. When everything settled, over two thirds of the war chief's nation had been swallowed by the island, which now stood once again as it had before; a jeweled palace towering over all that surrounded it. The gods had shown their displeasure by taking with them all the water of the sea and leaving only the sand.

"Naturally the war chief was furious, but it was not all terrible. He discovered that he and all his men now possessed magic just as the priests had. They could still make it back to the sea with their newfound powers and gather the remaining peoples of their home islands to move inland. But as they traveled, they discovered that the distance was much longer in the hot desert than it had been as a cool, breezy sea. Many of the men succumbed to the heat on their journey, and those who remained found that their bodies began to disfigure in strange ways. They grew in size and stature. At the same time their arms lengthened and they grew claws and sharp teeth. Finally their skin became hard and leathery, changing to match the sickly nature of their souls. But it was not only the Varhalla that had changed. The creatures that inhabited the sea had become cursed as well, turning monstrous and deadly to adapt to their new home. The gods did this to keep the Varhalla in fear and to make surviving the desert even more dangerous.

"When finally Hallumsha and his men reached the Southern Crescent, they were unrecognizable. The crews of the ships that remained in the waters feared their former chief and comrades. They fled back to their original islands and never returned to the horrid place, which they knew to be cursed. Even though it has been over two thousand years, the Varhalla are still recovering from their curse. They do still have a war chief, though no outsider knows who he is. Many believe that it's Hallumsha, considering how long they are said to live. More than likely, though, it's just a rumor designed to scare would-be invaders."

By now everyone had gathered around. They had all heard most of the story, and all seemed amazed, quietly contemplating the tale they had heard.

Clary was the one who finally broke the silence. "So, what happened to the palace? Has anyone ever seen it?"

Feryl looked at her for a second and then smiled. "Of course they have. The island was called Saroza. Now, since you all seem rested, let's get going. We've no time to waste."

Chapter 13

"So did you?"

"No! Of course not!"

"Oh come on, you mean to tell me you were alone up in the bell tower and the thought didn't cross your mind even once?"

"Well there wasn't exactly much time up there. Watching an army of Exiles storming the town was kind of a mood killer." *Thank the gods*, Clary thought. She'd never forgive herself if she'd let her first kiss be stolen by that lying coward, Valen.

Terra laughed.

It was another extremely hot day of traveling as Clary and the others trudged on through the Arid Sea. Oddly enough, however, their spirits were light. They had been traveling for days, and so far they had seen neither head nor tail of the Exiles. Everyone in the group was beginning to feel safer and confident in their successful escape. As fortune had it, there had even been a couple of small dust storms along the way. Not enough to be dangerous, but certainly sufficient to cover their tracks and provide cover.

On this evening Clary and Terra were walking together, talking. They had discussed the events of the night of the attack. Now that Terra had turned to teasing Clary about her time with the prince, and as much as she pretended to hate it, Clary was happy to be talking about something as simple as boys and gossip. It was nice to feel at least a modicum of normality, talking with Terra like this. It was a small comfort, but it almost made things feel normal, as if she Terra and Sisti were back home, going through their usual routine.

They tried not to talk about Sisti too much. The pain was too great. At some point during the first couple of days, Terra sat Clary down to ask her about what happened. She wanted to know everything, no matter how much it hurt. Clary reluctantly gave in and told her everything about the discovery of the horrid scene in the small house that night. However, she left out the details of having to hide in Sisti's blood. She thought that would be too much, even for honesty's sake. Terra was silent for a couple of days after Clary explained what had happened. When she finally started talking again, it seemed that there was an unspoken agreement between the two of them to put the topic behind them and move on, at least until they were able to get out of their current predicament.

"Who'd have thought that little miss 'I don't have time for silly boys' Clary would be the one to snatch up the prince that night? You really do have all the luck," Terra teased.

"Ugh, please. I didn't 'snatch up' anyone, and if I did, it definitely wouldn't be him."

"Clary?" Hilda interrupted, walking up behind them. "Are you okay? I don't know what you're talking about, but I could feel your embarrassment and nervousness from back there. You really should try to be more honest about things. Emotions like that are painful for me, you know?"

Terra burst out laughing, and Clary went bright red. Though she had grown close to Hilda, sometimes Clary wished her friend could turn her empath ability off. There really was no getting past her.

"Yeah, yeah, I get it, Hilda." she said, speeding up her walk.

Shouting came from the front of the group. "I'm telling you, we need to adjust our heading more northwest. If we keep hugging the side of the desert like this, then we are going to run into the Pronged Sea in the north and it will take far too long to cut west around it. The Exiles will cut us off!" It was Valen, arguing with Feryl again. The two of them were like oil and water. It seemed like they were always at each other's throats over something.

"And I'm telling you, if we stray too far west, there will be fewer oases, streams and game," Valen retorted. "We'll probably starve, if we don't run into a Varhallan village first!"

Everyone stopped. When these two picked up an argument, it would be a while before they could move on. Fortunately, however, they had started to use these times to mark their breaks, which was good – if it weren't for the fights, Feryl would keep on marching until the rest of the group passed out from exhaustion.

"I don't know why Valen tries to argue with Feryl all the time. I mean it's obvious that Feryl has the most field experience," Clary said.

"How do you mean? He was just a slave before, wasn't he?" Terra asked.

Clary had almost forgotten that Terra didn't know Feryl's true identity yet. "Oh, uh…well, I mean he's been out here for longer, and I'm sure he learned some stuff from the Exiles. Plus the prince has never been out in the field like this."

"I can understand that," Harvel said. He had now caught up with the girls, along with Sir Garrett and Gerald. "But truthfully there is some merit behind the prince's words… Terra, are you feeling ill?"

Terra had turned a little red at his arrival. Only moments earlier, she had been describing how close the two had gotten over the course of their time together and how she thought she was falling for him. Clary laughed. No doubt Terra was wondering if Harvel had heard anything. Had he arrived a few minutes earlier, she would have been completely exposed.

"Y-yes!" Terra stuttered. "I'm great, it's uh, just the sun! Yeah, just some sunburn. Er, what were you saying again?"

"Oh right, as I was saying," Harvel continued, "once the Exiles figure out where we are going – and you can be certain that they will – they will head straight for the point where the Pronged and Arid Seas meet, in order to cut us off. I'm sure they will have left some spies along the edge of the desert anyway, to monitor any movements by possible royal forces. They'll spot us at some point, if they haven't already. It doesn't take all that long to send a message back by hawk."

"And how does the prince know this?" Clary asked skeptically. "Surely he hasn't put that much thought into it."

"Of course he has. In fact, that big fellow would do well to consider the prince's advice more seriously. The sons of the Drakewil line are all extremely well educated. Their father insisted on it. From the time they are born, they receive the best education in the entire kingdom, from the best tutors. When they are old enough, they begin training to become military leaders. They learn everything – not just physical combat, but navigation, tactics, naval strategy and much more."

"Really? You're telling me Valen is some kind of military genius?" Clary scoffed. "You think way too highly of him, Sir Harvel. I've seen how he is. I'm sure you're just being loyal, but even you have to admit he's just a coward."

"True. He has acted cowardly recently, and he's lied more times than I can count, but he wasn't always like that."

"What do you mean?"

"There was once a time when he was kind and true. He was even quite chivalrous, but a couple years ago an attempt was made on his life."

"So what?" Gerald cut in, having finally caught his breath. "He's supposed to be this great military leader, yet a failed assassination attempt set him off his rocker?"

"Not exactly. You see, at the time the king was talking about opening up relations with the Varhalla. He said he thought that by sending small bands of emissaries to small Varhallan villages, we could build trust and open up better trade routes. Much of the nation was split over this idea. Those who had served under the king's father still remembered the battles they had fought against the Varhalla. Years before any of us were born, the Varhalla made an attempt at taking the southern portion of the kingdom. We were able to fight them off, but the war took its toll. When the king finally made the announcement that he was going to start sending emissaries and would in turn allow the Varhalla to cross our borders openly, there was an uproar. Eventually a certain group of people decided to take revenge on the king. They attempted to take the life of Valen. One night, when he and the queen were out in the market together, they were set upon by a band of rebels. In the confusion the rebels were able to kill Valen's men, but when they turned their attention to the young prince his mother leaped in to stop them. Instead of killing the prince as they intended, the assassin's blade struck the queen. She died on the spot. Valen shut himself away for a while after that. Since then he hasn't truly been the same."

Clary furrowed her brow, surprised by a newly emerging sense of guilt. She hadn't realized that Valen had been through so much, and had assumed that he had been just a pampered prince. Still, it did not justify his behavior. She understood the source now, but that didn't make it okay. He had still lied, and tried to sell everyone out.

"Even so, I still don't understand why you hold him in such high regard," she said, "especially given how he's acted. Surely even you can see what kind of person he his. Who he once was doesn't excuse him now."

"Yes, you're right in a sense," Harvel responded, frankly. "I do know how he is now... how he acts. However, I do still respect him and love him as a lord and a brother, but it's not who he was that makes me feel that way. It's who he can be. I see the fear, the uncertainty, the façade of lies he wears like armor, but I know that the man underneath it all is still capable of being the great leader he was meant to be. I have hope that one day, that man will surface and when he does, I want to be right there following him."

By now the sun had almost set, so they decided that it would be best to start making camp. At night, though the desert was so brightly illuminated with starlight that they would still be able to see, there were too many nocturnal threats to travel without better protection. A large number of desert species spent most of the day buried under the sand, hiding from the heat. At night, they would surface to hunt. This included creatures that lay just beneath the sand, waiting for prey to step on them, before dragging them under with snapping jaws and spikes.

They began rolling out blankets in the sand and dropping their things. The armory cart from which they had stolen their weapons had also contained several quick-escape bags, filled with various supplies and small bits of food and rations. According to Feryl, it was standard practice among the Exiles to keep these kits stored in case of emergency. This also meant that the escapees were able to change into fresh clothes after they left the caravan. Clary and Terra were very happy about this, as they had been wearing their dresses, which were not well suited for travel, since the night of the attack.

Clary got up and started heading towards the nearest sand dune. She always gave some excuse before walking off, but really she was going to train by herself. If she had gained anything from her time as a captive, it was her experience with a sword. While Thymey hadn't actually instructed her on form, her reflexes and her feel for the art had improved tremendously through simple trial and error, as painful as the "error" part had been.

Every night and every morning she would go off to train for a while. It was exhausting, but she didn't want to lose what she had gained. She knew that if Sir Edgrum hadn't been there to save her, that Exile would have killed her. She wouldn't let it come to that again. She was tired of being rescued. She vowed that the next time such a situation occurred, she would not give her opponent the chance to surprise her.

Once she had found a spot she deemed acceptable, she dragged the scabbard around in the sand to ensure there were no creatures waiting below, and then began. She swung her swords, dancing from left to right and trying to imitate the moves that had been the most successful against Thymey and the other Exile guard. She also tried to remember, as best she could, the lieutenant's moves that he had used on her.

After a few minutes a voice made her jump. "If you don't widen up that stance, you'll never be able to last long in an actual fight. And who taught you that light on your feet dancing rubbish?" It was Sir Rorian. He was sitting atop a hill of sand, laughing at her.

"Sir Rorian, why did you come over here? I was just—" Clary started.

"You were just what? Taking a piss for half the night? Who do you think you were fooling with that? I may be old, lass, but I ain't senile." He grinned. "I know exactly what you were doing, or at least what you were trying to do, pathetically. Been keeping an eye on you, I have."

"What, you think it's pathetic for a woman to try to learn to fight?"

"Ha ha, don't try to hit me with that bull, lassy. I'm far too old for that, and I've met women who could take on the Treacherous King himself. I don't know who you've been watching, but they've got you using styles that just don't match your physique. I will say you seem to have a good sense of the thing, though."

"I don't care if I'm not meant for two swords, I want to use them. If you're just going to sit there and make fun of me, I'd prefer if you'd just go away." Fighting in this way felt necessary. It was a way of keeping Sir Cloin's memory alive.

Once again the knight laughed. "That's exactly what I'm talking about. You don't even understand what I'm saying, but you still want to challenge me. I notice you like to challenge everyone. A word to the wise, dear, when someone's offering to help you towards a goal, it's best not to insult them or drive them away."

Clary just glared at the old man, not knowing what to say.

"And that's the main problem right there," said Rorian. "I can tell you've been fighting with a sword, but you haven't been practicing swordplay.

Whenever you swing those things it's just attack, attack, attack. It seems to me that whoever you trained with just wanted you angry. That's no way for you to fight. It may work with Fjoren magic, but not with a sword. When I said you didn't have the body for that type of fighting, I wasn't talking about how many swords you have. I was talking about the way you use them. Perhaps if you were the size of that Feryl boy then you could fight like that, but at your size, I don't see you overpowering a well-built warrior using pure strength. Do you?"

Clary furrowed her brow. "Well I'm not getting bigger anytime soon, so what would you have me do?"

"I'll have you trained properly, lass. That's what I'll do," he said sternly. "You're smaller and weaker than almost any soldier, but that doesn't matter. We won't have you fight with brawn, we'll have you fight with your brain. Technique and speed, those'll be your strengths, understand?"

Clary nodded fervently, making no attempt to hide her growing excitement. She would finally be able to defend herself.

"Now come on, show me a bit of what you can do with those butter knives!"

They trained for over an hour. At first, Sir Rorian let Clary come at him full force. After a few rounds, he stopped her and instructed her in various techniques, correcting her stance and form.

"Looks like we've got a lot to do, but now that I can see what we're working with, I'll have you whipped into shape in no time!" he said. "We'll take it slow at first. I'll teach you one combination each night. We'll review it in the morning."

After the sun had set completely Sir Rorian called for a stop.

"But I can keep going!" Clary protested. She was smiling confidently, even through her labored breaths.

"Aye, I'm sure you can, but if you do, you won't have energy for the morning, or tomorrow's travel. Rest is just as important as training, you know."

Clary groaned, but grudgingly sat beside her new mentor as he fell back in the sand.

"There is something you have to understand," he began. "The skills I teach you will only take you so far. Edgrum told me about your fight back in the camp. You were lucky that Exile was a newer recruit. They wouldn't force anyone half decent to take on a simple patrol job. If you come into contact with an experienced swordsman – that is to say, one who has been training since he was a boy – you won't be able to hold your own. Not without years of practice."

"So what's the point then? I won't be of any use if I can't defeat an Exile." Her expression now changed to one of exasperation rather than satisfaction.

"Hold on there. I wasn't finished. You don't need to go at this from only one angle. I know about your father, and I know what you can do. You need to work on the magic side of things as well. Unfortunately, I don't have much of a head for mystic arts and such. You'll have to figure that out separately."

Clary groaned again. "But I've tried using it on my own. I can't get any of it to work."

"Then you've got to stop trying to do everything by yourself." He stared at her expectantly.

Clary knew he already had an answer about how she was to train, but he would not give it away. He was waiting for her to give him an answer.

"Well… I suppose I could have Hilda help me."

"Who? The empath? Bah!" Rorian scoffed. "That girl may be decent at magic, but a battle mage she is not."

Clary realized where he was going with this line of thought. "But I can't work with him!"

"And why not?"

"Because he's the Chained King! He invaded my village. He killed my friends and neighbors. It's his fault we're even here." She was breathing heavily in frustration. Clary hadn't had the chance to express these emotions yet. It was the first time she'd really been able to talk about Feryl at all. Whenever she was alone with Hilda – the only other person who knew the situation – Feryl was rarely far away. When he was at a distance, there was always someone else nearby listening in.

"But you know that's not true, don't you?" Rorian said, in a surprisingly soft voice.

"Do I? How can I trust anything he says? For all I know he's leading us right into a trap." When Rorian chuckled, she blurted, "What are you grinning about? I'm serious!"

"No you're not, lass. In fact I think you don't believe a word you just said."

"And why not?"

"Because… I know you're a smarter girl than that, Clary." He was grinning.

It was the first time he had addressed her as anything other than 'girl' or 'lass'. Clary hadn't expected this sort of answer. She had assumed he would just retort with some joke or sarcasm. It caught her off guard.

"Think now," he continued, "why would this boy free us from the Exiles, just to take us right back to them? Why would he push so hard to get away from them that he's running himself ragged overusing his powers? And more than all of that, why would he watch you like a hawk, the way he does every time you so much as stumble during this journey?"

Clary blushed. She hadn't realized that Feryl had been paying attention to her. "I don't know. Maybe he still wants to turn me into the Chained Queen."

Sir Rorian laughed. "You know damn well that if that were true, the empath would have picked up hints of malice in his intent. That girl can hardly keep her mouth shut."

Now Clary was the one laughing. "I guess she does have a problem with privacy sometimes. But still... why do I still feel this way? Why do I feel so uneasy around him?"

"Well now, I don't think that's rightly my place to say. You'll have to work that out on your own," Rorian said, lying back and staring up at the starry sky. "Maybe it's something to do with you two being the last of your kind 'round here. Or maybe he's just upset you aren't going to be his Chained Queen." He laughed.

Clary blushed from embarrassment. She grabbed a handful of sand and threw it at the old man. He sat up and sputtered, brushing the sand off of his face, and the two laughed together. It had been a while since Clary had laughed this hard. Her sides were starting to ache from the strain.

After they had both finally calmed down, Rorian said, "Either way, I think it's time you two got started on that training."

"Well, it's late. I don't think I should go ask him now."

"Ah, that's okay, lass. You don't have to." He stuck two fingers into his mouth on either side and blew a loud whistle.

Clary jumped. The sudden sharp noise had startled her. "Hey! What was that for?"

Sir Rorian gestured over toward the end of another large mountain of sand. After a few seconds, a large figure, who could only be Feryl, came from behind it and approached them.

"Wait, was he spying on me this whole time?" Clary's heart raced with embarrassment. Fortunately, the hill from which Feryl had appeared was far enough away that he couldn't have heard her words.

"No, he wasn't spying," the old knight said with a laugh. "He's been doing patrols around the camp sites every night, with Sir Garrett. Apparently after he came across you training one night, he decided to keep an eye out to make sure you were safe. Don't worry though, I've already explained the situation to him. He'll be working with you from now on – and look at that! You didn't even have to ask!"

Clary buried her face in her palms.

Once Feryl arrived, Sir Rorian wasted no time in getting them started. Feryl was quiet, as he usually was whenever he was around her. He seemed almost like a different person when they were together. Anyone seeing the pair together would never suspect that he was the same person who was constantly fighting with Valen, let alone the most feared leader known to man.

It was strange to her how he could be so kind, yet so powerful. Perhaps that was the reason she didn't trust him. One moment he was perfectly calm, the next he was filled with rage, demonstrating his power. The way he put it, the key to utilizing Fjoren powers was to draw upon one's anger.

"It is truly dangerous. Most other mages try to avoid fighting this way, but for us, it's a necessity. You'll need to learn to switch back and forth in order to blend it with your swordplay."

"But I don't get it," Clary said, confused. "What's different about us? Why can't others use magic like ours?"

"I suppose it goes back to our ancestors. No one's really sure how they did it, but most people say that they were able to make deals with earthly spirits in order to gain the attributes of those spirits. In all honesty, I'm not really sure how much bearing that idea holds."

"But that still doesn't answer why it's so special."

"For most mages, altering one's own body is near impossible. Occasionally, you might see a mage use illusion magic to appear different, but that's about as far as it goes. I'm sure even you have seen that."

Clary remembered how Hilda had appeared to be an older woman when they had first met.

"But then what about medical magic?" she asked. "I've used that to alter bodies before. You know, stopping bleeding and healing small wounds and stuff like that."

"That's just it. When you perform medical magic, it's always done on someone else."

Clary still didn't understand.

"Here, think about it this way. Do you understand how magic flows through your body?"

"Yes, kind of," she replied. "My father said it was like an interwoven thread of energy passing through your body, and that it was different in each person."

"Exactly. This is why some people aren't able to use advanced magics, while other people are. It's like a system running through you that needs to work in a very specific way. When you use magic, you open up that system and release some of the magic in a controlled stream, usually by feeding it into a conduit. Whether it is a weapon or an item, the magic is altering the new system. The problem with altering one's own body is that you start to change that system, by using your *own* system. Imagine trying to perform surgery on your wrist using the hand it's attached to. It's impossible. Suddenly things stop working the way you intend them to and the outcome is horrible. It's the same thing with magic. You could try to enlarge your right arm with your left and then it may explode unexpectedly."

Clary finally understood. "So our ancestors found a way to get past it somehow?"

"Yes and no. They weren't able to figure out how to alter themselves. Instead, they somehow found a way to alter their offspring. They weaved the magic into their blood. The original Fjorendel were divided into separate villages, and once the technique was discovered, the different villages worked to develop their own types of alterations. It started with simple increases in strength, size and other physical attributes, but eventually they each started to develop individual techniques, settling on different powers. After a few generations of repetition, the abilities became ingrained in their heredity. We lost the means to create new powers but the magic in our blood became passed down the same way that hair color or athleticism is."

Clary was starting to understand now. "So then we are from different villages?"

"Yes. My clan's families worked mostly on further developing the ability to grow in size and to harden our bodies like stone. We increased our strength to the maximum limits."

"Then what about my lineage?" Clary asked. She was unsure how using fire equated to body alteration magic. There were many mages who could hurl fire and do other similar things.

"I thought that would be obvious," Feryl said. "Your father displayed it against me on the night of the attack. You have the ability to change the temperature of your body to incredible extremes. With enough training, you'll be able to melt through steel just by touching it. Not only that, but it is impossible for you to be harmed by flames. Breathing fire is impossible for most other mages. The intense heat would scorch their throat and kill them. Did you not notice how the flames your father poured on your wrists during the activation ritual didn't burn you?" Now Feryl was staring at her with a puzzled look on his face.

Clary thought back to the night when her father gave her the tattoos that related to her powers. "But the flames weren't hot, were they? I mean you and Hilda didn't—" But now that she thought about it, she couldn't remember what they were doing. She had been so upset at leaving her father behind that she had not been paying attention to them.

"You didn't notice that I had to step back and was covering my face to protect myself from the heat, or that Hilda had to hide behind me to avoid being burned? Those flames gave off more heat than a roaring bonfire. I'm sure that to you they were cool, weren't they? Maybe they produced just a warm tickling feeling."

Clary nodded, looking down at her hands in disbelief.

"The ritual he performed is unique to your people. It is used to activate the abilities to a higher extent, giving you further control. It also keeps you from accidentally killing everyone around you, should you go into a rage and start spitting out flames everywhere.

"Usually, as children, we are instructed on how to write the ancient runes of our people before going through the ritual around the age of eight or nine. It is supposed to be a joyous rite of passage for us. The entire village shows up for the final test, and there is a huge celebration. I'm sorry you had to have yours rushed like that."

"So did you have one? A celebration, I mean." Clary asked. She couldn't imagine what it would be like to have an entire village of people joining together for her benefit like that.

Feryl gave a genuine, happy smile as he looked towards the ground. He seemed to be reminiscing. Clary had never seen him like this before.

"Yes, I did have mine," he said. "It was one of the best days of my life. My whole family was there. My father had been gone for a few years but I was sure he was watching over me. My mother was so proud. I was set to begin combat training a few days after the celebration ended." His expression suddenly changed. "Only I never did. I was taken by the Exiles two days later."

Clary could tell he was replaying the events in his head. She wasn't sure what to say. "Uh… hey, are you alright?"

His eyes snapped towards her. "Oh, er, yeah. I'm fine. Anyway, I'm sure they'll want to celebrate your return when we get to Harsgard. You may have your ceremony yet." He smiled, though this time it appeared more forced. "But first, we need to teach you how to bring out the seals on your arms. That is what allows you to channel the ability in its various forms."

"And how do I do that?"

"You need to start by learning how to read and write them." Feryl drew his sword and started tracing the same markings in the ground that she had seen her father draw. Clary couldn't believe it, but there were four times as many characters as in the common alphabet she was used to.

"I sure hope you're a good student," Feryl laughed. "If not, this could take a while."

Chapter 14

Clary and her friends had been lucky throughout their journey so far. They
had been so fortunate, in fact, that it was beginning to cause worry among the
more seasoned travelers of the group, particularly Sir Rorian, Prince Valen
and Feryl. The three of them were well aware of the frequency with which
sandstorms plagued the Arid Sea – a higher rate than any other desert in
existence. Though their journey had been riddled with dust storm after dust
storm, they had yet to experience the thunderous hurricane of sand for which
the land was known. Valen knew of the weather patterns of the area. During
his tutelage he had read a book of desert stratagems written by Field
Commander Peyton, a knight who had served under his grandfather during
the last great Varhallan war, which had detailed storm patterns and how to
predict and utilize them to one's advantage. It was essential knowledge when
presented with Varhallan adversaries, who were equipped from birth to deal
with such conditions. The tome gave warnings of the desert appearing calm
for unusual lengths of time. Over the years in which the war was waged, Sir
Peyton had noticed that such calm times – which he dubbed 'building
periods' – would often lead to monumentally disastrous sandstorms which
even the Varhalla refused to brave. Should a building period last more than
thirty days the resulting storm would be too large to survive without solid

shelter. If a building period lasted more than forty-eight days, even solid shelter would not guarantee safety. Clary's group had traveled for fifty-three days already. If they were unable to find shelter soon, they would surely perish in the ensuing storm. Even if they survived, their fate was still uncertain.

As it happened, Gerald was the one to bring their worries to an end, finally demonstrating his worth even if it was unintentional. During a break for one of Feryl's and Valen's endless arguments, he left to relieve himself then, after only a few moments, there came a shout: "Help! Help!"

At his cries, everybody in the group stopped what they were doing and rushed over the sand dune.

On the other side there was an even larger hill. This yellow mountain was too tall to see past and was completely smooth save for a single hole in its side. At the mouth of this cave were two large, insect-like creatures. Each had hundreds of small legs, supporting long, armored carapaces. They were three times as long as a man, with bodies that jutted up from the forward end where one would expect their heads to be. The bodies lifted upright like cobras, with long, razor-sharp pincers reaching out from either side. The creatures were snapping at Gerald, who was scooting backward as fast as he could through the sand.

"What in blazes are those?" Ingrum shouted.

"Millipincers!" Feryl and Valen answered in unison.

After Edgrum, Harvel was the next to make it over the hill. His mind was already at work. He turned towards Edgrum. "Get their attention now!"

Edgrum did not even take time to answer. It seemed that before the words had even left his superior's mouth he had nocked and loosed an arrow. The attack was pinpoint accurate, as Harvel had expected it to be. The arrow pierced the eye of one of the millipincers, making it lose balance and fall back onto the other creature.

"Sir Garrett! Sir Morton! Mr. Feryl!" Harvel commanded. "Get under those monstrosities and keep them occupied! Draw their attention away from him!"

These three would be the best choice for keeping the creatures at bay. Sir Garrett was one of the best spearman the royal guard had ever known, and Sir Morton, one of the three other knights whom they had freed in their escape, was no slouch with a pike. Accompanied by Feryl's two unusually long swords with their immense reach, the three had the ability to keep the creatures at bay without risking falling within range of their tremendous claws.

"Edgrum, keep up the volley. Sir Ellerbe, get in there and retrieve Gerald."

Sir Ellerbe was the other knight freed along with Morton. Though these two men were a few years Harvel's senior, it was clear that Harvel had earned their respect, for the two followed the young man's orders without question. Ellerbe ran to Gerald with much haste and began to pull him away from the insects.

"Come on! Get up!" he urged Gerald. "We need to get moving!"

"I can't!" Gerald cried back.

Ellerbe had become used to Gerald's complaining, just as the others had, and took his response for cowardice. "Quit your whining and— oh!" He stopped as he caught a glimpse of Gerald's leg. The sand around it had turned a dark red and the leg of his trousers was wet and torn open. Ellerbe turned back towards the others. "I need help. He's hurt bad!"

Unfortunately this call for help gained the attention of more than just his fellow soldiers. One of the millipincers turned on him, swinging a scissor-like arm at the knight, who did not have time to release his grip from the wounded boy and retrieve his sword. Before the creature could claim Sir Ellerbe's life, however, Sir Rorian stepped into the fray. His shield caught the creature's blow just in time. While the shock was enough to send Rorian flying backward, it caused no real damage.

At the sight of Sir Rorian being struck, Garrett seemed to go into a blind rage. Clary, who had arrived last, with the other two girls, found this to be even more troubling than the sight of the monsters themselves. Sir Garrett was a man of few words. He was usually silent, in fact, and his manner always composed. Even when Clary had seen him take a life, he had always maintained an air of nonchalance. To witness the knight fly into such a rage was unsettling.

Garrett leapt onto the back of the creature and drove his spear between the first joint of its shell that he could find, pinning it to the sand and making it difficult for the creature to move. He then drew his short sword and jumped forward onto its body, driving the metal point into the soft crease at the nape of its neck, over and over again. The millipincer writhed in agony, eventually bucking the man from its back. It continued to squirm and roll around on the floor until it finally fell still. When Garrett recovered his bearings, he charged upon the corpse of the beast and continued to stab it repeatedly. Even after the other millipincer had been thoroughly dealt with, he continued to attack the deceased insect.

Though she was scared, Clary called out to him. "Sir Garrett! Sir Garrett, please! It's already dead!"

But the knight did not respond. For some reason none of the other knights did anything to stop him. Clary stepped forward but was stopped before she could reach him. To her surprise, it was Valen who had placed his hand on her shoulder. She turned to him ready to argue but he only closed his eyes and shook his head.

She didn't understand. Garrett seemed to have become completely feral, consumed by hatred and bloodlust. Though he had never been a particularly jovial person, he had never been crazed like this.

It wasn't until Sir Rorian got involved that Garrett's frenzy abated. The old knight, who had been dazed from the millipincer's attack, had only just regained his footing and caught sight of what was going on. He darted straight for the crazed warrior, embracing him from behind. He held Sir Garrett tightly, pinning his arms to his sides as the young warrior screamed. Sir Garrett's sword flew from his hands as he thrashed, heading straight towards Clary. She barely had time to raise her hands to defend herself, but at the last second Valen was able to pull her out of Garrett's trajectory. She was safe, but not unscathed: the blade's tip slid across her palm.

"Its's alright boy! It's alright!" Sir Rorian said firmly. "You've done enough! The job's over, you're safe. I'm okay. You don't have to go back there. That's not who you are." The boy cried and screamed, struggling to escape. Sir Rorian continued, "You've protected me, Garrett, you've done well."

Garrett quietened. He seemed to have snapped out of it. It was as if he didn't know where he was, or how he'd gotten there. He looked down to see Sir Rorian's arms wrapped around his torso and then looked up with an expression of shamed comprehension on his face.

"How long was it this time?" he asked the older knight.

"Not too long."

"Did… did I…"

"No, everyone's fine."

When Rorian released him, Garrett turned to face the rest of the group, a look of sorrow and embarrassment on his face. His eyes met Clary's, then his gaze fell upon her bleeding hand as she cradled it in pain. Realizing what he'd done, Garrett strode away in silence. No one followed him or even watched him leave.

Clary didn't understand what was going on, but from the solemn air she knew that it would not be right to press the matter further. She thought about how odd it was that even the obnoxious and selfish Valen had reacted in the way he did, until she remembered something from their time together in Vinvale. Valen had been quick to boast about the men who followed him. In fact, since meeting him, Clary was sure that the praise he'd given his friends was the only genuine thing he'd uttered. He was truly proud and never held back from touting the prowess of each member of his personal guard. Each member, that was, except for the quiet, wavy-haired knight.

"Give me that," Valen demanded, pulling her hand towards him. "No, this won't do. We're going to have to find a way to close this up. I'll search the supply kits for any medical supplies. I doubt they'll have anything we can use to clean it, knowing those barbarians, but perhaps a needle and thread at least."

Clary looked up at the prince, utterly bewildered. She couldn't believe the man was actually doing something nice.

Valen responded with an expression of annoyance and surprise. "What's that for? Do you want my help or not?"

She nodded and turned away, stifling a laugh.

"Just sit still and be quiet!" he fumed as he tore a piece of fabric from his shirt. Wrapping it around her hand and pulling it tight, he tied the cloth off so as to keep it in place. "This will have to do for now."

The wind had picked up. "Alright everyone, grab your things and move into the cave now!" Sir Rorian called out. "We'll be staying here for a while."

Clary looked around. Apparently Feryl and Sir Morton had been able to dispatch the second millipincer fairly easily under cover of Edgrum's arrow volleys, once it was separated from its partner. By the looks of it, Feryl had almost cleaved the arrow-riddled creature in two.

As Valen helped her up, Clary heard a shriek of pain. It was Gerald. Rorian and Ingrum were making attempts to get him on his feet, but his leg wound was obviously worse than they had thought. Feryl had rushed forward at the sound. He picked Gerald up and brought him into the cave while the others retrieved their gear. All the while the wind was becoming stronger and stronger. This was no ordinary dust storm. It was the one which they had feared – but fortune was in their favor. They had discovered the shelter at the perfect time.

As they entered the opening, they discovered that it wasn't the entrance to a cave at all but rather a former Varhallan home, long since abandoned. It was a large dwelling with multiple tunnels and rooms and, fortunately, the supply kits contained a few simple light crystals. Anyone with basic magic control could power them, even someone like Gerald. These crystals were convenient but they were fairly cheap and unable to retain energy. They would require constant work to keep illuminated. Clary, Feryl and Hilda each ignited one as they entered. The two millipincers had begun to build a nest inside the main room of the structure, but judging by the lack of remains the creatures had only been there for a few days – not long enough to have brought any prey inside.

Gerald was wailing in pain again as Feryl set him on the ground. Clary came over to him, shining the light upon his injury. At first, she assumed that Gerald was just overreacting as usual. However, upon further inspection she could see that the situation was far worse than they had initially suspected. The original wound, visible beneath his torn breech, did not seem deep enough to have produced the amount of blood that ran down his thigh. It didn't make sense.

"Hand me your knife!" she shouted, unable to disguise the panic in her voice.

Feryl, who did not have much of a head for medical magic or surgical treatment beyond basic field dressing, recognized the firmness in Clary's demand. It was evident that it would be best to leave it up to her. He pulled a small iron blade from his boot, which he kept hidden for emergency situations and handed it to her. Taking it, Clary began to cut her way along Gerald's trousers. Doing so confirmed her suspicion: the first wound had not caused the bulk of the damage. It was merely the point at which the beast had grabbed hold of him. The true attack had been higher on his inner thigh and, judging by the blood, it had struck the femoral artery. Fortunately for Gerald, Clary was the daughter of two great physicians, both of whom had taught her a great deal. Though she had never actually operated on anyone before, she had learned many spells for treating basic wounds. She'd read all of her parent's textbooks and often practiced what she'd learned with her father.

"Can you help him?" Hilda asked.

"Maybe, but we have to act fast, and I'll need your help," Clary replied, all the while tracing invisible inscriptions over the wound, which was now spurting jets of scarlet.

"Okay. J-just tell me what to do," Hilda stuttered.

Clary, having finished her spell, was holding her now glowing hands over the wound in an attempt to stop the flow. "First, I need you to put pressure on that cut there." She nodded toward the lesser of the two wounds. "Do you know any basic medical spells?"

"Like what?" Hilda removed a piece of cloth from her pocket and forced it onto the laceration.

"Can you slow down or stop bleeding?"

"I-I-I... I don't know. I m-mean, I do b-b-but I've never tried. I don't know if I should—"

"Hilda!" Clary shouted, cutting her off. "I need you to calm down. It will be okay. If you can't do it, it's okay. Just keep applying pressure and try. Leave the rest to me."

Hilda was clearly not adept at dealing with blood and was having trouble coping, but Clary's words seemed to have struck home and brought her back to her senses. "I... I'll do my best!" she said, mustering up her courage.

"Shouldn't we just sew it up? I mean, can't we?" Feryl cut in.

"No, it's hit a vital point. It should be okay though. The spell I'm using should work well enough to keep him alive, at the very least. We need to stop the bleeding internally before we can—" Clary paused. Something was wrong. She was using the same spell on Gerald that she had used on her mother. It was one specifically meant for targeting artery damage and heavy bleeding by stopping the bleeding and increasing the rate of tissue

177

regeneration in a targeted area. It was one of the most world-changing spells ever developed in the medical field. It had saved countless lives since its conception a mere century ago. She had seen her father perform it time and time again. He had even told her that she had been very good at it for her age, when he had seen her practice it. With all of this in mind, Clary couldn't understand why now, when she finally needed it, the spell was failing her. The blood just kept spilling and now she was truly panicked.

For whatever reason, the spell wasn't working, but Clary did not have enough time to figure out what she was doing wrong. Instead, she decided the only option would be to reach into the wound and fix it manually. This was something she had only read about in books. In fact, she had never seen this done before, since her father had always had the option of magic readily available. She hadn't even discussed this technique with him, as she never imagined why she would need to perform it. It was a last resort, but it was all she had.

"What's wrong?" Feryl asked. He must have noticed her shaking.

Clary knew she was short on time, but she was scared. She didn't know if this would work. By this point the others had entered the dwelling and could see what was going on. She was feeling the pressure more than ever. What if she couldn't do it? What if she messed up? She knew she wouldn't be able to save Gerald's leg, even in the best-case scenario.

She felt a hand on her back. "Clary. It's okay, you can do this. You're the only one who can. Just do your best. We are all here for you." It was Feryl. Somehow his voice calmed her in a way that perhaps only he could. It was odd having her own words turned on her, but it worked.

"Alright, I got it." She looked back at the others who were all standing there, as if awaiting her orders.

Taking a deep breath to gather herself, she turned to Valen, who was carrying the two supply kits he'd retrieved. "Valen, I need you to see if you can find a pair of clamps or something to that effect."

He nodded, and went straight to task.

"Ingrum," she continued, "I need your belt."

"What? Why?" Ingrum began.

Sir Rorian cut in. "Just do it, you idiot."

"Ellerbe and Edgrum," Clary said, "I need you to hold him down."

The pair hustled across the room to hold the still moaning Gerald.

"Here!" Ingrum shouted, handing her the belt.

Clary snatched the belt and wrapped it around the thigh of Gerald's injured leg.

"Alright, brace him," she commanded Ellerbe and Edgrum. "Here we go. One, two, and three!"

"Gaaah!!!" Gerald screamed as Clary pulled the belt as tight as she could, twisting the belt to create a makeshift tourniquet.

"Clary!" cried Valen. "I can't find any medical clamps, but we do have these." He presented her with two large iron tools, which she recognized as being meant for forcing bent swords into shape.

"That will work," she said.

It wasn't ideal. She would have to tie the tools shut in order to keep them clamped down on the artery, but the sheer size of them was already enough to complicate things. This was not even considering the amount of pain it would cause Gerald. It was, however, her only option at this point, and she had no time to search for an alternative.

"Hilda, if you think you can manage it, I need you to calm him. I know you can't always get it to work, but try. I'm going to start now regardless. Somebody put a rag or something in his mouth. This is not going to be pleasant."

"Here I go." She took a second to prepare herself and then plunged her fingers into the wound and began feeling around, trying to find the vessel.

"Aaaah! Aaaah! Shtopf! Pleathe Shtooopf!" Gerald screeched in pain, but there was no helping it. He attempted to thrash around, but Rorian and Harvel jumped upon his legs. With four knights holding down his limbs and now even Feryl placing one massive hand on his torso, the boy's struggling was getting him nowhere.

Clary continued to feel around, her fingers squelching as she reached in deeper until, "Got it!" Finally she felt the artery but as she grabbed it, she felt that it hadn't been severed. This was a good thing. It may have just been ruptured. If the damage wasn't too bad she might even be able to save his leg. But as she pulled on it in an attempt to bring it to the surface, she realized that she couldn't feel any sort of cut or laceration at all. When she could see it finally, she saw that it was perfectly intact. Shocked, she released it. If the artery wasn't severed, then there should not have been this much blood. It simply didn't add up.

"Clary what's wro—" Feryl began, "Clary! Your hand."

Clary looked down at her hand in confusion, only to discover that it was now bleeding profusely through the piece of cloth which had previously been covering it.

"Oh… Oh no!" Clary finally understood what was going on. She was certain. There could be no other reason. "It's the venom from the millipincer. It's some kind of magic-based anticoagulant!"

"What does that mean?" Feryl asked.

"It means the bleeding won't stop on its own and spells won't do the trick either."

"Can you stop it?" said Sir Rorian.

"I don't know. I mean, I think I can, but we only have a little longer. We're going to have to heat a sword and cauterize it – but using what we have in here… we won't have time to get a blade heated enough before he bleeds out."

"Right, then." Sir Rorian said. "Valen, Ingrum, Morton. I need you to search the other rooms, find something to burn."

Tears ran down Clary's cheeks. "No, you don't understand. We need it *now*. There's not enough time."

At this, even Sir Rorian seemed disheartened.

"No, Clary," Feryl interjected. "There is still one option."

Clary turned to meet his gaze and immediately understood his meaning. "But I still can't…"

In all her time training with Feryl, she had not even been able to heat her hands enough to hurt someone, let alone enough to match the temperature of a heated sword to seal flesh.

"Clary, you said it's all we have left. We have to try. And I know you can do it. You're much stronger than you think. You just have to stop doubting yourself. You haven't been able to get this power working with me, but you told me yourself, you were able to burn Thymey before even having your activation. If that doesn't tell you something about how powerful you are, I don't know what will."

Feryl's smile was a rare sight, but it was genuine. Clary thought that it was the most calming sight she'd ever seen. She suddenly felt warm. It was as if everything else had melted away and all she could see was his reassuring smile. He was right. She had to try, and if it didn't work, then at least she gave it her best.

She lifted up her bleeding hand and, taking a swipe of blood from the slashed palm she began to inscribe the symbols which she had practiced so many times with Feryl. She thought of the when her father had breathed multicolored flames onto her forearms, allowing her to access this hidden power. There was no way he had done that with a sense of anger inside him. His expression had been one of pride and love, and at this moment, she felt that way too. She focused on that emotion and closed her eyes as she finished the inscription. When she opened them and looked down at her hand, she saw that it was glowing a deep orange. It may not have been the blinding white of her father's hands when he fought against Feryl, but it was enough. Before she had the opportunity to lose focus, she plunged her hand into Gerald's open wound.

"Gaaaaaah! G—" Gerald finally passed out from the pain.

When Clary removed her hand, she knew that it had worked. Not only had the blood ceased flowing from Gerald's wound, it had also slowed the bleeding in her hand. Though her resistance to heat had kept her hand from cauterizing itself, the venom on the wound did not share the same resistance. The extreme heat had burned it away and had cauterized Gerald's wound at the same time. She wasn't done yet, however. Next, she took her still glowing finger and stuck it in the smaller puncture closer to Gerald's knee. She was happy that he had already passed out. She didn't want him to have to deal with the pain any more than he already had.

She fell back and let out a long sigh. She wasn't sure if it had been enough, but at this point she had done absolutely everything she could for him and she was exhausted.

"We're going to have to find a way to move him quickly if we are going to keep pace. I just wish we had time to rest," she said, realizing that they now had a whole new slew of issues to deal with.

"Well I think we can arrange that," said Edgrum. "Looks like we're going to have a good bit of time before we can even leave this place. While you were in here playing doctor, that sandstorm finally started up. That wasn't your ordinary dust storm. No way they can follow us in this."

Clary couldn't believe it. Their fortune had kept up after all, at least for most of the group. She looked at Gerald, and tears began to well up again. It wasn't fair. Even if it was by accident, Gerald had saved their lives. If he hadn't found this shelter, they wouldn't have lasted a day in the storm.

"Now don't you start that, lass," Rorian said, frowning. "The boy will pull through. You did well. Now that the venom's out, this is nothing more than a paper cut. I've seen way worse in my day."

Clary looked up at Sir Rorian and, seeing the sincerity in his eyes, she felt better.

"Now you rest up," he said, smiling down at her, "and when you're ready you can start working that magic of yours on the boy, and we can speed things up. Leave the camp to us – we'll take care of the rest."

Chapter 15

"It's not too bad really, once you get past the crunchy bits," Edgrum said, sinking his teeth into the charred piece of millipincer.

"Is there really nothing else?" Terra responded, turning green as she stared down at the chunk of crustaceous flesh she held in her hands.

"Well, we've been stretching the field rations thin as it is," Harvel said. Once we leave here, we're going to have to make what's left last even longer, and it's hardly enough for a couple of days."

"But they're just so disgusting. It feels like I'm eating some sort of giant cockroach or something."

"Ha! That's nothing, lass!" Sir Rorian laughed. "Why, once when I was a young buck in the expeditionary forces I spent three weeks living off of actual bugs! Crickets, maggots, night crawlers... one night I even celebrated catching a rat. To me and my men it was a feast. We would've been lucky to have a beast such as this."

At this Terra only turned even paler than she already was. Everyone laughed as she put the meat back on the cloth where the rest of the cooked meat lay.

They had been in the old Varhallan dwelling for about three days and could still hear the storm raging outside. Knowing that they would be hunkered down for a while, Harvel had made the decision to brave the deadly winds in order to bring in the corpses of the creatures that had previously inhabited the shelter. Fortunately Feryl had been on hand to help, and the close proximity of the bodies made things a good deal easier as well.

After everything settled down with Gerald, they were able to more thoroughly explore the abandoned structure and discovered that it was not a single home, but a vast compound that stretched deep beneath the sands. They were even able to find a large supply of old wooden furniture in the various rooms, which made for perfect firewood. If anything positive could be said of the Varhalla, it was that they had mastered the art of functional desert architecture. The dwelling was complete with ventilation pipes, which still worked and kept the group from suffocating in the smoke from their fire. There was also a central well, which, while not completely clean, was good enough to refill their depleted reserves.

The largest room they had found seemed to be some kind of dining hall. They ignited the fire pit in the center of the room and were now seated around it, relaxing and laughing. As horrible as things had been, it was nice to have a place all to themselves where they could forget all the tragedies which had befallen them, at least for a few days. They all knew that the future was uncertain; that eventually the storm would end and they would be forced to face an unknown, which they would most likely not all survive. For now, however, the destructive force of the sandstorm, which would spell only terror and destruction for anyone else, acted as a protective cloak. In their isolation it was as if time itself had been halted. For as long as the storm raged, no enemy could pursue them, no monster could hunt them. In every aspect that mattered, they were safe.

Every now and again, a combination of curiosity and boredom would drive somebody to venture into the rest of the compound to see if they could find anything useful. Just as the laughter over Terra's struggle to come to terms with her meal died down, Edgrum and Morton returned from one such expedition, grinning and with full burlap sacks slung over their shoulders. Edgrum, who was sitting closest to the door, turned to his brother and, noticing his dubious look, said, "What've you got there? Why do you look like you're up to no good?"

At this, Ingrum stopped and gave his twin an exaggerated look of being appalled. "How could you be so cold, brother? You know I would never engage in any act that could be considered anything less than knightly!" He puffed out his chest and turned up his nose in a caricature of pompous righteousness.

"Oh, don't you give me that crap." Edgrum shot at him. "Come on, out with it!"

Behind Ingrum, Morton was clearly struggling not to laugh. Once again, Ingrum looked at his brother in sarcastic shock. "Honestly brother, I sometimes wonder what kind of man you consider me to be. And after all the effort Sir Morton and I went through to secure such rare and valuable provisions… Why, I'm almost inclined not to share any with you." As he said this, he reached into his bag and pulled out a green bottle filled with a dark liquid. Everyone cheered as he and Morton began removing more and more of them from the bags and passing them out.

"Looks like whoever left this place was in a hurry and forgot to take the essentials with them!" Morton laughed.

"The tragedy of the fortunate is the grace of the scavenger," Sir Rorian added.

186

Just as everyone was about to start drinking, Sir Rorian interrupted. "Wait! Before we enjoy this happy discovery I think we should give a toast."

"Sir, I really don't need your thanks," Ingrum responded.

"Not to you, idiot," Rorian shot back, to everyone's amusement. "To Clary!"

Clary immediately stopped laughing. She flushed with surprise and embarrassment as the others turned to her with smiles of agreement.

"What? No, why would you do that?" She felt cheeks her going bright red in the firelight.

"Ha ha ha, it's precisely because you have to ask that you deserve it!" Rorian continued. "All of this is thanks to you, lass." He must have noticed her confusion. "Look at all you've done for us. It was you who planned the escape from that godforsaken camp. It was you who so creatively devised that distraction that kept the Exiles off our trail. And if it weren't for you, that lad over there would be buried in the sand out there, where not a single person would ever be able to even visit his grave. And the most admirable part of it all is that you don't even realize that all of these actions are exceptional."

During his speech there were silent nods of concurrence around the room. Clary wanted to deny it all but she could see that she was outnumbered. All she could do was turn an even brighter shade of red.

"With that being said, thank you, Clary. If it weren't for you none of us would be here."

"Hear, hear!" Edgrum called, and they all raised their bottles.

"To Clary!" Sir Rorian called.

In unison, everyone responded, "To Clary!"

Then everyone took swigs from their bottles and, also in unison, coughed.

"What is that?"

"That's just awful."

"Definitely weren't known for their proficiency in wine, were they?" Sir Rorian laughed.

As they continued to drink the terrible wine, Clary found herself looking frequently toward the corner where their injured traveling companion lay resting. Sir Rorian's speech had her thinking about what she'd done. She still felt that she had not been able to do enough. Even though she knew that she had done everything possible to save Gerald, she could not rid herself of her guilt.

Her glances did not go unnoticed. "You know Clary, I always thought you would be more of an eagle type, but maybe you should join the doves. I mean when this is all over, you know?" Hilda said.

"The what?" Clary asked.

"Oh, that's right, I never told you about the smaller guilds."

On the first day they had met, Hilda had described to Clary the meaning of the three talons shown on the mages' banner. She had explained that they were called the king's claws, with each of the three representing one of the major royal mages' guilds in the capital that were funded by the crown. The first, a gold eagle's talon, represented the eagle's guild, which focused on training battle mages, researching combat magic and developing new combat magic. The second was the silver talon of the owl's guild which focused on the study and education of magic, running the mages' university and library in the capital. The last was the black talon of the raven, accepting only the elite, delving into dark magic and focusing on secretive research.

"There are other smaller guilds outside of the king's claws," Hilda continued. "One is the doves – they run the capital medical center. It's made up of a lot of medical mages. They'd go crazy for someone like you."

Clary hadn't thought about the other guilds. Typically, it was only the owl's guild that traveled with the pilgrimage in order to spread magic and seek out those who otherwise would never realize their potential. For the first time in weeks she was thinking about what she might do when they finally made it back. She wondered whether she would even still want to join one. She'd been focused so much on saving her parents that thoughts of a life afterwards had evaded her.

"Are there any other guilds?" she asked.

"Oh, yes of course!" Hilda responded. "There's the gull's talon, who work with maritime magic. They're more in the southern kingdom, though. Then there's the hawk's talon. They work with nature magic and magical botany. They're especially good with beast taming. The cardinals work under the church and the woodpeckers build magical tools and items. The vultures are known for their potions. Oh, and the crows… you know, I'm not really sure what they do, to be honest. There's even a group known as the parrots who work with entertainment magic."

"Put on a mean show, those ones do. Trust me I've seen 'em all!" Sir Rorian laughed, grabbing another bottle to replace the empty one at his feet. He was becoming more inebriated by the minute.

"I actually considered joining them for a while too," Hilda said, "but I decided the owls would be better suited to help me with my abilities as an empath."

"Hm, I hadn't even considered any of that yet," Clary responded thoughtfully. She had heard that the capital city was huge. It shouldn't have been any surprise that there was still a lot she didn't know about life there.

They continued drinking and laughing for several hours. By the time Clary had begun to sip from her second bottle, she could feel the alcohol going to her head. The heat from the fire wasn't helping either. She felt so warm and cozy in what was a surprisingly drafty structure. She was starting to get sleepy and slowly began to nod off during a conversation about the parrot's guild's district in the capital, until she could no longer keep her eyes open. As she drifted off she found herself wishing that she could stay awake just a little longer, that this night would never end and they could put off returning to the horrors that awaited them in the scorching sands of the outside world.

*   *   *

When Clary woke several hours later she found everyone else still asleep. Judging by the number of empty bottles on the ground, she assumed it would be a while before anyone else woke up. Her skull was pounding from the night before. After sitting for a while in silence to collect herself, she decided it would be best to take a little walk and clear her head. Grabbing one of the illumination crystals and a skin of water, she took off into the dark to explore. Even though they had all agreed not to wander off alone, she was tired of sitting waiting for someone else to awaken.

She ventured through the halls, passing chamber after chamber, each varying in layout and design. Most appeared to be bedrooms or storage rooms, but occasionally she came across a room with an unknown purpose. Old bones and strange mosaic words hung on the walls, perhaps for some sort of ritual or magic. She was already curious about the Varhalla, but the more she explored the dwelling, the more questions she had. At the same time, she hoped she would never be close enough to one to ask.

Just as the thought of meeting one of the fiendish creatures from her childhood nightmares crossed her mind, she heard a noise from far along the hall ahead. She was so startled at the sound that she jumped, dropping her illumination crystal. Without the crystal she couldn't see a thing in the pitch darkness. She dropped to the ground and felt around on the floor.

She heard another crash.

In her panic she darted into the nearest room. It had the feel of some sort of supply closet. From outside she heard a strange scraping noise. It was slowly approaching her hiding place. Her mind raced at the possibilities. What if it was a Varhallan taking shelter from the storm? But if so, surely they would have run into it by now, or else it would have heard their revelry the previous night. Then an even worse thought crossed her mind. What if it was another millipincer? They hadn't searched all of the rooms, and it was possible that one could have burrowed in through another entrance.

The sound grew closer and closer. She was starting to hyperventilate.

Should I scream? No, then it'll definitely know I'm here. But it might have heard me gasp — that's probably why it's coming this way. Could the others reach me before it does? They're all dead asleep, they might not even hear. But it was too late. Whatever was making the noise was already outside the closet. She realized that a light shone under the door. Now she was sure it must be a Varhallan.

She knew this was the end for her, but she was determined to make sure the others were not taken by surprise. Just as she had committed herself to scream to warn the others, there came a voice.

"Hey, what are you doing in there?"

In her relief Clary let out the deep breath she had taken in order to scream. She knew this voice. It was Garrett. *Of course,* she thought. Garrett had been the only one who had not drunk with them last night.

"Sorry, I... I just dropped my light and was looking for it," she said. She opened the door, trying to hide her embarrassment.

"Oh... it's you." Sir Garrett seemed a little dejected at seeing her. Though she had told him about the crystal, he seemed to recognize that she had been afraid up until that point. It was a little awkward for a moment. Clary realized that not only was this the first time that they had been alone together, but it was also the first time she had heard him talk since the fight with the millipincers – though admittedly the knight rarely said much more than the occasional "Okay" or "Got it." Even so, he had been even more reclusive than usual during their stay in the underground dwelling, and had seemed intent on avoiding Clary at all costs.

"What are you doing back here?" Clary asked, "and what was that scraping noise?"

"Oh, uh, well... I was trying to get some more firewood." He gestured towards an overturned table stacked with other pieces of broken furniture. He had tied rope around it, using it as a sort of sled. "Here it is, by the way," he added, handing Clary the crystal she had dropped in the hallway.

"Oh, right. Thanks." She wasn't sure how to break the silence that fell. "Can I help you find some more? I wanted to keep looking around."

"No!" he responded quickly, taking Clary aback. "I mean... I don't need your help."

"You don't have to be rude about it."

Now it was Garrett who appeared angry.

"What? Why are you getting mad? What did I do to you?" She demanded.

It seemed as if he was about to crack. "No, you don't understand. I... I know you're just forcing yourself to be nice."

"Excuse me? What kind of person do you think I am? You don't know anything about me!"

"No, that's not what I meant, it's just..." He trailed off.

"Just what? Why won't you just spit it out?"

"I'm a monster, okay!" Garrett shouted. "I'm a monster, and you saw it... and because of what I am, I hurt you."

Despite her surprise, Clary said, "Are you still upset about that? It was an accident."

Garrett appeared dumbstruck. "Of course I am!"

"It's really not that big of a deal."

"You don't understand!" he shot back.

"Then why don't you tell me what's going on? Stop beating around the bush and say what you mean!" Clary was getting more and more frustrated by the second.

"I betrayed the commander!" Garrett finally shouted in exasperation. He was panting. It seemed as though he had been holding this in for a while.

Clary calmed down. There was something else going on here that she was missing. She tried to adopt a more understanding tone. "You saved him, didn't you? He didn't seem upset. And my hand... that was an accident." She paused. "Look, I understand that you don't know me and you may not like me, but I'd like to get past this. If you really don't want to talk I'll understand."

Garrett seemed genuinely puzzled. "Why would you think I don't like you? I've sworn to protect you."

Clary was completely lost. "When did you do that?"

"When you became precious to the commander," he said bluntly.

His response completely threw her off guard. This must have been what Valen was talking about. If she wanted to know the truth she would need to be more direct. "Can you explain what's going on to me? I'm sorry I got mad, but I want to understand."

Garrett sighed. It seemed as though he was finally giving in. "Sir Rorian… he's like a father to me. Actually, it would be more correct to say he *is* my father. He adopted me. Or rather, he saved me. I don't know. The two are one and the same."

It was clear to Clary that he wasn't the type to share his personal feelings with others. This was no surprise, given his usual silence.

"When I was a child," he continued, "I lived in the northeastern part of the kingdom. It's a cold wet place, almost always covered in clouds. My parents abandoned me out in the hills, leaving me to freeze. I don't blame them – a lot of people had to do that up there," he added, noting the expression of disbelief on Clary's face. "Once Thandessa fell to the Exiles, the northeastern villages were all but abandoned. People were starving, and a child was another mouth to feed. Anyway, I was found by some merchants. They took me in. You would think that's where things turned for the better, but the fall of that southern port brought more than just poverty to the eastern lands. When I was only a few years old, they started throwing me into fights. Gambling matches where they would give orphans weapons and pit them against each other, with the promise of food and life for the victor. Looking back on it now, it's almost funny how often the value of those two prizes switched places." He gave a soft chuckle at this morbid statement. "It wasn't only orphans. Sometimes it was dogs, or snakes, any small creature they could get their hands on that would draw a crowd. I can't even count the number of times I came close to dying, and I hadn't even reached eight years yet. One day my owner got word of a high roller in the capital and packed me up to take in and cash out."

"But isn't that kind of thing illegal?" Clary asked in disbelief.

"Yeah, but my owner wasn't exactly a law-abiding citizen." He chuckled again. "Anyway, even so young, I thought it was strange that they wanted to give so much money to watch a couple of kids kill each other. This guy was rich but not dumb. When they finally opened my crate and let me out into the pit, I saw what was worth so much money. It wasn't another kid, or a dog, or even a snake. It was a damned zabo."

Clary gasped. She couldn't imagine how someone could do this to a child. Zaboes were well known even in the western kingdom. They were large feline predators with serrated teeth and claws and they were particularly vicious. Not something a child could ever kill.

"I realized that this wasn't meant to be a fight. It was a hunting expedition. They didn't even give me a weapon. It would have killed me. It almost did. Lucky for me, zaboes like playing with their food. It sliced me open everywhere it could. It chewed my limbs like I was a toy. I was in so much agony I didn't hear the shouting from outside the pit. I didn't notice anything had happened until the thing fell on top of me with a spear sticking out of its side. Apparently, the guard had been following my master since he'd entered the city, after identifying him as being from Thandessa. The king had ordered any visitors from that city be followed until they could be proven innocent. Sir Rorian was the one leading the squad. When he saw me, he abandoned his entire mission to rush me to the doves. It was the first act of kindness I'd ever seen. He saved my life."

By this point Clary was tearing up. She never thought anyone could survive so much.

"It wasn't easy at first. I barely knew how to speak and, on top of that, my body was badly mangled. I was in recovery for months. But each day, the commander was there. I was violent to everyone. As soon as my body could manage it, I even lashed out at the doctors. Still, when I was finally healthy enough to leave, Sir Rorian took me into his home readily. I trashed the place. I threw tantrums day in and day out when I couldn't escape. I was like a wild animal. No... I *was* a wild animal... I was completely feral. But no matter what I did, no matter how bad it got, he never abandoned me. Even when I struck out at him or cursed his name, he only cared more. I didn't find out until later, but by the time I left the doves he had already adopted me.

"He's always been that way. He never quits when someone becomes precious to him. As I grew, we were able to stifle my savagery. When I was finally old enough to understand all that he had done for me, I promised to serve him until the day of my death, protecting all that is dear to him. The only problem was that sometimes, the savagery would come back. I'd lose control."

"You mean... like the other day?" Clary asked.

"Yes, just like that. And when that happens, only he can calm me. I view every episode as a failure... as a betrayal of that promise," he said, now looking ashamed.

"But if this has happened before, and you can't control it, then why should you be this torn up by it?"

"Because this time I hurt you, someone who is precious to him in the same way that I was when he saved me."

"I don't understand. Why would I be that important?"

"He cares for the tortured. He always see the good in everybody, even if they are too broken to see it themselves. He told me about what they did to you... the Exiles. He also told me about Mr. Feryl... yes, I know who he really is," he said in a reassuring tone, noting Clary's concern. "He said that you were like me. That I should think of you like a brother and sister. He told me I needed to protect both of you. He said from now on, I needed to do what I could to help you, just as he helped me... I expect he knew that both of you needed a family in a time like this, but... truthfully, I don't know if I know how to be part of a family." Now even Garrett was beginning to tear up.

Tears rolled down Clary's cheeks. For a time she had feared Sir Garrett. He had given her the impression that he was cold blooded, that he enjoyed killing, that he lacked emotion. But the man before her was nothing like what she had imagined. He was a tortured boy who had been sent through hell and back. She hardly knew him, yet he had opened up to her and poured out his soul. Even though this was the first time that she could truly say that the two had really met, this boy was ready to protect her and even Feryl with his life. Just the thought of hurting her, a complete stranger, seemed to cause him a great deal of agony, such was his love for the man whom he now called father. She knew that no matter what she could say or do, this boy would never turn away from them.

The memory of Sir Cloin's vow to protect her on the night of his death flashed across her mind. She remembered how hard he fought to defend her. Someone with whom she had shared only a few words had been willing to give everything he had to save her life. It was this selfless, undying devotion to protecting a stranger that she admired above all else, and now she saw it again in the sad, broken boy before her. Clary had always regretted not being able to show Sir Cloin, that greatest of knights, her gratitude. She wished to this very day to have been able to show the swordsman how much she appreciated him. She would not fail to do so a second time, in similar circumstances. Leaning forward, she grabbed Sir Garrett and pulled him into a loving embrace. She had never had a younger sibling, but she imagined that the way she felt now is what it would be like.

"It's alright," she whispered. "I understand now. You don't have to worry about any of it. We're okay."

At first the knight seemed shocked. Clary could tell that he was unused to the idea of a soft, comforting hug. Eventually, however, he hugged her back. Perhaps this was long overdue for the boy. After a few moments, the pair released their embrace. Clary placed a light kiss on the top of his head, then stood back.

"Alright," she said softly. "Let's head back,"

Then she caught a glimpse of something further along the dark hallway. She tilted her head. "What is that?"

Garrett turned around to find the point she was staring at. "I'm not sure."

Something was shimmering at the far end of the hall, beyond the room in which Garrett had been gathering firewood. Whatever it was, it had not been there before. Garrett started moving towards the light, drawing his short sword.

"Stay behind me," he said, as he noticed Clary following.

As they drew closer, the shimmering light became brighter. Only when they reached it could they see that it was a hole in the wall at the end of the hallway. Light shone through it. At first, Clary feared that it was the light of a fire made by another being, but when she peered through the hole she saw that it was sunlight. The storm had ended.

Their relief was short lived, and was soon replaced by frantic excitement. Sir Garrett raised his sword and began to bash the pommel against the hole, attempting to break through. The wall chipped away at a much faster rate than Clary would have expected.

After a few minutes of repeated hammering, she understood why. As more sunlight poured in, she could see that the outside of the wall was charred. It had been burnt with magic. In fact, the entire Varhallan village before them was burnt, still smoking from whomever had lain siege to it. There were bodies everywhere.

They stood in silent shock until finally Sir Garrett broke the silence with three simple words.

"Get the others."

Chapter 16

"These marks... they are magic in origin," Sir Harvel said, crouching over a pile of black rubble.

"What makes you say that?" Terra asked.

It had been a while since Clary and Garrett had exited the Varhallan compound to discover this razed village. They had since retrieved the others and were now examining the area cautiously, searching for possible survivors or clues as to what had happened. Their fear was that it might have been an Exile unit who had been tailing them and who had happened upon the unsuspecting village.

"Well, for one thing; the smoke is still flowing, and... look there, you see that?" Harvel pointed towards what appeared to have been some sort of desert cargo sled. "There are still some flames here and there. Ordinary flames wouldn't have been able to withstand the winds, especially for such a long period of time."

"But what if it happened after the storm?" Terra looked around nervously as if to check that the attackers were not still in the vicinity.

"Not likely," Harvel answered. "These buildings are far too gone for this to have happened very recently, and there's quite a bit of sand built up inside the ones that are still partially erect. No, more than likely it happened just before the storm commenced. It might have even concluded during the storm."

Clary had been listening in. "Do you think it was the Exiles?"

"It could've been, but something seems a little off about that, to me."

"What do you mean?" Terra asked.

"Well, we know the Exiles have a deal set up with the Varhalla, right? So then why would they have killed an entire village of them? I mean, that would only cause problems once they retrieved us and returned. Most likely they would've avoided the fight. On top of that, I doubt any party sent to hunt us down would have been sizable enough to take on this many Varhalla – and even if they were, they would have only fought those who attacked them. If we assume that this was an opposing tribe who did not acknowledge the truce, it still doesn't add up. Even for the Exiles it would make no sense to kill civilians or burn down homes in a defensive struggle. It would be a waste of resources. I suspect this was a coordinated attack. The perpetrators planned to annihilate the entire population."

Clary was impressed. Once again Sir Harvel was living up to his reputation. It was hard for her to comprehend how he could have derived all of that information during the few moments they had spent examining the area. As much as Harvel had deduced, it seemed he was not finished.

Before he could continue, though, there came a call from up ahead. "Hey! Hey, Sir Rorian! I think you should come have a look at this!" It was Sir Edgrum. His urgent tone made everyone run over to him.

When they finally rounded a collection of half-burned huts, shock was evident on the faces of all of the knights. Sir Ingrum, in particular, seemed stunned at what they had discovered, turning green and gasping at the sight. The only ones who didn't seem to understand what they had found were Clary, Terra and Feryl. Though the three did recognized the gruesomeness of the sight before them and were justifiably disturbed, it seemed as though the knights recognized something particular about the bodies strewn out across the sand.

A human man knelt in the sand before them. Though he was undoubtedly dead, a Varhallan spear was run through his chest and into the ground behind him, propping him up in a kneeling position.

Then Clary saw something that should not have been there. Instantly she understood the knights' shock and confusion. Behind the kneeling man was a group of bodies dressed in similar armor and matching, deep-purple tabards. These tabards mirrored the tattered standard in Sir Edgrum's hands: a golden eagle's talon.

"I don't understand. What are they doing here? Why would the eagles be attacking the Varhalla way out here?" Clary asked, in desperate confusion. "Do you think they were looking for us and stumbled into the wrong place?"

The knights remained silent. It was as if no one was sure how to approach this unfathomable situation. Even Sir Rorian appeared at a loss for words.

It was Harvel who finally spoke up. "No, unfortunately, Clary, it's as I said… this was a premeditated extermination." He looked completely dejected.

"Well, that one did always have it out for them," Sir Rorian added, staring at the kneeling man. "It was no secret that he disapproved of the king's leniency with the Varhalla."

"What do you mean?" Clary asked. "Do you know him?"

Sir Rorian did not take his eyes off of the kneeling man as he spoke. "Aye... or at least I *did* know him. He was Sir Hathafurd, a former knight who ended up leading the eagle's guild. The man was deadly enough without magic. With it, he was almost unstoppable. Almost."

Clary couldn't imagine what kind of power this man must have displayed in order to receive such high regards from Sir Rorian. Then again, if this man truly was the leader of the eagle's guild then it was to be expected. It also explained how they were able to lay waste to such a sizable force of Varhalla.

"I never thought the old bastard had it in him," Valen added. "I mean, everyone knew that his loyalties remained with my grandfather and that he didn't trust the Varhalla... but to go this far..."

"But it's not like he could've believed that he could take on the entire Arid Sea by himself," Edgrum interjected.

"You're right," Harvel said. "However, he may not have acted alone. Some of these are regular knights, not battle mages. I expect that he had a following, and maybe a few high-ranking co-conspirators. The eagle's guild is very large and many of them are always looking for an excuse to fight, so there may still be a larger force out there."

"Still," Feryl cut in, his tone skeptical. "I'm not buying it. You said this Hathafurd was a seasoned veteran. Anyone with halfway decent experience would know that it would be impossible to take on the entire Varhallan nation without a nation's army of your own."

"Aye, you would be right on that, if his goal was to defeat them with just this force," replied Sir Rorian. "You don't wipe out civilians for the sake of defeating the Varhallan forces. You use guerrilla war tactics, taking out supply lines, ambushing caravans and hunting parties. You aim for the resources and the warriors."

"So it was revenge then! What does it matter?" Valen shouted. It seemed to Clary that he was becoming unusually angry with the dead man before him.

"Could be," Rorian replied, "but it's been too many years since the great war to rile up this kind of support, and as Harvel said, many of these bodies were regular soldiers, not eagles. No, I don't believe Hathafurd would have thrown his life away so easily. He was far too intelligent for that."

"Are you trying to defend him old man? He's a traitor!" Valen shot back, even angrier.

At this, Sir Rorian finally drew his gaze away from the body of his former brother-in-arms to face the young prince. "Boy, I am fully aware of the implications for you that come with this discovery, but if you cannot keep your head straight long enough to think about what this means for the world as a whole, then you can go wait back by the compound with the injured boy and the others!"

Whenever Sir Rorian used this tone, it had the effect of squashing any resistance. Valen was no exception, reluctantly giving in and letting the old knight continue his investigation.

"There's only one reason I can think of for choosing a target such as this," Rorian continued. "This man wanted to start a war. I'm sure he believed he of all people would survive the attack, but sometimes all it takes is one lucky strike."

"But it does seem odd, don't you think?" Sir Morton interjected.

"W-what do you mean?" Sir Ingrum stuttered, finally snapping out of his trance.

"Just the timing of it all. What are the chances of something like this happening right after the attack on Vinvale? I mean, it sure seems like a lot of unusual movement in a short time, and all on the same side of the kingdom."

"What?" Ingrum spluttered. "No, I'm sure it has to just be some kind of coincidence. There's no way Hathafurd would ever work with the Exiles, and someone would have noticed if he was moving that amount of money from the eagles' accounts with the imperial banks, right?"

"Not unless he funded it privately, or if there is someone wealthier partnering with him, maybe some sort of senate backing," said Sir Rorian.

Ingrum turned green again. He was clearly worried about what this meant for their return home. Clearly, they were all scared about the implications of the conspiracy, but Ingrum in particular seemed more distraught than usual. He had often talked about how he could not wait to get back to the kingdom and take some time away from combat. If a war broke out, there would be no such option. Worse still was the possibility of a wealthy backer, which would no doubt drag the situation back to the capital. Finally, Clary understood the reason for his fear. As Valen had explained upon their first meeting, Sir Ingrum was well trained in the art of subterfuge; it was in fact, his specialty if Clary was not mistaken. No doubt his mind was already turning with all of the terrible possibilities that surfaced along with this discovery.

Just then Sir Morton called out to the group, "Hey, over here!" He had wandered off to continue the search during the latter part of the conversation and was now standing over a smoldering pile of what seemed to have been half of a dwelling. He was pulling a body out of the rubble by its arm with great urgency and seemed shocked by whatever it was he had found.

"Is it a survivor?" Sir Rorian asked, hurrying over.

"No, he's dead, but I think it's a—"

Sir Morton was interrupted before he could divulge his new information. Sand flowed up and out of the cadaver's sleeve. Sir Morton let go of the body and tried to jerk his hand away from the danger but it was too late. The sand had already coiled around his wrist and up his arm like a great snake. He tried to run, but all he could do was struggle as the sand began to climb up his legs. He drew his sword with his free hand and tried to sever the sand which tethered his arm to the ground, but as the sword made contact it too was pulled in.

Clary ran towards the trapped knight to save him, but he shouted, "No! Stay back!"

It was clear that Sir Morton knew it was too late, and that anyone who tried to lend him aid would only be sucked into the same fate. The others seemed to understand this, and Sir Rorian and Feryl both jumped in Clary's way. Finally the sand reached Sir Morton's head, forcing its way into his mouth, suffocating him. There were a few gasps before finally the mound of sand, which only moments before had been the valiant Sir Morton, fell still.

Tears welled up in Clary's eyes as she turned away from the horrid scene. She saw that she had not been the only one who had sprinted in to rescue their fallen comrade. Valen was writhing in anger, tears pouring down his cheeks, and he was screaming. Even as the man lay buried and dead, the young prince was struggling with all his might to go and save him. If it hadn't been for the four knights – Harvel, Ingrum, Edgrum and Garrett – restraining him, he would no doubt be digging the knight out at that very moment, regardless of the danger. In fact, Clary was sure he would have eventually succeeded in breaking free of the knights' grip had it not been for the frightened words which Harvel now spoke: "Sire, ambush!"

Harvel and Rorian appeared to be the only two knights to realize what was going on, as they were the only ones with weapons drawn. Feryl hadn't even begun to activate his magic when an arrow, which seemed to have emerged from thin air, pierced just below his shoulder. Without so much as a wince, he snapped the shaft off and drew his two massive swords from their scabbards, shoving Clary behind his back as he did so in order to place himself between her and the danger. Clary felt relieved – at first glance she had believed that Feryl's lung had been pierced but now she saw that the projectile had struck high.

There were bloodcurdling shrieks from every direction as the enemy burst forth from behind ruins and sand. Clary's heart sank. Though she had never encountered one in person, this could only be a scouting party of Varhallan warriors wielding their long curved blades and hooked spears. They were just as the stories described. Though their shape vaguely resembled that of a human, they were anything but. The Varhalla were tall and slender, covered in a greyish leather like skin. Their arms were extremely long, and tipped in razor sharp claws. Three of the beasts held back as the others charged Clary and the still confused knights. The Varhalla were chanting incantations in an unfamiliar dialect.

"Edgrum! Don't let them finish!" Sir Rorian commanded.

Sir Edgrum reacted without hesitation, pulling a small knife from his vestments and hurling it at one of the casters. The blade struck its mark, as was to be expected, interrupting the Varhallan warrior though failing to kill it. These creatures possessed incredible fortitude. The other two continued their ritual and were apparently quite enough of a force on their own: the sand began to stir and rise between the Varhalla and the knights until finally a wave of sand blasted the entire group, forcing them all off of their feet – with the exception of Feryl, who had managed to gather his magic in time and bolster his defenses.

It was clear that the Varhallans' intention was for the few at the head of the charge to swarm the downed knights and finish them off quickly, but they were not prepared for the likes of Feryl, who swung his sword into the first of the enemy, catching him square in the torso. Under normal circumstances, a strike such as this would have cleaved a warrior in two, but these Varhalla were not of the same cut as humans. The creature caught the sweep with his own blade and though the impact sent him flying back several feet, Feryl was not able to break the Varhallan's curved sword, nor did it even seem to rattle him, as would usually be the case with such a powerful blow.

Feryl then swung at the next aggressor, only to miss as the creature spun under his sword, lunging at him with his spear. Feryl managed to avoid the thrust successfully, but as the hooked tip was retracted it caught his side, pulling him toward the Varhallan, who in turn used the momentum to stick his long claws into the Chained King's chest. Had Feryl been a normal man, these razor-sharp claws would no doubt have run him through, tearing his heart out with the strike, but his fortification magic stopped the claws at the surface of his skin to leave no more than a flesh wound. This leniency, however, did nothing to stave off Feryl's mountainous rage. He roared, grabbing the clawing creature by the same arm and kicking its head into the sand until the limb was ripped from its socket. Sir Rorian then dealt the final blow, burying his sword into the writhing Varhallan's throat.

By now the other knights had regained their composure and leaped into the fray. The visceral display by Feryl seemed to have startled the other

Varhallan warriors. They now adopted a much more cautious stance towards their prey. Sir Edgrum had gained control of his bow and was nocking and loosing a shower of arrows in the confusion. He struck another one of the casters in the throat, and managed to force two Varhallan archers standing near a charred house back into cover.

Sir Garrett had also managed to do some damage, leaping onto a Varhallan bearing down upon the distracted Sir Rorian and Feryl, and running him through with his short sword. The warrior shrieked in agony, grabbing the small knight and throwing him to the ground with one whip-like arm. Unfortunately, due to the creatures' long, clawed appendages, it was near impossible to escape contact with one unscathed. Sir Garrett's back was covered in bloody punctures. The scuffle was enough to alert Feryl, who then swiped back; rending the Varhallan's head clean from his shoulders.

Sir Harvel was pulling Terra back towards the compound. On the front lines she was in great danger and it would be easier to defend her at the mouth of the compound, with the aid of Sir Ellerbe, where he and Hilda were looking after Gerald. Edgrum, Valen and Ingrum were covering their retreat, though there was only one Varhallan in pursuit; the remaining three warriors had made Feryl their top priority. The trouble wasn't so much the warrior they faced, but the last of the casters that had begun to assault them with a new spell, conjuring up hardened projectiles of condensed sand and launching them at the knights. Fortunately the caster's aim was not as true as Sir Edgrum's, and the projectiles failed to strike the fleeing knight. Just as Sir Harvel's retreat seemed assured, his feet became stuck. Sand rose up and trapped his legs. The other caster, the Varhallan that Edgrum had failed to kill with the first strike earlier, was unable to make it to his feet, but still had the energy to cast one more spell. As Sir Harvel struggled to escape, he was struck twice. The first bolt of sand pierced the right side of the small of his back, and he dropped to his knees, blood splattering the sand. Sir Harvel turned to face his attacker, but as he did, he was smashed in the side of his jaw, and he fell to the ground motionless.

The sight seemed to light a fire under Sir Edgrum. With sudden stone-faced concentration, he nocked and loosed three arrows with pinpoint precision. The first struck the injured caster directly between the eyes, and the following two pierced the remaining caster's heart, striking almost directly on top of one another. Finally Sir Edgrum was able to turn his attention back to the two Varhallan archers whom he had already suppressed once.

As Feryl struggled to fell one of his three adversaries, Rorian and Garrett managed to isolate another. This left a single unattended Varhallan, whose attention was turned to Clary. She had already drawn her swords and begun to make her way slowly towards Terra, keeping her guard up. Clary knew that the battle taking place before her was of a higher level than she was prepared for – what was more, she had only ever trained against humans. The long whipping arm movements of the Varhalla were like no attack any human could perform, and she didn't even know where to begin to formulate a strategy. She also wasn't confident that she could force her abilities as she had done to save Gerald. Even if she could use them again to such a degree, in that earlier instance they had been only hot enough to burn flesh, not melt steel and bone. She could injure but not kill, especially with razor-sharp claws and steel between her and the enemy.

She had no option, though. The third Varhallan darted straight at her as soon as he registered her hesitation. He slashed the air with his blade and Clary just barely managed to avoid it. As he did so, he whipped his free claws erratically in such a violent fashion that it could not be anticipated or dodged.

A claw caught Clary's ankle and she tumbled to the ground. The Varhallan turned to face Clary, slowly approaching her, perhaps to savor the kill. Clary tried to stand but the sharp pain in her ankle, combined with the soft sand beneath her, made her stumble backward. She held her sword before her as she slid backward, away from the danger, until she hit a wall.

She turned to see that she was pressed up against a half-burned hut. She had nowhere to go and there was no one to help her. Everyone else was still busy with battles of their own.

The beast inched closer and closer, slowly raising its sword to strike.

Then Clary felt something odd: a warmth beneath her hand, different to the uncomfortable blaze of the desert. Smelling smoke, she glanced down to see that she was sitting in a pile of white-hot coals. Opportunity had finally presented itself, and she knew what to do as if by instinct. She may not have been able to reach the Varhallan with her hands, but she could still burn him. As he stopped to stare at the flames emanating from the back of her shirt and trousers, Clary took advantage of his confusion, grasping handfuls of coals.

She began pelting the Varhallan in the face and neck. He was so shocked that he did not have time to protect himself. Varhallans may have been strong and resistant, but any creature would writhe in agony when struck between the eyes with a burning coal.

Clary was pleased with herself. She had only ever thought of using her abilities as she had seen her father use them before, not even considering that it could be used in such a simple yet effective way. She would have to consider other such uses later.

Though the Varhallan had dropped his sword, his flailing arms were still a threat. In order to avoid them, she took her sword and stabbed it through the blinded creature's ankle. Then, rolling out of the way, she picked up the Varhallan's discarded weapon. Though smaller in comparison to the blades wielded by Feryl, Varhallan weaponry was still much longer than weapons used by the average human. Clary used this to her advantage, moving around to the other side of the creature and bringing the weapon down upon its head. The warrior's flailing stopped immediately and his body went limp. Clary couldn't believe her luck. If her aggressor had not hesitated in confusion at the sight of a burning girl who failed to scream in pain, he might have seen the intent in her eyes and thought to strike before she could pepper his face with the near-molten rubble.

Clary spun to return to the rest of the battle, but it seemed that her adrenaline had run out. The pain in her ankle, which she had forgotten during her fight, returned and she collapsed.

Luckily the battle appeared to be over. Feryl was pulling his sword from the last of the archers. Another two arrows protruded from his back and arm.

From what Clary could see, everyone was bloodied and battered – but everyone appeared to be alive. *Everyone except for Sir Morton,* she thought, and she recalled the night before when he had smiled and shared that awful wine with her and the others. Before she could shed a tear, a thought came into her head. *Sir Morton and Sir Harvel! Harvel! Is he okay?* The last she had seen of him, he had collapsed into the sand, blood leaking from his head. She needed to tend to him immediately. She knew that she would be busy taking care of all of the wounded for a while, but if she did not see to Harvel first, she might not be able to save him. That is, if he wasn't already dead.

She struggled to get up. "Feryl, come help me!"

"You should stay down," Feryl replied as he hurried towards her.

Clary felt instantly guilty. Feryl was in need of attention as well – his body was covered in lacerations from claws and swords, there was a tear in his side from where the hooked spear had caught him, and three broken arrows stuck out of him. Any normal man would have been dead. It was clear to see how this boy had come to be feared by so many, and he wasn't even armored. She shuddered to imagine what a fully armed and armored Chained King would have been capable of when not completely drained from exhaustion and sleep deprivation. However, there was no time to dwell on this, nor to begin to deal with his injuries.

"Feryl! Harvel is dying! He needs me now!" she shouted.

Feryl complied without asking again.

Though Clary had not yet evaluated Harvel, one thing was evident, everyone else was standing and he was not. That meant he was first. She was scared of what his condition might be after witnessing the hit he took. She had seen head trauma before. When Feryl lowered her next to him, she first had to deal with the crying Terra who was draped over him.

"Is he okay?" Terra sobbed. "Clary, do something! He's not waking up!"

"Terra, I'm going to do everything I can, but you need to back off of him and let me examine him." Terra seemed to understand. Clary felt oddly calm and collected in such a dire situation, and her tone carried weight with it. After the incident with Gerald, no one was going to question her. Clary realized she had gained confidence. While she was not cocky, she now felt that she knew what she had to do, and knew that everyone was relying on her so she had to be strong.

She sighed in relief. "He's breathing normally, and he doesn't appear to be bleeding too badly, but I'm going to treat him with an internal bleeding reduction spell just in case."

At these words, Terra fell back onto the floor, tears still flowing down her face, though she was visibly calmer.

"Those of you still able, spread out in pairs and keep an eye out. We need to make sure there are no more hostiles in the area and then we need to move out quickly before there are! Move as quickly as you can!" Sir Rorian ordered, but the others had already begun. Though they were injured and worried about Harvel, they knew the protocol. If there was a scouting party, it meant that more would be on the way.

After a few moments, Sir Ellerbe and Hilda joined the rest of the group. Ingrum, who had gone to retrieve them, was carrying Gerald over his shoulder. He was conscious and confused, but explanations would have to come later.

Valen was the first to shout. "There's another one over here, but something's strange. He's tied up!"

For some reason, Valen sounded happy. He was even laughing.

"I really think you should come have a look, too. This may be our best luck yet. We might even be saved."

Chapter 17

"We should kill him. It's too much of a risk," Ingrum said. It was obvious that he was still devastated by the loss of his friend.

"He's right. Gut the bastard. The last thing we need is another one of those demons taking up our food and trying to kill us in our sleep," Valen agreed.

"But he may prove useful. He might be able to clear up what happened here," Edgrum protested.

"You think he'd tell us anything?" Valen shot back. "And would you actually believe him if he did? You can't trust these monsters."

Even Sir Garrett, who was usually quiet in such discussions, spoke up. "I'm sure we could make him talk. You'd be surprised the truths you can bring out when you apply the right leverage."

"Fine, so we get what we can from him, then we kill him," Valen conceded.

"What are we even discussing?" Hilda interjected in a tone of disbelief. "You're talking about an execution!"

"He'd do the same to us!" Ingrum shot back. "We should just kill him now and be done with it!"

"Can't we just leave him?" Clary cut in. "We'll be long gone by the time anyone finds him, so it won't matter. He wouldn't dare follow and attack us on his own."

"No," Feryl responded. "If we free him then chances are a following scouting party would find him quickly and catch up to us, especially if they have gandovors. We'll never outrun them."

Clary still didn't understand what it was that had made Valen so happy. All she could see was an old covered wagon pulled by two particularly large bull-drages. This would be helpful for their supplies and would help take care of their wounded, but it hardly seemed something to be giddy over, especially considering what was bound to the back of the wagon. Being led behind the wagon by a long rope was a Varhallan prisoner. Deformed as Varhalla looked when compared to humans, Clary could still tell that this individual had been put through hell. His face was swollen and bloody. Though bruises were not as visible on his body as they would be on human skin, Clary could see contusions on his face and beneath his clothes. He was kneeling silently, staring down at the sand, but he did not appear frightened. Quite the contrary, in fact: he wore a blatant look of hatred and disgust for his captors.

Voices were beginning to rise as the group continued to argue over the fate of the prisoner. Finally Sir Rorian, who had been sitting on the side of a nearby sand hill, cleared his throat to silence everyone. "We cannot afford to let him go. The risk is too high, but taking him with us will also be too dangerous."

Clary saw Hilda's face fall at the words.

"That being said," Rorian continued, "he could be invaluable, both for his information and as a witness to the courts back home in the capital."

Clary felt relieved to hear this. Killing in battle was one thing, but she did not like the idea of slaughtering a captured enemy in cold blood.

"But sir—" Ingrum started.

Sir Rorian interrupted him. "We will take him with us, and that is final. We are not murderers, boy." His stern tone made any opposition impossible. "Now let's get a move on. We don't have much time. Strap everything you can to your backs and grab anything that looks like it'll fit in that little wagon the prince found. Don't forget, though, we will still have to put Harvel and the other boy in the back, so there won't be much space. We can't bring too much. Maybe we can strap some water sacks to the bulls over here. We'll have to figure something out."

Everyone was worried about the lack of food. Most of the provisions in the village had been reduced to ash or buried in the sand. There may have been a well somewhere in the town, but if there was, the sandstorm had buried it under one of the hundreds of hills that covered the area. Clary had no idea if they had enough water or food to make it to the north. If worse came to worst, they would have to kill the bull-drages to eat, but they would likely perish from dehydration long before then – if exhaustion didn't get them first.

It seemed that this thought had crossed everybody's mind at once. Everyone was quiet until Valen let out a laugh. He was grinning from ear to ear.

"What? What are you on about, boy?" Sir Rorian said, evidently irritated.

"Well, that's what I was excited to tell you about," Valen replied. "I don't think supplies are going to be an issue for me anymore, and I think I'm done walking for now."

"Why you pompous little—" Sir Rorian was visibly annoyed now. "If you think we're going to let your royal arse climb into that wagon over the injured, just because you're a prince, then you've got another thing—"

"Calm yourself, old man." Valen laughed again. "Clary," he called out, "why don't you go have a look in the wagon and tell me what you see?"

"Me? Oh… okay," Clary was embarrassed to have been put on the spot. She was standing the closest to the wagon with her back to it. Hopping up onto the step on the front of the wagon, she opened a latch and peeked inside. Immediately, Clary understood Valen's meaning and was speechless.

"Well, lass, what is it?" Sir Rorian demanded, losing his patience.

Clary pulled her head back out and gazed at Valen, mouth agape. Then she stuck her head back in for a moment and pulled it out again, now looking at Sir Rorian, her expression of amazement never leaving her face.

"Come on! Out with it!"

"It's, er, well… I'm not really sure how to say. It's like some sort of large Varhallan tent structure."

The group stared confusedly up at her. Only Hilda seemed to have an inkling of what might be going on. "You mean like spatial magic?" she inquired.

"I…I don't…" Clary wasn't really sure what that meant, but she could not find better words to describe what she was seeing. Inside the wagon appeared to be an entire dwelling with canopied walls and filled with Varhallan carpet and bedding. It was even sectioned off into areas with tables. The whole set-up was luxurious, and was centered around a fire-pit on a sand floor. What she saw couldn't be possible, all within the confines of a crummy old wagon. What's more, she could see food and water in baskets and barrels stored in one of the compartments, sectioned off by a canopy wall. The most confounding of all of this was the natural sunlight penetrating the top of the tent. It was as if she had been transported to a tent in some far off corner of the desert.

Finally Valen had enough of his smug game and decided to let the others in on his discovery. "You're quite right. It's a special kind of spatial magic, actually. The Varhalla like to pull this little trick to hide their numbers during travel, as well as to create comfort in this horrible place. Fortunately for us, it means that the rest of this journey should be a breeze."

Hilda, however, looked quite frightened at this revelation. "Doesn't that mean that the other Varhalla will know that their comrades were defeated? They'll simply come through the other end and attack us. If that's the case, then we have to destroy it now! This probably leads back to their camp!"

The others became visibly worried. Clary even jumped back off of the cart, fearing that another Varhallan warrior might pop out at any moment. She understood now. This was the same kind of magic that she had seen when Hilda had pushed her through the rear of the tent at the mages' camp. The portal she had fallen through had led to the mages' garrison. If this was the same, then it meant that she had been in a tent at the center of a Varhallan caravan.

Valen laughed at their nervousness. "You should've paid more attention in your studies, mage."

Hilda stared at him, perplexed.

"Varhallans don't use the same type of spatial magic as us," Valen continued. "Leaving behind a bedouin such as this would involve recasting the spell every time they moved the camp, or risking the unguarded tent they left behind being destroyed by whomever came across it."

"Then what is it, boy?" Sir Rorian demanded. It was clear that he was at the end of his temper. "Enough with your games!"

Valen laughed. When he spoke again his voice had a clear undertone of superiority. "The Varhalla created a new space for this. They built a luxurious bedouin tent somewhere in the desert and then linked the entrance to this wagon. The difference is that afterwards they would've covered the outside in their ancient runes and enchantments. Then they destroyed the tent from the outside, crushing it into dust while the entrance was connected to this cart."

Hilda still looked confused. "But that should have destroyed the wagon as well, if the two were spatially linked."

"And therein lies the problem with your magic schools in the owls. You presume that your magic is the ultimate form and that if you can't do it, then nobody can. The Varhalla are an ancient people with centuries of magical experience, different from our own. Their inscriptions do not work in the same way as ours. Either way, they discovered a way to protect the integrity of one structure not by simply linking the entrances, but by completely swapping the interiors. That bedouin tent exists all on its own."

Hilda seemed amazed, apparently never having considered this as a possibility. With magic like this, one could hide an entire fortress in a broom closet. It had endless possibilities. Even Sir Rorian seemed impressed.

Clary found herself feeling the same way. Though Valen had been arrogant in his delivery, she admired his knowledge. She never would have expected him to know so much, spoiled as he was. Had he not been there, they would probably have burned the cart and made off on foot, carrying the injured. Now they could travel not only fully supplied, but in relative comfort.

They were safe for the moment. This wagon was a gift no one had seen coming, on top of having defeated a group of Varhalla – no easy feat. It was a bittersweet victory, however. The air was still heavy with the weight of losing Sir Morton. They took a moment to grieve, but it was short-lived. Everyone wanted to bring his body with them, but they couldn't be sure that the magic trap cast on him by the Varhalla wouldn't take whoever tried to dig him out of the sand as well. They each said their goodbyes, finished packing up into the wagon and left.

Sirs Ingrum and Ellerbe seemed to be the most affected by recent events. Knights in the guard usually worked in pairs, from training all the way up to squad formation. It was a tradition to ensure camaraderie since the founding of the nation. Sir Ellerbe and Sir Morton had been one such pair. The loss of one's partner was akin to losing a family member, and though Ellerbe was as strong as knights come, even he could not keep from shedding tears. Ingrum and Morton had been particularly close as well. Though they had never been in the same squad, they had been drinking buddies for quite a while, frequenting every pub, tavern and bar they could find. Ingrum sat on the roof of the wooden wagon, watching the still smoking, nameless Varhallan village where his friend would rest until the end of eternity.

Sir Rorian had been unsure of how to handle their new Varhallan guest, but was still quite wary of the danger he might pose. He had asked Hilda to use her magic to construct two platforms on the wagon – one on the back and one on the side – using spare wood taken from the compound. The Varhallan was now seated on the back platform, which seemed kinder than forcing him to continue walking on his already burnt and bleeding feet, and also made him more easily watched. He did not say much, and what he did was not in any language they understood, though from his tone it was not difficult for them to imagine what he was saying. He sat quite comfortably on his platform, awaiting his fate. Sir Rorian sat on the second platform, keeping one eye on the prisoner and also watching the landscape behind the wagon, to ensure they were not being followed.

The bull-drages seemed not to mind the change in ownership and simply trudged on, dragging the wagon at a comfortable pace. There were a few sectioned-off areas within the wagon, which served as makeshift rooms. There were not enough for everyone, but still enough for the girls to have their own, plus a few extras. There were, however, many floor beds and pillows, so no one was without a comfortable sleeping place. They each took great pleasure in selecting for themselves the perfect place among the soft gold, red and brown patterned cushions and carpet.

By the time evening turned into night, Clary had finished tending to everyone's wounds and injuries, using not only her medical magic, but also the medical supplies and disinfecting herbs stored by the Varhalla. The mood had lightened, particularly once they had found a case of more awful Varhallan wine to drink. The knights had taken to drowning their sorrows and then decided to celebrate their newfound luck. Even Gerald and Harvel, who were both now awake and aware of the situation, had joined in on the revelry, lying around the fire pit, drinking and singing with the others.

Clary decided to take the opportunity to slip outside and bring some wine to Sir Rorian, who was still sitting outside, keeping an eye on things. It had been several hours since their departure, and from what the others had said, he had been questioning their prisoner the entire time. She opened the wagon door and climbed out into the vacant driver's seat. Hilda had enchanted the reins to steer the bull-drages on their own. Though she hadn't much opportunity to use her magic on this journey, one could not say that she was not a talented mage. She was actually quite knowledgeable in every-day magic. This trip simply had not given her much chance to show what she could do. After all, she had never claimed to be a battle mage, nor a survivalist.

Clary could hear Sir Rorian talking to the Varhallan, who had yet to give any response other than grumbling under his breath in his native tongue, no doubt more profanity. She climbed around the wagon to sit with Sir Rorian. It was clear that he was exhausted from the day's events. He flinched, startled, as Clary sat down next to him on his platform, jumping as the wood creaked with her weight, then groaning in pain. Clary felt awful; she realized that her mentor had yet to be treated for his injuries. He was, in fact, still bleeding visibly from various wounds.

"Sir Rorian!" she gasped. "Why didn't you say anything?"

"It's nothing, girl. Just a few scrapes and bruises." His voice was raspy from the battle and the constant interrogation of the captive.

"Don't give me that, you old goat." Clary scowled at him with an expression learned from her mother. "You need treatment." Sir Rorian began to protest but she wasn't having it. "Take this wine, and lean back. It's nothing for me to heal 'a few scrapes and bruises'," she said sarcastically. "Don't worry, he'll still be there when you wake up. I'll keep an eye on him."

Sir Rorian laughed. "Well, I guess there's no arguing with you." He took the wine. "Where'd you even learn to talk like that?"

"From the best," she responded, smiling at him. They both laughed. "Honestly, I'd expect this kind of behavior from the boys, but not from the great high commander himself."

Sir Rorian chuckled as he leaned back for his treatment. "Well, lassy, I may be old, but no one makes it as far as I have without a little recklessness

– not too much, but just a little. Eventually, the greats grow up but all of us knights were brazen boys at one point."

"I'm sure you were," Clary laughed. She began drawing inscriptions in the air over his wounds, and her hands began to glow gold as they had before, energy pouring from her hands onto the bleeding areas, speeding up his natural recovery. Fortunately, none of the wounds were too serious, so it was not long before the lacerations began to shrink and heal over.

After a while Clary spoke, knowing that the healing process would exhaust him even further, soon putting him to sleep. "Is that why you're so hard on Valen? Because you think he's too reckless?"

The old knight opened an eye and said in a tired voice, "No my dear, it's quite the opposite, in fact. Take young Harvel, for example. He's a great leader, with a good head on his shoulders. I have no doubt that one day he will make a great commander, one who will surpass even me. He only lacks confidence and practice. The problem is that Harvel will not be able to go much higher without a cause." He started to trail off and Clary could tell the fatigue was taking effect.

"So what does this have to do with Valen?" Clary asked, a little louder, trying to regain his attention.

Rorian yawned. "Well, the cause that Harvel will latch onto is that boy."

"And you don't think Valen will be able to live up to it?"

"No, I think he will go far beyond what anyone ever expects of him. I've watched that boy and his older brothers grow up," he continued. "Each of the boys are valiant and formidable leaders, but none show as much passion and willingness to change the way things are done as that one. Sure, he is arrogant and self-centered and sometimes a downright pompous idiot, but when it comes down to it, he truly cares. More than that, he's not the type to change his views just to satiate those around him. Maybe these are just the ramblings of a delirious old soldier, but…" He paused to yawn again. "I truly see something in the boy. There're a lot of mysterious happenings in the world right now, and I believe he could be the one to set them right. He's already got all the support he needs… if only… he could just get… his head out… of… his… own… arse…" And with that, Sir Rorian began to snore.

Clary continued to heal the old knight and giggled silently. She was surprised to hear such endearment from him towards the prince. She expected it from Harvel, but she couldn't see why this renowned warrior had such respect for the prince. Then again, perhaps even she was beginning to see it…

She snapped to her senses. How could she believe that cowardly, selfish ass had any good qualities? Sure, he was knowledgeable, but that was it. These knights had to be blinded by his position of royalty or something. Still, maybe there was *something* she'd noticed. Just a small *something*, but *something* all the same…

"Pfft, first they leave a senile old man too watch me, now a simple girl, barely parted from her mother's teat. These humans truly are imbeciles," said an angry, heavily accented voice from behind Clary. It was the Varhallan, speaking the common tongue. He spat on the ground. "The gods must wish for my humiliation."

Clary was shocked to hear a response from him other than angry muttering. Normally she would have been offended at such words, but it wasn't as though she would expect kindness nor cooperation from a prisoner towards his captors.

"I didn't know you understood our language," she said, unsure of what else to say to such a dangerous monster.

"There are many things you children do not know," he responded defiantly.

Now Clary was beginning to lose her patience. "I'm not so much of a child. I've experienced more than most two or three times my age."

"Ha! Those who are twenty times your age are still but children to me, whelp," he laughed. "The lives of humans are but fleeting moments to the ancient desert people."

"Well, these 'whelps' just defeated an entire scouting party of 'ancient desert dwellers', so maybe you shouldn't be so full of yourself," Clary shot back. No matter what he said, this creature could not take away their victory. "Your warriors couldn't even handle a couple of these 'children'."

Again the Varhallan laughed. "It appears that naivety is common among your people. But one could not expect much more from lesser beings, as I said. They were no friends of mine, and what's more, those were no warriors. They were but desert salvagers, practically vagabonds. Their casters knew but simple combat magic – even our young are proficient enough to perform such feats. To use such a victory to compare humans to the mighty Varhalla is laughable."

"I wouldn't be so quick to belittle humans if I were you. I've heard your legends. You were once humans as well."

The Varhallan chuckled. "Yes, but then we learned better." He grinned at her with his razor-sharp teeth. It sent shivers down her spine.

"In the story it was a curse. How could you say this is better?"

"A curse? Is that what you were told? Trust the apes to change a story to fit their simple perceptions. It was a gift to be given the power that we possess. Now we can crush humans as we please. Humans like your friend in the village. I heard your people mourning him. What was his name again?"

Clary became instantly furious. The Varhallan had crossed a line. She raised her fist to strike him. She knew he wanted her close so that he might try something, and that he was riling her up on purpose — that much was obvious. Still, she didn't care.

Before she could throw her first punch, she felt a hand grasp her wrist. There was a sizzle and a hiss.

"Clary, no!" Clary looked up to see Feryl grasping her glowing hot arm. Hilda was with him. She must have felt Clary's rage and brought Feryl out to check on her.

Clary calmed immediately, embarrassed at her loss of control and feeling horrible for having burned him. "Feryl, I—"

The Varhallan cut her off. "Fjorendel! I have been captured by demons!" he yelled. Even after all these years, it seemed that the Fjorendel were still the natural enemy of the Varhalla.

"I thought you said we were children," Clary said, spitefully.

"You are still a child, but a child of evil, and I will converse with you no longer!" he snarled.

"That's the first pleasant thing I've heard come out of your snout!" Clary retorted.

Clary remained on guard, refusing to let him win. The two were silent for the rest of the night.

Chapter 18

"Why is it still so hot? Haven't we traveled far enough north yet?" Clary plopped herself on the ground next to the wagon, panting. "It's been so long since we left the compound. I thought we were already pretty close."

"Ha! Quit your whining, lass," Sir Rorian replied. "It shouldn't be too many more days now. This is nothing! Why, when I was your age I once spent a full two years in the field fighting against the Silver Army in the freezing cold ice and mud, with nothing to eat but rocks and—"

"Rocks and rats," Clary interrupted, rolling her eyes and grinning. "You and your ancient war stories. I think I've heard them all by now."

"You shan't be hearing any more, then. I'll save them for someone who might appreciate them. Perhaps our leathery-skinned guest over there!" Sir Rorian pointed at the Varhallan, who spat at them and cursed in his native tongue.

Clary chuckled at his joke, but she didn't look at the creature. She had tried to avoid it as much as possible. Sir Rorian had insisted that they continue Clary's training near the wagon, where he could keep an eye on the prisoner. Clary couldn't stand it. When the beast wasn't shouting at them in Varhallan, he was laughing at Clary for her inability to control her powers fully. While it was evident that he hated all of them, he seemed to hate Clary the most. She believed that it had something to do with the ancient story of the Varhalla and their rivalry with the men in the north. It seemed to confirm the theory that the warriors who defeated the Varhalla were in fact the ancient Fjorendel. The prisoner hated Feryl for the same reason, but he seemed to be aware that Feryl had control over his powers, so he knew better than to test him too often. It would have been a much more bearable situation had the Varhallan kept his resolve to avoid conversation with her, but in fact Clary was the only one with whom he would speak in the common tongue, albeit in insults and rude remarks. As a result, Sir Rorian, who spent the majority of his time questioning the monster to no avail, often made Clary take the watch when he was too tired, hoping the creature might slip and give up some piece of crucial information.

"Besides," Sir Rorian continued, "I thought you couldn't feel heat, lass."

Clary laughed. "You'd think that, wouldn't you. No, for some reason I can feel heat from the weather, but that's about it."

"It's a trait to help you be aware of your surroundings," Feryl cut in. "Once you've mastered your abilities, you will be able to control that too. It could be dangerous not to understand how weather and heat works. Imagine if someone from your clan went into the wilderness with others and couldn't figure out why everyone else was suffering or freezing to death. Our ancestors spent millennia perfecting these powers to ensure the survival and power of their clans. They fine-tuned them to the smallest degree."

"Stupid boy, your ancestors were murderers and imbeciles. You do not know a damned thing!" came an irritated, heavily accented voice from the back of the wagon.

"Shut it, Sheckem," Feryl shot back, silencing the Varhallan. "Sheckem" was a Varhallan word that they often heard amidst the creature's shouting and mutterings. Sir Rorian did not speak enough Varhallan to create even half of a sentence, but he did understand this word to be a vulgar insult. As a soldier and a self-proclaimed "connoisseur of profanity", he knew how to swear and insult in all of the world's languages. Everyone had taken to calling the Varhallan, who refused to give his true name, by this well-deserved title.

In the weeks since their departure from the village, things had continued much in the same manner as before. Clary's training became even more productive now that she wasn't forced to march through the desert all day and had more energy. The additional time even allowed her to learn about throwing knives and archery from Edgrum. Terra and Hilda often joined in as well. Now that they weren't literally running for their lives, constantly worrying about starvation and dehydration, they were granted the privilege of boredom, something Clary never realized she had been missing. Everyone was finding ways to fill their time. Harvel and Valen had begun deciphering a strange Varhallan board game found in the wagon. The other knights spent their time training to keep their skills honed, and drinking what wine and spirits they had stored in barrels in the wagon. Ingrum, perhaps, was drinking too much.

Gerald, who was now healed enough to limp around, seemed to have gained a good deal of humility. He was no longer his former irritatingly loud and snarky self, though whether that was due to the comfort of the wagon or actual gratitude towards the people who had saved his life, no one was sure. Hilda had even begun to warm up to him a bit, including him in her magic lessons, which she had been giving to Clary and Terra. The lessons contained nothing particularly amazing. Hilda taught them to move small objects, making them levitate or switch places, more for fun than practicality – though she did show them a defense spell which allowed the user to project a concussive force into their enemies. Though Hilda used it only lightly to knock over a stack of mugs from a table, she warned them that at full force it was like getting kicked by a horse or smashed with a large club.

As the three were sitting by the wagon cooling off, Sir Edgrum came out with water and some Varhallan daggers, ready for some target practice. They all turned to look up at him. He had dragged his brother out of the wagon as well, saying something about fresh air and sunlight being good for him.

"Well that's not good!" Edgrum frowned. "Looks like we won't be able to do much today, not with the wind picking up like this."

The wind had been picking up for a while now. They had all become familiar with the telltale signs of an oncoming dust storm. Sure enough, in the distance they could see the sand start to rise against the orange sky.

"Guess we'll just have to practice inside then!" Clary joked.

"Yeah, no way. Not with your aim!" Edgrum replied immediately.

Everyone laughed, with the exception of Ingrum, who for some reason was staring past them into the distance, his mouth open with a look of confusion and fear. Eventually the others noticed.

"Hey, are you alright, lad?" Sir Rorian asked.

Ingrum seemed unsure how to respond to what he was seeing. He stepped back.

There came loud Varhallan shouting and cursing from Sheckem. Then there was a trumpeting blast that shook the wagon and made everyone's hands shoot to cover their ears. Those seated by the wagon turned to look in the direction of Ingrum's gaze.

Instantly, they saw what it was that had garnered such a reaction. Emerging from the red haze of sand swirling in the distance was a reptilian creature of titanic proportions. There could be no mistaking its intention. This behemoth of a monster was lumbering directly towards them, eyes trained on their position.

"What is that thing?" Edgrum gasped.

"Why don't you go ask it, and you can tell us later? Me, I'm not sticking around to find out." Sir Rorian shouted. The wind began to whistle and roar even louder. "Alright! Pack it up! We need to move, now! Whatever that thing is, it can't keep up with us at that pace."

"No sir. We can't outrun it. It's not moving slow, it's just that monstrous and far away," Feryl protested. "It'll be on us within the hour. We're going to have to face it – it's our only chance. That thing is hunting us."

Feryl had a habit of speaking in this frank manner. Clary always found it odd how he could remain stoic even in the face of insurmountable odds. She would even go so far as to say she admired that quality about him. It was comforting in a way. The confidence of his demeanor and voice made her believe that they might be able to pull off some kind of strategy, even against such a beast.

She looked again at the creature. Feryl was right. Their eyes had been fooled by the sand and heat. It was even larger than they had initially anticipated, but at a greater distance. It only appeared to be moving slowly because of its immense size. It was taking huge strides on its six trunk-like legs. It was even larger than the mobile garrisons had been. Clary had never imagined that a creature of such size could be possible.

She wasn't the only one beginning to panic. The others were now emerging from the wagon, inquiring about the booming noise the creature made. They all displayed the same reaction of bewilderment and fear at the sight of the creature.

The knights were already preparing under the instruction of Sir Rorian, who was now strategizing with Sir Harvel. The last person to emerge from the wagon was Prince Valen. Though Valen was not the bravest soul by any definition, he usually had faith in his men and their ability to handle such unexpected situations, especially as their escape progressed and they proved their capabilities time and time again. It was for this reason that his next words caused such concern.

"We need to leave! We need to leave now!" he shouted, grabbing hold of Sir Harvel.

"We can't, boy," Sir Rorian answered, obviously vexed. The prince's reaction wasn't good for morale. "We'll never outrun the thing. We have to face it, so stop yer whinging."

"What are you talking about? Are you insane? I know you're a good warrior, but there's no way you can possibly think you can take them! Those are sand rovers! Walking plagues! That thing is creating this dust storm. They're Varhallan super weapons!"

This wasn't just cowardice. The prince knew what he was talking about. The prince's studies had yet to fail them, but one thing Valen had said stood out to the old knight. "What do you mean 'them'? There's only—"

He was cut off by another resounding blast, even louder than before. Looking back, three of the creatures were now visible. Two of them had

previously been hidden by the mountainous dunes on the horizon. "Oh…
Oh no,"

Sir Rorian looked scared. It was the first time Clary had seen this
level of uncertainty in the man. "Run… We must run."

"There is no point!" Sheckem shouted. "You will all die! He knows
where you are now! He sees through the beasts' eyes! Release me! I have done
nothing to you. Do not make me die along with you!"

"What are you talking about?" Sir Rorian shouted back. "Who sees
us? Were those things sent after us?" Clary admired his relentless search for
information that might help to evade death.

"It does not matter now, you fool! They have betrayed you! He
thinks you attacked the village!" Sheckem shouted, desperately trying to break
free from his bindings. "Free me! Free me now!"

Another blast came from the direction of the sand rovers. This one,
however, was noticeably different from its predecessors. It was much higher
in tone and more gentle, though a little eerie. It almost even sounded musical.
Looking down at the rovers, they saw not another six-legged reptile marching
toward them, but a pod of new, equally large creatures surfacing from
beneath the sand, directly in the path of the rovers.

"By the gods, is that a whale?" Sir Rorian gasped, unable to believe
his eyes.

"Not quite," Prince Valen replied sounding incredibly relieved. "It's a
pod of Arid Sea leviathans."

"A pod of what?" Clary asked.

"It is about the only thing in the world that could save us, demon,"
Sheckem answered. "You mongrels really do know nothing."

"Running into those creatures is an almost mythically rare occurrence, even in their territory here in the north," Valen explained. "In almost every case, it would mean death for us, but with prey as enticing as rovers, they won't notice us so long as we get moving."

"They don't look all that dangerous," Clary added. "They're almost beautiful."

But even as she said this, the leviathans refuted her statement. They grouped up before the rovers in an attempt to surround them, and began to suck in air. This caused incredibly large, spear-like spikes to protrude from their backs.

"They're highly poisonous," said Valen. "They surround their prey and can wait for extremely long periods of time until it either starves or tries to cross over the backs of the leviathans and dies in the attempt. Usually they wait beneath the surface of the sand and ambush whatever walks over them before they can even be noticed – but prey this large requires a more aggressive approach."

The first of the three sand rovers reeled up onto its hind legs, trying to back away from the advancing field of spines – but it was too late. The other two rovers were in the way. As its feet came crashing down, they met hundreds of lance-sized protrusions, causing the giant to crumple to its knees. The beast had no time to fight or writhe, as the poison instantly began working itself through its system. It fell, paralyzed, onto the spikes while its two companions fled for safety. The leviathans did not hunt their retreating prey however, choosing instead to turn their attention toward the fallen giant before them.

"The gods must have plans for you heathens, though the reason is beyond me," Sheckem growled, returning to his usual demeanor.

"I think you know more than you let on, you filthy snake," Sir Rorian shot back. He was not going to let the Varhallan's panicked outburst go unaddressed. Rorian had got the slip-up he had been looking for.

First, however, they needed to put some distance between themselves and the titans on their trail.

*   *   *

After traveling for about four hours the wagon pulled to a stop. The bull-drages had already been exhausted before they had run into the titans, so pushing them even half of this distance was already a stretch. They needed water, food and rest, so they had no choice but to make camp.

Sir Rorian had sat on his same platform for the entire ride as usual but this time he had not said a single word to the prisoner. Instead, he simply sat, angrily contemplating something. Clary had never seen Sir Rorian act this way. It was a far cry from his usual composed and generally happy nature. The only ones close enough to understand what the Varhallan was shouting over the roar of the dust storm and the cries of the rovers hours before had been those sitting by the wagon when the battle occurred. Clary hadn't been able to make heads nor tails of it, and everyone else was still in too alert a state, fearing the return of the sand rovers, to discuss it. Sir Rorian had apparently picked up some meaning and was trying to mull over the pieces of information. Still, he was showing more strain in his demeanor than just worrisome news. Clary, who was sitting on the driver's platform, could tell he was weighing a heavy decision.

When they finally stopped, all of the knights and Feryl gathered before Sir Rorian to await orders or a plan of action.

"I don't have enough information here," Rorian began. "I know nothing of these creatures, and know neither who's coming for us nor when.

We are going to have to rely on the prince's information for this one." He gestured towards Harvel. "Lad, I am going to need you to organize everyone for this. There're too many unknowns for me to handle this one right."

"But Commander!" Harvel protested. "If you are unfit for this job as you say, then how could I hope to take proper charge? What will you be doing?"

"First, lad, don't count yourself too short. You're perfectly capable. Second, it'll only be for a moment. What we have here is an unfortunate information deficiency. I plan to rectify that problem immediately."

Sir Rorian marched directly over to the bound Varhallan and ripped him from the wagon. He began dragging him back over towards the other knights. Unexpectedly, the prisoner did not say anything, though he did protest physically, refusing to make it easy. He knew exactly what was going on, which was more than the others could say.

Clary looked around for answers. Most of the other knights seemed confused about the commander's intentions. She could see, though, that Feryl grasped what was about to happen. An expression equally as upset and conflicted as Rorian's spread across his face. Other than him, only Garrett, who knew the commander better than any other, and for some odd reason Ingrum, seemed to understand what was going on.

"But sir," Ingrum said nervously, "don't you think we should wait until we get him back to the capital? I-I mean we really shouldn't be making those kinds of decisions on our own. What if something happens?"

"Come on boy," the old knight responded. "Now's not the time to lose your composure. I don't like it any more than you do, but we are far past the time for niceties. This is war now. More important things are on the line."

Ingrum fell silent, looking down at the floor. Whatever was about to happen, it was clear that Sir Rorian had made up his mind that there was no other way.

"Ingrum," Rorian called to the young knight, "I know you haven't been yourself since Sir Morton's death, but you need to get your sense back. I'm going to need your help. You were squire to Sir Vacarro, were you not?"

"Y-yes sir," he replied.

Clary had no idea who Sir Vacarro was, but the mention of his name caused a change among the knights. If there were any doubts among them as to what was about to happen, the mention of his name appeared to erase them. Clary still had no idea what was going on, but it was clear the knight for whom Ingrum had squired held some kind of meaning to all of them.

Sir Rorian continued, "Then I know you were taught how to deal with these situations. Surely he taught you more than just how to sneak around and sabotage things. You know how to conduct his style of interrogation?"

"Aye, sir. He taught me… everything," Ingrum replied meekly.

"Then let's get to it, lad. Come with me. The rest of you stay focused on the tasks you're assigned. I don't want any disturbances unless we're under attack." With that he nodded towards some nearby hills, signaling Ingrum to follow. They walked off into the darkness of night, dragging Sheckem along with them.

Clary wanted to ask what was going on. She had so many questions. What were they doing to Sheckem? Why was Sir Rorian bringing Ingrum to do it? Who was Sir Vacarro? What was so bad about his interrogation? But it seemed that no one wanted to discuss it, and they were all busy making preparations for the potential attack.

While most of the other knights were out keeping watch, Clary was left to guard the entrance to the wagon, which housed Gerald, Hilda and Terra. She sat on the driver's platform, waiting for the first word of attack so that she could warn those inside and wake up the bull-drages as quickly as possible. Prince Valen was also assigned to guard the cart, but he chose to sit on top of the wagon to afford him a better vantage point.

Clary was still terrified, though she supposed everyone was after the sight of the sand rovers only a few hours earlier. However, what had made her most nervous was the way Sheckem talked about the creatures. It sounded as if he knew there were more than just those creatures on the way. If those monsters were nearby she was sure she would hear them before they got too close, but if more Varhalla were on their tail, she was not so sure that they could survive the standoff. They had barely survived the last encounter.

As the thought crossed her mind, she felt a large, warm hand on her shoulder. It made her jump, but only for a moment. It was Feryl. He had a sort of endearing look about him as his eyes met hers.

"It's going to be okay," he said softly. Feryl was almost always a man of few words, especially since they had departed from the Exiles' camp. In fact, as far as Clary could tell, he only ever really opened up when the two of them were alone together. He always said only what he needed to and no more. It was for this reason that he had the strange effect of managing to calm her, no matter how bad the situation. He smiled. "I won't let anything happen to you. Not that you need much looking after."

Clary was glad for the darkness just as she had been when they first met, so that Feryl could not see the shade of red she was certain she was turning. She was now just as nervous as before, but for an entirely different reason. Feryl was not one to smile unless they were alone during their training, to reassure her that she was doing well or, sometimes, when they talked about returning home. This smile, however, was different. It was unlike his usual stoic self to risk such a gesture in the middle of camp where anyone could see. Still, she suddenly felt safe, just having him around. She knew he had to keep patrolling the area, but she wanted him to stay.

"Feryl... I..." she began.

Before she could finish, he answered as if he had read her mind. "Do you need me to stay with you for a while?"

Clary only nodded; embarrassed that she hadn't been able to ask this herself. It was strange. She had never gotten nervous like this around someone before.

Feryl climbed up onto the seat next to her. She giggled as the wagon sank when he got on. Varhallan structures were clearly not meant to support someone of Fjoren size. The platform was small, so they were forced to sit very close together. Given the cold of the desert night, it was nice to lean up against someone so warm. Clary was exhausted from the day's events, and the sudden warmth was getting to her. Feeling bold, she leaned her head to rest on his shoulder. Feryl's posture stiffened for a moment, but he did not protest.

"Do you think they'll catch up with us?" she asked, drearily.

"Honestly... I'm not sure," Feryl admitted, staring up into the night sky, "but do you really think it matters at this point?"

Clary was puzzled. "What do you mean? Of course it does. I still want to make it out of here."

Feryl chuckled. "I have no intention of dying in this wasteland either. What I meant was, look at everything we've been through. We've run into a million different life-threatening situations: dangerous monsters, bandits, the

Varhalla. Hell, even the weather tries to kill us out here. We've nearly starved and died of thirst. You were on the brink of death the night I first met you."

This time it was Clary who chuckled. It was strange how long ago that felt now.

"Yet somehow," he continued, "through all of that, we've managed to survive, especially you. You've done such amazing and brave things, Clary. You went against the Exiled Regiment and freed us all. Ha – I mean, you even liberated the terrible Chained King. You've saved so many lives all by yourself."

"I didn't do all that much!" Clary cut in. "You know as well as I do that those things were mostly thanks to everyone else. I was just helping. We couldn't have escaped without you and the other knights. We would've died so many times if you hadn't been there to save us, Feryl. Besides, I hardly think a little bit of first aid could be called amazing or brave."

Feryl looked down at her. "I think you'd be hard pressed to find anyone here who wouldn't agree with me."

"I don't know why. I'm always scared and nervous. I always wanted an adventure, but I never imagined it would be so terrible. I've made it this far just doing what anyone would to survive and staying out of everyone's way."

"And that is precisely why everyone would agree with me. You don't even realize how important you are to the group. It's for precisely that reason that I don't think it matters if the enemy does catch up. I don't know if I believe in the gods. I mean, does anyone really? But it does seem to me as if someone up there is watching out for you. Something has been keeping you alive time and time again, whether it be god, demon, fate or just plain luck. I don't think they'd let anything happen to you just yet. You're too special."

Feryl stopped abruptly, seeming embarrassed at his words. He looked down at her again, perhaps trying to think of a way to shrug off what he had just said, but it was too late. Clary was staring up at him. She knew exactly what he meant, and there was no getting past it. Only now were they both fully aware of how close they were, and the exact atmosphere of the situation, but oddly enough, neither one protested. Instead, they simply looked into each other's eyes. Clary didn't realize it until after she had already started, but she was drawing closer to him, and Feryl was reciprocating. She closed her eyes.

Suddenly she heard a yell from within the wagon. "Clary Help! Something's wrong with Hilda, Terra too!" It was Gerald. He stuck his head out of the wagon to call them in. Valen had hurried to join them, having heard the screaming from atop the wagon. Clary and Feryl still had their arms around each other, so it was fairly obvious what was going on.

"What's wrong?" Clary asked, making her way into the wagon. She did not look back as she did. Had she done so, she would have seen the standoffish looks that Feryl and Valen were now trading. With the doors open the yelling was much louder and completely distracting. There was no time to address the awkwardness of the interruption, nor the brewing argument between the two boys behind her.

As she entered the wagon she was greeted by even louder screams. Both Hilda and Terra were curled up on the ground, clutching their heads. Clary rushed over to them immediately. Gerald limped over to them as well, kneeling beside Clary.

Just when they were closer to their adversaries than they had been in months, just as they were on the verge of a possible attack, some unknown ailment had afflicted two of their members. To think that Clary had entertained Feryl's idea that someone might be looking out for them.

"Gerald, I'm going to need you to get some water and rags," she ordered. "Also some wine if you can find any."

"Right! I'm on it!"

Clary turned to Terra first. "Terra! Terra, what's going on?"

Terra only yelled more.

"Terra, I need you to tell me where it hurts," Clary said with more urgency.

"I-I don't know! It just hurts everywhere. My head! My body!"

Clary wasn't sure what to make of it. She could tell this was no ordinary illness, not with the both of them in such pain at the same time and without anyone else being affected. She turned to Hilda, hoping she might be a bit more coherent. "Hilda, what's happening?"

Hilda was only slightly more composed. She was straining from the pain but managed to fight down her screams for a few moments. She looked up at Clary and said, "Th-th-the e-enemy is nearb-by! Th-they are torturing someone very close. I can f-feel it. Such pain. I've never felt so much pain." She went back into her groans of agony.

Clary sat back. If Terra was reacting to this situation in the same way as Hilda, then it could only mean one thing: Terra was an empath as well. It explained so much about their friendship.

She turned to go and warn the others. She would have to tend to Terra's and Hilda's pain afterwards, if they all survived. Before she could even stand up, she was greeted by Feryl and Valen standing right behind her. In all the commotion, she hadn't heard them enter. Just as she started to tell them what was going on, Valen stopped her.

"We heard what she said."

Clary was confused. Valen didn't seem at all urgent about the matter. If they knew the enemy was nearby then they should be out telling everyone and preparing for the fight to come. Instead, the pair remained inert, with sullen looks on their faces.

"If you know, then why aren't you—" Clary began.

"Because there is no enemy nearby." Feryl said in a somber tone.

"But you heard her! They're torturing someone!" Clary couldn't understand why they didn't believe her. The two men just looked at each other uncertainly. "Fine! If you won't tell the others, then I will!" She started marching around them towards the door, but before she could make it, Feryl grabbed her by the hand. She stared back, furious.

Finally, the Chained King sighed. "Clary... someone *is* being tortured... but it's not the enemy doing it."

Clary couldn't believe how stupid she was. How could she be so naïve to think that 'interrogation' just meant asking questions? This wasn't some local constable back in Vinvale. This was survival in the midst of a war outbreak.

"Look," Valen said, "we can talk about this later, but right now those two need your help, especially your friend. She doesn't understand her powers yet. She must be terrified. This is why they took the Varhallan further away. They wanted to make sure the mage didn't pick up on it. Obviously it wasn't far enough." He seemed irritated at this. "Either way, you can at least sooth their pain with your magic. We'll go tell him to move it."

"You need to tell them to stop," Clary muttered, returning to her writhing friends.

"We all wish it were that simple," Valen said dejectedly.

244

As the two left the room, Clary set to work in silence. She didn't want to talk to either of them right now. When she thought about it all, it made sense. Ingrum did specialize in subterfuge. It was the first thing Valen had told her about him. This Sir Vacarro they mentioned must have been his master. No doubt he would have taught Ingrum about torture tactics during his training. Judging from everyone's reaction to his name, Sir Vacarro must have been infamous for his abilities in the practice. Clary really didn't know enough about their world. When they returned, she would make sure she talked to Sir Rorian. They should have discussed all of this together.

*　　*　　*

After spending so much time and magical energy trying to help ease her friends' pain, Clary promptly fell asleep. When she woke up, most of the others were asleep. She got up, quietly walked over to the entrance, and slipped out before anyone could stop her. She still wanted to confront Sir Rorian, knowing he would be on his platform as usual by now. She had been asleep for only an hour or so and it was still dark out. However, when she turned to the side of the wagon where Sir Rorian usually sat, she found nothing but an empty seat.

"He's set up another camp for him and Ingrum to stay at while they go over the information."

Clary jumped at the voice, as there was no one around.

"I'm up here." It was Edgrum, sitting atop the wagon.

"Oh, hey. Why is everyone asleep? Shouldn't they be on the lookout?" Clary asked, looking up at him.

"According to the commander, we aren't in danger for now. He learned a good bit from the Varhallan."

"Really? What else did he say?"

"Couldn't tell you really," Edgrum said frankly. "He didn't give us any other details. Just told us the coast was clear and that we could relax."

"And that's it?" Clary asked, a little irritated that there wasn't more. "He didn't say anything else?"

"No. Well at least not about the information. He just seemed really worried. I think he picked up on something big. Told everyone that he would be making camp farther back to mull over the information with my brother. Don't be too worried, though. It's kind of standard procedure since we don't have an officer's tent."

Clary couldn't believe how casually the torture was being handled, even by such a kindhearted person as Edgrum. She was starting to wonder what kind of other horrors these knights might have lived through.

"Is there anyone else out there? Or just them?" she asked.

"No, just those two and the prisoner. Oh, and Garrett is out patrolling as well."

"Well good, I'm going to have a word with him," Clary said, determined to give the captain a piece of her mind.

Edgrum jumped off the wagon, clearly intending to argue, but he must have seen something in Clary's eyes that suggested there was no room for negotiation.

"Alright, fine," he said, "but at least let me go with you. There're a lot of strange things out there. No one should go alone."

Clary nodded in agreement, and they set of together.

After a few minutes they rounded a particularly large dune. Now Clary could see the light of a fire. She hurried ahead, ready to give the old knight an earful, but when the campsite finally came into view she screamed, her hands shooting to her mouth, and froze.

246

Ingrum was standing over Sir Rorian, a large ornate dagger plunged into the old knight's gut all the way up to the hilt. Sheckem was knocked out on the ground, untied. Edgrum came up behind Clary and nocked his bow, pointing it at his own twin who was completely taken aback at having been discovered. Ingrum went to draw his sword, but as his hand reached for the hilt, Edgrum's arrow pierced the center of his hand.

Clary saw a tear glisten on the young archer's cheek. There was no room for interpretation here. His own brother, Ingrum, was attempting to assassinate Sir Rorian and had intended to place the blame on their prisoner. She made to run to her mentor's aid, but as she stepped forward Sir Garrett rounded the other side of the hill to appear beside Ingrum, obviously having hurried to investigate the source of Clary's scream. Sir Garrett hadn't even looked at Sir Rorian, who was gasping on the floor, and before he had time to comprehend the situation Ingrum leaped behind him, pulling another dagger from his vest with his remaining hand and putting it to a confused Garrett's throat.

"Now let's talk brother," Ingrum shouted. "I know this looks bad but there's a reason for all this. You just have to trust me. We can both walk away from this, I swear." He sounded nervous, and deranged. It was like he was a completely different person.

Edgrum did not respond at first, but after a moment he let out a single solitary word, which held more anger and commanding power than Clary could ever remember hearing from anyone.

"Speak!"

Chapter 19

It was the middle of the night and though Sir Rorian had given the okay for a few hours of sleep, Feryl did not think it wise to risk it while an encroaching, unknown force lay behind them. Feryl had experienced more time at war than any of the others here, save for the old man. The lack of experience of the group was evident in their ability to sleep without worry, upon the simple word of a superior. Feryl took it upon himself to lie awake in wait for any possible attack that could come. His senses were, after all, much more acute than most of the others. He would be able to hear any combat even from within the wagon.

He stirred at a light shuffling of feet and creaking of the wagon door. It had come from within the wagon. He peered around the room to search for the source, and to ascertain where everyone was so that he could be prepared.

He stifled a groan. It was Clary who had woken up. *Why does it always have to be her?* he wondered, silently. He wasn't sure if Clary attracted trouble, or if she went looking for it – either way, he didn't like her wandering off on her own. However, Sirs Garrett and Edgrum were outside, so surely she couldn't get into too much trouble. He decided to let her be.

Even as he made this decision, thoughts of their earlier conversation began to spring forth in his mind, and he felt an unfamiliar pang of embarrassment. His stomach tightened as he thought of what had *almost* happened on the driver's seat of the wagon. He could still feel her warmth at his side where she had rested her head. He had never had much time for these kinds of feelings when he had lived amongst the Exiles, and given his position as a slave he had never had much hope of surviving to share that kind of interaction with someone.

His mind flooded with all of the things he had said, and he felt nerves well up within him. He was not used to sharing his thoughts with others, let alone his emotions. Had he been strange or said anything wrong? He was beginning to feel pathetic, overanalyzing the entire situation as he was, but it was all so new to him. For now, he would just have to put it from his mind. There were more important things to worry about. Perhaps the tension of their escape and the stress of the situation was getting to him. If it meant anything to Clary, surely she would bring it up again once they were safely at their destination.

Feryl's train of thought shifted. *Where is Clary?* He had heard her faintly speaking with Edgrum outside, but that was a while ago. It was strange that she would wander off for so long alone. Edgrum must have gone with her. Then it dawned on Feryl that she must have gone off to speak with Sir Rorian and the others. After what had happened with Hilda and Terra, he was sure that this would have been her initial intention on leaving the wagon. This calmed him slightly. She would be safe with Rorian, Edgrum and Ingrum at her side.

After a few moments, however, his worry returned. *Perhaps I should go check on her, just in case. There's no harm in that.* He did trust the others, but he had a strong need to ensure her safety personally. After all, she had been the one to free him from his lifetime sentence under the heel of the Treacherous King and the burning whip of his former handler, Turk.

He got up and made his way out of the wagon as quietly as he could, so as not to disturb anyone. Peeking over the top of the wagon, he saw that Edgrum was gone. Clary and the knight were nowhere in sight either. Feryl turned to dismount, moving as gently as possible to diminish the creaking that always occurred when the wagon was relieved of his immense weight.

As his boots hit the sand, he was greeted by a different noise, something he had not expected. A scream.

He knew immediately that it was Clary. The scream was full and uninterrupted, which meant that she most likely had not been injured. At least, that was what he hoped.

He sprinted in the direction of the scream. It seemed to have come from the place where Sir Rorian had made camp. This must mean that the old knight was with her – a relief, as Feryl did not want to take time to summon help from within the wagon.

He saw a hint of firelight beyond the large dune which hid the camp. Feryl sighed in relief as he recognized Clary's silhouette. It was short-lived, however. Moments later his gaze fell upon Edgrum, whose bow was fully drawn and aimed at some unseen attacker. Something was wrong, but Feryl could not quite tell what was happening. The dune still obstructed his view of Edgrum's target but Feryl was sure that he was facing a low number of foes, given the young knight's stillness. Perhaps the prisoner had escaped, or maybe there was an enemy scout, or some new kind of creature. Whatever the case, Feryl had remained unnoticed, having stopped out of range of the fire's glow. He planned to take advantage of the darkness to assess the situation.

He made his way around to the other side of the dune, concluding that his best chance of seizing the advantage, as well as discovering the identity of his foe, would be in flanking to the rear. As he approached he could hear Ingrum talking quietly. Sir Rorian, if he was with them, was not speaking, and the prisoner was oddly quiet as well.

Finally, Feryl made it to the other side of the hill of sand and had a better view of the situation. He was not prepared at all for the scene before him.

Sir Rorian was lying back on the sand, the hilt of a dagger plunged deep into his gut. He was grasping at the wound, struggling to withstand the pain, blood pouring down his sides. He was still alive, but Feryl was not entirely sure just how much longer he would last.

It was too dark. Sheckem was lying nearby, unconscious. Feryl almost certainly would have believed that the Varhallan had been the one who attacked Rorian, had he not seen Ingrum holding Sir Garrett at knifepoint. It was obvious what had happened. Sir Ingrum had attempted to kill the commander and lay blame on the Varhallan prisoner – though for what reason, Feryl could not say.

Sir Ingrum's voice quavered as he said, "I'm sorry. He has to die. If we let him live, we'll be killed!" Though Feryl could not see his face, he was sure that Sir Ingrum was crying or at the very least he was struggling not to. "It's not my fault!"

"Don't give me that, Ingrum!" his brother shouted. "I'm not stupid! Just look at yourself!"

"Please, you don't understand!" Ingrum sounded more and more panicked. "It was an order. I didn't want this. If we had just killed the damned Varhallan, none of this would be necessary!"

"What are you talking about?" Clary demanded. Ingrum's ravings were only making the situation more unclear.

"This doesn't concern you! It's your fault too! If we had just stayed with the Exiles like we were supposed to then we would've been fine! But no – you had to come along and mess everything up by bringing the goddamned Chained King himself, along with—" Ingrum stopped short. It was obvious that he had said something he shouldn't have, but it was too late for him to try and smooth it over. Both Clary and Edgrum noticed.

"Wait a second, the Chained King? What are you talking about?" Edgrum said in confusion. So far only a few among them knew of Feryl's true identity: Rorian, Garrett and Hilda. None of the others had been told, and Clary knew that none of those who did know would ever share that information unless it was absolutely necessary.

"How… how did you know who Feryl was?" Clary asked.

"I… uh…" Ingrum stammered. As clever as he was when it came to lying his way out of a situation, he had dug himself too deep. This was not the kind of mistake he would ever make were he not staring down the wrong end of a bow held by his own brother.

Feryl had a sudden realization about Ingrum, and it was all the information that he needed in order to decide upon his next move. He crept up behind the panicking boy, while at the same time activating his enhancement magic. It made a slight noise when he changed, as it usually did. In the hushed tension of the conversation Ingrum heard the subtle yet unique sound and turned just as one of the giant's hands closed around his throat.

252

Feryl'd had no time to grab his blades from the wagon. He held his palm on the back of Ingrum's neck, the fingers of his massive hand easily reaching around the entire circumference of his throat. A deadly aura was emanating from the giant that would cause most men to fall to their knees in despair.

When he spoke, it was no longer Feryl, the kind and silent boy – it was the commanding and unwavering power of the man feared as the Chained King. "If you know who I am then you're aware of how easily I could end your worthless existence right now." His eyes glowed a soulless red.

Ingrum was visibly shaken, knowing full well that the Chained King could crush his throat easily with one hand, quicker than the slash of a sword. "Y-yes b-b-but there's poison in this blade. It's extremely potent. Even a nick will be enough. If you don't let go I'll kill him!" He was trying to summon whatever courage he could to survive. It seemed that he was determined to live.

"That may be, but if you kill him then you lose your bargaining chip, and I'll just kill you all the same," Feryl responded. In truth, however, he was bluffing. He didn't want anything to happen to Sir Garrett and even if he killed Ingrum before he could slash his hostage's throat, the knife was pressed too closely to Garrett's skin. The slightest twitch from Ingrum, even the weight of his fall, could leave a scratch on Garrett, flooding his body with poison. Still, one did not question the power of the Chained King. Ingrum would not question this bluff.

Ingrum had not anticipated that kind of answer. He did not let go of Sir Garrett but it was clear that he would not try anything, at least for the moment. "So then, what do we do now?" he asked.

"We talk," Feryl replied calmly. "First, you are going to tell me who hired you to work for the Exiles. Who set up the contract on the prince?" He saw that Ingrum was about to protest. "Don't deny it. I know the Exiles didn't hire you."

"Hold on," Clary interjected. "What do you mean? He was working with the Exiles? Why didn't you tell us before?"

"Because I didn't know it was him. We had someone inside Vinvale who opened up the guards' tunnels on the night of the attack. Captain Turk didn't like to divulge too much information to me, so I didn't know what our inside man looked like. All I knew was that he worked for our employer. I assumed he was released back to his master following the incursion, if he even survived. I never thought that he would remain hidden as a prisoner. I'm sure Captain Turk kept him hidden amongst you all to keep tabs on you. I could never have imagined that the traitor would accompany us in our escape. I expect that this means your employer didn't truly care whether the prince was captured or not. If we are being pursued by Exiles, then it isn't because of the prince."

Ingrum's face filled with a combination of anger and shame. "No, it's not. They want their Chained King and his new Queen back. That's why this is your fault too." He spat.

"So the Exiles didn't decide to attack on their own?" Clary asked, shocked at this new revelation.

"Not exactly," Feryl replied. "The Treacherous King wanted it, but we needed a financial backer for the supplies and ships to the desert. On top of that, we sent an incredibly large and well-equipped force just to take one village. Someone else must've had the same goal and gone along with it. Given Ingrum's willingness to go along with the rest of the group, my guess is that he had auxiliary orders in case of an escape. In fact, I imagine that had we not tortured Sheckem, he would have gone all the way back to the capital without hindrance." He saw Clary's confused look. "I'm guessing that the Varhallan spilt a bit of information that we weren't supposed to hear – which means that this one's employer is most likely also connected to the attack on that Varhallan village a ways back. Since Sir Rorian found out, no doubt he had to silence him and blame it on Sheckem."

"Shut up!" Ingrum growled. "You can't say anything more!"

"But still," Clary began, "it doesn't make sense. Even if he was inside the city, the entrances to the guards' tunnels are magically locked. Only their individually enchanted keys will work for the doors. You can't even pick those locks. He was only there a day. I mean, how would he even have been able to…" Clary stopped at a sudden realization. Her face flushed and her hands began to glow brighter than ever before. The sleeves of her shirt, which did not even cover her forearms, began to smoulder from the intensity of the heat. "You bastard! I'll kill you!" She erupted in a blind rage, sprinting towards him.

She understood how the Exiles got into the village. She understood where Ingrum had gotten the key. But most importantly, she now knew how Sisti and her family had met their end.

"You murderer!"

Edgrum made an attempt to stop her, grabbing her by the shoulder. The heat was far too intense, forcing him to release her almost immediately. His hand was burnt badly, and he let out a yelp of pain. This cleared Clary's head slightly.

Ingrum seemed distracted by the sudden outburst. Perhaps his instinct was to help his brother. He momentarily loosened his grip on Sir Garrett.

Feryl took the opportunity to grab Sir Garrett, pushing Ingrum and his poisoned blade away from the hostage. Ingrum flew to the ground from the force of the shove, also losing his grip on the dagger, which landed in the fire. He scrambled to his knees, but it was too late. He was now surrounded and unarmed. The situation was in their favor, but Feryl knew that they weren't out of the woods yet. Ingrum was near enough to Sir Rorian to be able to pull the dagger from his gut. If he went for it, there was a possibility that Rorian would bleed out. Feryl must keep the conversation going, now with the added concern of Clary's anger. If she lost it again, Ingrum might start making risky moves. "Clary, what's wrong?" Feryl called out. "You need to calm down."

"Calm down? How could I calm down?" she shouted back. Angry tears were pouring from her eyes, evaporating into steam as they made their way down her cheeks. "He killed her! He killed Sisti and her parents on the night of the attack! That's how he got the key. Sisti's father was a member of the village guard. How could you do that to her? She trusted you. She liked you, and you used her!" She remembered staring into her best friend's cold, lifeless eyes as she lay in her blood, hiding from the Exiles.

Ingrum looked down at the sand, exhibiting an even greater amount of shame. He clutched at his side.

"How? How can you be so sure?" Edgrum finally asked. Even though he now knew his twin to be a traitor, he still couldn't believe his brother would have gone so far. "He may have messed up, but I can't see him killing an innocent civilian."

Clary answered sharply, indicating Ingrum's side. "On the night of the attack Ingrum appeared in the village square with a wound on his side. He said it was the Exiles, but I think it was Sisti. She had a bloodied knife with her. She managed to injure her attacker before he killed her."

Edgrum didn't ask any further questions. It was clear from Ingrum's expression that what Clary had said was true.

Finally, Feryl spoke again. "Then I'm guessing that since you still tried to flee with the prince, it means that he wasn't our goal at all. If that's the case, then what was it the Exiles were truly after? Why did we attack the village?" Feryl had believed fully that the entire point of their mission was to take a shot at the royal family and the nobles, but now it didn't add up. There must have been other reasons for the mission. Up until now these goals were known only to the higher-ups but no longer. His only orders had been to capture nobles and wipe out opposition.

"It doesn't matter now. If I tell you, then we all die." Ingrum shot back.

"Come on, brother," Edgrum pleaded. "Please, just tell us what's going on. You may still survive this. Stop fighting it and tell us who hired you and what their plans are."

"No, Edgrum. The only way we make it out of this is if those who know too much die. You should be helping me! He promised that when this is over and he rules everything, we would have honored positions in the kingdom! He promised protection for the two of us. But if I fail he'll kill you and I both." It seemed that Ingrum was running out of room. He was making a last ditch effort to get someone on his side.

"Who are you talking about?"

Just as Feryl asked this, there came noise from behind him.

"Hey, you brute! What's going o—" It was Valen, along with Ellerbe, Hilda, Terra and Harvel. Evidently, the two empaths had sensed the raised emotions and come to investigate with backup. Clearly, however, they had not expected to come across this scene.

At the same time, Sheckem stirred and woke. "What is happening?" he asked, still delirious.

In the confusion, Ingrum saw an opening. He pulled back his sleeve, above where Edgrum's arrow had struck him earlier, to reveal an intricate web of tattoos. He had been drawing the incantation for his spell in the sand under his cloak while they had been talking. In his hand opened a small dark hole, which appeared to be a portal of some kind, and from it he drew another ornate dagger.

He leapt towards the Varhallan.

The only people close enough to react were Clary and Edgrum, who had not taken their eyes off Ingrum. Clary leapt instinctively, throwing her body over Sheckem. She hated the foul-mouthed creature, but if he died then they would never gain all of the information for which Sir Rorian had been stabbed. Ingrum hesitated for a moment, giving his brother enough time to nock and loose his bow, despite the pain of his burnt hand. The arrow pierced Ingrum between the ribs on his right side. It was a perfect hit.

Ingrum dropped his dagger and fell to his knees with a gurgling cough, spattering the sand with even more blood. Edgrum threw his bow to the ground and ran to his brother's side, catching him in his arms as he slowly fell backward. "Ingrum... Ingrum... I just don't understand why. Why would you betray your friends? How could you betray me? Just for power?" Edgrum was weeping openly. Ingrum was no longer a threat, and evil as his actions had been, they were still brothers.

Ingrum looked up at his twin, and tears of his own began to flow from his eyes. He was wheezing, only moments from death. With the arrow lodged in his lung, speaking was no simple task. Utilizing his last bit of strength, he reached toward his own neck, grasping his collar, pulling it down to reveal what could only be a slave's contract brand.

Edgrum was shocked. "But why? Why would you let someone do this to you? What did they have to use against you?"

Ingrum was unable to form a complete sentence due to the blood pouring from his mouth. His time was at an end. All he could do was slowly raise his bloody hand, placing it on his brother's cheek, and splutter three words. "Th-they... had... y-you." With that, his hand fell lifeless to the sand.

Edgrum's eyes widened with understanding as the light in his twin's eyes faded. It was clear what had happened and why his brother had done such terrible things. Someone high up had threatened to take Edgrum's life if Ingrum did not cooperate with his plans. For this, Edgrum had killed his own brother.

Edgrum began to lose all self-control. "Ingrum! Ingrum please, no! Wake up! I'm sorry! Please don't leave me here alone! I didn't know! I-I didn't mean..." But his brother lay lifeless in his arms. Finally, Edgrum snapped. He cried out, wailing to the night sky as he pulled his fallen best friend into a tight embrace. It was the saddest sound any of them had ever heard.

Hilda stepped forward, hoping to calm him with her empath abilities, but Feryl stopped her. "No... he needs to feel this." The group stood and watched, consumed in the sadness of what had happened.

The only ones who moved were Clary and Garrett, who both rushed to Sir Rorian's aid. There might still be time to save their mentor. Clary immediately began miming magical scripts over the wound.

"Clary! Clary, please save him!" Garrett panicked. He seemed to be losing himself. "You have to save him! Will he be okay?"

"I'm trying. I think I'll be able to stop the bleeding." It was working. The bleeding was slowing.

"I'll go get the medical supplies!" Terra said, running back to the wagon.

Clary began to believe she might remove the dagger and patch Rorian up at the rate things were going. *But still... something doesn't feel right,* she thought. This was going too well. What was more, the dagger appeared to be identical to the poisoned one, which Ingrum had used to threaten Garrett. She examined it more closely and saw that there was a pommel, unusual for such a short blade. It had a strange glass portion to it, perhaps a compartment for poison. Yet as she worked on Rorian, he seemed to be springing back to life. This shouldn't be possible without the antidote. Even her magic couldn't neutralize an unknown poison.

Finally, Sir Rorian spoke. "It's a magical assassination poison. It's extremely rare and expensive."

Clary looked at him in confusion. "I don't understand. How could you—"

Feryl cut in, to allow Rorian to save his energy. "It's a time-delayed poison. It's meant for anonymous assassinations. It enters the bloodstream and shows no symptoms, remaining dormant in the host's body until it activates, killing them suddenly, hours after the assailant has disappeared. All it takes is a prick of the finger or a drop in your food and you're doomed.

Dead before you even knew it was there. If you heal him, he will continue as normal until it activates and then he will most assuredly die. Though, I doubt Ingrum intended to let him live long enough for the poison to activate."

Garrett became frantic at this news, tears welling up in his eyes. "What do you mean? How long? Is there anything we can do? There has to be a way to stop it! You can do it, can't you, Clary?" But she just shook her head. Tears began to drip from her nose. "How...how long do we have?" Garrett asked as his face fell.

"There's no telling," Feryl admitted solemnly. "Could be minutes, hours or even a day or two."

"But we're not that far from Harsgard. Surely, they'll have a full apothecary there! We can definitely—"

Garrett was interrupted as Rorian placed his hand on the boy's. "We aren't that close, my boy. I'm afraid this is going to be it for me." The old knight seemed worried as he said this, but not for himself. He worried only for the children he had watched over until now.

"B-b-but... sir..." Garrett began.

"I know Garrett... I know. I can't say I'm too thrilled about it myself, but I suppose it's my time. Besides, I'm not a young buck anymore. I can't keep up with the likes of you lot." He laughed weakly. "It's going to be hard, I won't lie, but it's part of life. It's only natural that I would eventually have to turn over the guard. It's time for my generation to move on, I think." He reached into his pocket with his free hand and pulled out a small silver medallion attached to a long chain. As he did so, he looked up at Sir Harvel, who had joined them along with Valen. "I kept this hidden because I had a feeling that I would need to hand it over at some point soon, and I didn't want to deprive you of the moment." He handed the medallion to Harvel. "Take it. You will be the high commander now."

"But sir! I don't think I'm suited for such a—" Harvel started.

"Bah! Nonsense!" Rorian shot back. "It's for exactly that reason that I believe you are suited for it. You are humble and gallant, lad. More so than any knight I've ever met. So many lose that as they age. Don't make that mistake, as so many of us seniors have."

"Aye, sir!" Sir Harvel accepted his duty, pressing the medallion to his heart. He would not deny what he knew to be his leader's dying wish for him.

"Feryl..." Rorian continued. "I haven't known you long, but I can see that you are troubled by your past. You're shy, and lonely, but I sense greatness inside of you. Please take care of the rest of these kids. With your power behind them, I can rest easy and know they're safe."

Feryl simply nodded.

Next, Rorian turned to Valen. "Brat, you're spoiled rotten, and sometimes your skull is thicker than a rock." He laughed. "But damn it all if you don't have a greatness inside you that exceeds what even you think of yourself. You can save this kingdom. I know it. You just need to see in yourself what everyone else sees in you. It's time for a little growing up, understand?"

Valen looked down, ashamed.

"And most importantly, you need to stop that," Rorian continued. "Stop being so hard on yourself. Your mother... she loved you, and she would be proud of you no matter what. It's time you worked to be worthy of the sacrifice she made for you."

Valen opened his mouth, but Rorian stopped him. "You don't need me to tell you. You've got a strong set of friends who will follow you to the ends of the earth. They trust you, so just put your faith in them."

Terra returned with the medical supplies and gave them to Clary. "Here! This is everything I could find."

Clary thanked her, taking the kit and removing some bandages and a small bottle with a blue liquid inside. "Here, take this, it'll ease the pain," she said, handing the bottle to Rorian.

"Thank you, lass. I don't know how we'd make it through all of this without you."

Clary was still crying.

"Now stop all of that, lass. You've got nothing to feel sorry for. This is all thanks to you. Why, if you hadn't freed us all, none of us would have made it this far. Besides, you've got to save your parents. You've come so far from who you were in that small outer village. You've saved so many lives. We are all so grateful. Don't let anyone make light of what you've done, not even yourself. Keep getting stronger and keep practicing with your swords and your magic. I have no doubt that you'll be a key player in the days to come. Keep pushing, and I know you'll be able to change the world if you want."

"Thank you, Sir Rorian. Thank you so much!" Clary cried.

"And lastly, Garrett. I know how much you hurt inside. I know that the coming days will be some of the hardest you've ever faced. You've always viewed yourself as some kind of beast of destruction, but that isn't you. You fear your own power, but that's because you don't realize what it's for. You are one of the fiercest warriors I have ever met, yet at the same time, you have a kind and gentle soul. I figured out long ago why you were granted such power." The old knight smiled up at the crying boy. "It's because you are a protector. From the moment I saw you, I could tell that you would be the shield that would protect this kingdom and its people."

"But sir, how can I do that without you?" Garrett blurted out. "How do I continue by myself?"

At this, Sir Rorian laughed. "But my boy, you aren't by yourself. Don't you remember what I told you?" He gestured toward Feryl and Clary. "They are your family now. Treat them as though they were your own flesh and blood. They are just like you. I want you to protect them. Trust them. They will take care of you in turn. You do not know each other too well yet, but I feel in them the same strength I felt in you. Promise me you will do this."

"Y-yes sir," Sir Garrett sobbed. "I promise you, I won't leave their side."

"Good. Now I have one more thing to say to you, and then I want you all to pack up and leave, before the enemy gets here."

Garrett nodded and listened intently.

"My boy, at some point you may find yourself feeling guilty over what happened tonight or wishing you could have had more time with me before it happened, but I want you to know that firstly, it's not your fault, and secondly, that I have always been proud of you and cherished all of our time together. But most importantly… I want you to know that I loved you with all of my heart, son." And with that, he reached up and pulled the crying boy towards him, giving him one final hug.

"Now, I think I'd like to see the sun rise one more time before I go," Rorian said, letting go of Sir Garrett. "So take this damned thing out of me already and sew me up. Then sit me against that hill over there so I can see

264

it." Before anyone could protest, he stopped them. "No arguing! If I'm going to die, it'll be on my own terms."

It was the last time any of them would ever hear his commanding tone, and no one would argue with him.

Clary prepped him and removed the blade. She started sewing him up. She had stopped the bleeding and any pain. He would feel completely normal until the poison activated.

"Ellerbe!" Sir Rorian called. "Do me a favor and grab one of those crates of liquor for me. I know none of you children have the stomach for the strong stuff anyway, and I'd like to die drunk. I've no idea when it'll happen, so just bring the whole crate would you?"

Ellerbe did as instructed and left for the wagon to grab the food, water and alcohol for their commander. As he did, the others began wrapping things up, and Feryl lifted the old man in his arms, carrying him over to the spot he had indicated.

When Ellerbe returned with the crate, they all said their goodbyes, one by one.

"Good luck, lads and lassies, I'm sure you'll do great things," Rorian said with a swig of the bottle.

And then off they went, leaving him alone in the night.

Sir Edgrum had already collected his brother's body and buried it in the sand while the others were talking with Sir Rorian. Valen, who was the last to leave, approached the grieving knight to have him move along. As he did, however, he finally got a good look at one of the ornate daggers, which Ingrum had used to cause such havoc in the night. He picked it up to examine it.

Valen froze, barely able to believe his eyes. On the hilt of the blade was a sapphire-encrusted symbol of a silver-horned ram. His heart sank, and his eyes went wide.

"Lorious…" The prince uttered in disbelief.

His mind raced as the pieces began to fall into place. It was the symbol of the third eldest Drakewil son, the symbol of one of his beloved brothers. Valen now understood. Ingrum's employer, the conspirator attempting to incite a war was Lorious Drakewil. He was planning to take over the kingdom of Belderan.

Chapter 20

"Lieutenant, one of the relay men from our forward scouting party has just reported in! He says they've found signs of the target."

"Have you listened to the report yet?"

"No, sir. I didn't want to risk letting our guests overhear anything that they shouldn't."

"Good work, Mr. Sproles. Have him brought to me directly."

Thymey was glad that he was allowed to bring second lieutenant Sproles with him. He was quite young and new to the Regiment. Most other Exiles would consider his lack of time with the regiment to be a fault, but it eliminated any insubordination and difficulty that usually came with members who had been part of the regiment before they turned from the Drakewil legions. It was hard to convince men to follow orders when they themselves assisted the power structure through their betrayal.

Sproles, on the other hand, had been street scum prior to his induction into the Exiles. He was a war orphan who never knew when the next meal might arrive. This bred an unwavering loyalty and grateful attitude into the boy towards the Regiment. He worked with an unparalleled diligence that had proved invaluable on difficult missions such as these. Moreover, he was adept in a few types of sensory magic, specifically in the manipulation of sound waves. He could eavesdrop on the soldiers to keep tabs, and he could muffle sound within a room to prevent anybody from listening in. These tools were extremely helpful to those who knew how to utilize them effectively. The boy was, admittedly, a bit too soft, but Thymey had never enjoyed a more competent right hand. He was glad that he brought him in.

Captain Turk had not permitted Thymey to take anyone too valuable with him on this mission. The group that the Exiles had amassed for the entire Arid Sea expedition was quite sizeable for such a small raid, with over fifteen hundred soldiers and about two hundred slaves at the start of their journey in Thandessa. This was only a minute portion of their true forces across the sea, but for a mission that required naval tactics, it was unusual for the Exiles to risk such a number. They were after all, primarily comprised of land-based infantry. This was clear proof of the importance of this mission to the Treacherous King.

By the end of the assault on Vinvale there were just under twelve hundred soldiers remaining. The majority of the men who fell did so in that attack and in a storm that had ravaged their warships as they crossed the Crescent Ocean. From this remaining army, Thymey had been permitted a company of only a hundred men, most of whom were considered expendable. Turk would not risk parting with any of the high-quality warriors or battle mages that bolstered his ranks. Thymey suspected that this was not only to keep up the appearance of strength in the eyes of the Varhalla, but also to punish the lieutenant for his ineptitude. Such was the demeanor of the captain that he would gamble with the outcome of a mission just to dish out an extra bit of suffering to Thymey.

Sproles had been correct to keep the report silent up until now. The Varhalla may have been marching separately from the Exiles, but he was sure that they were observing them every chance they got. Thymey wanted to ensure that they did not act without his information or, for that matter, his permission. For this reason he insisted that the scouting party be composed primarily of Exiles, with only one Varhalla emissary. His company was split into three platoons of about twenty-five each, with his at the center while the other two were to the front and back. There were eight men in the scouting party and two relay-men who ran back and forth between the main force and their group. They had lost about ten men to the heat of the dessert and the sandstorm, but that was to be expected.

The Varhalla numbered about thirty, and they remained split into two groups who stayed on either side of Thymey's platoon astride brightly-colored gandovors. They were there as an escort to aide Thymey, sent from Beyond, the main Varhallan City, by Turk. Apparently they were from a much larger group of elite mages who answered directly to the Varhallan king, and who possessed magic specifically withheld from the general public and which required access to secret royal scriptures to learn. It was comforting to have such powerful reinforcements, but for a while now, they had seemed concerned. Thymey's men had reported unrest among them for the past week or two. He could not be entirely sure why, but judging from the way they observed Thymey and his men, coupled with their dramatically increased interest in catching their prey, he suspected that they knew something about the Exiles' other mission in the Arid Sea. However, if they did, then they surely did not know that the Exiles were involved or else they would have pulled back to warn their superiors at Beyond… or they might attempt to wipe the company out first.

Thymey had made efforts to avoid the small Varhallan village which their auxiliary group had moved to destroy while the main force was in

Vinvale, but he could not be sure whether or not they had discovered the wreckage. He had been acting so far as though the ruse was a success, and the Exiles shared no blame. He felt especially safe after the leader of the Varhallan group, a particularly ornery old caster named Marashal, insisted on using what he called "The King's Pestilence" to eliminate their targets. This was an intensely terrifying bit of magic that involved summoning from the desert immense creatures, known simply in the common tongue as sand rovers. They breathed decay and had the strength to destroy cities. Unfortunately, they were summoned directly into a sand leviathan feeding ground. It was a million to one chance, and the worst possible situation, one of the only ways the attack might fail. It took almost all thirty of the Varhallan casters to pull off the attack, and it left them completely drained. When one of the beasts was killed, it reverberated and three of the casters died, with one being left critically injured. They had known ahead of time that this move would be incredibly risky, which is what cemented their desperation in Thymey's mind. He was sure that Marashal had discovered what happened to the village and blamed the boy, Feryl, and his group. It was laughable that they believed the boy capable of such a feat. He was, after all, an idiot. Still, it had left them weakened, which was a concern.

Finally, the relay-man arrived along with Second Lieutenant Sproles. Thymey signaled to his second in command, who promptly began chanting under his breath and drawing magic scripture in mid-air. "*To thee who would seek to gain knowledge meant not for peasant's ears, seek thou not the property of gods who graciously bestow upon thee a life which hath not been earned, lest thou submit unto them the senses which they hath humbly granted unto thee…*" he chanted. Most mages chanted in ancient languages when performing incantations. It was the mark of a young mage to utilize the common tongue when casting. What was more, most men would never be able to understand a caster's chant-speech due to its rapidity. Thymey was only granted such a clear rendition of the young boy's spell because of Sproles' sound manipulation magic. He always made sure to bind his speech to Thymey, amplifying the clarity by channeling the sound waves directly between them. With this spell, Thymey could understand even a whisper from the second lieutenant from opposite ends of the formation.

Once Sproles' sound barrier spell was complete, Thymey turned his attention to the scout. Fortunately, this early in the morning it was too dark for the Varhalla to gain any real intel by sight. "What have you got for me, grunt?"

"Sir, we've found traces of a campsite only a couple hours away. There were remnants of a small fire, hot coals and embers."

Thymey smiled at this new information. They were so close. Tracks had revealed the children they were hunting to be traveling in a wagon pulled by bull-drages. There was no way that they could outpace Thymey's company, especially with the gandovors in their possession. If he wanted to, he could send the Varhalla ahead to catch them, but he didn't want to take any chances. The desert dwellers were still weakened and had their own plans to boot. No, there were too many variables. He would be sure to overwhelm them with far superior numbers. It was better to be safe, given the recent luck of the small group.

"We will pick up pace then and catch them before the next two days are out," Thymey concluded. "Is there any other pertinent information at this time, soldier?"

"Yes, sir. At the campsite, there were traces of blood and what appeared to be a burial site. We dug it up to reveal one body, male, late teens.

Also, there is a dense fog rolling in from the north. Our Varhallan cohort informs us that this is a normal occurrence in the northern Arid Sea, caused by evaporation off of the Pronged Sea. It will reach us as the sun rises, before we reach the campsite."

Thymey was extremely satisfied with the relay-man's report. Their prey had now been weakened by at least one member. Whether it had been an accident or, even better, dissent amongst the group, the diminution of their group was good news for the Exiles. This fog was an added bonus. For a while now they had been tracking their prey by scent. The gandovors were exceptionally good at this. Decreased visibility would hide their force of numbers, raising their advantage to even greater heights.

"Private, I want you to spread the word to the two sergeants of first and third platoons. Second Lieutenant Sproles here will assist you. When that is done, return to me and we will inform the Varhalla. These next few hours may very well determine the success of this mission."

Thymey grinned, certain that very shortly he would have his revenge. If all went well, he might even send a hawk to the Treacherous King himself. That fool, Turk, may have provided these weak soldiers to punish Thymey, but he had also unwittingly given Thymey an opportunity to prove his worth to their king. *Captain Thymey...* he liked the sound of it.

*   *   *

The fog was upon them. It was a blinding mist thicker than Thymey had ever seen, even denser than the white haze that rolled in from the morning sea back in their port city of Thandessa. This was admittedly more than he had hoped for, but the lieutenant had confidence in his company's ability to hold a formation, which would minimize the risk of losing soldiers in the reduced visibility. As long as they did not run into any more unwelcome surprises, they would be fine.

It had been several hours since they had received the information regarding the newly-discovered campsite, and they had made all efforts to act on the news. Thymey was becoming restless, this close to redemption. He had sent Sproles up to the head of the forward platoon, to maximize visibility and communication. This would compensate for the lieutenant's inability to see the entire company within the fog. Sproles was reporting every bit of information from the front. Thymey had also set two runners to relay information between himself and the rear guard. He allowed the Varhalla to play their own game, giving them the illusion that this hunt was theirs, but he would ensure that any glory would fall to him.

As the twilight hours finally waned, Thymey gained his first bit of good news from the forward post.

"Sir, the scout from earlier has found the tracks left from the enemy's wagon. He says it shouldn't be long now."

"Excellent, Mr. Sproles. Does the grunt have an estimate?"

After a pause, Sproles answered, "He says it should be any moment now. We are closer than he thought."

"Good work, boy! I'll have to remember to reward that one when this is all over." Thymey laughed. Sure this relay-man was nothing more than a tracking mutt to him, but the lieutenant was not so ignorant as to stiff those who did their jobs properly. In fact, today he was even feeling benevolent. Perhaps he would give the little flea some sort of promotion.

Just as he was patting himself on the back there came word from the front again. "Lieutenant, we've made contact, I think you should come have a look at this."

"You've found the target?" Thymey exclaimed.

"No sir, it's the scouting party," Sproles explained. "But sir, they—"

"Stay right there!" Thymey was feeling downright giddy at their progress – so much so that he couldn't contain himself to the center-line anymore. It may not have been the escapee brats yet, but if the scouting party was this close to the main force, then it meant that the Feryl boy and his lot couldn't be much farther ahead.

"Alright, Mr. Sproles, I'm coming to you!" Thymey hopped on the maroon gandovor, which the Varhalla had presented to him as a sign of trust, and began making his way towards the front.

"But sir, wait, it's…" Sproles began, but Thymey did not hear the rest of his statement. Before Sproles could finish, there came an exasperated call from behind the lieutenant.

"Lieutenant Thymey! Sir!" the man gasped. "Sir, stop! Urgent news!" It was another relay-man from the rear guard.

Thymey halted his mount and turned on the man in irritation at his good mood being interrupted. He couldn't see the man in the thick fog until he was within a few arms lengths of him. "What? What do you want, grunt? If this isn't anything good, so help me I'll—"

"Forgive me, sir, but this needs your attention. We've lost communication with several of our men from the rear guard."

"What? Several men just went missing at once?"

"Well, no sir, not all at once. Two went missing from the lattermost rank, and then the squad that went to find them didn't report back either. We also had a few on the western file go missing as well."

Thymey scowled. The last thing he wanted was to deal with idiot men losing their way in the fog. "Tell that damned sergeant commanding the rear guard to tighten his formation and keep a better eye on his men, or I'll have his ass! I don't have time to worry about a few drunken soldiers getting lost in the fog just because they couldn't hold their piss in for a few extra minutes. They'll just have to wait until it clears up in a couple hours and then follow our path. If they can't follow the trail of a hundred-strong company in the sand, then they aren't worth going back for. Now hurry back, I'm moving to the forward platoon." It was to be expected that a few men would lose their way in such diminished visibility. There were no other threats in this area, save for the Arid Sea leviathans that they had passed weeks ago, and if one of those were nearby then they would know about it. The Varhalla did not settle this far north, and no other creatures would attack a group this large.

He put the interruption from his mind and returned to his excitement at the discovery waiting for him at the front of the formation. He was very much anticipating a talk with the scouting party. He was sure that these men would have good news and valuable information on their prey. Finally, he would be able to leave this godforsaken desert and put all of this behind him.

As the lieutenant approached his destination, he saw his second coming into view. "Mr. Sproles, I have arrived. Now where are they?"

Second Lieutenant Sproles sprang to attention and saluted. Thymey never got tired of the respect he received from his right hand, but something seemed amiss with the boy.

"At ease, Mr. Sproles. What's going on? Where are the members of the scouting unit?"

Sproles gestured toward a figure on the ground in front of him and his men. "The first man is here, and the others are scattered around the area.

I have instructed the men not to touch them so as to preserve evidence for your viewing, sir."

Thymey's mood immediately changed. What he was looking at was the remains of his scouting party. "Why the hell did you not tell me the scouting party was dead? What happened?"

Second Lieutenant Sproles regarded his superior in confusion. "But sir, I did tell you when you informed me that you were on your way."

Thymey recalled that he had not heard the rest of Sproles' report because of the rear relay-man's interruption. *That damned grunt. He'll be getting a flogging by the end of this, I swear.*

"Very well, Mr. Sproles. My mistake. Have your men locate all the bodies and bring them to me immediately. I want to know what happened so that we can get moving right way." Thymey was seething, but he had to take control of the situation immediately. He did not want their prey slipping away while he was puttering around here. He was still confident in their safety in superior numbers – any attack on such a force as theirs would be a suicide mission – but it still paid to be a little cautious.

Sproles finished delegating roles to his men, and they began making their way to the other bodies in the area. Sproles then turned to inspect the body nearest to him, but interrupted him. "Wait a minute, Mr. Sproles. I want a full report of everything that happened."

"Oh… right, of course sir, right away," Sproles replied. He turned to one of his men. "You there, tend to the corpse, and see if you can't find anything."

"Yes, second lieutenant, sir!" the soldier barked, before making his way to the dead scout.

Sproles turned toward his commanding officer and opened his mouth to begin his report, but before he could get a single word out, he was interrupted by an ear-piercing scream. It was the soldier to whom he had just given orders. As the man had rolled the corpse of the scout over to examine it, the sand below him had given way and he had fallen to his knees in a shallow hole. The hole was filled with sharpened wooden stakes, which penetrated the unlucky soldier's shins and thighs. The sight was truly gruesome. Someone had booby-trapped these bodies, but neither Sproles nor Thymey had the time to warn the other soldiers. More screams came from within the mist. It seemed that all of the others had fallen victim to similar traps.

Sproles rushed over to help his man but Thymey ordered him to stop. "There may be more traps in the area! Everyone remain still!" This was the worst possible situation. Whoever had killed the scouting party was attempting to slow the company down, though whether those responsible were the party of escapees or someone else, Thymey couldn't be sure. They would have to wait out the fog before they could see any other traps in the area. This meant that they would lose valuable time.

Sproles called out, "Sir! It seems this trap was made from sharpened planks. They are improvised. The wood appears to have been salvaged from a wooden storage crate or box."

Who would use an old damned crate to create a trap for an army? This was clearly either someone mad or someone with too much time on their hands. It couldn't have been their prey. They would not risk taking the time to sharpen bits of wood from a cheap crate and set traps. It would take away their lead advantage.

Just as Thymey worked this out, there came another scream from behind.

"Gaah!" from the back right. Then a few moments later from the left, "Aaaah!"

"Mr. Sproles, what the hell is going on?" Thymey shouted, but Sproles had no answer.

Were there more traps? No – if there were, they would not be activating so late. Nothing as advanced as a time delay could be rigged out of spare box parts. There had to be someone attacking, but as long as they maintained formation they should have been safe. Then Thymey realized that they were not in formation. They had spread out the first three or four ranks to survey the area.

"Get back in formation, now! We are under attack!" he commanded. "Shields! Face shields outward! They can't do anything if we group together!"

"Ahh!" came another scream as he said this. Judging by the intervals in between the screams, there could only be a few people attacking them, three or four maximum. Their attackers were picking off soldiers who had become separated in the fog, one by one. Whoever these people were, they were extremely skilled and battle hardened. They must have had great experience and confidence to take on an entire company with such a small number. But it hardly mattered. The attack was over now. Their tactic would not work against a tight formation. As long as the Exiles remained close together, the enemy would not be able to separate individual targets. Thymey had won.

"Mr. Sproles, use your abilities and send word down the line to the other platoons. We cannot afford to use runners – they will just be picked off. Tell the rear and mid sergeants to tighten up formation as we have done, and inform them of the situation. Also send for the Varhalla to lend us some mages! We will smoke these bastards out! They are in our arena now."

Just as Thymey said this, there was a crash in the distance. An orange light became visible through the fog. *Fire mages?* Thymey thought. No, this was something else. He had faced fire mages in battle many times before, and he had never known an attack to make this sort of noise.

There was another crash, and another. Whatever this attack was, it was splitting up the men. Thymey heard more screams, and smelled burning flesh.

"Sir – look out!" Sproles shouted, grabbing Thymey by his tunic and pulling his head down.

Finally Thymey saw what the attack was. Furthermore, he now knew what had been stored in the broken crate. What appeared to be a Varhallan liquor bottle flew past his head, only for an instant, but there was no mistaking it. The bottle had a torn bit of rag sticking from its mouth, ignited in flame. It was such a clever and simple trick, yet incredibly effective in this situation. Whoever this was, it was clear that they were not heavily armed. They were using improvised weapons.

It would have been preferable to wait for the assistance of the Varhalla, but they were losing men every second. Instead, Thymey decided on a new plan.

"Mr. Sproles, they are low in number, and for a while now their attacks have only been coming from the northeast. Can you pinpoint their exact location with sound?"

"Aye, sir. That I can do!" Sproles replied confidently.

The distinct flapping sound of something on fire flying through the air is unmistakable even to an average person, but with Sproles' magically enhanced abilities, the bottle bombs would sound like cannons. He could trace the flapping noise straight to its origin quickly, knowing the enemy's location better than the attackers themselves did.

As Sproles chanted and mimed his inscriptions, Thymey spoke quietly so as not to give anything away to the enemy. "What have you got? How many are there?"

"Just one, sir."

"Just one? Are you certain?" Thymey couldn't believe that this could be just one man.

"Are you questioning my abilities, sir?" Sproles replied.

"Watch your tone, boy!" Thymey shot back. It was annoying, but this display of disrespect was confirmation that Sproles was confident in his determination. He would never give the slightest resistance to his lieutenant-savior otherwise.

"Sorry, sir. But I have him now." Sproles opened his eyes and pointed northwest.

"Good. Take this." Thymey pulled a bow and a quiver of arrows from the saddle of his gandovor and handed it to Sproles.

The boy accepted it and turned to face his target. He nocked his first arrow and pulled it back. As he did so, he closed his eyes, listening intently.

"Everyone shut up now! That's an order!"

Most of the men went quiet. It wasn't completely silent, but the volume level was significantly lowered. Sproles continued aiming, eyes shut tight, breathing slowly. It this state, the young Exile was skilled enough to hear even a drop of water hitting the floor from forty yards. He already knew the attacker's location and was locked on to his footsteps and panting breaths, but he was waiting for his prey to make a move that would give away the positioning of any part of his body.

Then it happened. The attacker picked up a bottle of liquor and ignited it. That was all Sproles needed. He loosed his arrow and there was a grunt of pain in the fog as the arrow struck its target. The bottle bomb was thrown, but the arrow had made contact with the target before he could get the bottle airborne. As such, it only went about half of its intended distance, crashing to the ground between the attacker and the Exiles.

As the flame erupted the man tried to make a run for it, but Sproles was too quick, nocking and loosing an arrow towards the sound of the attacker's leg dragging through the sand. It was another hit. This one immobilized the bombardier in his tracks. They had him.

"Sir! He's just ahead," Sproles shouted. He nocked another arrow and prepared to finish the target, but Thymey placed his hand before the boy.

"Hold it, Mr. Sproles. That's enough. Keep him alive. I'm not done with this one. We are going to squeeze every ounce of information from him that we can." He smiled. "We may not have the captain's pain magic, but I think we can manage the old-fashioned way. After all, a good leader musn't be afraid to get his hands dirty from time to time."

With that, they inched forward toward the grunting, panting victim of Sproles' bow. Almost as if on cue, the fog began to lift as they approached.

"Wait a minute, I know this old bastard!" Thymey shouted as the old man came into view. "You're the high commander of the royal guard!" The lieutenant became more and more excited. As angry as he was at the situation, the chance to torture such a high and mighty knight was not something he wanted to miss.

The old knight was kneeling on the ground panting. An arrow pierced his right hand and thigh.

"Good work Mr. Sproles!" Thymey said. "You didn't hit anything vital! I'm gonna have a lot of fun with you, old timer!"

The old man simply looked up at him and smiled as he gasped. "Oh... I... don't know... about that, lad."

Thymey hated being talked to like that, especially by a weak, injured old man, who had just taken out so many of his men. "What the hell did you just say to me, you old bastard?" he growled, stepping forward and lifting the knight up by his shirt. "I swear I'll kill—" but the lieutenant wasn't able to finish his threat. It was too late. The old knight's eyes stared into the sky, his mouth frozen in a grin of satisfaction. He moved no more.

"Poison," Sproles concluded.

His commanding officer threw the body down to the floor in anger.

At that moment the Varhalla finally arrived at the scene, riding their gandovors.

"Are you in need of assistance, lieutenant?" Marashal asked, his tone almost sarcastic.

"No, not at all," Thymey growled, stifling the choice words he had for the lazy, useless bastards. "I handled it."

<u>Chapter 21</u>

"Clary, calm down!" Feryl called as Clary's sword reverberated from his. "Clary!"

"Aaah!" she roared, bringing her sword down as hard as she could. As the two blades met, sparks flew, and the metal shaft of her sword bent around Feryl's.

"That's it, we're done for the day!" Feryl announced.

"What? No! Why?"

"Because you can't control yourself! That's the third one you've bent this week! You need to cool off!"

"What are you talking about? I'm fine!"

"Are you serious? Just look at your sword. What if it had broken? We can't keep doing this. You may be fireproof, but the heat of the thing would be the least of your worries if it snapped and stabbed you," he pointed out.

They had been training for a while and Clary's emotions had been getting the best of her. So much so, in fact, that the sword she had been using had turned red hot from the heat of her grip after so long, causing it to become malleable.

It had been the same for everyone these past several days since they had lost Sirs Rorian and Ingrum. Morale among the group had never been so overwhelmingly low.

"What does it matter? I'm fine!" Clary shouted.

"Clary, I'm worried about you. I know you're upset about what happened. We all are, but—"

"You don't know anything about what I feel," she interrupted, "and stop worrying about me! What has it got to do with you anyway?"

"Well, I just don't want to see you in such pain and—"

"It's none of your business. Besides, it's not like you haven't caused me pain before," she spat.

Feryl frowned. "Clary, that's not fair. I thought we were past that by now."

"What? Past you attacking my village and getting my family captured by Exiles? Why? So we had one moment, and you think that you have some kind of connection to me or something?" Clary regretted it even before the words left her mouth.

"No, you're right… Clearly we don't. I'm going to check the perimeter with Garrett. You can stay here and train. You're clearly getting the anger part of the magic down." With that, the giant turned and walked off.

"W-wait… Feryl, I didn't mean…" But he had already disappeared around a nearby dune.

She felt awful. She hadn't meant to say such terrible things. In truth, she didn't believe a word that had come out of her mouth, but she was just so angry. She felt she was partially to blame for what had happened to Sir Rorian. She kept thinking about how obvious it was that Ingrum was the traitor. If only she had seen the signs sooner. If she had spoken up and gone to see Sir Rorian a few minutes earlier, she might have been able to wake him up and warn him. None of the others could have done a thing, only her.

Still, she hadn't meant to take it out on Feryl. After all, he was there for her more than anyone else. What was more, lately she had spent more time at his side than even Terra's. Not only had Clary said such unforgivable things to him, she also ruined the memory of the moment they shared on the wagon that night. Though they had not yet addressed it because of all the other events that had occurred on the night in question, she did remember that part fondly from time to time as one of the few nice moments of their trip. All of these thoughts only made Clary hate herself all the more for what she had done.

She sat in the sand, put her face to her knees, and cried. It was hard not having Sir Rorian around. He was always able to calm her down in situations like this. He always knew exactly what to say. If he were here now he would be able to give her advice. He would tell her how to handle things. Then again, if he were still here, she wouldn't be feeling this way in the first place. She just missed him so much. They had spent so much time together over these few months. They trained together every day, but that wasn't all. She missed his stories. She missed his stupid jokes. She missed sitting on the wagon platform with him and watching the stars together. He somehow managed to take this hellish wasteland that would make even the strongest of warriors fall into despair and make it seem almost as if they were simply taking an extended camping trip with friends. Tough as the old man was, it had been his warmth and guidance that kept them all together.

"Wow, that seemed a bit harsh, don't you think?" came a familiar and annoying voice from behind Clary.

Clary shot up, hurriedly wiping away her tears. "What do you want? How long have you been there, Valen?"

"I got here right about the point when you nearly gutted yourself on your own sword. You know, right before you shouted off the big oaf just for worrying about you."

Even though Clary knew she deserved it and that he was completely right, she couldn't stand to see him acting all high and mighty. "I don't know what you're talking about. I thought you hated Feryl anyway."

"Oh please, I saw everything. You're not fooling anybody. It's no secret that he and I don't mix well, but even I wouldn't take the man's legs out from under him like that."

"And what do you know about it?" Clary shot back. "You said yourself that you don't like him. How could you know how he's feeling?"

"It doesn't take a genius to know how much that giant cares about you, especially now that I know who he is."

Following Sir Rorian's passing, they had decided that it was time the rest of the group found out about Feryl's identity as the Chained King, given that so many of them already knew. Valen was really the only one who seemed angry about it, but that was to be expected given the relationship between the pair. This made it all the stranger for him to berate Clary for how she had treated the war tyrant.

"What has him being the Chained King got to do with anything?" Clary asked.

"Really? You mean you haven't realized it yet?" Valen rolled his eyes in his usual irritating way. "Fine, I'll spell it out for you. That big idiot has been a slave damn near his entire life, right?"

Clary nodded in agreement.

"In fact, he still would be if it hadn't been for you."

"So you're saying he cares about me because I found out his contract had been broken?"

"Maybe," Valen admitted, "but I think it's more than that. You were probably the first person in that guy's life to treat him with respect and kindness. I mean, truly, you are the only one he even really gets to talk to."

"That's not true!" Clary interrupted. "He talks to you!"

"Yeah? I don't think shooting insults back and forth between each other quite amounts to pleasant conversation."

"I guess you're right." Clary actually smiled for a second, upset as she was, when she thought about how much the two fought. "Well, what about Garrett?" she asked, remembering how often she saw the two together.

"Ha! You're kidding, right?" the prince laughed. "You're talking about probably the two least talkative people in the history of Belderan. Have you ever been around them while they are together?"

Clary thought back to the times she had seen them interact. She laughed in agreement.

"Exactly, it's not exactly a night in the king's opera with those two. I've heard conversations between brick walls that were less reserved," Valen joked.

Clary laughed again. She didn't always get along with the prince, but he did have his more charming moments. Nobody else could make her laugh now of all times, when she was at her lowest.

"Look, I guess what I'm getting at is that you are his friend – his *first* friend. Even if he doesn't exactly know how to express it."

Now Clary felt even worse. She hadn't realized how much she meant to Feryl. She had never really thought about their relationship like that. *How do I feel about Feryl?* she wondered.

"To think that the almighty Chained King, scourge of eastern Belderan, feared by all kings and rulers, has been tamed by a teenage farm girl from a no-name town in the middle of nowhere."

This time they both laughed.

"I don't know how you do it," Valen continued. "Clary, Daughter of the Firedrake of the North. Her charm knows no bounds. It works even on the most terrifying beasts out there." His voice was comically over-exaggerated, as though he were announcing some great performance. "They sure worked on me," he muttered as she continued laughing.

"What? Was that last bit? I couldn't hear," Clary asked, gasping from laughing so hard.

"Huh? Oh, nothing, never mind. Anyway, I came here to tell you we're about to start moving, so you might want to hop back up on that little platform of yours. If I'm right, we should be just on the border of the Fjorenlands."

"Really? You mean it?" she said excitedly.

"Yeah, we're almost out of here."

"Finally! I can't believe it!" she exclaimed, jumping to her feet.

"But hey, don't forget what we talked about, okay?"

"I... I won't. You're right. I should go apologize right way." She calmed down for a minute. "Thank you, Valen... for everything."

"Wait a second. Is that gratitude I hear? I can't tell, it was a little hard to hear."

"Oh shut up, you! I said thank you, you jerk!" She punched him in the arm.

But she was grateful. Valen could have just kept quiet or made fun of her, but he really had done his best to help her feel better and figure things out.

"Ouch! Hey! Jerk? Is that any way to talk to someone who helped you out?" he continued. "I mean—" But before he could deliver another rude remark, Clary pulled him into a hug. He was shocked, but then she did something that left the prince even more astonished. She kissed him on the cheek.

"Don't ruin it, you big idiot," she said quietly, before releasing him and walking back toward the wagon.

The prince stood for a moment, still facing away from the wagon. He was so surprised he didn't know how to respond for once.

"Hey, aren't you coming? If you don't hurry up I'll tell them to leave without you," Clary joked, snapping the prince out of his trance.

"Oh... yeah, right. Ha ha," he stuttered, turning and jogging to catch up with her.

They didn't say anything for a bit as they walked. Clary was thinking about what she would say to apologize to Feryl. Then a random thought crossed her mind. "Hey, Valen."

"Huh? I mean yeah?"

"You know all about this desert, right?"

"I'd say I know more than most in Belderan. Why?"

"I was just wondering, if we're so close to the Fjorendlands, which is supposed to be some sort of frozen place covered in snow, then why does it still feel just as hot as it did all the way back at the Exile camp?"

Valen thought for a moment. "To be honest, I'm not entirely sure. No one is. The last war with the Varhalla took place primarily in the southern parts of the desert, so not many books in the capital contain much information about the north. But I can tell you that the temperature around the rest of the Arid Sea doesn't differ from place to place. It is constantly ablaze. It's one of the endless mysteries of this place. Though I suspect by the time we cross into the northlands, we'll know more than any scholars in the kingdom."

"Yeah, I guess we will," Clary said with a smile.

When they reached the wagon, Clary climbed up to her spot on the side platform where Sir Rorian used to sit. She had taken it upon herself to assume this duty, and no one had objected. When she wasn't watching the prisoner, Garrett would take over. It seemed that having something to do was the only thing that kept him from falling apart these days, and in doing so he was helping Clary as his master had instructed.

Even Sheckem had seemed changed after the events of that night. He no longer fought back against them or shouted insults at Clary. In fact, the old Varhallan was silent, for the most part. Clary was not sure what had caused this sudden change, but it was welcome.

Clary would be sure to apologize to Feryl at their next stop. He would be walking ahead of the wagon to keep an eye out, so she wouldn't have the chance for a while. For now, she would just sit and think. They spent a lot less time taking breaks, in order to maintain their lead over any possible pursuers. Clary felt bad for pushing their bull-drages – whom they had taken to calling Thump and Bubbles – so hard lately, but they had no choice. It wasn't so bad, since Clary had realized that her healing magic could be used to sooth the creatures and aid in their recovery each night. Hilda even made attempts to use her empath abilities to keep the creatures as calm and relaxed as possible, when she wasn't working with Terra on her newly-discovered powers. With these advancements in their efficiency, they were able to cover more ground than anyone would have expected.

Clary enjoyed her time on the side platform each day. She liked having the time to herself. Privacy had been a rare commodity on their journey. Wandering off on one's own was too dangerous to risk, so everyone usually had to have someone else with them at all times. Here, however, Clary had time to herself where she could just enjoy the ride and even practice the occasional spell or two. She may have been struggling with her Fjoren magic, but she found the common Belderanian spells which Hilda had taught the group were much easier to grasp. Today she decided to work on the first two spells that they had learned together as the wagon kicked into motion.

"As one day, all things shall lose their form before the power of time, so you shall become weightless before me," she chanted under her breath, stretching her hands toward the sand. Just as it had done so many times before, a ball of sand rose before her. She would try to hold it for as long as she could while they moved along, until all the sand trickled away. This was the most basic of levitation spells. The goal was to practice the incantation out loud, learning how she felt about each part of the sentence, until she could invoke the same emotions and feeling while reciting the incantation in her head. Eventually, once she mastered it, Clary would be able to use this spell without speaking even a word. Gerald and Terra, who didn't have to worry about things like extra combat training or watching prisoners, had much more time to practice these spells and had each managed to reduce the lengths of incantation required to perform the spell. Gerald could do the same spell, only saying, *"Become weightless before time and me,"* and Terra only needed to say, *"Become weightless!"*

and she could levitate almost anything. They could both also hold up much heavier objects than Clary could.

Clary wasn't completely left behind, as she had surpassed them both on the first defensive spell that they had learned. As the last grain of sand fell from her levitation spell, she decided to practice this second spell. Though the usual incantation was, *"May the force of the gods' divine winds aid me against my enemies, repelling them a thousand times over,"* all Clary needed to chant was, *"Divine wind!"* and a concussive force shot forth from her hands, blasting a hole in the ground and shooting sand up into the air. The other two seemed to struggle a bit more with that spell. Clary supposed that her combat experience so far had helped her to become more in tune with the emotions necessary for combat magic. *Now if only I could get my Fjoren magic to work that well, then we'd be in business,* she thought.

As if he had been reading her mind, Sheckem spoke for the first time in weeks. "I don't understand you, she-demon. You seem to have figured out that bit of children's magic so easily, yet you still struggle to use the powers that infest your own blood."

"Oh yeah? And what would a Varhallan know about Fjoren magic?" she shot back, unsure whether his statement had been an insult or not.

"Far more than you know, and far more than that big stupid monkey who has been failing at training you knows. Don't underestimate the Varhalla. We have been fighting and killing your kind for millennia," he said proudly.

"Killing someone isn't the same as knowing them," Clary retorted.

"Are you so sure?"

Clary had no idea what he meant. Not only that, but this was without a doubt the most pleasant conversation she had ever had with the Varhallan.

When she didn't speak, Sheckem answered for her. "To defeat one's enemy, you must know them better than you know yourself. To know them better than yourself, you must face them as much as possible. I've fought with your demon race more times than I can count and killed even more than that. I can tell you that you cannot truly know someone until you have crossed blades with him."

"What does that mean?" It almost seemed as though this Varhallan, who hated everything about her, was trying to be nice in his own way and actually help her.

"You really are a pathetic race. You are weak even for a demon child and stupid to boot."

Yep, that sounds more like his usual self, Clary thought.

"Very well, I shall explain my meaning, so that even a brat like yourself could understand. No doubt you have been taught that magic is made possible through four things: emotion, control, scripture and recitation."

"Well, not in so many words, but yes, basically," she admitted.

"Scripture, the words which you draw in the air with your fingers, and recitation, the words you speak, are so self-explanatory that even you seem to be able to grasp it. And as I just saw, in your exchange of words with the large monkey boy, you clearly have intense emotions to capitalize on. So the part you need to focus on is control."

Clary wanted to slap him for the constant insults peppered into his explanation, and his jab at her fight with Feryl, but she was so desperate to control her powers that she shrugged it off. "But I was told that Fjoren magic works by letting your anger run wild."

"I suppose that in a sense, yes, it could be put that way. But just as your powers involve fire, you must remember that only a controlled flame is useful to its wielder. While rage is part of the equation for any Fjoren magic, it is in controlling and directing that rage that you will find power."

He said this simply, as if it cleared things up, but all it did was make Clary more confused. She tried to hide her confusion, but it didn't get past him.

He sighed. "I wonder why I even thought someone like you would be able to comprehend such a thing. To put it in terms that a beast such as yourself could understand, you need to find out what your rage is for."

"What my rage is for?"

"Yes, its purpose. It is different for everyone. That boy uses his rage for a different purpose than you will. It is up to you to find that out."

"But how do you know all this? How could you possibly know how Fjoren magic and emotions work?"

"How? I would think that would be obvious, demon." He smiled. "I know because our ancient Varhallan magic works in the same way as yours."

Clary couldn't believe what she was hearing. She'd been struggling to figure out her powers for the entire journey, and the entire time he'd been sitting there, laughing at her ineptitude safe in the knowledge that he could have taught her very easily.

"So why are you telling me this now?" she asked. "I thought you hated me and all of the Fjorendel."

"Oh, but I do, little demon. Don't think that has changed. I just do not like being in anyone's debt. It is unbecoming of a higher being such as myself. Don't feel special. We even reward our animals when they have done something useful." With that, Sheckem turned his head away from her as though to say, "I am done talking with you."

Clary consider pressing him further, but decided against it. She knew why he had helped her. In his own weird way, he was saying thank you for jumping in front of Ingrum's dagger that night. Sure, his speech had been filled with insults and crude language, but one couldn't expect much more from someone like Sheckem. *Baby steps,* she thought.

Before she could say thank you, someone called from the front of the wagon. "Hey everyone, come out here! You've got to see this! It's amazing!" It was Hilda. Apparently she had stuck her head out of the wagon door to see how things were going outside when she spotted it.

Clary looked in the direction they were heading to see what Hilda was talking about. She didn't even have to ask. Coming into view in the sky far ahead were clouds – but something was strange about them. They were grey and heavy, unlike anything they had seen in the rest of the desert. In the Arid Sea one was lucky to even see a small wisp in the sky. Still, though, the density of these clouds was not the only thing that appeared strange. What made them amazing was the fact that they all seemed to stop at a specific point, as though there was an invisible wall that separated them from the burning, cloudless, blue sky above the desert. This wall of clouds stretched as far as the eye could see and the separation of them from the blue sky also never seemed to end.

As the hours went by and they drew nearer and nearer to this anomaly, it only became more apparent that this weather pattern was not a natural occurrence. They concluded that it was something that had to be magically influenced. Beneath the clouds it was snowing. They could see a mountain range and forests glazed in white powder. It was a far cry from the flat desert, where the closest thing one could find that even resembled mountains were sand dunes. Furthermore, despite the snow they could see, the burning sun still hung above them, and the temperature had not lessened even slightly.

When they arrived at this great divide, it was all the more magnificent to behold. They pulled the wagon up just before the point where the snow started. Everyone exited to have a look. Clary couldn't believe her eyes. Here she was, a stone's throw from snow, yet she was sweating from the heat in the air. The snow was piled up to knee-level, but at a certain point it stopped as though some sort of giant invisible glass wall was holding it in place.

Feryl was the first to try anything. He walked up to the invisible wall and slowly stuck out his hand. It passed through with no resistance, and Feryl jumped.

"What? What's wrong?" Harvel said, rushing to his side.

"Nothing. It's cold," Feryl said, astounded. He grinned.

After that everyone wanted to try. One by one they stepped up to where the desert ended and the snow began. They stuck their arms into it, each surprised at the frigid air. Clary was the last one to stick her arms through. She couldn't believe it. She could almost cry. It was freezing, but the cold was welcome. For so long, she had feared that she would die in that desert, hot and dehydrated, but now she was actually feeling cold. As she looked in either direction she could see no point where the snow and sand mixed. It was as though someone had drawn a line and separated the two.

"I guess you have your answer, then."

"What? Oh! Valen!"

He had come up next to her – she didn't know how long he had been standing there, she had been so lost in thought.

"I guess the Arid Sea really was cursed," he said, looking up to where the sky was split between snow clouds and scorching desert sky.

"Yeah, and this must be the point where the curse ends."

"That makes us the leading experts then, doesn't it?" Their eyes met and they both laughed.

Just then Clary felt herself shoved from behind and she went flying forward, landing face first in the snow. She screamed as the temperature fell sharply, and the snow got into her clothes. She jumped up and turned to see her attackers, Hilda and Terra, standing behind her on the desert side, laughing.

"Oh, you think you're clever, do you?" Clary shouted. She reached down, grabbing a handful of soft white snow, and packed it into a ball. "How do you like this?" she said, throwing it at them. But as the snow reached the point between desert and forest, it flattened and fell to the floor, unable to cross the border into the Arid Sea. This failed attempt made them burst out into even more laughter. Not to be outwitted, however, Clary took this opportunity to reach out and grab both of them, pulling them into the snow with her, where they would be in range of her snowball attack.

The three of them launched snowballs back and forth for a while, and before long Harvel, Gerald, Valen and Garrett joined in. Harvel even managed to pull Edgrum and Feryl into the fray. Sir Ellerbe, who was keeping an eye on Sheckem, watched and laughed. It was such a simple and childish game, but to those who had suffered for so long in the desert, it was a gift from the gods, a sign of hope, just as the Varhallan compound and the wagon had been; things that brought back a sense of normalcy. For the first time since Sir Rorian's death, they were enjoying themselves and having fun.

They played in the snow until their fingers went numb and decided that they should return to the wagon for robes and better clothing. Clary soon learned that she could only get cold to a certain degree; her temperature-control abilities kicked in when the effects of the snow and icy air became low enough to cause injury. She could feel the cold, but frostbite and hypothermia were not an issue for her. Still, she decided to don the robes and furs that they had in the wagon for the sake of comfort.

They prepared swiftly for their ascent into the Fjorenlands. Harsgard would be the first major city when approaching the Fjorendels' nation from the west. Once they reached the city, they knew all would be well. No matter how many soldiers the Exiles sent – and Feryl had assured them that it would not be the entire army that had been with the caravan – they would not be able to take an entire Fjoren city. On top of that, any Varhalla that might be chasing them would be at a disadvantage, as their sand magic would be limited in that terrain. Lastly, they knew that they would be safe from any more dangerous monsters like the sand rovers.

Unfortunately, however, the Arid Sea was not finished with them. Just as Clary was relishing their luck, Hilda dropped to her knees right in front of her.

Clary rushed to help her up. "Hilda! What's wrong? Are you okay?"

"Y-yes, I'll be fine, but we've got a problem," she replied, clutching at her head.

"What's going on?" Harvel asked, as he and Valen made their way over.

"I can sense a lot of emotion. It's many, many people. They're still pretty far away but the fact that I can sense them from here means that there are a lot of them. I can sense a lot of bloodlust."

Valen looked back into the desert, but he couldn't see anyone. "How close?"

"I can't be sure, but I can tell you that once Terra starts sensing them, then we are in trouble," she warned.

They all looked at Terra. She shook her head.

"Alright, everyone! We need to leave now! They're on our tail!" Harvel shouted. They all quickly packed into the wagon as Hilda started up her magic steering again. For a moment Clary had almost mistaken Harvel's commands for someone else's. It was strange how much like the old knight he was beginning to sound. She didn't have time to dwell on this, though. She hopped up on her usual platform, handing some extra blankets and robes to Sheckem.

After they ascended for about an hour or so, there was another call from Harvel. Clary hadn't even noticed, but he had been sitting on top of the wagon with Terra at his side the whole time, watching the horizon with a spyglass that he had found among the wagon's supplies.

"I can see them! Look there!"

Clary looked back, trying to see whatever it was that he had spotted. "I see them! Oh no, there are so many!"

They had already ascended far above the level of the dunes, and Clary could see for miles. Their pursuers were just specks, but as they emerged from between a range of particularly large dunes, it was clear that this was a small army, and that they were headed straight for them, fast.

"Are they Exiles or Varhalla?" she asked the commander.

"Looks like both, and that's not all – they have gandovors."

"What? No! We'll never outrun them!" Clary said, panicking. With the speed of the army following them versus the slow-moving wagon that they were riding, it was almost certain that they would be overtaken before they could reach Harsgard.

"We don't have much of a choice," came Feryl's voice from behind her. He had been walking in front of the wagon, keeping watch and helping with navigation. "We'll just have to pick up the pace."

"Harvel, I'm so scared. I can feel them," Terra said, burying her face in his chest. "It's something like excitement from them, but it's dark and morbid."

"I feel it too," said Hilda, who was sitting in the driver's seat, helping with the steering. "That's bloodlust… overwhelming bloodlust. I haven't felt anything like this since the sand rovers showed up."

Just as she said this, something miraculous happened. At the base of the mountains, where the sand and snow collided, the sand started to move and shift in a very familiar way. Suddenly, large spikes began to burst from the sand. Clary and the others were in awe at what they were witnessing.

"But that's impossible!" Clary shouted. "How could that happen twice?" She gasped in disbelief as the leviathan slowly made its way in the direction of the pursuit force.

"Hahaha!" Sheckem doubled over laughing. "I cannot believe this!"

"What's so funny? What do you know?" Harvel demanded.

"To think you had such powerful empaths here among you. I had no idea they were this attuned."

"What has that got to do with anything?" Clary asked.

"Little demon, do you know why there are almost no empaths among the Varhalla?" Sheckem asked, to no response. "Because the king decreed that it is a royal privilege to be one. Any child discovered to be an empath is executed upon discovery."

"That's horrible!" Terra shouted. "Why would he do something like that?"

"Because, children, the king maintains his control of the great desert beasts with this ability. Apparently, your two little emotional mages have garnered favor and protection among the leviathans. You were safe the moment you crossed into their territory. I cannot believe I didn't see it before. A millennia here, yet this desert never ceases to offer new surprises."

All Clary and her friends could do was stare in awe as the old Varhallan's former comrades and the Exiles scattered to avoid the massive field of poisoned spines that lay before them. It would not be enough to finish them off, but now the group would have enough time to reach the gates of Harsgard without being captured. Finally, after all this time, they were safe from their pursuers.

Chapter 22

The Harsgard of Feryl's memory was an amazing and brilliant city. It was not as sophisticated as the capital of Belderan, nor as large as the port city of Thandessa which he had come to call home for so many years, yet still it had a beauty which he felt outshined the other two cities. Feryl had not actually grown up in the city, but he had been there quite a few times as a child with his father, Balthazar. It was the meeting place where all clans of the Fjorendel gathered each year.

The Fjorendel had no formal king; instead they had a council of earls, hailing from the scattered villages throughout their lands. These villages were each comprised of multiple clans who had banded together ages earlier and established homes in the Fjorenlands. Balthazar was one such leader, which meant he had often been required to make trips to Harsgard for the Congress of Earls. He always brought his family along with him.

More than anything, Feryl remembered marveling at the sheer scale of the place. It wasn't large in population or size, but the height of its features was a marvel to behold. The city was set between two large black mountains, which resembled manmade towers rather than geological formations. He had always been astounded at the grand wooden gates which connected these two massive spikes. He remembered his father telling him that they were built by giants, who ripped out enormous trees and banded them together with iron. He believed his father to this very day, for he could not imagine any other way in which such an intimidating structure could have been constructed. Even the buildings within Harsgard appeared to have been made for giants. The structures were built as though their occupants were expected to be at least twice the size of even the tallest men.

Now, years later, as he faced the great city once more, he found himself saddened and confused to find that the giants' craftsmanship had fallen to ruin. The great wooden gates were ripped open on one side, burnt and rotting after years of neglect. Feryl's heart sank as he observed what was left of the unbreakable fortress of Harsgard, which he had so loved. He couldn't imagine what had happened. The idea that any force was great enough to destroy such a powerful Fjorendel stronghold was unthinkable.

"This is amazing!" Gerald gasped, as they passed through the fallen gates. "I've never seen walls like this. They must be two— no, at least three times the height of the gates around the capital. Ouch! Hey, what was that for?"

Terra had elbowed him in the ribs. "Seriously? Not the time," she whispered to him.

"What do you— Oh, right… sorry," he responded as Terra gestured towards Feryl, who was walking a short way ahead of them. Though Feryl noticed their unsubtle exchange, he paid it no mind. His thoughts were preoccupied elsewhere.

The devastation in the boy's eyes was apparent, or at least as apparent as emotions could be with Feryl. He was usually so stoic around the others, but even the great Chained King couldn't completely hide his emotions in the face of such a tragedy. As they entered the city proper, it was evident that it had been years since anyone had lived there. There were signs of battle everywhere. Most of the buildings had long since burned and crumbled from where they had been set ablaze. Arrows and weapons remained where they had stuck years earlier, rusted and rotting. Snow and ice covered every visible surface, something that would never have been allowed during its reign.

As they continued toward the great drinking hall and gathering chamber at the center of Harsgard, there was no noise other than the slight wind that passed through the city streets. To experience such silence in a large city was chilling. There was no sign of life anywhere.

A sense of nervous tension was beginning to grow the more time they spent there. They had traveled all this way to seek asylum in this ancient fortress, and had expected a warm welcome with fresh food and drink, warm beds and, eventually, a guarded escort back to Belderan. Clary seemed particularly distressed by the current predicament. In previous days as they traveled through the Arid Sea, she'd often spoken to Feryl of how excited she had been to learn about her heritage and to meet others from her clan who might aid her in controlling her powers. Instead, they had found only death and decay, an empty city where they were now trapped. Still, for Feryl's sake she remained quiet, giving him time to process what he was seeing.

"What do you think happened?" Edgrum asked as they continued forward. "I mean, obviously there was some sort of attack, but this is on the scale of a full-blown war."

"I'm not really certain," Harvel replied. "Whatever this was, it couldn't have been recent and still gone unnoticed. If there was a war, then surely we would have heard something about it in the capital."

"I wouldn't be so sure," Valen cut in. "The Fjorendel have always been extremely reclusive. Occasionally some of their better warriors would be given out to Belderanian militias to show support as allies, but we never had much open communication with them until Balthazar and Cartus joined up. When that went south, father said that they shut themselves off even more than they had before the two made their names. It's been a long-standing policy to allow the Fjorendel to govern their own lands as they pleased. Apparently many generations ago, one of my ancestors made an attempt to take the Fjorenlands and suffered an overwhelming defeat."

"The Fjorendel are that strong?" Edgrum asked, clearly surprised to hear that these mountain people could reject the might of Belderan.

"Yes, they are incredibly strong warriors, but that wasn't all. They understand the harsh terrain here better than even the animals do. Any time he made an attempt to push into the mountains the Belderanian army would experience heavy losses in the ice and snow. Those who didn't succumb to the conditions were left completely exhausted and malnourished due to the lack of resources in the area. On top of all of that, it was so hard to maintain formation when pushing through the mountains that the Fjorendel were able to pick the invading soldiers off only using small tactical groups. The only way to attack without running into the harsh terrain would be to enter from the west as we just did – and that great gate was considered impenetrable when it still stood."

"Yes, it was," Feryl said, his expression becoming sadder by the second. "It was unimaginably strong. Makes it even harder to believe that it was somehow broken through."

"But it wasn't broken through," said Terra from the back of the group.

"What are you talking about?" Sir Ellerbe retorted. "Didn't you see that huge entrance we walked through? That was the gate."

"No… Well, I mean yes it was, but that's not what I meant," Terra replied, to confused looks. "That big door up there, it looked like it was blown up from the inside. As if it got pushed outward from the inside, not from the outside in."

The knights looked back at the giant structure, still visible even this far into the city. She was right – they had been too distracted by the destruction to notice that it was blown outward, not inward. At first glance, the wall had appeared to have simply collapsed in on itself, as though it had been set ablaze and rammed through. Upon further inspection, it did seem to be leaning outward.

"We'll have to figure that out later. For now I want to search the main hall. We should be able to find some information about what happened here," Feryl said as they arrived at the large central structure. "Or at the very least we might be able to figure a way out of this mess."

The central drinking hall was large and constructed from black stone. Its great wooden door seemed to have been modeled after the city's giant gate. The only differences were the size of it and the massive set of antlers that stuck out above the center. They appeared to have been taken from some kind of deer or elk, but they were many times the size of normal antlers. Clary thought that the creature that carried them must have been half the size of a warship.

Feryl ascended the steps and pushed open the large wooden doors, revealing the remains of what looked to have once been an extravagant and warm mead hall. There were burnt remnants of pelts and other animal-based furniture everywhere. Tables and chairs had been thrown about and most appeared destroyed. Barrels of whiskey, mead and ale were still laid out from whatever event had been happening right before the attack, though they had become frozen and rotten over time. More terrible than these sights, however, were the bodies. Most of them were mummified, frozen solid in the same positions they had died in. The majority of the dead appeared to have been violently thrown to the outer parts of the room, where they now lay. This was the first chance any of the group had to really see any of the residents of the city, as most of those outside were buried in layers of snow.

"It looks like they were having some kind of party when they died," Sir Ellerbe suggested. "I don't think the people in here knew they were under attack."

"But that's not possible," Feryl replied. "They would've had to notice something. This is too far from the gate for any attackers to have made it here without causing a stir."

"Unless they mistook the enemy for an ally," Valen suggested.

"You think they were betrayed?" Edgrum asked.

"Maybe. Hard to say."

"Here, let me get some light going in here so we can actually see what we're looking at," Clary offered, grabbing an old lamp. "Look! This still seems to have some oil in it." Starting the lamp up with her glowing fingers, she walked toward one of the walls, which still bore a few torches. As she walked around igniting what torches were still viable, the illumination slowly began to reveal the truth.

"What in the blazes could have caused that?" Sir Ellerbe asked, pointing at a large crater in the middle of the hall. Now they knew what had thrown the other bodies around in such a way.

"It looks like some sort of bomb blast." Valen said. "But how could someone have detonated something like that in the middle of a party without anyone stopping them? Think it was some kind of magic?"

Sir Ellerbe knelt down to inspect the blast site. "Nah, it looks like more of the conventional sort. A barrel or box of flammable powder or liquid."

"They probably dropped it from the ceiling. The platforms up there are accessible from the roof. Used to be used for adjusting the light fixtures and decorations," Feryl said. "This wasn't the only one either. I noticed similar signs on many of the buildings on the way over. Whoever this was must've set bombs like this all over the city. It looks like it was someone who knew the place well. It had to be some kind of betrayal. They set off a bomb of some kind in the midst of a welcoming celebration, at the same time as others throughout the city."

"But who were they welcoming?" Clary asked.

"I can't be sure. There are only Fjorendel bodies in here."

"Do you think it was some kind of civil war? Or perhaps it could've been a coup or something," Ellerbe suggested.

"Yeah, that could explain why we hadn't heard about it," Edgrum added.

"Not likely," Feryl responded. "If it were, they would've taken the city for themselves. It would just be under different leadership. No Fjorendel would ever abandon the great gate of Harsgard like that. And if that were the case, I'm sure the new power would have informed your people immediately as well. Besides, look. All of the earls' seats at the council table have bodies in them. If one of the clans was turning traitor, then they wouldn't have killed their own earl." He gestured toward the long table at the head of the room, which was raised up on a stage so that whoever was sitting at it would be able to watch over the entire hall. There were several large chairs at the table, each with the body of a former earl of a different Fjorendel village. Their throats had been slit, their faces still frozen in expressions of complete shock as though they had been attacked from behind.

"What's that?" Clary asked, pointing to a large set of armor chained up on the wall, behind the central chair. It was large and made of a dark, shining metal. Fierce and terrifying, it was covered in what Clary recognized as Fjoren runes of protection. It was also adorned with a heavy fur cape that hung around the shoulders.

"It's the armor of the elected head of the Council of Earls," Feryl answered. "My father's armor."

"But if they weren't trying to take over, then what was this?" Ellerbe asked, still focused on the mystery of the city's tragic fall.

"It was genocide," Feryl answered coldly. "And I know the bastard that did it, too."

He walked up to the seat at the center of the earls' table, where it appeared that the head of the council would have sat. The body in this place appeared to be as well-preserved as all of the others. The only difference was that the head of the council was leaning over onto the table, where he had fallen forward at the time of his assassination.

"This was my uncle Bethel. He was elected to lead the Congress of Earls in my father's stead while he was away fighting for the King's Militia," Feryl explained.

He lifted the body upward into the sitting position. There were gasps of shock from all around the room.

"By the gods!" Ellerbe exclaimed in disgust.

"Is that a hand print?" Edgrum asked, covering his mouth.

"What the hell could have done something like that?" Valen asked.

"The Treacherous King," Feryl said. "This is his ability."

"What kind of ability does something as gruesome as that?" Harvel asked.

"The cursed kind," Feryl answered bluntly.

Bethel's body had been horribly disfigured from the top of his forehead all the way down to his naval. It appeared as though something had eaten away at his flesh, starting at a large hand-shaped indentation on top of his face. It was as though his body had decayed over the course of time, only something was off. If it weren't for the perfect preservation of all of the other bodies, one might have assumed that this was the case with Bethel's body too, but it didn't add up. There was a pattern to this decay, and the flesh was frozen in place. If the conditions were such to promote this type of breakdown of the flesh, then it would have done the same to the other bodies as well. Even those that had been ripped apart by the bomb had not decayed in such a manner. What was more, it wasn't only Bethel's skin and muscle that had dissolved; the bone also seemed to have melted away.

"Balthazar and Cartus weren't the only Fjorendel to fight in the King's Militia back when it turned into the Exiled Regiment. If they were, then they might have been able to quell the rebellion."

"So you're saying that some other Fjorendel from the Exiles did this," Clary concluded.

"Yeah, and not just any Exile either," Feryl answered. "This was the work of the Treacherous King."

"What? The Treacherous King is a Fjorendel?" Clary asked in shock. "But my father never told me anything about another powerful battle mage being a soldier in the militia."

"I'm not surprised. It probably would have been far too painful for him, especially in regards to that one."

"What do you mean?" Clary demanded.

"You probably heard that before the Treacherous King rose up in rebellion against Balthazar and Cartus, he was Cartus' protégé and right hand. But what most people don't know was that before all of that, he was Cartus' ward."

Clary couldn't believe what she was hearing. It was surprising enough to find out that her father was the legendary battle mage, Cartus, but now to find out that his own ward had been the one to betray him and form the Exiled Regiment... It was so much to take in.

"But I've never heard of any power like this, even in my studies of the Fjorendel," Valen said.

"That's because his power is considered a curse among the Fjorendel," Feryl explained.

"You're saying an entire Fjorendel clan is considered cursed because of their powers?" Harvel interjected. "That seems a bit odd."

"No, it's not a clan. The powers he possesses belong to no clan in particular. It's like a sickness that occurs in the Fjorendel. It appears maybe once every other generation. Sometimes it takes even longer than that. It's a very rare power, and it is believed that those who possess it are cursed because it's usually followed by great calamity within the nation."

"So what exactly is the power then?" Clary asked.

"It's hard to explain. I've only seen him use it a few times myself. The Fjorendel called it the power of pestilence," Feryl replied to further looks of confusion. "From what I've seen he can make anything he touches decay and rot away instantly – though I've heard he can do more than that. He also maintains the abilities of the clan that he was born into."

"And what clan was that?" Valen asked.

"The Night's Bane clan."

"Night's Bane? Who are they?" Clary asked.

"I've read about them," answered the prince. "Pretty nasty group of mages. I've heard that they sweat venom and breathe poison."

"Exactly. They've altered their bodies to be completely toxic weapons. To make things worse, they are impervious to all other forms of poison. They were feared as warriors even among the Fjorendel, but they were also a very kind and intelligent clan as well."

"So, you're saying that not only can you not touch this Treacherous King, but he can't be poisoned either," Valen surmised.

"Exactly," Feryl answered. "You even have to worry about breathing the same air as him if he gets too close. That's why he was able to run off even Balthazar and Cartus."

"I can't believe such a powerful combination of magic exists," Hilda said in disbelief. "It sounds like it shouldn't even be possible."

"I know, but unfortunately it is," Feryl said darkly.

"But if my father was from the Firedrake Clan, then why was he looking after a Night's-Bane?" Clary asked.

"Well, like I said, his powers are considered cursed, and for good reason. I remember hearing stories about him as a child. His father died a few weeks before he was born, during a skirmish with some Varhalla at the border. On the day of his birth, his powers killed his mother. After that, no one was willing to even go near the child, let alone raise him. Cartus, though, as I'm sure you know, was kinder than most. He took him in without a second thought and raised him as his own."

"That explains the name," Valen said. "Can't think of anything much more treacherous than that."

"That's so sad," Terra added. "Do you think that he was the one who did this?"

"Absolutely. It's unmistakable. The only question is how," Feryl said, still examining the corpse. "He had to have been the one who attacked, but I don't understand how he could have caught them so off guard like this."

"I know this is hard for you Feryl," Valen interjected, "but we are going to have to address it later. Right now we have to figure out what we are going to do about the Exiles. That leviathan may have cut them off back there, but it most likely didn't stop them entirely. They probably just went around it, so we don't have much time."

"No, you don't have *any* time!" came a crazed shout from the shadows behind the earls' table.

At that moment a large mass of wood sprung forth from the crater where the bomb had gone off, as though a tree had grown in mere seconds. Its branches pushed outward, enveloping everyone in the room, trapping them one by one. The only one out of range was Feryl, who was still up on the stage. Then, behind him, a smaller tree started growing upward and wrapping itself around his legs.

"Careful!" he shouted as it began wrapping up his torso. "This is Fjoren magic, the caster must be nearby!"

"I'll see if I can sense him," Hilda shouted as she struggled with the branches entangling her.

"Oh, now I don't think yer gonna' be needin' to search me out, you filthy Varhalla," shouted a large man, stepping out into the open. He was tall and emaciated looking, with long black and hair and a beard, both as matted and dirty as his clothes. The more frightening and unusual aspect of his appearance was that from his forearms down, his arms seemed to be made of wood, and were covered in bark. One of these tree-like limbs was reaching towards Feryl, stretching and growing until it wrapped around his throat.

"Kill them! Kill them! Kill them! Kill the filthy monsters! Ha ha ha ha!" The man sounded completely deranged as he talked to himself.

Fortunately, however, he hadn't counted on Feryl being a Fjorendel as well. Feryl's body expanded as he activated his powers. To the surprise of the strange wood-man, he broke through his restraints quickly, then leapt forward striking the stranger square in the jaw with his massive fist. As their attacker flew backwards onto the ground the plants that he was controlling began to release the others. It seemed that the force of Feryl's strike was enough to loosen his grip on his magic. The Chained King still wasn't finished, however; he jumped on the man and struck him two more times.

"Stop, please! I didn't mean it, I swear! I swear! I thought you were Varhalla!"

"Liar! We look nothing like Varhalla!" Feryl shouted, holding the crazed man by his throat.

"B-but you have a V-v-varhalla with you like the last ones d-did, so you must be Varhalla I think, I think, think, think." The man's way of speaking was strange. It was hard to tell if he was talking to Feryl or himself as he continued muttering under his breath.

"What are you talking about? Who were the last ones?" Feryl asked.

"The time when they blew up the city. Balthazar, Balthazar, Balthazar! His army came with the cursed boy and they l-l-let in the Varhalla. J-j-just like you and your Varhalla friend." As he spoke the man's eyes darted around the room, as though he was watching out for something. It appeared that he wasn't entirely sure what was reality and what wasn't. "They came here pre-pre-pretending to be friends. Everyone cheered as the great Balthazar and Cartus army walked through the great gate. Only no Balthazar or Cartus with army. Only cursed brat. Still, earls hold big party to welcome. Celebrate f-f-friendship. Ha! Makes me laugh, it does. Then suddenly at night, everywhere explode during party! Even the great gate explodes! Then Varhalla come, we think the cursed one and his army will help Fjorendel fight, defend Harsgard. No, they help Varhalla. With everywhere on fire, it not possible to fight back. So many people dead in explosions while they sleep."

"So, it was the Exiles," Feryl concluded. "And you've been here since then?"

"Exiles? What's Exiles? No one's Exiles here. N-no, I don't know Exiles. We were attacked by the Belderan king's men. His militia. Balthazar's men. Balthazar the traitor. Traiter Balthazar. Balthazar the abandoner."

"You shut your mouth about my father before I rip your tongue from your head," Feryl shouted. "You don't know a damned thing."

Once again the man cackled. "Rips my tongue from the head he says. Rip, rip, rip Ha! I bet a good crunch noise that'll m-make."

By now the others had all managed to break free from his ensnaring tree branches and had gathered around Feryl.

"Feryl, ease up," said Valen, kneeling down beside him. "He's clearly mad. You're not going to get anything from him like that."

Realizing that he was inches from choking the life out of the man, Feryl calmed himself, loosening his grip and lifting him up. Now he spoke much more calmly than before. "Look, my name is Feryl. I'm a Fjorendel like you, from the Stone Giant Clan."

"Ha!" the man sneered. "Fjorendel, he says. That'll be the day, I says. No more Fjorendel left. Fjorendel is me and only me. Well, me and the cursed boy, but he is no true Fjorendel. And the young lord Feryl is gone. Gone, gone, gone, gone, gone. Just like the rest of his clan."

"What? You know me?" Feryl said in shock.

At this, the crazed man's eyes locked onto Feryl and he seemed to have a moment of clarity. "F-f-feryl? The young lord, come back to life? After all these years."

"Yes, I am Feryl, I swear. Who are you?"

"Wh-wh-who am I? I think the true young lord would recognize m-me of all people. Played together with the young lord many times I did, I did, I did. Got in t-t-trouble too for knocking over—"

"For knocking over the butcher's chicken coop when you were showing me how your magic had started to surface. You're Turly, aren't you? We stayed at your father's inn every time we visited Harsgard. You were a few years older than me, but we used to play together whenever I was here." Feryl was astounded. He couldn't believe what had become of the boy before him. "What happened to you?"

Turly's eyes began to water as he looked up at Feryl. "Young lord, young lord, is that really y-y-you?"

Feryl nodded, and then Turly sprung forward, wrapping his arms around him. "Praise the gods! They've brought someone back. They saved the young lord."

Feryl was shocked by Turly's reaction. He felt horrible for what had happened to him, but he was still weary of him. He may have been the innkeeper's son at one point, but now he was crazed. Feryl wasn't sure when his childhood friend might snap again and lash out.

"Turly, look, I'm glad to see you too, but we're in trouble right now, okay? We've got some Varhalla and other men called the Exiles coming after us. They are the ones you said did this to the city. We are going to need your help, okay? Is there any quick way out of here? I need you to concentrate now."

Turly was wincing. He seemed to be struggling to stay in the moment. "W-w-way out, young lord? N-n-no, all the escape tunnels are frozen over. Can't leave this time of year. Not without Firedrake Clan to keep the ice melted."

"Well that's convenient," Ellebe said. "Good thing we've got one of the last two members of the Firedrake clan with us."

"No, that's still no good," Feryl said coldly. "Even if Clary's powers were working fully, it'll take us days with just one Firedrake."

"Damn!" Edgrum exclaimed. "If that's true, then what do we do? There has to be another way out."

"No, there isn't," Feryl said, falling into despair as he continued. "The only way into this city is through the great gates that we already passed through, or the large tunnels at the rear end of the city. Those used to be maintained by Firedrake Clan members year round.

"So what do we do then? Just sit here and wait to be killed?" Valen asked, starting to panic.

"Calm yourself, prince. We shall do no such thing!" Harvel shouted.

"Are you suggesting we turn and face them?" Edgrum interjected. "There are loads of them. We'll never defeat that many."

Even the others were beginning to lose faith at this point.

"I know, but it might not be so bad," Harvel responded.

"Might not be so bad? What are you talking about?" Valen argued. "You saw for yourself, there's an army of them!"

"There *was* an army of them!" Harvel shot back, raising his voice against the prince in a way that was completely out of character for him. Everyone went silent. The air around the new commander was as it had never been before. In an oddly familiar tone, the young knight spoke in a way that commanded silence from his peers, garnering their full attention. "There were a great deal of enemies after us, yes. I'd estimate anywhere between eighty and a hundred, including the Varhalla, from what I could see. By even the best odds, we would have no chance against them in a fight under normal circumstances." He paused for a moment, registering his friends' confusion and fear. "But these are not normal circumstances."

"How do you mean?" Valen asked, having calmed down a fair bit at his most trusted advisor's words.

"Think about it. They may have had some gandovors, but they were mostly on foot. There's no way that all of them could have made it past the leviathan. Undoubtedly they will have lost a few men. Even if it's a minimal loss, it still means fewer of them to deal with. Next, they will be exhausted from the climb and the cold. We, on the other hand, will have had time to rest here in the city. Furthermore, we have the city itself and the great gate to help us."

"Yes, but the gate is broken. It won't be keeping anyone out anytime soon. So it's no help at all right?" Clary cut in, but it seemed that it was only she, Hilda, Terra and Gerald who hadn't grasped Harvel's meaning. All of the warriors had looks of understanding and excitement at the prospect he was suggesting. "Did I miss something?"

"Clary, fortress walls don't simply dispel enemy forces through sheer size alone," Harvel smiled. "There is much more to their fortification than that."

"Such as a high, protected point from which one can shoot arrows without worrying about being hit from below," Edgrum added.

"And ducts from which one could poor boiling oil," Ellerbe continued. "Would they still have any after all this time?"

"I can't see why they wouldn't. They used to store oil under the wall," Feryl replied.

"Exactly," said Harvel. "And that's not even our biggest advantage."

"What is?" Terra asked, excited to see Harvel in such confident command.

"Our greatest advantage is that they will never expect us to turn and fight them, not in a thousand years."

"How do you know that?" Valen asked, far from convinced.

"Because they don't know that we're stuck here." Harvel explained. "As far as they're concerned, we are going to continue through the city's back tunnels. It's not like the Varhalla would have any extensive knowledge of what happened in the city, and the Exiles were able to sack this place in one night. They have no idea how the seasons affect this place. For all they know, the tunnels are melted all year around. If we play this right, then we can get the jump on them. Separate them, surprising them with hot oil, and showering them with as many arrows as Edgrum, Terra and Gerald can loose – then we might be able to come out of this alive."

"But even if we manage to split them in half, they still have numbers on us, especially if they don't lose any to the leviathan. I mean there're only nine of us, a prisoner Varhalla, and a crazy tree-person," Valen cut in.

"Yes, but out of the nine people we have here, two are Fjorendel. If anything, they each count for a few men."

Clary blushed to hear Harvel say that. They all knew her powers weren't fully functional. But she didn't want to ruin Harvel's speech. It was stirring confidence in the others. Plus, it wasn't as though they had much other choice now. They would fight or let themselves be captured.

"We have three Fjorendel," came Feryl.

"What do you—"

"We have three, including Turly," he finished, but the others didn't look convinced. It was obvious that none of them really trusted the crazed Fjoren man. It was no secret at this point that he didn't have a stable grasp on reality. Feryl saw this in their faces, and turned to his childhood friend, who was still looking around as though he didn't know what was going on. "Turly, do you want to help us kill Varhalla?" he asked bluntly.

"Oh yes, yes, yes, please let me kill many Varhalla. I haven't eaten meat in w-w-weeks," Turly blurted out, snapping to attention.

"See?" Feryl smiled.

"Well, close enough, I guess," Harvel said. "Can't really turn down help at this point."

"Good, now let's start with the preparations," Feryl stated, before turning and walking back toward the stage.

"Where are you going?" Clary called after him.

"To get my armor. I'm going to need it."

<u>Chapter 23</u>

Clary sat leaning against a large pile of snow beside the great gate, where she had been posted to wait for the impending arrival of the Exiles and their Varhalla escort. Her location was the entrance to an alleyway which led to stairs leading to the top of the gate. She and the others had covered this entrance with snow and fallen debris from the surrounding buildings to hide it from the enemy. One of the most important advantages they needed to maintain was the perch at the top of the gate, which now housed Edgrum, Terra, Hilda and Gerald. From this strategic height, they would be able to launch arrows, attack spells and even heavy objects down onto the heads of the enemy without putting themselves in danger. They had spent a good amount of time gathering large icicles, old spears, swords, rocks and whatever other sharp, heavy things they could find within the ruined city, to lob at the Exiles. This would mean that the Exiles would be forced to focus on the sky whilst being attacked by those on the ground at the same time, rendering them distracted and defenseless. They had also managed to find oil in the storage rooms, which they had boiled ready to drop on the heads of the enemy as they passed through the downed portion of the gate. It was only two cauldrons full, though, as most of the containers had ruptured and cracked over the years, but it was better than nothing.

The gate not only served as a high point from which to attack the enemy, it also kept Terra and Gerald – who didn't have much in the way of fighting skill – out of the way. This also meant that they wouldn't have to worry about Gerald's injuries, which, while mostly healed, still gave him a limp that would most likely remain for the rest of his life. This didn't mean that he would be totally useless, though. He had become quite skilled at the few spells he had learned and could defend their position if anyone managed to make it up to their level. There was only one entrance to reach their position, and it wouldn't lend would-be attackers much room to maneuver or dodge. Clary laughed, thinking about how much she used to hate the annoying know-it-all boy that Gerald had been. She remembered how much they used to fight, and how satisfied she had been when Hilda had told her he didn't have the spirit to become a proper mage. Now she actually worried about him, and she was happy to have someone else from home at her side. When Clary had asked Hilda about Gerald's newfound powers, the mage told her that she suspected the arduous journey, coupled with the loss of his father and his near-death experience at the hands of a desert monster, had changed his spirit. She had sensed a shift in his spirit and his priorities. Clary, too, could tell that the boy had changed; she didn't need to be an empath to figure that out. In fact, she could detect differences in everyone in the group. None of them were the same bunch of kids that they had been back in Vinvale. If they were able to talk with the kids who partied and laughed and drank back during the festival the night of the attack on the village, they probably wouldn't have much in common. She and her friends had now seen too much of the world.

Clary was startled from her thoughts by the sound of hasty footsteps crunching in the snow. It was getting dark after their many hours of preparation and waiting, and they were expecting their pursuers to show up at any minute. Fortunately, however, these were not the sounds of an approaching Exile, or at least not any soldier currently in their ranks. Clary held up a glowing hot hand, illuminating the confined area.

"Using your all-powerful and ancient Firedrake Clan powers as torchlight?" Feryl said. Clary chuckled. "Better be careful or you'll end up sitting in a puddle."

"Hey, it's better than sweating myself to death in a desert," Clary said with a smile.

"You might be the only one with that opinion right now. The others are starting to miss the desert, but then I guess they don't have your temperature resistance, or a super-heated pair of hands to keep their fingers from freezing off."

Clary chuckled again. "So what do you need?"

"What? Oh yeah, right. I was just coming over to check on you, and let you know that everyone's all set." Feryl stepped into the light and sat down beside her.

As Clary got a good look at him, strapped into his father's armor, she couldn't help but recall the first time she had seen him dressed as the Chained King. The resemblance to his current appearance was strikingly similar. In the strangest way, it was oddly nostalgic. That had been such a traumatizing night, but when she had thought back on it over the course of their journey, she realized that it had been the second time Feryl had saved her life. He had been looking out for her even then, when they barely even knew each other.

"Couldn't get the chains off it?" Clary looked down at the various places where the armor had been chained up to its display in the Fjoren drinking hall.

"I might be able to. I hadn't really thought about it since I pulled it off the wall. I was in such a hurry, but it's alright. It's kind of better that way for me. I've fought wearing chains my entire life – no reason to stop now."

"It suits you." Clary said.

"The chains?" he said with a chuckle.

"No, the armor." She laughed too. "It seems like it was made for you. You look even better in it than the knights did in their royal armor."

"Oh, ha ha. Well, thanks." Clary couldn't see his face in the darkness, but she imagined he was blushing, if Feryl even could blush.

"But won't it be too tight once you activate your magic?" she asked, remembering how much bigger he grew when he used his abilities.

"No, not at all. This armor was specially designed for Stone Giant Clan members. It's a special metal that is affected by the user's magic. It'll grow with me. The armor I used back when I was still the Chained King was similar, though its iron was crude and the blacksmiths who made it couldn't quite figure out the Fjoren formula correctly, so it wasn't quite as easy to move in and it restricted me a lot."

"Is it really that special?" Clary asked, curious to hear more about the lives of her ancestors.

"I guess this set in particular is very well-made, but all Fjoren clans have their own developed techniques for building armor and weapons that accentuate their powers." Feryl suddenly became excited, as though he had remembered something obvious. He reached into his bag. "Speaking of which, I've found something I think you might find useful." After a few moments of shuffling through his posessions, he pulled something out. "I found this earlier when I was gathering supplies in the old armory, and packed it away for you, but we've been so busy that I hadn't the chance to give it to you. Here, I hope it fits."

As soon as Clary took the set of armor from him she could tell something was different about it. Its leather was amber colored and it was covered in Fjoren runes, just like Feryl's. "Is this Firedrake armor?"

"Exactly. It's made from the hide of a creature that lives up in the large volcanoes on the other side of the Fjorenlands where your clan lives. I can't remember what it's called, it's been so long, but it's already highly resistant to heat, and with Firedrake inscriptions protecting it, it won't melt even when you use your powers to their fullest. I know it's not as strong as their metal armors, but it's much more flexible, and can still ward off most things. I think it'll help." He seemed excited, as he sat there waiting for her response.

Clary didn't know what to say. It made her feel much safer knowing she had something to protect her. Unfortunately, her powers didn't lend themselves to protection and defense as Feryl's did, but she was happy he'd thought to prepare this for her.

"Thanks, Feryl, I love it. I'll put it on right now." She stood to don her new apparel. There wasn't much to it. Hard leather greaves, cuisses, kneepads and boots covered each leg from foot to hip, and a leather cuirass with pauldrons and matching bracers protected her upper body. A leather headband covered her forehead and cheeks, coming down the sides of her face and jaw. It all fit well over her clothes. She felt stronger just knowing that it was there.

"So… what do you think?" she asked, now that she was fully dressed.

"Wow, you look… perfect." Feryl said, his mouth agape. "I… I mean, it looks like it fits well. Definitely will help keep you safe in battle," he stammered.

"Thanks, Feryl," she giggled, sitting down next to him again. "I think I know what you mean."

They waited in silence until something that had been nagging Clary's mind for a while occurred to her. Here was Feryl, looking out for her again, making sure she was safe, protecting her before all else, and she still hadn't apologized for her behaviour. This boy never stopped caring for her even after she had said such terrible things. She wanted to say something, but she was nervous. If only she weren't so stubborn, it would be so much easier. She had always hated admitting when she was wrong, but even she couldn't deny how awfully she had treated him. Given the danger they were about to face, there was no guarantee that she would have another chance to speak her mind. She had to do it now, before it was too late.

"Look, I've been meaning to talk to you about earlier." she began.

Feryl looked up at her as though he wasn't sure of her meaning.

"You know, when I said all those horrible things."

"Oh you mean *then*," he said.

"Yeah, I mean then." She hung her head guiltily. "Look, the thing is—"

But he didn't let her finish. He smiled at her. "Clary, you don't need to say anything. I know you didn't mean it. After everything that happened, you were just upset. I know it's not your fault."

She couldn't believe it. After everything she'd done, he wouldn't even get a little mad at her. It was unfair. In fact, it actually made her upset with him.

"Damn it, Feryl!" she shouted, though still quietly enough that it wouldn't give them away. "It doesn't make any sense! I'm trying to tell you I'm sorry. I said such horrible things to you, but you still act like it was somehow your fault! Why are you so nice to me? Why do you do so much just for me? Nothing I did or said to you then was okay. Sure, I didn't mean any of it, but that only makes it worse. It means that I only said those things because I wanted to hurt you, and all you were trying to do was help me. So can't you just let me say I'm sorry? I'm sorry, Feryl, I'm so sorry!" She was right up next to him now, her head on his chest.

She realized she had been beating his chest and shoulders over and over again. Not to hurt him – she knew it wouldn't through the intensely durable armor he was wearing – but from frustration. She clutched her hand from the pain of smacking the metal repeatedly. "Say something. Say something, please."

Feryl simply sat silently, then put his arms around her gently. Once she had calmed down he loosened his embrace, then lay her down, placing her head in his lap, just as he had done on the first night they had met.

"Clary, I wasn't trying to deny your right to apologize. I'm sorry that I confused you. I know that high tempers run in our people's blood. That still doesn't excuse what you did. I'm just saying that I understand. But the truth is I already knew that you regretted what you said immediately after you said it. I knew you would apologize eventually and I even knew that you have been thinking of ways to say you were sorry ever since that moment. To be honest, even Valen told me to forgive you for some reason, though I'm not sure why. But it was already too late. I forgave you right away – though I won't lie, that temper of yours is the same as mine, so I needed some time to cool off as well." He gave a guilty smile.

"As for why I treat you the way I do," he continued, "to tell you the truth I'm not really sure myself. I've just wanted to protect you from the first time I saw you in that forest."

Clary looked up at him, making no attempt to hide her surprise. He had never really talked to her about that night. To hear him bring it up now of all times was completely unexpected.

"I was out trying to kill that monolith bear in order to make sure that the Exiles' cover wasn't blown. According to their protocol, I should've let you die there, and I definitely shouldn't have given you the last of my phoenix tears. I must confess, I was so scared to go against orders that I almost did leave you be. But the second I saw you, I was drawn to you. From what I've seen, you seem to have that effect on most people. Anyway, I didn't care anymore, even if they'd torture and kill me for it. I needed to make sure you were okay. I feel the same now as I did then. Even today I can't really explain why – I just feel that it's something I'm meant to do. After that night, I never thought I'd see you again. I was completely shocked when I found you there that night in that house. When I did, all I could think of was how I was going to get you out of there. When we captured you again, I was happy to be near you but still, I knew I had to make sure you were safe. When you freed me, my first thought wasn't about getting myself out, but about making sure you were safe. I never thought that somehow all that would lead to where we find ourselves today." He paused, as though considering everything that had happened in their time together all at once. "I guess the reason why I'm so kind to you all the time is because after everything that I did to you, and all of the pain that I caused you and your family, I am just happy that, in the end, I got to be your friend."

This was a conversation that they had needed to have for a long time, and the relief was evident in both of them. Clary was still processing the huge amount of information he had laid out before her. It was a lot, and she would have to think it over later if they somehow survived the night, but for some reason, right now the part that stuck out was when Feryl had said that he was happy to be her friend. It wasn't the statement itself that confused her, but rather the emotions that she felt upon hearing that they were just friends. For some reason, it stung, but she wasn't sure why. Did she want to be more than that? She didn't have time to consider it now. She had to respond.

Clary was so grateful to the boy that she wasn't sure what to say, but she did her best. "Thank you, Feryl. I don't know what I'd do without you, so just... Just promise you'll stay with me through all this."

He smiled. "So, you still want my protection, then?"

Clary shook her head. "No. I want to be the one to protect you in the future, for everything you've done for me. You can't always be the one saving everyone else, you know. Someone needs to look after you sometimes." It may have been her imagination, but she felt as though her hands were beginning to heat up and glow stronger than before.

"I guess I could try to stick around a little longer," he said.

The sun finally set, revealing an arctic sky filled with dancing lights of green, pink and an array of new colors that Clary would not have thought possible. Her jaw fell in amazement as she gazed upon the wonderous sight before her.

"Feryl, it's beautiful." she said.

"Yes, it really is," Feryl responded without looking up.

Before either of them could say anything more, Clary heard a whisper from nearby. "Feryl, is that you?"

Ellerbe came into view. He was panting. Clary presumed he had been running around, checking the positions where each member of the group was waiting.

"I've been looking all over for you!" he shouted. "We've spotted the Exiles. They've come within view of the gate. They should be here any moment!"

Clary and Feryl were already on their feet.

"Alright," Feryl said. "I've already checked to make sure that everyone's ready. Did you find a place to leave the wagon and Sheckem?"

"Yes," Ellerbe replied. "Harvel said it would be best to keep them stored together in the old stables next to where the inn used to be."

"Good, he should be safe in there. I doubt they'll have any reason to search back there. I'm sure if we don't make it out of this, he'll find something to cut his restraints with, and take the wagon," Feryl said. They had all been worried about what to do with the Varhallan earlier.

"What's to stop him from cutting himself loose and running?" Clary asked.

"I'm sure he won't try to escape right now, knowing he'd just find himself in the midst of a battle in which neither side will defend him." Feryl said, putting on his helmet. "He's already branded a traitor to the other Varhalla for letting himself be captured, and for helping us. Since he's committed no crime against Belderan, he should know his best chance to get out of here would be through the kingdom or by attacking us while we are weak – if we do somehow manage to make it out of this battle alive."

"I want to stay here with Clary," Feryl said. "There's a much better view of things from this position. From here I'll also be able to give her and the others up top the signal to get things started."

"Right, I'll leave it to you then." Sir Ellerbe said. He turned to leave, then paused. "I almost forgot to mention. It seems that we're in luck. Harvel got a good count this time through the spyglass. They've lost a good twenty men and about half of their Varhallan escort as well. They're down to about sixty or seventy. So let about thirty through before you give the signal."

"Great news. It's not much, but it'll help." Feryl said.

Ellerbe nodded in affirmation before departing for his own position.

All was silent for a while as they waited for the Exiles to arrive. The sky was perfectly clear, revealing a great sea of endless stars, coupled with the largest full moon that Clary had ever seen. The dancing lights in the sky lit the city as if it were early morning rather than the dead of night.

After a time in which the only thing Clary could hear was the thumping of her own nervous heart, she saw the light of torches appear through the gate and heard the shuffle of armor and weapons. This was followed very quickly by the appearance of the first of the Exiles. As they slowly marched through the opening in the great gate, Feryl felt the warmth of Clary's hand in his own. She was nervous, and so was he, but knowing that the other was there had a calming effect on both of them. Clary squeezed even tighter, and the warmth turned to heat. Feryl looked down and saw her hand glowing. Fortunately his armor protected his hand, but even so, it was still incredibly hot. He realized that Clary was no longer hot from fear or anxiety but from anger. Sitting atop a gandovor and surrounded by other Exiles was the man who had tortured her repeatedly for weeks, the worst possible person that the Exiles could have sent after them. It was Lieutenant Thymey.

It seemed that a couple of soldiers noticed the glow from Clary's hand in the alleyway and stopped to look. *Damn!* Feryl thought, hiding her hand behind his back. But it was too late.

"Wait a second, sir! I think I saw something over there," one of the men shouted, raising a spear to point toward their position.

Thymey held up his hand, signaling for the Exiles to stop. "You three, go have a look," he ordered. Then he continued talking to someone who Feryl couldn't see. "Second Lieutenant, we may have a spot of trouble here. Hold the others at the back, and tell them to be on guard."

Sproles, Feryl thought. *Of course he would be here. If he detects us then we're done for.* If Sproles went on guard and started listening, he might hear the others, or even the bubbling of the boiling oil. He might easily pull everyone back. Only a handful of Exiles had come through the gate. If they dropped the oil now, then they would only be able to take out a few, and would still be vastly outnumbered by a fully-aware army. They would lose their strategic advantage.

Even if the second lieutenant didn't figure them out, there was the more pressing concern – the group of Exiles were now approaching Feryl's location. He struggled to contain his panic. With so many eyes on his position, there was no way he could stop these men without giving everything away. He needed to think of something right now. He began to draw his sword, ready for the worst, but suddenly a loud shout from the other side of the courtyard drew the attention of all of the Exiles.

"You filthy traitors! Bringing Varhalla rats into Turly's city! Turly will kill you all! He will feast on your eyes tonight!"

The crazed Fjorendel had leapt out into battle on his own, his tree-like arms growing rapidly to become sharp branches that skewered the first few men before him. Apparently his first sight of the Varhalla after all these years had been too much for his feeble mind to bear, sending him into an insane rage.

"Mr. Sproles, it's an insane bark-skinned Fjorendel. Seems we missed one. Get the men moving but be on guard, there may be more." As Thymey called this order, the army began moving into the city at an increased pace, the front ranks surrounding the Fjorendel.

Turly was still sending his wood and tree magic into the enemy forces. His branches pierced some men and wrapped around others, strangling them and breaking their necks. His bloodlust and fury was a terrible sight to behold. Unfortunately, his onslaught wouldn't last forever. As the Varhalla made their way to the front of the formation, it became clear that the lone Fjorendel would soon be be outmatched. Each Varhalla carried large bags at their hips. As they began to work their magic, sand started to flow from the bags. The sand made its way through the trees and branches and began barraging Turly, beating him senseless, but still he stood, trying to fight. Even as it started to wrap around his neck, squeezing his throat, he would not let himself fall. However, despite his determination, he was unable to hit the Varhalla casters, who were far more experienced in battle.

It wasn't until Thymey took action that they were able to stop the man. He leapt off of his mount, landing on one of Turly's tree trunks, and made for him. As more of Turly's plants started shooting out, attempting to skewer the lieutenant as they had his men, Thymey bobbed and weaved, dodging every strike with perfect precision. Finally, he reached his target, and with one quick strike, lanced Turly in the center of his chest.

Turly froze immediately, dropping to his knees. It had been a perfect strike. Thymey kept his blade in his victim's chest, knowing that once he pulled it out from where it was lodged, the bark-skinned man would bleed out and die.

"Who are you? Are there any others with you? Tell me and I will let you die. Refuse and I will make sure that you suffer first."

"Others?" Turly asked. "There has only been Turly here for years. You followers of the cursed one and the filthy Varhalla have seen to that. Turly is the only Fjorendel left."

Thymey stared at Turly, trying to assess the veracity of his words. Interrupting this tense moment was a cry from one of the Varhalla, causing the lieutenant to flinch. He looked at the mage, who had gotten too close to one of Turly's plants. Another sharpened branch had shot out and pierced the Varhallan directly through the heart. When Thymey looked back at the Fjorendel before him, he could see that Turly had his hand raised in the direction of the one who had just died. Thymey evidently hadn't thought much of it while he was questioning Turly, believing him to be too near to death to muster up another attack. From where he was standing, it appeared to be simply a last reach for life.

"Tricky little one, aren't you?"

"Turly has finally killed the Varhalla. Turly has avenged the great Fjorendel. Ready... ready to die now finally," he wheezed. It was clear he had given all of his remaining energy toward exacting his vengeance.

"To think, the mistake of missing one Fjorendel beast all those years ago would have repercussions on us even now," Thymey said. "If only they'd let me kill the others when we catch up to them, then we'd truly be rid of your miserable race. Guess I'll just have to settle with you."

With that, he ripped his sword from Turly's chest, and the Fjorendel fell to the floor, limp. He died almost immediately.

The Exiles had ceased moving through the gate when the Varhalla made their move, as it would have been too crowded, but now they started to push through slowly. It seemed that Turly's outburst had caused just the distraction that the besieged group needed, and he had managed to take eight men, as well as one of the Varhalla.

"Thank you, Turly," Feryl whispered, watching as the Exiles made it about halfway through the gate. "Leave the rest to us."

Feryl pulled on a rope that hung between him and Clary. The other end was tied to a small stack of rocks atop the gate, that toppled over signaling Hilda and the others to commense the assault. Hilda, Gerald and Terra used their levitation spells in unison to lift the first of the two oil-cauldrons over the far side of the gap in the gates, while Edgrum grabbed onto a lever that would release the second one from their side. Then, all at once, they released, sending scalding hot oil down onto the Exiles below. There were screams of pain as men's skin melted from their bodies.

"Now Clary!" Feryl shouted.

With a great deal of fear, but not a single beat of hesitation, Clary reached down and touched a trail of oil that they had poured from the gateway to her position, igniting it. A wall of fire burst forth separating the Exiles outside of the Gate, from those within.

Their plan so far had been a success. Now the real fight was beginning.

Chapter 24

An attack? Thymey thought. *Are there more Fjorendel? No, that's not possible. We made sure to search the city thoroughly before we left. One mad Fjorendel I can believe, but not enough to attack a force this large.*

He stood paralysed with confusion as the dark entrance to the ruined city of Harsgard suddenly burst into a roaring blaze illuminating him and his men. There was shouting all around him as men started dropping like flies. He turned back toward the fallen great gate where the rest of his men should have been entering the city streets. In its place was a great wall of fire, engulfing at least ten of his soldiers.

"You there!" he shouted at one of his sergeants assigned to the forward platoon. "Gather the men into formation and—"

Before Thymey could even complete the order, the sergeant dropped to his knees and fell flat on his face. An arrow stuck straight up out of the top of his head.

Thymey looked around at the buildings, searching for a vantage point from which an arrow could have been launched to hit the man from directly above. Then another arrow fell, scratching his cheek. This time he had felt the angle of its trajectory.

"They're on the damned gate! Shields up!" he ordered. "Mr. Sproles!" he shouted, to no response. "Damn!" Only now did he realize that his forces had been separated and reduced to nearly half strength. Not only had the fire separated the men, but it had interrupted communication between himself and Sproles. Still, fortune seemed to remain in his favor. Whoever was orchestrating this attack had neglected to split the Varhalla's power from the main force. Their magic would provide enough strength to defend against a small-scale ambush such as this, at least until the fires died down and the other portion of their forces could make it into the city.

Beneath the roof of shields created by the Exiles, Thymey was able to calm himself long enough to survey the situation. His men surrounded and protected him as he peered through their ranks, trying to ascertain who was attacking them and from where. It seemed the ambushing force was smaller than he had initially thought. The Varhalla were engaging with enemies on either side. It was too difficult to make out their identities, but the attackers appeared to be human. From what he could tell, there were only a couple of them to his right. Perhaps three, give or take. From above he could see arrows, icicles, rocks and even old rusty weapons and tools dropping. It was spaced out, though, and couldn't have been the work of more than a few people, plus a mage shooting concussive bolts down into the fray. It wasn't an experienced mage, however, given the slow frequency of the attacks and the simplicity of the spells. Lastly, the lieutenant could see that a small number of the Varhalla were fighting some kind of large creature in the alleyway to the left of his formation. The figure moved further into the firelight, revealing a large, familiar face. *No… not a beast,* Thymey thought, *that's a man. It's—*

338

"It's the damned brats! It's the targets! We've found them!" He turned towards the Varhallan leader standing at the rear of his casters' formation, facing the former Chained King. "Marashal! We need to take those ones alive! Everyone, take as many of them alive as possible!"

Marashal had conjured a makeshift shield of hardened sand to protect himself from the archer above. He turned to face his Exile counterpart, furious at the notion that their enemy was to be permitted to live. "Alive? This cannot be allowed! These children have incurred the wrath of the Varhalla and must be executed immediately!"

"That's not the deal, mage! These prisoners are Exile property, and your king agreed that you would help us to capture them alive! They have information that is vital to our operations. Killing the wrong ones will impede relations between our forces."

"These Belderanian parasites have commited crimes of the highest degree against our nation and must be punished immediately!" Marashal argued. It was clear that the Varhallan was not going to let this slight go.

Thymey had to think quickly to appease his much-needed ally without losing important targets or giving away his knowledge of the raid on the Varhallan village. He knew that the Varhalla were furious, but he hadn't expected them to act so brashly. This wasn't exactly the best time for negotiations either. The longer they argued, the more men they would lose, and both the Varhalla and the Exiles were avoiding going on the offensive until their two leaders gave the order.

Finally, Thymey conceded for the sake of expediency. "Alright, you can have some of them to execute, but only after they've been captured and we discern the information they possess." He could possibly afford to spare a few of the prisoners, but if he played things right, he could kill the remaining

Varhalla afterward and chalk it up to losses in the battle. They had incurred enough losses by now to pass it off as such.

Marashal eyed the lieutenant for a moment, perhaps wanting to argue, but even he must have realized that a decision had to be made immediately. At the moment, he and his mages were pinned between the Exiles and the enemy. If he refused to concede he would be forced to face an attack on both sides, which even he could not repel with fewer than fifteen casters, having already lost a few.

"Very well," he said reluctantly. "Varhalla, sand restraints! Slow them down," he ordered before signaling Thymey to join in.

Thymey nodded in agreement and ordered his men to charge in and capture the enemy. As his men moved forward, the Varhalla's magic began to work. Sand was flooding out from their satchels and covering the enemies' limbs. It wasn't enough to stop or kill them, given the small amount of sand in their bags, but it was sufficient to work as weak restraints, impeding their enemies' movements. The main goal was to hinder Feryl, whose Fjoren strength made him nearly impossible to control, especially now that he was fully armored. It was as if they were facing some sort of invincible demigod. The majority of the sand was being used to restrain him, but even still, he was fighting off the Exiles.

This was going well. The enemy had gotten the jump on them, but the advantage was still theirs. The superior numbers held by the Exiles and Varhalla would allow them to outlast their prey. Only Feryl would be able to keep his strength up, but once they whittled down the enemy forces to just him, they could overwhelm him easily. Even those trapped behind the wall of fire would be able to join in soon. Second Lieutenant Sproles had begun ordering the men on his side to shovel snow onto the fire in an effort to put it out, and it was working.

Now it was time the lieutenant himself joined in. The forces within the city walls had been reduced enough that he could not afford to keep himself and the men guarding him out of combat. The Varhalla had managed to hamper Feryl's movements as planned, and though the boy would have outmatched him under regular circumstances, this edge would be enough to allow Thymey to contend with him, especially with the aid of his men. Including the Varhalla, those inside the walls had numbered about forty-five before the attack. Between the crazed Fjorendel, the oil fire, and the ambush itself they now numbered fewer than thirty and were losing more by the second. Thymey and his men would need to attack and pressure the enemy until the twenty or so men beyond the wall were able to rejoin the main force.

Thymey charged forward, pushing through the front line. With a great crashing of metal, he crossed swords with the boy who he loathed so much.

He noted the weakened state of the Chained King. "Feeling sluggish are we, boy? What's the matter? Missing your cage already? Thought that bit of freedom would've put a bit more pep in your step."

"Didn't think you'd miss me so much, Lieutenant," Feryl shot back. "Bringing a whole army just to pick me up? Or is it that you needed this much backup just to face a lowly slave?"

The force of their blows split them apart. In the momentary pause three of Thymey's guards rushed in, only for the first two to be cut down by the massive strokes of Feryl's blades. The last guard almost made it through, but before he could make contact, Clary's sword burst through his chest, having been plunged upward under the lower right side of his back. Most of the men were so concerned with the massive Feryl, who had been taking advantage of the narrow alleyway to keep himself from being surrounded, that they had disregarded the small female warrior crouched at his side as being under his protection rather than acting as his backup. When this soldier had made this mistake and lunged for the Chained King, he had mistaken Feryl's trust in Clary's capabilities for an opening.

"So now the slave's having his little girlfriend fight his battles for him," Thymey laughed, clashing blades with his enemy once more. "How cute."

"You keep calling me slave, but it looks like Turk's got himself a new errand boy, doesn't it?"

Thymey's laughing mockery ended to be replaced by an angry scowl. He was none too pleased to be compared to the boy whom he looked down on so much. "Without a slave to get his hands dirty for us this time, it's up to the master to go out and slaughter the escaped animal. You forget your place, boy!"

"Oh, I know my place quite well, Lieutenant. Do you?"

At that moment a ball of hardened sand blasted Feryl in the head, sending his dented helmet flying. It was a clear indication of his magical prowess that Marashal was able to launch the projectile with such force and density that it was able to do such damage. He wasn't leader of these elite Varhallan mages for nothing.

For any normal person this would have been instant death. Even for Feryl it was enough to stagger him. This allowed Thymey to take advantage of the confusion to slash Feryl across the face with his sword. Unfortunately, he'd been so caught up in his anger that he'd forgotten to consider Clary's position. He tried to retract his blade to defend himself but it was too late –

she made directly for the kill shot. However, just before she could deal the decisive blow, another bolt of sand came hurling into her shoulder, sending her spinning to the side. There was a loud crack as the joint disconnected from the force. She screamed as she hit the ground, hard.

"Clary!" Feryl shouted. He made a strained effort to reach her, but the enemy cut him off. This show of concern was his fatal mistake. Thymey smiled widely at the realization of this girl's importance to the Chained King. Feryl's cry signaled to the lieutenant a new strategy. He had found a weakness. It was a chink in the invincible armor of the most feared tyrant in the western kingdoms, and he would exploit it to the fullest.

"Seize the girl!" he shouted. "She's number one priority! Take her hostage and it's all over!"

"Clary, run!" Feryl shouted in desperation. "Get out of here, now!"

Clary reacted immediately. Given her dislocated shoulder, she would not be able to help anymore, and the presence of the Varhalla and Exiles did not leave much room for argument. Blocked from returning to safety behind Feryl, she was forced to run to the next street, which was clear of enemy and ally alike.

This is it, Thymey thought. *With the boy's attention focused elsewhere I'll have him beat. He can't protect her and the others when they're spread so thin.* Thymey started to make his way towards the alley to catch Clary, but then hesitated. He needed to stay and command the main force. *The Varhalla — they're quicker and their sand can trap her without touching her or worrying about getting burned.*

"Marashal! I need you to take some men and catch her!" Thymey dodged a large swing from Feryl, and two more Exiles got between them to hold the giant off. The Varhallan tried to protest, but Thymey wasn't having it. "It has to be you! She's Fjorendel! Firedrake Clan, she doesn't have full control of her powers, but still, be wary of the skin! And no killing!"

Begrudgingly, the Varhallan took six of his men and marched off down the dark street. It would have been too risky to take on Feryl without the Varhalla, but just as Marashal departed from the battlefield, the great fire that had engulfed the entrance waned enough for Mr. Sproles and his men to move in. It appeared that two of the three enemy warriors on the other side of the courtyard had been subdued. Even without the girl, the battle was won.

*   *   *

"Oof!"

Clary tripped over some rubble buried beneath the snow as she struggled to run down the dark street. Even though the snow was thick enough to break her fall, it did not protect her head completely. A hidden rock caught her forehead; she realized that blood was now running down one side of her face. She was dizzy from the pain in her shoulder, and as she clambered to her feet it was hard to tell whether it was her drenched arm or the new wound on her head that had been responsible for dying the snow red. She stumbled as she ran, barely able to keep her feet beneath her. It would be easier if she could reinsert her right shoulder into its socket, but she did not have the time to try, and the blood pouring from the joint made it slippery and difficult to manage.

She could hear enemies running close behind her. She hated leaving the others behind, but in her current state she would just be in the way. The best course of action was to lead some of the enemies away from the fight, lightening the load for her friends. If she could find a good place to hide, she might keep the enemy split up indefinitely. If this were to be a possibility, she would have to act quickly. Her pursuers were uninjured, meaning that they would not be slowed down as she was. The trail of blood she left behind would not help her remain concealed either.

She was beginning to panic. She could hear shouting and the crunching of snow. Her enemies were close, and she was out of ideas. She turned down one street, then another. All the while, her lungs were burning more and more, her panting increasing with each step.

Suddenly, she hit a dead end. This was it. There was nowhere else to go. She would have to make a stand here, facing her attackers and hope for a miracle. If she were lucky, they would take her as a prisoner, though she wasn't sure if that would really be better or not. Regardless, she drew her remaining sword and faced the darkness.

As she stared down the street, waiting for her attackers to appear out of the alleyway from which she had just emerged, she recalled a night long ago when another person had stood alone against the might of the Exiles in the darkness. She looked down at the blade in her hand and wondered if Sir Cloin had felt the same fear that she felt at this very moment. *No, Clary though. He was brave and ready to defend another. Summoning all his power to protect someone he hardly knew. I'll never be like that.* But she didn't have to worry about protecting anyone right now, only herself. Live or die, it would not help the others. She had way less to worry about.

Clary was prepared to kill who she could and let that be the end of it, but as the pursuers rounded the corner, all hopes of taking some enemies with her vanished. She now faced seven Varhalla, accompanied by two Exiles. She had no hope of taking on this many enemies by herself. She was done for.

Clary lowered her sword, ready to be taken prisoner, but as she stepped forward she was blasted in her left thigh with a hardened ball of sand from one of the Varhalla. The power of the blast knocked the leg out from under her, and she fell to her knees. It was nowhere near as powerful as the shot to her shoulder had been, but it still felt as though she had been smashed with a hammer.

One of the Exiles shouted at the Varhallan who did it. "Hey! The lieutenant said to take her alive! Are you stupid or something?"

"And she is alive!" the Varhallan shouted back. "But your lieutenant never said she was to remain uninjured."

With that, he turned back and shot another bolt of sand at Clary who was struggling to remain upright due to the intense pain. The shot collided with her stomach, causing her to cough up blood and knocking the wind out of her. Now she was on all fours, gasping desperately for air. She felt like she was going to pass out.

The Varhalla were all laughing as she cried silently, trying to think of a way to survive.

"Hey, that's enough! We need her alive!" the Exile protested again, to no avail. This rebellion was more than the two Exiles could handle. As the other Varhalla stepped in front of them, it became clear that the Exiles would have no say in what was about to happen.

"Don't worry, I am just going to put her to sleep before we take her back so that she is a bit more... manageable," the Varhallan said. He grinned, baring his razor sharp teeth. "That should be alright, shouldn't it Marashal?"

Behind him, the Varhallan who Clary guessed was the leader agreed. "I do not think that should be a problem. I am sure the lieutenant will be more than gratefull for such diligence."

"One more blast of sand to the back of the head, then. That should do the trick. I just hope I don't use to much power. You know, I don't know my own strength sometimes." A ball of sand gathered in the Varhallan's palm.

Marashal smiled. "Well, accidents do happen, don't they?"

Clary was still on all fours, staring at the ground. She could not catch her breath, and the pain was too great for her to try to run – not that she had anywhere to go if she could run. All she could do was sit there and accept her fate. Tears dripped into the snow.

She thought of her parents. "Mom, dad… I'm so sorry I couldn't make it back to you. I tried," she whispered.

"Goodnight, little girl," the Varhalla said, standing over her.

Clary heard a ripping of flesh and saw blood splatter on the floor beneath her. Strangely, however, this blood was not her own. She was utterly confused, until she heard a familiar voice that she never imagined she would be happy to hear.

"Ha! One of the proud Fjorendel warriors crying on the battlefield? I thought even you were stronger than that little demon."

"Sheckem!" Clary shouted, looking up to see their former prisoner standing in front of her, his arm stuck straight through the enemy mage's chest.

"True, it is the place of your people to be knelt before the Varhalla," Sheckem replied, "but when the time comes for you to kneel before my people, it will be before true Varhalla, not treacherous usurpers."

Marashal scoffed at Sheckem, "Who are you to call us treacherous when you have become the dog of these lesser beings? You even let them call you by such a disgusting name. It is you who is not truly Varhalla."

"Children really should learn how rude it is to interrupt their superiors when they are talking," Sheckem said, without turning away from Clary.

"And now you would dare talk down to me with your back turned! How dare you, traitor! You do not know to whom you speak!" Marashal shouted in anger before hurling a sand bolt at Sheckem.

"Look out!" Clary screamed as the bolt came speeding toward him. But Sheckem's smile remained undimmed, and he simply raised his hand behind him. Clary couldn't believe her eyes. The ball of sand had stopped in mid-air, mere inches from Sheckem's raised hand.

"You presume to use the sand of my own desert against me? How dare you, young royal caster," Sheckem said, turning to face his enemy. "Hold on, little demon. I will be but a moment."

"It… it's him! It is the wanderer! The Varhalla condemned to Exile. It is the Fallen King!" Marashal looked as though he were face to face with the most terrifying creature the Arid Sea had to offer, and in a sense, he was. "Attack! Kill him now befo—"

Marashal was cut off as the same sand bolt which he had launched at Sheckem flew back at him, compacted even smaller and harder than before. It flew with such speed that instead of smashing into him like other sand spells Clary had seen, it went straight through his shoulder like an arrow.

"Gah!"

"Do not dare call me by such names! I am Halumsha, true king to the Varhalla! To raise your hand against me is an act of treason, regardless of what your usurper who falsely calls himself king says," Sheckem shouted in the most terrifying voice Clary had ever heard. She couldn't believe that all this time, the Varhalla that they had been keeping on the back of their wagon was the legendary warlord who had created the Varhalla.

"Why would the Fallen King protect his most hated enemy?" Marashal asked, grasping at his shoulder.

"She has become my pet, and protected me when I was in danger like any domesticated beast should," Halumsha said arrogantly. "And like any good master, I protect those who serve me, no matter how lowly they may be. More importantly, I believe I told you not to call me by that name!" With that, he raised his arms to begin casting his magic.

While he was talking, the other Varhalla had begun casting as well. Their sand started to rise from their carrying bags and condense, firing at Halumsha. Even he could not control so many bolts at once, but the spell he had been casting hadn't been one of sand. He finished chanting just in time for a large hand made of stones and earth to be formed from the ground in front of him. It was large enough to shield both Clary and Halumsha easily, but it was not only a shield. As Halumsha moved his fingers, the giant stone hand before him mirrored it. He could control the hand and move it as he pleased. He reached his arm forward, swiping it to the side, and so too did the stone arm move, smashing the first three Varhalla into a nearby building. The force was such that two of them died instantly. The third might have survived had the rubble from the building not fallen onto him, crushing him in the process. The three remaining Varhalla assaulted him with more bolts. He managed to dodge the first two, but they were only a distraction. Sand now wrapped around his foot, holding him in place, and the third shot struck him. It hurt, but not enough to stop him. He motioned to attack and the great stone hand wrapped around the nearest Varhalla, crushing him to death.

"You children have so much to learn," he said, as the two Exile soldiers ran toward him, raising their swords.

Halumsha was still rooted to the ground by sand. Still, he managed to duck the first slash, grabbing Clary's sword from the snow and cutting down both humans. The only enemies left now were Marashal and the Varhallan who was maintaining the hold on Halumsha's leg.

"Do you really think that I cannot kill you from here?" Halumsha said, looking up at the young caster.

"No, but your hand cannot reach this far, and I will see any other attacks before they reach me!" the Varhallan replied confidently.

"Is that so?" Halumsha raised his hand, chanting under his breath in Varhallan.

Clary was confused when no sand or stone shot out at the enemy. Then the young caster began to choke and sputter. The sand from his own pouch had started to flow out and up his body, constricting around his neck and choking the life out of him. Finally, Halumsha released him, and he dropped to the ground.

"Now, child," he said, slowly advancing toward Marashal, his final enemy. "Will you face me by yourself and fall with some dignity? Or do you only know how to face an enemy with an army to hide behind? Do not worry. I will not judge either way. After all, you do not have that beast master king of yours with you like last time."

Marashal, who had been sporting an expression of astonishment and terror, snapped to his senses and stood firm to face his opponent. "If you remember me, then do not mock me! I was part of the group that defeated you the first time, and I will do so again! Killing my men was a gift to me! You have given me everything I need, and sealed your own fate!"

All of the sand that the other Varhallan had carried started to gather in the air between them, forming a wall of long sand spikes, now aimed directly at Halumsha and Clary.

"No matter who you may be, you cannot block all of these bolts, and you cannot dodge this many either!" Marashal shouted. "Now die, Fallen King!"

Clary braced herself for the worst. Surely it must be the case that Marashal's attack could not be stopped, now that Halamsha had dropped his stone hand spell to take on the two Exiles. But the attack never came. The wall of sand arrows fell to the ground, revealing what had happened to their master. Marashal was standing still, arms in the air raised toward his enemies. He had been stopped by the sand in the two satchels at his hips. He had been so focused on all of the sand spread across the field that he had neglected his own stores. Halumsha had taken advantage of this, casting a spell to make the sand form into long spear-like poles, which pierced through Marashal's sides to burst out from his shoulders.

Having defeated their foe, Halumsha turned back to Clary. "We must fix this arm quickly, before the rest of them arrive. I have used up too much energy to take on another group of my people and yours," he said, grabbing Clary and leaning her back.

"Wait, I don't understand. Why did you—" *Crack!* "Ah." He had popped her arm back in without warning.

"Here, take these herbs I took from the wagon, the same that you gave that old man. There's only enough left to numb you for a short while, but it will have to do."

"Wait, you still haven't answered—" Clary started again, but Halumsha would not let her finish.

"Demon! We do not have time. Your friends need us. Take the medicine first." Clary was still curious, but she understood what he meant. The medicine would take a few minutes to kick in. She took the herbs and began chewing.

"I know you are confused as to why I helped you," Halumsha said, as Clary chewed on the dry, bitter herbs. "As I'm sure you have gathered by now, I am indeed the original ruler of the Varhalla and the reason for our current state as a species. It is true that once I was human like you, as the legends state. But that is a story for another time. All you need to know is that it has been a few millennia since I sat on the throne. I was usurped, you see."

Clary finally swallowed the herbs and was waiting for them to kick in. "What does any of that have to do with me?"

"I... I'm not entirely sure. I guess I was angry to see that traitor Marashal, who was part of the coup that led to my expulsion. No, that is incorrect." It seemed as though the former king was struggling to figure out his own reasoning. "No, I suppose it is because you saved me that night, even though I am your enemy."

"But that wasn't—"

"Demon, I have no time or patience for your humble puttering. You showed an enemy kindness and asked nothing in return. It is sickening how trusting and merciful you are. It is something I myself have never been, even when I knew I should have been." He looked away. "More importantly, it made me think of when I was usurped. No one came to my aid. Not a single subject or retainer. Not even my family came to my defense. My punishment was to remain a wanderer forever, excommunicated from society. It has been centuries since I have been shown sympathy of any kind. My saving you was merely a whim brought of momentary gratitude for a nostalgic feeling. I suppose even a demon deserves that much."

Clary wasn't sure how to react. It seemed like the Varhallan whom she had known as Sheckem was trying to say that he'd become fond of her, though his message was interspersed with rudeness. It couldn't be helped. That much was to be expected of him.

"Thank you, Sheck— I mean, thank you, Halumsha." She smiled.

"Well, demon, if you're smiling then you must be feeling good enough to move," Halumsha said, as if trying to avoid her kind remark. "Let us tend to your friends."

Clary nodded, and the Varhallan lifted her to her feet, handing her the sword which he had borrowed. He made his way back toward one of the fallen Exiles to take his blade.

At that moment an Exile turned the corner into the street. "Mr. Sproles!" he called out, "I've found them!"

Halumsha reached down and grabbed the sword, then dashed forward to strike down this new enemy – but as he leapt forth, a younger Exile came from the alleyway, already casting his spell in common tongue. *This must be the 'Mr. Sproles' that the man called for*, Clary thought. She was fairly sure she had heard Thymey calling that name at the start of the ambush, and now she knew why. Just before Halumsha could reach him, he tripped sideways into the snow. He didn't appear to have tripped over anything. It was more like he had lost his balance and now he was rolling on the floor, clutching at the sides of his head.

Clary started forward to help him. The Exile, Sproles, turned his sights on her and raised his hand as though he were about to fire a spell at her, but nothing happened, so Clary kept running towards him to attack.

Then it hit her – a mind-numbing ringing sound, like nothing she'd ever heard before. It hurt, but it wasn't enough to stop her, so she kept pushing. If the painful sound was the main purpose of the spell, she might have been able to fight back, but as she discovered, pain was not Sproles' true intention. As Clary continued to charge forward, she suddenly fell over to one side. Just as with Halumsha, she hadn't tripped over anything. She was a little dazed but otherwise not harmed, so she tried once again to get up and run at the new enemy. All the while, Sproles just stood there holding out his hand towards her. Clary stood and wobbled again, falling to the other side, only this time the falling did not stop when she hit the ground. Everything kept spinning. She was having a fit of vertigo, and the sound just kept blaring. She couldn't figure out what was going on, but she was unable to orient herself or move.

"Funny thing, sound," Sproles said, squatting down beside her. "It's powerful enough to shatter solid objects, yet it can be gentle enough to go unnoticed by human ears. It can affect so many different facets of our lives, even changing our emotions when used correctly. You see, my parents were musicians before they died, and my father was always fascinated with how sound affects us, just as I am now. One day he even taught me the most peculiar fact. You see, sound does not just have the ability to affect us emotionally, but physically as well. In your ear there exists a part which controls the balance of your entire body. I know, amazing isn't it? how affecting one little tube in your ear of all places can hinder all of your movement. All you have to do is apply a little pressure in the right way, a sound even, if played at the right frequency. That's all it takes. Now, normally I don't take joy in using this ability on people as it's quite uncomfortable and even a bit cruel, but after all of the pain you've put the lieutenant through, and all of the comrades I've lost to this stupid little chase we've had to go on,

I think you deserve at least a little extra time in limbo. So, instead of releasing it once you're chained up, I'm going to keep you sedated with it all the way back to the city's entrance. I wish I could say it was my idea, but I must admit these are the lieutenant's orders, so I couldn't free you even if I wanted to."

Clary wanted to curse and scream at him. She wanted to attack this man, but she couldn't do a thing. She tried to lunge at him and ended up going the wrong way. She couldn't control her body at all, and the spinning caused her to throw up into the snow.

"I appreciate the effort, but that's not going to work. Chain them up, we've kept the lieutenant waiting long enough."

Clary was sure she imagined it, but as confident and cold as this Sproles person was acting, it seemed just that – an act. He didn't seem like he was enjoying it. It was as if he were trying to imitate Captain Turk, but he had missed on a few key points. Turk would never have brought up his comrades, even if he had any. This Exile seemed more like he was trying to convince himself that he was doing the right thing. Clary thought she even saw a flicker of remorse in his eyes as he watched the others shackle her, but she couldn't be sure due to all the spinning.

Finally the men had her chained and secured and began dragging her through the streets along with Halumsha. She wanted to talk to him, but with the constant ringing and spinning, she was sure that opening her mouth would just cause her to be sick again. She would just have to wait until they reached the others.

The others…

Chapter 25

Clary's shoulder was still bleeding as she was forced to her knees before the great gate of Harsgard once more. She was still sick from Sproles' sound spell, even though he had released it a while ago. Fortunately, she had nothing left to throw up, so she was no longer heaving as she had several times on the short journey back to the battlefield. As the spinning slowly came to an end, she was able to focus on her surroundings. The haze and confusion dissipated, allowing her surroundings to come into focus. The battle must have been over for a while. Long torches were now arranged around the area, illuminating everything to a greater degree than it had been during the battle. The Exiles had also brought in their gear, which had previously been left outside. It was clear they were planning on making camp in the city for the night.

Clary looked to either side and was relieved, even in this terrible situation, to find that all of her friends were relatively safe. None of them had been killed, but no one had managed to escape without at least some form of injury. It seemed that Sirs Ellerbe and Harvel had received the worst of it. Harvel's face was swollen as though he had been beaten repeatedly, and Ellerbe was missing fingers on his left hand. Even Feryl had been unable to escape injury. His armor had been stripped away, and he was covered in deep bruises where he had been shot with bolts of sand. His most painful-looking injury was a stab wound on the bottom-left side of his stomach. His hardened skin would have been sufficient to deter a lethal blow, but the gash still did not look pleasant. While most of them were chained up in a line with iron cuffs connecting their hands, Feryl had been chained in multiple places and his tethers were hard-rooted to the ground. All of these restraints were simply extra precautions, however, as the real bond keeping him subdued was the threat Thymey had made to kill Clary if he acted out.

There were a little over thirty Exiles remaining, and only five Varhalla. The surprise attack the escapees had launched had been truly effective, but in order to succeed, it needed an amount of luck that they just didn't have. Given the numbers, Clary could only assume that the fighting ended shortly after she was forced to flee. Sproles and his sound magic must have been what did it. Otherwise Feryl would have definitely been able to kill a much greater number of the enemy soldiers.

"Where's Marashal?" Thymey barked at his second lieutenant.

"Dead, sir, along with the rest of his party. This unknown Varhalla has killed them, I believe," Sproles responded.

"Really? How 'bout that? Must be one tough bastard to take on Marashal and six of his men... Alright, the head Varhalla is dead. Men!" Thymey turned and nodded as though he were giving a previously discussed order. All at once, the five remaining Varhalla had their throats slit from behind before they even had a chance to realize what was happening.

"Sir, why did you—" Sproles started.

"Couldn't trust them, could I? Without Marashal to reel them in, they might've caused problems. Not to mention they saw our handiwork in that little village and wanted to take some of our prisoners for their own. Without knowing what these brats know, I couldn't risk it."

Sproles seemed hesitant at first, but he accepted it in the end. "Right, as you say, sir. Good thinking."

"Good. Now back to you, girly," Thymey said, training his eyes on Clary. "You brats put me through a lot of trouble, dragging me halfway across the world, just to get yourselves cornered."

By this point Clary was thoroughly irritated. She knew he was going to drag this out to result in as much pain as possible. It was just the type of person he was.

"Bet you kids are feeling pretty stupid now ain't ya," Thymey said with a smile.

"Not as stupid as the man who lost half his men chasing a bunch of kids," Clary shot back.

Thymey didn't like that at all. *Smack!* He struck her hard across the face, but Clary just smiled back, knowing it would irritate her captor even further.

"Have you forgotten our play sessions already, little girl? Did you think those were over? Oh, no they've only just begun. I'm going to enjoy watching you scream in pain everyday. See, Turk wants to turn you into some kind of Chained Queen, but I'm sure you've already figured that out by now. Me, I think you won't be able to hack it." The lieutenant leaned in closer, speaking softly. "Yeah, I'll bring you back alive, like a good soldier, but who's to say my hands won't slip once I've had my fun with you?"

"Let them," Clary said. "If you keep hitting like that, it won't amount to much."

Thymey stood up and slapped her again with the back of his hand, knocking her to the ground. The other Exiles sitting or standing around Thymey and his prey were laughing at Clary. It was the same as it had been during her time in the Exile caravan. Clary knew she should stop egging him on, but knowing how terrible the future was going to be now that they'd been captured, she didn't care. If the worst happened and he did kill her there, then Feryl would lose his reason to hold back. He might even find a way to free the others while they returned to Thandessa. Clary definitely didn't want to end up as a bargaining chip to keep anyone under control, just as her mother now was for her father, and just as Feryl's family had been for him.

Thymey grabbed her by the shirt, pulling her back onto her knees. He produced a small knife, holding it up to her face. "Do you hear what I'm saying, you little bitch? I will hurt you. I don't care what it takes, I will find a way to break you down, and I will exploit it until there's nothing left of you." He let go of her shirt and grabbed her hair, pressing his thumb into the open wound on her forehead where the rock in the snow had hit her earlier.

"Don't you touch her, you bastard!" Feryl roared, attempting to break his chains to protect Clary. He lurched at Thymey, but the chains stopped him, creaking and straining under the pressure of the giant's struggling. Feryl would have broken the chains without much more effort, but before he could, Thymey jumped behind Clary, placing his knife to her throat.

"That'll be enough of that, boy. Don't forget who holds the power here."

Feryl stopped immediately, his eyes widening. Thymey had him.

"Now now, that's a look that could kill, isn't it Mr. Sproles?" Thymey asked his subordinate, staring at the giant.

"Yes, sir. I'd say it is."

"And remind me, what's the punishment for a slave who threatens his masters?" he continued.

"Why, that'd be death, sir."

"Right you are, Mr. Sproles, but we can't afford to be killing them. It's not like we can hurt the boy too much either, since we don't have the captain with us. So what do you do to a slave who deserves to die, but can't?" Thymey was being so obviously facetious that it was nauseating. Clary wished more than anything that she had her powers under control, not so that she could escape, but just so she could roast this man before she was killed. "Oh, I've got it," Thymey continued, "If you can't hurt him or kill him, then let's make him feel like dying, by hurting something he loves. I believe you can help us with that, girly."

"If you hurt her I swear I'll—"

"You'll what? Don't blame me, boy. This is all your fault. If you hadn't let yourself get so attached, then we wouldn't have to be doing this, now would we?" With that, he pressed his knife into Clary's skin right over her collarbone. He only cut the skin, making sure not to dig the blade deep enough to create a lasting injury. His goal was just to inflict pain. He smiled as Feryl struggled and protested while the Exiles around them pointed and laughed. "Come on, girly, give us a scream, would you?" But Clary didn't make any noise at all. In fact, she didn't even flinch.

Thymey looked at her in confusion, and tried again to hurt her, this time pressing his thumb into the other wound on her shoulder. Still Clary didn't show any signs of discomfort. She only smiled.

"What the hell is going on?" Thymey didn't understand. No matter what her pain tolerance was, Clary shouldn't have been able to react in such a way. "Wait a minute, you've taken something haven't you? You haven't been feeling any pain this whole time." Thymey was visibly furious. He threw Clary to the floor in anger. "Well, this was all pointless then, wasn't it?"

Clary laughed. She'd gotten the upper hand on her tormentor, even if it had just been for a moment. She hadn't been able to feel even the slightest amount of pain since Halumsha had given her the Varhallan herbs back in the city streets. The only thing that could cause her pain in this condition was Sproles' sound magic. Fortunately he didn't have any way of knowing whether Clary had been in such discomfort because of the terrible ringing noise, or just because of the vertigo. Thankfully she had absorbed most of the medicinal effects of the herbs before puking her guts out on the way over. The numbness wouldn't last much longer, but at least it had done its job so far.

Thymey stepped over to Clary, furious at being outwitted. Valen, Ellerbe and Edgrum all laughed at the lieutenant's idiocy, which only served to anger the man even further. This was supposed to be his moment of victory, but his own prisoners were taking the joy away from him.

"You little shits, the lot of you. You're all worthless. Hope you enjoyed that filthy little trick of yours, because it'll cost you. If I can't hurt her, then I'll just have to take the same approach I took with the big one. Looks like someone else is going to have to take her place."

This shut them all up. No one liked the idea of another one of their own being tortured. Thymey paced up and down the line, trying to figure out who his victim would be, holding his sword out towards each prisoner in turn as he weighed his decision. The other Exiles started getting into the spirit, calling out suggestions.

"Sir, do that ugly one! He was calling the shots!" one called out, pointing at Harvel.

"No, this one's too mushed up," Thymey replied. "They'll never be able to tell if he's in pain with his face all swollen up like that. Besides, I like my prey to see their punishment."

"What about that one, Lieutenant? He looks like the oldest. I bet they look up to him!" another called out, gesturing toward Sir Ellerbe.

"No, this one's already damaged. I like me a blank canvas when I do my work," Thymey grinned. Clary was sickened. He was like he was a child picking out candy from a store, the way he played with his decision.

"How 'bout that there Varhallan?" a third Exile called. "Might as well have fun with the last one."

"Are you thick? Who would care about seeing one of them monsters tortured?" Thymey laughed again. "The goal is to hurt the others, not entertain them, you dolt."

The rest of the Exiles roared with laughter as he continued down the line. Thymey seemed to be struggling with his decision of whom to toy with, until finally he turned to his second lieutenant. "Mr. Sproles."

"Yes, sir?" Sproles shouted, snapping to attention.

"I just can't make up my mind here. I trust your judgment more than any of this lot. So tell me, who would you choose? For maximum effect, of course."

Sproles seemed a bit uncomfortable at having this decision thrust upon him. He paused for a moment before answering. "Well, sir... It— er... It appears that this one here showed a similar reaction to Feryl when you began to work on the new Chained Queen. The prince gave a similar reaction as well, but I'm guessing you want to save him. Plus he seems to be the youngest, and a knight of little command. You wouldn't have to worry even if you accidentally killed him."

Thymey was impressed. "Very astute, Mr. Sproles. I knew I could count on you." He began walking towards Sir Garrett.

Valen leapt out in front of him. "Wait! Wait, please!" he begged. "Don't do it. Use me instead. I'm a prince of Belderan. I hold more value to these people than anyone here."

Clary was shocked. She had tried jumping to her feet to stop Thymey as well, but another Exile had put his hand on her shoulder and forced her back down before she could act. It looked as though a few of the others had made similar efforts, but they were all stifled as well. Only the prince had managed to make a move, as he was the first to act and the closest to them.

Thymey struck Valen in much the same way as he had struck Clary. "Don't you try to fool me, young prince. You insult my intelligence," he shouted. "I was there when we captured you all the first time. I saw your cowardice before your loyal subjects. No one would place all their value in a leader like that. Though I should thank you. You have confirmed the value of this little one with your outburst."

Thymey stepped over the prince and grabbed Garrett by his collar, dragging him forward. "Well boys, are you ready for a show?"

The Exiles cheered as he threw Garrett to the floor. Thymey held up his hands in a sort of victory pose, egging on his adoring followers. He loved this sort of blood spectacle, and he was second only to Turk in performing such torturous displays. He stepped over the boy, who was face down in the snow, and straddled his back, cutting open his shirt.

"Now, let's see, how shall I draw it out? What do you say boys? Slice or flay? What shall it be?" he shouted to thunderous applause and cheering.

The Exiles cheered and called out responses. "Good answer! Why choose when we can do both?"

Thymey bent over and began carving a bit of skin from Garrett's back. Garrett screamed in pain as the flesh was sliced off bit by bit.

"Stop! Leave him alone now!" Clary had likened this situation to her fights with Thymey under Turk's supervision, but she was wrong – this was much worse. She struggled to get to her feet, but the Exile holding her would not allow it. She was heating up, but her keeper was wearing thick metal gauntlets, and the heat was not enough to reach him through the metal.

Thymey held up another piece of skin and muscle, tossing it into the group like a piece of meat to the hounds, before returning to his screaming victim for another slice. Clary continued to struggle and cry. This was all her fault. Why couldn't she activate her powers like her father? If she could only do that, she could save everyone. She thought back to her first battles with the lieutenant, remembering the anger and rage she felt then. It was nowhere near as intense as the burning hatred that she felt now. So why, then, could she not use her powers? She felt a rage now that she did not think was possible. If her current state could not invoke the fires within her, then what could?

"Please!" she begged again. "Please stop this."

But her cries fell on deaf ears.

Clary wished she could be like Feryl, and go into a rage as he had. Even Halumsha managed to control his powers through heated emotions. Then Clary remembered when he came to her aid in the city. True, the Varhallan was angry, but he did not seem anywhere near as furious as she was now. *What was it he said?* she thought, trying to remember when he had spoken to her on the wagon. *It was something about finding another feeling than rage, something about directing it. What did he mean?*

"Gaah!" Garrett screamed again, as Thymey slashed his back once more.

Clary was thinking fast now. She had to do something before it was too late, and for the first time, she felt as though she was on to something. She thought about times when she had seen Feryl use his powers. Sure, he always seemed to be angered when using his powers, but he wasn't in a blind rage every time. There had to have been a connection between her father, Feryl and Halumsha. What was it that connected all of them? What was similar between all of their demonstrations of immense power? How could she figure it out in time to save Garrett?

Garrett... that's it!

Clary remembered a time when Garrett fought in a way that exceeded his own ability. When he had seen Sir Rorian injured in battle, Garrett flew into a fury unlike anything she'd ever seen. Though he had been acting on instinct, he had a similar look in his eyes to the three battle mages who had helped her. It was a look born from not just anger, but a combination of rage and a desire to protect someone who was important to him. Halumsha had wanted to protect Clary in the street, just as her father had wanted to protect her and her mother against the Exiles. Then she thought about Feryl. He had always done everything he could to protect her. Even the first night that they met, Feryl took on a monolith bear, without a weapon, just to save her. It seemed that for all these men, power came from a desire to fight not just to kill or to save themselves, but for someone else.

It all made sense now. This had to be it. Clary focused on Garrett's screams, as much as it hurt to hear them. She closed her eyes and let the rage take over, but this time she didn't think about her desire to murder Thymey and escape. Instead, she thought of her friends' faces and their pain. At that moment she felt that nothing else in the world mattered anymore except for her hatred of the ones who sought to hurt her friends. She gathered a bit of blood from her shoulder with her fingers while everyone else was focused on Thymey and Garrett. She began drawing runes on her forearms.

Finally she opened her eyes. Looking down, she cried one last tear, only this time it was a tear of joy. It sizzled, evaporating immediately as it hit her burning white hands.

The light did not go unnoticed.

"Sir! The girl!" one of the Exiles shouted, causing everyone to focus their attention on her.

"Mr. Sproles, subdue her now!" Thymey shouted.

Sproles immediately started casting the same spell as earlier, but it was too late. Clary melted through her chains, grabbing the wrists of the Exile who had been holding her, burning his forearms to ash, and jumping to her feet.

"Just stay back and she can't hurt you!" Thymey ordered, trying to keep his men from panicking. "She barely has control of her powers!"

The Exiles remained grouped together, raising their weapons in defense, but this was their fatal mistake. Remembering her father, Clary inhaled one great and deep breath and then exhaled sharply, releasing a flood of white-hot flames into the group, engulfing the majority of the Exiles.

Suddenly the ringing sound returned, and Clary dropped to one knee. Sproles had completed his spell. However, he was so flustered in his preparation that he didn't realize he was standing dangerously close to Feryl, who finally burst from his chains and caught the second lieutenant with a booming right cross, knocking him out instantly.

Thymey was terrified. He was losing control quickly. Clary had torched at least ten of his men and injured several others, and now Feryl was loose. Still, he had one card left to play.

"Stop or he dies right here!" he shouted, raising his knife, ready to end Garrett's life on the spot. Clary and Feryl both froze, making Thymey believe he had won, but he had made another critical error due to lack of information.

There was a shout from one of his other prisoners. *"Divine wind!"*

This was followed by a concussive burst of energy which blasted Thymey in the side, sending him flying from atop Garrett. The Exiles had neglected to bind Terra's hands and gag her properly, unaware that she had learned magic in the time that the escapees had been in the desert. Being able to move her fingers freely and chant, she was able to cast her spell, catching the lieutenant entirely by surprise.

Clary jumped towards Halumsha, Valen and Ellerbe and melted the chains that linked their wrists, before moving down the line to free the others. The distraction of the flames, and Feryl's rampage, provided cover while she worked. Before long, she had managed to free all of the others, and they turned on the Exiles to commence their counter-offensive. Thymey, who was just regaining his bearings, had yet to give an order, and his men were in complete disarray. Between Feryl, Halumsha and the knights, it was already clear that even with their superior numbers, the Exiles had lost the advantage. If they still had the Varhalla on their side there may have been hope, but this attack was too much for the remaining force.

In a fit of terror, Thymey tried to run toward the gate to make an escape, but he was cut off by the collapsing wall of a nearby burning building. Unable to make it over this flaming rubble, and cut off at the other end by his former prisoners, he took the only path left available to him: the main street which led to the drinking hall.

There was a wall of about twelve Exiles between Clary and the main street, but she did not want to let the lieutenant who had tortured her and her friends get away.

Apparently Feryl felt the same way. "Clary, let's go!" he shouted as he charged the line. Before Feryl could even come into contact with the group, a great stone hand appeared from the ground in front of him, smashing a clear pathway through the Exiles.

"Thank you, Halumsha!" Clary shouted, as the two young Fjorendel sprinted down the dark street.

"Did you just call him Halumsha?" Feryl asked in shock, deactivating his powers in order to save his already low energy reserves for the fight ahead.

"Yeah, I'll explain later!" Clary shouted back without slowing.

Just then Feryl screamed in pain. One of the Exiles behind them was determined to keep them from escaping. Before the two could completely disappear into the darkness, a spear had connected with Feryl's unenhanced hamstring, erupting from the top of his quad. Feryl collapsed to his knees, sliding in the snow.

"Feryl!" Clary shouted, stopping to help him.

"No! There's no time. I'll be fine. It didn't hit anything vital. I'm lucky." He snapped the head off of the spear and pulled it back through his leg.

"But Feryl, you're—"

"I'm okay. I just need to keep my enhancement magic up. It'll keep it pressured and stop the bleeding."

"Are you sure?" Clary asked, worrying that he was not being entirely truthful.

"Yes, now let's go," he grunted, clambering to his feet.

The two of them took off again, confident that they could still catch the lieutenant before he was able to hide. Losing him, even while he was trapped in the city, posed too many risks. He could attack them in their sleep, or even sabotage their escape. They didn't have the time to search the entire city, so it was now or never. What was worse, Clary could hear Feryl's panting growing louder by the minute, and she was beginning to regain feeling in her body again.

The tracks in the snow were leading exactly where they had predicted. Thymey was following the street directly to the main hall. As the immense building appeared out of the darkness, they could see that the lieutenant had run directly through its giant doors. He wasn't trying to hide. He was trying to barricade himself inside until he could find a way out.

"Are you ready?" Feryl asked.

Clary nodded.

Feryl turned to the great door and started kicking it. *Boom!* The door didn't give way, so he tried again. *Boom!* It shifted more with this blow. *Boom, Boom, Boom, Boom.* Feryl was panting heavily now. This door was designed by Fjorendel, and as such was strong enough to hold back a drunken Fjoren rampage, at least for a while. Still, Feryl kicked with all his might. *Boom! Boom!* He was almost there. *Boom!*

Crash! Finally the door burst open. Before Feryl's sight could adjust, a dagger came flying out from the darkness. Feryl caught it with his forearm. His increased density kept it from going too deep, but the blood loss and energy depletion was almost too much for him to withstand.

In the confusion they had gathered their weapons from the pile in which they had been thrown, but Feryl hardly had the energy to wield his two swords. As they entered the building he attempted to hold one of the two massive swords using two hands, as a normal-sized warrior would, but he was becoming increasingly sluggish by the minute.

"Come on out, Thymey! I know you're in here!" he shouted as he walked slowly into the hall.

Clary drew both of her swords, ready to back Feryl up. She knew that their odds were worsening with the passing of time. They needed to draw Thymey out and engage him quickly, before it was too late.

A loud thump in the darkness to their left made both of the young Fjorendel raise their guard.

Feryl grunted, falling back to his knees once again, as Thymey rushed out of the shadows behind them, slashing Feryl across the back. The sound they had heard was a distraction, meant to help him get in an extra hit. Not only was he successful, but this slash was the final straw for Feryl, who could no longer maintain his strength. Thymey took notice of this and went in for the final blow. Fortunately, however, Clary was able to stop him, parrying the lieutenant's strike with the sword in her left hand. It caught him off guard, so that Clary was able to strike at him offensively with the sword in her right hand. It would have caught the Exile as well, but as she swung, pain shot through her body from the wound in her left shoulder, causing her to falter and miss.

"Very good, girly," Thymey laughed. "Looks like you've improved a bit. Been practicing everything I taught you."

"Ha, don't flatter yourself," she replied. "The man who taught me was a million times the swordsman you ever were."

"Oh, I doubt that, girly. But even if he was, he's not the one I'm fighting, is he? No, you're just a little Fjoren child who's run out of magic."

He rushed at her. Their swords rang out as they collided over and over again. Clary couldn't believe she was keeping up with him. A few months ago, she couldn't hold a candle to this man, but now she was keeping pace with him, even with her shoulder injured as it was. Still, something wasn't right. Thymey was smiling as he fought, unfazed by her improvement.

"How does it feel, knowing you're going to be killed by the little girl you thought was so beneath you?" Clary asked during one pause of separation, attempting to get at the lieutenant's psyche. "You seem pretty happy, considering I caught up to you in just a matter of months."

"Oh, girly. You mean you haven't realized?" Thymey laughed. "You actually thought I was fighting seriously?"

"Now's not the time to bluff, Thymey. I've seen your skill before, remember?" Clary shot back, though she felt slightly unnerved.

"Oh, it's no bluff," he replied, becoming more serious. "You see, it's a point of pride that I won't go all out against such a weak opponent."

"That pride of yours didn't stop you from going all out against a chained-up prisoner. You sure you're not just weaker than you think?"

Thymey's smile turned into a scowl. She had struck a nerve. "You've never even felt my true ability. Fighting you has always been a game. A challenge of seeing how little power I could use while fighting, so as to keep you alive for Turk. But I guess you have improved enough that I can let loose a little. So how 'bout it then?"

Clary didn't take the time to answer. She dove straight into the fight, confident that Thymey was just talking a big game. From the first collision she knew her confidence was misplaced. As their swords hit, she felt the force of his blow send her blade bouncing backward. Thymey was taking an aggressively strong offensive. Now Clary understood what he meant. Against her, he had only been using his skill, and not any strength. She felt stupid for only considering it now. Thymey was, after all, a seasoned warrior. He was larger than her too, with much more muscle, and now he was showing it. He continued his assault, crashing down on her swords over and over again. Clary barely managed to defend herself, being forced back with each blow.

She looked to Feryl for help, but he was hardly able to move. It was all her now.

Finally she found an opening and tried to deal some damage to stop Thymey's onslaught, but as she attempted the slash, the lieutenant placed his boot square in her chest, sending her flying backward. She landed on an old wooden table, crashing through it to the floor. Before she could get up, Thymey was on top of her, kicking one of her swords away, and grasping the open wound on her right shoulder, forcing her to drop the other weapon.

He placed his sword on her throat. "You really are an idiot, girly. You actually thought that you could catch up to a swordsman of my caliber in just a couple of months? It's laughable. You are no swordsman. I've been fighting for years, against warriors who were far more skilled than you will ever be, yet here you challenge me, half bled to death and dangerously low on magical energy to the point where you can't even cast a spell. It's insulting."

Thymey's words did not insult Clary. He was right after all. She wasn't a swordsman. She did have far less experience and strength than him. She knew he was right, but oddly enough his words brought to her a sense of clarity, as she remembered someone else who had said a similar thing to her. Only this person had not meant it as an insult.

"You're right," she admitted. "I'm not a swordsman, and you do have much more power than I do. I could never hope to defeat you in a straight swordfight,"

"Then what are you smiling about?"

"I'm smiling because this isn't a fight between two swordsmen. It's a fight between a swordsman and a battle mage."

"Wha— Ahh!" Thymey yelled as the hand that had been grasping Clary's shoulder burned. It distracted him for a moment, but he still had his sword pressed to her throat.

Thymey tried to press the blade into her neck and kill her right then and there, but Clary had been prepared for it, heating the metal while they were talking and turning up the heat while he was distracted by his hand. It bent and then melted through over her neck. He tried to pull away, sensing the danger, but Clary caught the collar of his armor and pulled him back, her knuckles burning his throat.

"I'm not done with you yet!" she shouted as she sank her other white-hot hand through his armor, stabbing into his gut.

Thymey lurched with pain, but he was not dead yet. He rammed his knee into her stomach, making Clary lose her grip. Terrified, he ran for the exit, only to be met with a fist directly to the nose. He stumbled back, hunched over in pain, clutching at his wound.

"Thanks, Valen, but I've got it from here," Clary called to the prince, who was standing in the doorway with Edgrum.

"You... you brats! I'll kill you all! I swear it!" Thymey shouted, as Clary approached him calmly. "Get back! Stay away from me!" he cried, but Clary kept advancing. Out of desperation, the weakened Thymey pulled another knife from his belt and took a huge clumsy swing at his opponent. Clary didn't even have to parry it. She simply stepped out of the way and stuck the sword, which she had retrieved moments earlier, out. Thymey, too exhausted to stop himself, ran straight into it.

"Looks like you weren't as good a swordsman as you thought, Lieutenant." Clary said. She pulled the blade from his chest, dropping him in the process.

The battle was over finally, and they had won. Clary had no time to enjoy the moment, however, as she needed to get to work on Feryl's wounds.

"Clary, are you alright?" Valen asked, rushing in to help her.

"Y-yes, I'm...fine," she stuttered, approaching the injured Feryl.

"Clary, I don't think you are."

"Yes, I am. Just... used too much magic... that's... all."

She began to stumble forward.

"Clary, no! Clary!" Valen shouted. He jumped in front of her, catching her before she could hit the ground.

"I... I guess he was right... I really was... out of magic." She was so exhausted that she was struggling to speak. Everything was fading into darkness. Distantly, she could hear voices calling her name.

"Demon... Magic exhaustion...give her to me... dying."

Clary could hold on no longer. Everything went dark. She wasn't scared though. She just hoped everyone was okay.

*   *   *

Clary opened her eyes to blinding sunlight peeking through the canvas of a Varhallan tent. She was in the wagon. She started to sit up but she moved too fast.

"Woah there, take it easy." Ellerbe was sitting next to her, watching over her. "Look who's finally awake!" he said, with a big smile. Slowly, he helped her sit upright.

"What happened? Where's everyone else?" she asked, still confused.

The knight laughed. "What's the matter? I'm not good enough for you?"

"Ellerbe! What about the battle? Are the Exiles still after us? I'm serious!" Clary urged him angrily.

"Okay, okay! I get it, not the time for jokes. I've just been so bored waiting here all this time. Don't worry, everyone's fine."

"What about Feryl? Is he okay? I didn't have time to help him!"

"Calm down, Clary, he's okay. He's probably outside with the others. He woke up a few days ago."

"Wait, what do you mean? A few days? How long have I been out?"

"Well, I'm not going to lie. It has been a while." Ellerbe looked as though he was trying to figure out the most delicate way to break bad news to her.

"How long?"

"Look, I honestly didn't think I'd be the one on watch when you woke up so—"

"How long?" Clary demanded again, much more firmly this time.

"…about two weeks."

"What? How did you even keep me alive that long?"

"I don't really know the specifics. It was mostly that Varhallan friend of yours and Hilda. You succumbed to blood loss and magic exhaustion. You almost died. They've been taking shifts, running spells to keep you alive. It took a couple days before you were out of danger, but your body still needed time to rest." Ellerbe appeared very awkward about the situation. He and Clary weren't really that close, so this was naturally an uncomfortable situation for him.

Clary wanted to ask him more, but fortunately there was someone else there to clear the air. The door flew open, and Terra and Hilda came rushing in.

"Clary! You're awake!" Terra shouted.

"I knew I felt you in here!" Hilda shouted.

Both of them jumped in to embrace her.

Another voice came from the front door. "Glad to see you're okay."

"Thanks, Valen." Clary was too anxious and confused to wait any longer. She needed to know what the situation was. "Please, can you fill me in on what's happening?"

"Well, let's see. Where do I begin?" he started. "We won the battle against the Exiles."

"Yeah, I figured that, considering that we're still alive. But what are we doing now?"

"Well, I didn't get the chance to discuss it with you all before, because we were so focused on surviving, but the truth is I know who hired Ingrum."

"What? Who? How?" Clary gasped. She couldn't believe he had waited to tell everyone until after the fight.

"The special blades that he used that night. They carried my brother's emblem, the silver and blue ram."

"Prince Lorious sent Ingram to kill you?" Clary asked in shock.

"Not exactly," Valen admitted. "We've concluded that Ingrum wasn't supposed to kill anyone. His mission was to be the inside man for the Exiles, and then to ensure that I made it home safely without discovering anything I shouldn't. If I did discover anything, I was to be considered expendable. When he tortured Halumsha with Sir Rorian, the old Varhallan let slip that he'd seen the Exiles carrying off their dead and leaving the eagles mages' bodies to be found. When Ingrum realized that Sir Rorian would eventually inform the rest of us, he tried to kill him discreetly to save us all. We think the attack on Vinvale was intended to look as though it were a kidnapping, when really it was meant to wipe out as many mages and knights as possible while at the same time sending the kingdom into disarray and simultaneously setting up an alliance between the Exiles, who are under my brother's thumb, and the Varhalla. We think he's trying to start a civil war, so that he can gain control of the throne, and Thandessa, in the chaos."

Clary was astounded. She couldn't believe they had been able to piece together that much. "How'd you figure all that out?"

"It was pretty easy once we had the cooperation of Halumsha. We pooled his info with everything we already knew, and it all just kind of revealed itself."

"More like Harvel put it together for you," Ellerbe laughed.

"So if that's the case, then we need to get moving to warn your father don't we? I need to start melting that ice right now!" Clary started, attempting to get up. "We're lucky no more Exiles or Varhalla have shown up in all this time!"

"Hold on a moment!" Valen cautioned. "Has no one told you yet?"

"Told me what?"

"You didn't think we just sat here waiting for you two lazy bums to wake up, did you?" he laughed. "Here, come with me. Ellerbe, help her up, slowly."

The prince and the knight started to lift Clary, with the help of her friends. She was woozy, but with the help of everyone, she was able to make it to the front door. Valen opened it for her and held her hand, leading her out into the sunlight. She was expecting to step out onto snow, but instead she found herself standing on the wooden deck of a ship in the middle of the sea.

"What's going on?" she asked in confusion.

"We're in the Pronged Sea, on our way back to Belderan," someone answered from behind.

"Feryl!" she shouted, letting go of her supports to jump into his arms.

"Woah! Hey, be careful!" he said, smiling and holding her up.

"But how'd you guys get through the ice? I thought you needed Firedrake Clan members for that."

"You do, if you want to melt it quickly," Valen replied. "We did it the long way."

"The long way?" Clary asked.

"A lot of torches and old axes!" Terra said behind her with a laugh.

"We made it to a Fjoren harbor south of the city after that and commandeered an old ship. It may not look like much, but she's the best vessel the old bay had to offer," Harvel added, joining in on the conversation.

"Ah, I see the demon has finally risen," came another familiar voice.

"Halumsha? Guys – you can't still be keeping him prisoner," Clary pleaded. "He saved me!"

Everyone laughed at her cluelessness.

"I am no prisoner little demon," Halumsha said. "I am simply looking after my pet, as I said before."

"You mean you didn't want to go back to your people?" she asked.

"I do love my people, yes. Even though they have abandoned me, I still care for their well-being as any king should. It is for that reason that I must accompany you children. This war concerns my people as well," he stated in his usual regal tone. "Besides, you are in desperate need of a new magic instructor. This boy here has no talent as a teacher. It would be a shame to leave you in his hands," he continued, turning his nose up at them.

"Ha ha. I'm glad you're coming with us, your highness," she laughed, bowing towards him.

"It is not quite kneeling, but it will do for now, little demon," he said.

"And thank you again for saving me."

Halumsha turned away. "I don't know what you are talking about."

"Clary, I think we should all be thanking you," Feryl added.

"What? Why? All I did was worry you."

"That's not true, and you know it!" Garrett cut in, much to her surprise. "Your powers saved my life… and you killed that bastard, Thymey."

"Garrett…" she exclaimed. "I… I'm so happy you're okay!" She reached out and grabbed him, pulling him into a hug. "I was so worried."

"I'm fine, thanks to you, so don't worry one bit."

Clary was starting to tear up as she let go of him. She wasn't sure how to feel. She was just ecstatic that everyone had made it.

"Clary, come here. I want to show you something," said Feryl. Everyone else seemed to understand that she needed some space too. They went back to their duties, each saying thank you or hugging her before they left.

Clary was too weak to walk yet and was beginning to feel tired again, so Feryl picked her up in his arms, carrying her to the bow of the ship.

"Here, I borrowed this from Harvel when Terra and Hilda told us you were awake. Take it and look straight ahead." He handed her the small spyglass that Harvel had used to spot the Exiles on the day of the attack. Clary took it from him and did as he instructed.

She saw a shadowy line on the horizon, sticking up from the water.

"Is that…"

"Yeah… It's home," Feryl answered. "The key to saving your parents is just over there. We spotted it this morning."

"Belderan…" she said. "You think the king will help us?"

"He'll have to," Valen cut in, walking up to join them. "I won't take no for an answer. Besides, my father has to defend his kingdom. It's a ruler's duty."

"Then I guess we're almost there," Clary said, feeling truly relieved and safe for the first time since the festival so many months ago.

Mom… Dad… Don't worry… she thought. *We're almost there.*

Acknowledgements

Michelle

Thank you for your love and support and for constantly encouraging me to keep writing.

Liliana Hart and Scott Silverii

Without your guidance I never would have been able to figure this thing out! Thank you both so much for your words of wisdom.

Aunt Hope

Thank you for constantly asking me when the next chapter would be finished. It kept me focused, and your positive feedback helped me to get the job done!

About the author

D.A. Martin is a native of Louisiana. He has traveled extensively through Europe and Asia. After living in New York, Los Angeles, and Honolulu he returned to Southern Louisiana to pursue his dream of writing.

His love of fantasy began as a child through popular movies, television series, and comic books of the time. In his highschool years he began sharing stories with friends, but the thought of writing never occurred to him until his college years. While procrastinating during finals week, Martin was struck with the idea of a new story and had to write it down. When he finished the first chapter he sent it to his parents, who were completely unaware of his passion for storytelling. They immediately encouraged him to spend the next year putting his stories down on paper, having fallen in love with what they read. That single chapter began the Clary saga.

www.ingramcontent.com/pod-product-compliance
Lightning Source LLC
Chambersburg PA
CBHW021431240626
47153CB00001B/96